D1295915

Hardy and His Readers

Other Books by T. R. Wright:

THE CRITICAL SPIRIT AND THE WILL TO BELIEVE (*co-edited with David Jasper*)
D. H. LAWRENCE AND THE BIBLE
GEORGE ELIOT'S *MIDDLEMARCH*
HARDY AND THE EROTIC
JOHN HENRY NEWMAN: A MAN FOR OUR TIME? (*editor*)
THE RELIGION OF HUMANITY
THEOLOGY AND LITERATURE

Hardy and His Readers

T. R. Wright

First published 2003 by
PALGRAVE MACMILLAN
Houndmills, Basingstoke, Hampshire RG21 6XS and
175 Fifth Avenue, New York, N. Y. 10010
Companies and representatives throughout the world

PALGRAVE MACMILLAN is the global academic imprint of the Palgrave
Macmillan division of St. Martin's Press, LLC and of Palgrave Macmillan Ltd.
Macmillan® is a registered trademark in the United States, United Kingdom
and other countries. Palgrave is a registered trademark in the European
Union and other countries.

ISBN 0-333-96260-5

This book is printed on paper suitable for recycling and made from fully
managed and sustained forest sources.

A catalogue record for this book is available from the British Library.

Library of Congress Cataloging-in-Publication Data
Wright, T. R. (Terence R.), 1951-
    Hardy and his readers / T. R. Wright.
        p. cm.
    Includes bibliographical references and index.
    ISBN 0-333-96260-5
    1. Hardy, Thomas, 1840-1928–Fictional works. 2. Hardy, Thomas, 1840-
1928–Criticism and interpretation–History–19th century. 3. Fiction–
Appreciation–England–History–19th century. 4. Authors and readers–
England–History–19th century. 5. Books and reading–England–History–19th
century. 6. Hardy, Thomas, 1840-1928–Technique. 7. Reader-response
criticism. I. Title.

PR4757.F5 W75 2003
823'.8–dc21   2002192493

10 9 8 7 6 5 4 3 2 1
12 11 10 09 08 07 06 05 04 03

Printed and bound in Great Britain by
Antony Rowe Ltd, Chippenham and Eastbourne

Contents

Acknowledgements

I would like to thank the Arts and Humanities Research Board and the Leave Committee of the University of Newcastle for between them funding a year's paid leave from the end of January 2001, which enabled me to complete the writing of this book. I am also grateful to the Small Grants Research Fund of the University of Newcastle for funding two visits to the Dorset County Museum and one to the British Library. I would like to thank the librarians of those institutions, in particular Jessica Plane of the Robinson Library and Lilian Swindall of the Dorset County Museum for their unstinting help. The staff of the Literary and Philosophical Society of Newcastle upon Tyne were also very helpful throughout the time I worked there. I would like to thank Mr de Peyer of the Dorset County Museum for permission to quote from the Thomas Hardy Memorial Collection, the British Library for permission to use details of an illustration from the *Graphic* on the cover of the book, and both Michael Turner and Felicity Stimpson for permission to quote from their dissertations.

Among the many academics who helped and encouraged this research I would like to thank Michael Millgate for his advice at any early stage of the whole process, Roger Ebbatson and John Schad for reading sections of the book and providing helpful comments, Philip Mallett and other members of the Thomas Hardy Society for sitting through my lengthy paper on *The Hand of Ethelberta* at their Spring Conference of 2001 and providing me with feedback, Laurence Lerner and other members of the International Association of University Professors of English for their comments on my paper on the 'minor' novels in Bamberg in July 2001, Adrian Poole and Cedric Watts for supporting my proposal to the AHRB, Michael Turner for talking to me about Tillotson's Fiction Bureau and showing me their surviving notebooks, and my colleagues in the Department of English Literary and Linguistic Studies at the University of Newcastle for helping me through the many stages involved in a project of this sort. I would also like to thank Emily Rosser, my editor, for ensuring the smooth transition of this book from typescript to press, the anonymous readers for their helpful suggestions, my copy-editor Anne Rafique for her careful attention to detail and my research assistant Laura Daniels for her work on the index. My family, especially my wife Gabriele and my children Catherine and Andrew, deserve my deepest thanks for putting up with holidays in Dorset, compulsory visits to the British Library and the many other side-effects of research on Hardy. My sister Gail Wright even helped with research into library borrowing figures.

Abbreviations

All page references to Hardy's novels are given in brackets within the text with the following abbreviations. Unless otherwise specified they refer to the new Penguin Classics edition (General Editor Patricia Ingham), which takes the first volume edition as copy-text in all cases except *Far From the Madding Crowd*. This is the edition that Hardy's original readers would have encountered. Previous modern editions have been based on the Wessex Edition of 1912, which is often significantly different. The date of the first volume edition is given in square brackets. *NW* refers to the New Wessex Edition, published by Macmillan 1974–5.

AL   *A Laodicean*, ed. John Schad, 1997 [1881].
DR   *Desperate Remedies*, ed. Mary Rimmer, 1998 [1871].
FMC   *Far From the Madding Crowd*, ed. Rosemarie Morgan, 2000 [1874].
HE   *The Hand of Ethelberta*, ed. Tim Dolin, 1996 [1876].
JO   *Jude the Obscure*, ed. Dennis Taylor, 1998 [1895].
MC   *The Mayor of Casterbridge*, ed. Keith Wilson [1886].
PBE   *A Pair of Blue Eyes*, ed. Pamela Dalziel, 1998 [1873].
RN   *The Return of the Native*, ed. Tony Slade, 1999 [1878].
T   *Tess of the D'Urbervilles*, ed. Tim Dolin, 1998 [1891].
T-M   *The Trumpet-Major*, ed. Linda M. Shires, 1997 [1880].
TT   *Two on a Tower*, ed. Sally Shuttleworth, 1999 [1882].
UGT   *Under the Greenwood Tree*, ed. Tim Dolin, 1998 [1872].
W   *The Woodlanders*, ed. Patricia Ingham, 1998 [1887].
W-B   *The Pursuit of the Well-Beloved and The Well-Beloved*, ed. Patricia Ingham, 1997 [1897].

Other published writings of Hardy are abbreviated as follows:

CP   *The Collected Poems of Thomas Hardy*, London: Macmillan, 1930.
Letters *The Collected Letters of Thomas Hardy*, ed. Richard Little Purdy and Michael Millgate, 7 vols, Oxford: Clarendon Press, 1978–88.
Life   *The Life and Work of Thomas Hardy*, ed. Michael Millgate, Athens: University of Georgia Press, 1984.
LN   *The Literary Notebooks of Thomas Hardy*, ed. Lennart Björk, 2 vols, London: Macmillan – now Palgrave Macmillan, 1985.
PN   *The Personal Notebooks of Thomas Hardy*, ed. Richard Taylor, London: Macmillan, 1978.

PW   *Thomas Hardy's Personal Writings*, ed. Harold Orel, London: Macmillan, 1967.

References to manuscript collections are abbreviated as follows:

BL   British Library.
DCM   Dorset County Museum.

References to specialist journals:

THA   *Thomas Hardy Annual.*
THJ   *Thomas Hardy Journal.*

1
Hardy's Contemporary Readers: Some Introductory Questions

Questions of reading: towards a sharper reception theory

The subject of this book is not quite as simple as its title might suggest. It *is* about the relationship between Hardy and his readers but neither half of this partnership constitutes a straightforward, easily defined object. Reception theorists have argued that the process of reading involves the construction of an 'implied author' responsible for the final form of the text, a mental object clearly distinguishable from the historical author. But in practice, as we shall see, there have been as many Hardies as readers, each producing an imaginative projection of the author, a myth: 'My Thomas Hardy' (Widdowson 1989: 2). Even the historical Hardy is not that easy to pin down since each biographer produces a modified image of the inhabitant of Max Gate. Michael Millgate, for example, writes of a Hardy so wrapped up in his work and his elevated Shelleyan conception of the role of the artist that he was often unaware of the likely impact of his work upon his readers (Millgate 1982: 374), until, that is, the reviews appeared. I will attempt to modify Millgate's model of Hardy, suggesting that he was fully aware of the likely response of his readers but increasingly risked challenging and antagonising them. My Hardy is also a somewhat bolder figure than that of Robert Gittings, 'a cringing, insignificant fellow, towered over by Oxbridge men, metropolitan editors, and worldly sophisticated lords and ladies' (Neill 1999: 4). He bears a family resemblance to the Hardies constructed by critics such as John Goode and Joe Fisher, similarly 'marked by radical alienation' (Page 2000:78) and resentment of his middle-class literary masters, but is in other respects my own construction.

The same difficulties beset the attempt to identify Hardy's readers, who are by no means a homogeneous group. Hardy, it has been claimed, spans 'the entire range of readers as no other writer', not only 'ordinary' readers of all kinds but conscripted readers of all ages within the educational institution (Lock 1992:3). Hardy, as we shall see, appears to have followed friends such as Gosse in believing that his admirers were mainly male. He certainly resented the idea that he had to imagine his reader as a young girl whose blushes of embarrassment he must never deign to provoke. The second section of this introduction will give some indication of the range of Hardy's audience in terms of gender and of class, drawing both on the records made by individuals and on the assumptions we can adduce on internal textual evidence about the readers of the magazines in which his novels first appeared. Like most writers, I will argue, Hardy had a clear mental picture of his imagined audience. In his case, however, it was a patronising male upper-middle-class audience he actively disliked. The third section of this introduction will consider the class base of his audience while the fourth raises questions about its gender.

Part of my purpose is purely historical: to record the way in which Hardy was received by his contemporaries. As with an earlier book entitled *Thomas Hardy and His Readers*, it will involve quoting contemporary reviews, though my coverage is much broader than that of the anthology edited by Laurence Lerner and John Holmstrom, which includes only one review of *Desperate Remedies* and none at all of the other six novels then classified as 'minor' (Lerner 1968). The same clear weighting towards the 'major' fiction can be found in similar collections of early criticism edited by R. G. Cox (Cox 1970) and Graham Clarke (Clarke 1993). None of these volumes pays sufficient attention to the fact that Hardy carefully preserved many of these reviews in a scrapbook which survives in the Dorset County Museum, clearly demonstrating his acute interest in and knowledge of his contemporary reception. These scrapbooks furnish much of my evidence, supplemented by material listed by Gerber and Davis in their bibliography of writings about Hardy and by the large collection of unpublished letters to Hardy, over five thousand in number, which have recently been catalogued in the Dorset County Museum.

The 'extent to which Hardy was influenced by the attitudes of his readers, or by what his editors and publishers thought those attitudes to be', is the subject of an article on 'Hardy and His Readers' by James Gibson. His main concern is Hardy's 'duel with Mrs Grundy', a duel which began with Alexander Macmillan's rejection of Hardy's first novel *The Poor Man and the Lady* in 1868 in the belief that readers would 'throw down the volume in disgust' and only ended with Hardy, sickened by the hostile reception of his last three novels, resolved to write fiction no more (Gibson 1980: 192). Gibson's article did not have the space fully to consider how this stormy relationship with his readers was mediated by material factors comprising the general literary field within which he had to operate: the conditions of the marketplace, the variety of formats in which he was read and prevalent attitudes to fiction. Part of my own concern is to shed light on this whole field, to place each of Hardy's novels in the immediate context of the precise publishing conditions in which they were initially produced and consumed. This book, in other words, aims to contribute to the now fashionable 'history of the book'.

Each of the following chapters of the book examines the reception of Hardy's individual novels in the order that he wrote them, attempting to bring together the historical evidence of actual readers' response and the literary-critical reconstruction of the activity of 'implied readers'. In each case I will begin by outlining the contemporary response to each novel before proceeding to critical questions about their reading raised by the text. The point, in each case, will be to highlight the changing dynamics of reading; 'changing' because different readers at different times ask different questions, approaching the text with differing assumptions, 'dynamic' because there is a genuine dialogue between text and reader which I hope to capture. Hardy's uneasy relationship with his contemporary audience, I will argue, left permanent traces in his text.

My approach, in other words, is both historical and literary-critical, although whether the gap between these two approaches to reader response is capable of being fully bridged is a moot point. Patrick Brantlinger acknowledges that 'no sociology of readers can fathom exactly how actual readers responded to texts' while 'a strictly rhetorical approach' based upon an analysis of the text can never 'get at real readers' since 'the actual reader is always "outside the text"':

> It is partly this obvious fact, with its correlative uncertainty about how actual readers would react to their novels, that leads novelists so insistently to try to conscript, interpellate, or guide their imaginary 'dear readers' in the direction they wish them to go.
>
> (Brantlinger 1998: 16–17)

Hardy may be much less obvious in the ways in which he attempts to manipulate his readers than his immediate mid-Victorian precursors. He rarely addresses them directly in the manner of a Brontë or a Dickens.

That does not mean, however, that they are not inscribed in the text in more subtle and complex ways, which it is my aim to explore.

My attempt to bridge the historical and literary approaches to reader response will necessarily draw upon reception theory, although the work of its initial exponents, Iser and Jauss, will be supplemented both by the critique of phenomenology involved in deconstruction and an awareness of ideology more characteristic of feminist and cultural materialist criticism. At the heart of the relationship, however, is the highly personal textual encounter of reader and text, which Wolfgang Iser attempted to describe. *The Act of Reading*, to employ the title of one of his books, is nothing if not personal. Books without readers, in Georges Poulet's memorable image, are mere 'objects' on shelves in bookshops, like animals in a pet-shop, waiting for someone to buy and read them, to 'deliver them from their materiality' (Poulet 1980: 41). Iser's own phenomenological description of 'The Reading Process', in the final chapter of the English version of *The Implied Reader*, draws on Poulet's observation of the extraordinary way in which, 'Whenever I read' I am taken over by an 'alien consciousness', so that 'the *I* which I pronounce is not my own' (Iser 1974: 294). Poulet emphasises the vulnerability, the lack of control of the reader, whose 'interior world' is thus invaded by alien 'mental entities'. When I read a novel, he claims, 'I deliver myself, bound hand and foot, to the omnipotence of fiction...I surround myself with fictitious beings; I become the prey of language' (Poulet 1980: 43). Hillis Miller, in his summary of the beliefs of the Geneva School, to which Poulet and for a while Miller himself belonged (including the period when he wrote his study of *Thomas Hardy: Distance and Desire*), identifies this personal relationship between author and reader, a 'reciprocal transparency' of two minds, as central to their account of the reading process (Miller 1966: 321). In post-structuralist hindsight, they may seem to have underestimated the opacity of language, its materiality, and to have exaggerated the extent to which there can be any 'unified or homogeneous, generating or receiving consciousness' (Spivak 2000: 478). Both author and readers, I accept, are ideologically constructed, belonging as they do to what Stanley Fish would call a range of interpretive communities. But the textual encounter between them is a personal one and it is this encounter which remains at the centre of all critical analysis.

Hardy himself, in an essay on 'The Profitable Reading of Fiction' for the New York *Forum* in 1888, described the process through which 'the perspicacious reader' will 'by affording full scope to his own insight, catch the vision the writer has in his eye' (Widdowson 1997: 247). In the more complex terminology of the Polish phenomenologist Roman Ingarden, the reader is said to 'concretize' the 'intentional thought' projected by the author. The problem, as Matei Calinescu recognises, is that

> No two concretizations of the same work, even by the same reader, can ever be identical, primarily because of the temporal-historical dimension in which all reading occurs. Seen from this point of view, each act of reading is 'absolutely individual' (*Cognition*, p. 402) and as such is incommunicable. Hence, in order to make a reading experience communicable, the necessity to reread and thus try to limit the individualizing effect of (personal) time and history.
>
> (Calinescu 1993: 28)

The aim of criticism (as opposed to the initial act of reading) for Ingarden lies precisely in the reduction and limitation of the personal elements involved in the act of reading in order to construct a notion of the work of art itself, an aim also dear to the young phenomenologist Jacques Derrida, whose state doctorate, attempting to define the ideality of the literary object, was 'inspired by reading of Husserl and phenomenological aesthetics' (Norris 1987: 240). If we compare 'several aesthetic concretizations of the same literary work...and find what is constant in them,' Ingarden argues, we can arrive at 'the common aspect of several concretizations', a 'correct' reading of the work, stripped of its more personal and historically contingent aspects (Ingarden 1973: 403). Few later critics, of course, have accepted that this is either possible or desirable, which may explain why Derrida abandoned his thesis, proceeding to found a mode of double reading – deconstruction – alert both to the author's intention and to the way in which it is always necessarily unfulfilled, undermined by factors beyond the author's control, complicated by the contingencies of language and the conditions of reading (what the reader consciously or unconsciously brings to the text). The text always (happily) exceeds both authorial intention and 'correct' realisation.

Phenomenology and structuralism between them spawned a frightening array of theoretical readers including Iser's 'implied reader' and Jauss's 'actual reader' (Freund 1987: 4). What I hope to achieve here is a balance between the two, accepting both the necessary difference between every historical reading and the desire of critics to find a common object to discuss. Iser begins his analysis of 'The Reading Process' by insisting, like Ingarden, on the two poles of the literary work, the artistic and the aesthetic, the former referring to 'the text created by the author', the latter to 'the realization accomplished by the reader' (Iser 1974: 274). It is only in the mind of each party to the literary transaction that the literary work as such can be said to exist. Readers necessarily bring to the texts a whole repertoire of expectations but these are 'scarcely ever fulfilled in truly literary texts', which are capable of surprising and even shocking their readers into new insights, revised beliefs (278). Without this prior 'repertoire of familiar literary patterns and recurrent literary themes', of course, no texts would be readable, generically identifiable or followable. But authors deploy a number of 'strategies . . . to set the familiar against the unfamiliar', forcing readers to modify premature realisations of the text's meaning (288). This capacity to surprise and shock while still operating within conventions familiar to his readers, as I hope to demonstrate, is of particular importance in Hardy, who often lures his readers into the text by appearing to promise the fulfilment of familiar generic expectations (such as those of sensation fiction) before requiring of them a more complicated response. Not surprisingly, as we shall see, he often leaves them puzzled and frustrated, particularly in his 'minor' fiction (for which the best definition may be those novels which failed to meet his readers' expectations).

Iser's 'implied reader', then, as he explains in *The Act of Reading*, is not so much a person as 'a textual structure' or 'a network of response-inviting structures' brought into being by the interaction of an historical reader with the text (Iser 1978: 34–5). The secret of all textual power, according to Iser, lies not so much in what is explicitly formulated as in what is left implicit, to be supplied by the reader: the gaps, blanks, indeterminacies, vacancies and negations of the text. Iser uses all these terms to describe the indirect means by which an author stimulates a reader to supply meaning, to make connections and to resolve contradictions in the text itself. The slightest withholding of information (even something as trivial as the colour a character's hair) counts as an indeterminacy which readers will want to resolve. More significantly, the 'blanks' between opposed perspectives in a novel, whether of characters, narrators or ideological norms, positively demand to be resolved, as we shall see in relation to the distance between the narrator's explicit perspective and what appears to be implied. Again, as I hope to show, it is the very unreliability and inadequacy of Hardy's explicit narrative comments, his diegesis, as opposed to the power of his mimetic representation, his involvement of his readers in a world they help to construct, which accounts for some of the apparent contradictions in his work.

Some of Iser's more recent work analyses the way in which literature can be said to interrogate ideology, manifesting itself in 'a continual repatterning of the culturally conditioned shapes human beings have assumed'. For literature, as Hardy also insisted, refuses to imprison itself in any existing systematic frameworks (Iser 1993: xi). What Iser calls the 'fictive' is neither simply true nor untrue; it is 'an operational mode of consciousness that makes inroads into existing versions of the world', keeping in view 'what has been overstepped' but simultaneously disrupting it (xiv–xv). Again, this seems to me an appropriate framework within which to place a writer such as Hardy, who aims to challenge or at least subvert the ideological framework of his readers without having a systematic alternative with which to replace it.

'The American Reception of Reception Theory', as Robert Holub has demonstrated, underestimated its engagement with ideological and historical issues, being transformed there into yet another method for the close reading of texts (Holub 1992: 22–36). Both Iser and his colleague, Hans Robert Jauss, however, recognised that readers were 'differently encoded according to the period at which the text was written, and according to the audience originally envisaged for it and its particular "horizon of expectations"' (Flint 1993: 34). One of the seven theses articulated in the opening chapter of Jauss's most important work, *Toward an Aesthetic of Reception*, emphasises the importance of this 'horizon of expectations, in the face of which a work was created and received in the past', which helps to establish 'how the contemporary reader could have viewed and understood the work' (Jauss 1982: 28). Jauss's 'contemporary reader', of course, is still a hypothetical entity, but is constructed along genuinely historical lines.

Jauss himself, for example, analyses the contemporary debates over *Madame Bovary*, including arguments presented at Flaubert's trial, to illustrate the way in which the new narrative technique of free indirect speech caused a realignment both of reading practice and of moral attitude. The prosecuting counsel misread Emma's celebration of herself as an adulteress as reflecting the author's view, failing to perceive the intermediate layers of narrative and focalisation which represent Emma's perspective. Flaubert, of course, *was* challenging his readers' assumptions about sex and marriage but in complex indirect ways characteristic of fiction:

> the impersonal form of narration not only compelled his readers to perceive things differently... but at the same time thrust them into an alienating uncertainty of judgment. Since the new artistic device

broke through an old novelistic convention – the moral judgment of the represented characters that is always unequivocal and confirmed in the description – the novel was able to radicalize or to raise new questions of lived praxis. (42–3)

Hardy, as I hope to show, finds similar ways in which to challenge the assumptions of his readers, to make them rethink their attitudes, particularly in matters of sexual morality.

During the 1980s and 1990s, as Andrew Bennet has shown, theories of reading built upon the foundations provided by Iser and Jauss, increasing their 'recognition that readers are historically or socially constructed, rather than abstract and eternal essences'. The deconstruction of notions of stable identity also led to 'a problematization of the very concept of "reading" and "the reader", a recognition not only that readers are different from one another, but that any individual reader is multiple', a product of more than one interpretive community (Bennett 1995: 4). As Diana Fuss puts it, 'Readers, like texts, are constructed; they inhabit reading procedures rather than create them *ex nihilo*' (Fuss 1989: 35). Readers, as James Machor insists, 'are subject to 'historically specific conditions' and to 'ideological, political, and material factors' which define and structure their role (Machor 1993: viii–ix).

The study of reader response has been further historicised by the recent rise of 'the history of the book'. When the Society for the History of Authorship, Reading and Publishing (SHARP) was founded, there was much debate about the word 'history':

> 'History,' desirable for its place in a catchy acronym, might be thought to preclude theories of authorship prominent in gender studies and in deconstruction, theories of reader reception, and whatever else might emerge in the near future from thinking about publishing as more than a commercial, or even as a commercial, enterprise.
>
> (Jordan 1995: 11)

The truly SHARP critical practice, I want to suggest, involves using all these interpretive strategies. Any study of the relationship between author and reader requires *both* a critical framework akin to the phenomenological account of the reading process I have outlined *and* a historical consideration of the empirical evidence of the sort provided by the 'history of the book'. That at least is the assumption on which I will proceed, beginning with an attempt to characterise Hardy's contemporary audience both in terms of the historical records which have survived and in terms of the material conditions under which they operated.

Questions of history: who were Hardy's readers?

The contemporary audience for Hardy's novels, stretching from the mid-Victorian era when he began writing to the Georgian admirers of his revised editions of 1912 and 1920, cannot be treated as homogeneous. These years registered massive changes in literacy (the sheer numbers able to read texts of this complexity), and in physical mode of reading (from serials and three-deckers to paperbacks) as well as in horizon of expectation. Hardy's first readers, in the anonymous editions produced by Tinsley, would not have attached any significance to his name, had they known it, while those who bought his later collected editions would have been only too aware of the myths attached to the Grand Old Man of Letters he had by then become.

The individual circumstances under which people read Hardy also varied dramatically. It is difficult, for example, to find much common ground between the supportive if patronising local rector's wife, Emily Smith, who wrote to him in June 1873 'recognizing many of your vivid descriptions' in *Under the Greenwood Tree* (DCM 5271) to a Mr Herbert who wrote in 1924 to tell Hardy that he had left a copy of that novel with a relative in the Notts County Asylum, to find on subsequent visits

> that the copy had passed through the wards and been eagerly devoured. In that place of gloom it caused so much merriment and happy talk as to constitute a real uplift in the condition of the patients. The medical staff then borrowed it and were equally interested and amused.
>
> (DCM 3402)

Mr Herbert proceeded to report that his relative was 'later discharged and has continued one of the sanest and happiest of mortals'. John Cowper Powys received similar benefits from Hardy's work. Disturbed by 'devilish' moods, he would sit up 'for hours and hours' eating 'piece after piece of chocolate out of my bag' until 'by degrees as I listened to the wind in the chimney the genius of Hardy would drive my demon away' (Powys 1934: 224–5, 309). Siegfried Sassoon read him on active duty in the trenches, while Bartos Zoltan, who translated *Tess* and *Jude* into Hungarian, read him in a Siberian camp in freezing fog with 'flocks of ravens shrieking above' (DCM 5674). Perhaps his most captive audience was in a German prisoner of war camp in East Africa about which the novelist Howard Spring heard from a retired naval officer:

> They had one book: Hardy's *Tess*. He did not know from whence it had come, but there it was, and every man read it and re-read it; and, as year followed year, bits of paper frayed away, chunks of print were obliterated by thumb-marks; pages, stuck together by food, wouldn't come apart without disaster. But, whenever a new prisoner turned up, and was given the book, someone could always help him over stiles, reciting the missing bits.
>
> (Spring 1942: 85–6)

These may be extreme examples but they serve to demonstrate the difficulty of making generalisations about Hardy's readers.

The many unsolicited letters sent to Hardy by unknown admirers across the world include some from readers who clearly identified all too closely with his characters. William Blatchford, for example, nephew of the militant atheist Robert, reported that *Jude the Obscure* 'appeals to me so forcibly because I am in a way one of the many Judes there are in the world' (DCM 1094). Like, to adopt one of Norman Holland's mottoes, appears all too often to have appealed to like. There were also, unfortunately, a number of Tesses who wrote to the well-known address to confide their own undoings. There are two envelopes full of letters on *Tess* in the Dorset County Museum, including one from a girl in The Hague who unburdened her trouble to him, because 'you *understand* a woman' (4605). A girl from New York City also confessed, 'some of my experiences of life have been not unlike hers' (4684). Others demanded to know why he had written such a sad and immoral novel. One of these is neatly annotated in pencil 'unanswered' (4603); another (from Chicago) reports waking up at night 'screaming at the impurities' in the novel (4611). These, again, are individual responses, necessarily varying according to temperament and belief.

Partly in the interest of good public relations, Hardy tended to reply politely to such letters. He was also, as we shall see, as quick to thank reviewers for good notices as to rebuke them for the opposite. Many of these letters indicate a clear sense of the audience he had in mind. When his friend Edmund Gosse published a fairly critical review of *Jude*, for example, he explained that the story was 'sent out to those into whose soul the iron has entered, and has entered deeply, at some time of their lives'. The problem, he added rather plaintively, was that 'one cannot choose one's readers' (*Letters* II 93). He also wrote to thank Laurence Alma-Tadema (daughter of the painter) for her 'generous estimate of *Jude*'. The acquisition of 'an imaginative reader like you', he assured her, contrasted markedly with 'the prior expectations of readers who wanted something comfortable, resigned and conforming' and were consequently 'disappointed' when a writer furnished something different (VII 128).

Even the mid-Victorian audience for which Hardy began writing covered a vast social spectrum. Trollope's much-quoted claim of 1870, 'We have become a novel-reading people, from the Prime Minister to the last-appointed scullery maid' (Trollope 1938: 108), reflects not only the dominance of the novel at that time but the necessary differences between such socially distant readers. Prime Ministers, as one might expect, have left better records. Gladstone's voluminous diaries, for example, record his initial excitement at *Tess*, which he at first found 'a plum pudding stone full of faults and merits' but on finishing called provocative and disgusting, 'a deplorable anticipation of a world without a Gospel' (Gladstone 1994: XIII 23). It was Asquith who nominated Hardy for the Order of Merit on the basis of his prose rather than his verse (Asquith 1928: I 43). Macmillan, however, who began his career with the family firm, thought him 'a very bad stylist', betraying his 'self-educated' bad manners by a tendency to 'produce classical quotes, as if he had just discovered them' (Horne 1990: 62).

The only maid who appears to have recorded her experience of reading Hardy is Edith Hall, whose brief autobiography, *Canary Girls and Stockpots*, published by the WEA in 1977, recalls being encouraged by reading *Tess* in the 1920s to reject the stereotype of the working class promulgated by '*Punch* and other publications of that kind...as stupid and "thick" '. Hardy's 'story of Tess, a poor working girl with an interesting character, thoughts and personality', Hall records, was 'the first serious novel I had read up to this time in which the heroine had not been of "gentle birth" and the labouring classes as brainless automatons. This book made me feel human' (Hall 1977: 39–40). The WEA, as we shall see, was one of the twentieth-century organisations which helped to expand the class base of Hardy's readership. It is arguable that the growth of newspaper serialisation in Britain, the United States and Australia in the 1870s and 1880s (in which Hardy was involved first through his American publisher Henry Holt, then through Tillotson's Fiction Bureau and finally through his agent A. P. Watt) would have brought his work to a wider range of readers than previously suspected.

But there can be little doubt that Hardy's first readers in Britain (the ones of which he was most aware) were the middle and upper classes who subscribed to the monthly magazines in which his work was serialised and to the circulating libraries such as Mudie's and W. H. Smith's who bought the majority of the expensive three-volume first editions. It would have been through such libraries that the small print-runs of his work before the 1890s would have found their main readership.

Hardy was all too painfully aware that his career as a novelist had been 'founded upon his capacity to mediate between essentially rural material and a predominantly urban audience' (Millgate 1982: 265). An essay on 'The Profitable Reading of Fiction' for the New York *Forum* in 1888 accepted that most readers turned to fiction for 'pleasure', for 'relaxation and relief'. This necessarily involved an element of escapism, the 'town man' finding 'what he seeks in novels of the country, the countryman in novels of society' (*PW* 111). Hardy appears to have been happy, to begin with, to meet this need. As his career developed, however, he came increasingly to rebel both against the role of entertainer and against the limitations imposed by his publishers on that role. His contribution to a discussion of 'Candour in English Fiction' in the *New Review* of 1890 identified the problems raised by the dominance of 'the magazine and the circulating library'. These catered for 'household reading' and the standard set for the novel had become the youngest members of the family (128).

There are, of course, positive things that can be said about serials and circulating libraries. Both encouraged publishers to risk new material by unknown writers, the former by providing a ready-made audience and prestige (that of the magazine itself), the latter by guaranteeing sufficient sales at artificially inflated prices and so minimising the risks of publishing new authors. Laurel Brake cites an article of 1879 in *Blackwood's* explaining that subscribers to that magazine 'were predisposed to look kindly' on the authors that its editor considered worth publishing. This ensured that 'the *debutant* had the encouragement of knowing that he addressed himself in the first place to a friendly audience' (Brake 1993: 84). As opposed to book publication, which is predicated on named authors, the serial has a more collectivist ethos, appealing to readers of the whole magazine (93).

The dynamics of serial reading, as Linda Hughes and Michael Lund explain, were altogether different from those of a volume, stretched out as they were for over a year, with breaks between reading. Under these conditions, the time of the reported experience often dovetailed better with the time of the reading, especially, as we shall see, in the case of *Far*

From the Madding Crowd, which incorporated corresponding seasonal details month by month. There were other ways too in which the conditions of reading a serial accorded with the beliefs and values of its middle-class audience:

> the perseverance and delay of gratification necessary for middle-class economic success were, in a sense, echoed in serial reading, which required readers to stay with a story for a long time and to postpone learning a story's outcome. Readers approaching stories within a single volume can 'cheat,' thumbing ahead to a mystery's solution; serial readers could not.
>
> (Hughes 1991: 4–6)

Many Victorian novelists attested to the sense of intimacy established with their audience over such a long period, when they would hear exactly how certain characters were being received. Trollope famously killed off Mrs Proudie after overhearing a conversation between two clerics at his club while Mary Elizabeth Braddon altered the ending of her adaptation of *Madame Bovary* as a result of what she heard from her readers (Jordan 1995: 145).

The corporate character of the nineteenth-century periodical, however, with its anonymous writers and reviewers, also furnished the means of controlling both its writers and readers. Laurel Brake cites Adorno on 'the process a literary text has to undergo, if not in the anticipatory manoeuvres of its author, then certainly in the combined efforts of his readers, editors' and others, which 'exceeds any censorship in its thoroughness' (Brake 1993: 131). Hardy made precisely this point to Edward Garnett, who seemed to think censorship applied only to the stage: 'The Editor is the Censor' in the other forms of English Literature, Hardy explained, referring to the recent rejection of one of his poems by 'one of our chief editors on the sole ground that his periodical was "read in families"'(*Letters* III 278). The editors in question always argued that they were serving the interests and responding to the complaints of their readers but they functioned 'explicitly as a mechanism for guiding readers in their selection of appropriate reading matters' and implicitly 'to create readers and appropriate, class-specific reading practices' (Mays 1995: 167).

Some of Hardy's publishers warned him of the dangers and difficulties of serial publication. Henry Holt, the American publisher of *A Pair of Blue Eyes*, writing in May 1873 to congratulate him on that novel, whose 'melancholy ending works as much against its popularity as its elevation above the popular taste', and on the acceptance of his next novel by the editor of the *Cornhill*, confessed,

> it is almost a source of personal sorrow to me that he is going to begin the publication of your next story before you finish it. You can't take your time about it, you can't afford to be sick, or lazy, or really at ease, and you give up control of the beginning before you have reached the end – you lose all hope of the happy second thoughts that arise as the work progresses.
>
> (DCM 3474)

Hardy would experience for himself the difficulties of sickness, telling Frank Hedgcock in 1910 that 'he always recalled with a shudder the writing of *A Laodicean*', dictated to Emma from his sick-bed. He explained further,

> writing a serial was no joke; in order to sustain the interest each instalment had to contain some striking incident; and editors often insisted on alterations to suit the taste or to avoid shocking the susceptibilities of their readers... To be ready with the necessary portion of manuscript at the proper date was often a trial and, when one was ill, a nightmare.
>
> (Hedgcock 1951: 224)

Hardy at times sounds almost embarrassingly subservient (or perhaps cynically pragmatic) towards his magazine editors. Sending the first 15 chapters of *The Return of the Native* to John Blackwood in 1877, and making no mention of the fact that Leslie Stephen had found the developing triangular relationship too dangerous for the *Cornhill*, he claimed that 'by changing into another periodical occasionally one acquires new readers'. He offered his prospective new editor *carte blanche* to revise it at will:

> should there accidentally occur any word or reflection not in harmony with the general tone of the magazine, you would be quite at liberty to strike it out if you chose. I always mention this to my editors, as it simplifies matters.
>
> (*Letters* I 49)

Even with this concession, however, the novel proved too risky for Blackwood, and Hardy, as we shall see, was forced to turn to monthlies with a more 'bohemian edge' (Law 2000: 194).

Hardy's dealings with his serial editors, the first readers of his work (after Emma) have been seen to have 'directed the course of his career in prose fiction . . . more than any other single factor outside his own creative powers' (Taylor 1982: 150), from Leslie Stephen of the *Cornhill* perpetually reminding him of the parson's daughter to the Reverend Donald Macleod of *Good Words* warning him that *The Trumpet-Major* should avoid 'anything – direct or indirect – which a healthy Parson like myself would not care to read to his bairns at the fireside' (DCM 2625), Editors were always telling him that his work was too miserable. C. J. Longman, for example, rejected "The Withered Arm" as 'a ghastly tragedy from beginning to end' with 'no relief in the incidents', reminding Hardy that the 'majority of magazine readers are girls' (DCM 3911). A similar reminder came from Arthur Locker of *The Graphic*, who rejected the original version of *A Group of Noble Dames* as appropriate enough for 'the supposed circumstances of their narration . . . the robust minds of a club smoking-room; but not at all suitable for the delicate imaginations of young girls' (DCM 2629).

Hardy, as we shall see, continued to receive explicit instructions from his editors about what was and was not acceptable to his readers. Mowbray Morris, editor of *Macmillan's Magazine*, in which *The Woodlanders* first appeared, grew anxious about the philandering Fitzpiers and rejected *Tess* outright. Chapter 5 will recount Hardy's difficulty in finding a periodical publisher for *Tess* and the changes he was forced to introduce into the story when it was finally published. The *Graphic* 'had always been rather more circumspect in its menu of fiction' than many of its rivals, such as the *Illustrated London News'* (chosen by Hardy for his next serial, 'The Pursuit of the Well-Beloved') which was then running Hall Caine's *The Scapegoat*, complete with 'loosely-attired harem girls' and 'the dramatic rescue of the heroine from imminent rape by the evil Sultan' (Law 2000: 192–3). Hardy's choice of the *Graphic*, in fact, and the drastic changes he introduced for the serial as opposed to the book form of *Tess*, may have been designed more to protest against the censorship imposed by the magazines than to find the most appropriate outlet for his work.

Each of the magazines for which Hardy wrote appealed to a particular audience, which I will attempt to characterise in greater detail in subsequent chapters. These journals, according to Norman Feltes, did not simply 'address social groupings as it found them . . . but rather reconstituted their members into a specialized clientèle' as consumers of 'branded goods' (Feltes 1986: 64). The difference between an intellectual magazine such as the *Cornhill* and the glossier *Illustrated London News*, for example, is apparent not only from the fiction they chose to publish and the way they presented it but from other articles and even their advertisements. Richard Ohmann's study of American magazines of the 1890s is able on such evidence to characterise *Harper's Monthly*, in which *Jude* appeared, as both implying and reaching 'an audience of the leisured and affluent, with culture given by birth and education, rather than achieved in spare moments as an adjunct to new and precarious respectability'. Even its cover was iconic:

> The publisher's name is inscribed on a pedestal that bears scattered musty shards of culture: two piles of books bound in morocco, parchment scrolls, an artist's palette, papers, an inkstand...On top stand two toga-clad children with baskets on their heads...
>
> (Ohmann 1996: 6–7)

Harper's published 'Literature' with a capital L (296), likening its function at one point to that of a university, devoted to 'culture' rather than the merely 'timely', which could be found in the ten-cent magazines (234). It deliberately excluded politics and religion (254), and catered for women but not blacks (267).

From the late 1880s, as we shall see, from the time he started writing for the *Graphic*, Hardy began consciously to address a dual audience, revising the serial significantly for the more serious audience he clearly envisaged as reading the volume. Letters of his from the 1890s frequently distinguish between the censored magazine and authentic 'book-form' of his novels (*Letters* II 48). He told friends not to read *Jude* 'in the Magazine, for I have been obliged to make many changes, omissions and glosses' in it (II 70). He even asked the publisher of the book to advertise it (with its new title) as 'a forthcoming new novel...the magazine form of the story being considerably mutilated' (II 69). By this time, however, his career as a novelist was in its final phase, the financial security he had achieved enabling him to write what he chose (poetry) rather than what would please an audience he had come to despise.

One form in which Hardy achieved a broader audience (both in mind and in numbers) was through newspaper serialisation. The expensive literary monthlies, such as the *Cornhill* and *Belgravia*, founded with a flourish in the 1860s, were already on the decline by the 1870s when he published in them. By 1882 the *Cornhill* could only claim a circulation of 12,000 (less than half of what it was when Leslie Stephen became editor). *Belgravia* had fallen to 3500 by 1887. From the mid-1870s, according to Graham Law, the dominant mode of initial British periodical publication (whether measured in terms of the number of works issued, the size of the audience reached, or the remuneration offered to authors) had shifted gradually but unmistakably from serialization in single metropolitan magazines . . . to syndication in groups of provincial weekly papers with complementary circulations.

(Law 2000: 32–3)

Henry Holt appears to have arranged for the serialization of some of Hardy's early novels in newspapers in the United States in the 1870s: the *Semi-Weekly Tribune* (owned by the *New York Tribune*) serialized *A Pair of Blue Eyes* in 1873 and *Far from the Madding Crowd* the following year while *The Hand of Ethelberta* appeared in the *New York Times* in 1876 (Weber 1946: 18, 285). In the 1880s he began to issue work through the most enterprising British syndicate, Tillotson's, who had begun syndicating fiction in the Lancashire weeklies in the 1870s and by the 1880s were supplying a wide range of provincial newspapers. 'Benighted Travellers', for example, later to be called 'The Honourable Laura' and to be collected in *A Group of Noble Dames*, first appeared in the *Christmas Leaves* supplement of the *Bolton Weekly Journal* in December 1881, to be followed by 'A Mere Interlude' in October 1885 and 'Alicia's Diary' in the *Manchester Weekly Times* in October 1887. Even *Tess of the D'Urbervilles*, as we shall see, was first designed for Tillotson's.

A provincial newspaper such as the *Nottinghamshire Guardian*, in which *Tess* appeared could boast a circulation in excess of a hundred thousand. In addition to this, *A Daughter of the D'Urbervilles* (a version of *Tess* similar to but not identical with that in the *Graphic*) found its way into papers as far afield as the *Sydney Mail*. Elizabeth Morrison has shown that Hardy was already by this time

a familiar and popular author in Australia, with his novels serialized in many papers throughout the 1880s: to name but a few, *A Laodicean* in the *Sydney Mail*, *Two on a Tower* and *The Mayor of Casterbridge* in the *Leader*, and the novella *Emmeline* in the Melbourne *Weekly Times*.

(Morrison 1995: 312)

Tillotson's syndicate also did business in the States, selling to a whole range of newspapers in the 1880s. Charles Johanningsmeier calculates that with only eight to ten full-time employees in Bolton and small branch offices in London, Berlin and New York, but with a single work appearing in up to a thousand newspapers simultaneously, Tillotson's

was 'reaching millions of readers on almost every continent' (Johanningsmeier 1997: 53).

These figures, of course, are hard to prove. It would be a massive
labour to discover which of Hardy's works appeared in which newspapers at any given time, since many provincial papers delayed publication until long after buying them from the syndicate. But the readership
that at least some of his work attained in newspapers was clearly different in both numbers and composition from that which he achieved in
the metropolitan monthlies. In the 1890s, it is true, the *Illustrated
London News* (which published 'The Pursuit of the Well-Beloved') and
the *Graphic* (which published *Tess*) could rise on occasion to half a
million readers (Law 2000: 133). An article of 1890 calculated up to
18 million readers worldwide, starting from a base in England of 3
million copies of all provincial weekly papers (127) while a survey in
the *Economic Review* in 1904 into reading habits in the industrial district
of Lancashire discovered Tillotson authors such as Rider Haggard and
M. E. Braddon being read in weekly papers on a Sunday by men who 'sit
akimbo on their door-steps, clad mostly in their shirt-sleeves' (Turner
1968: 110–11). It is possible, in other words, that Hardy's work reached
out beyond the middle classes through such newspapers.

A similar broadening of readership seems to have taken place in the
volume publication of Hardy's work, from the expensive small print
runs of the early work, designed to achieve 'select' readers through the
circulating libraries, to the cheap reprints in much larger numbers
through which later novels such as *Tess* achieved sales of 100,000 at
the beginning of the twentieth century. As with serialization, there was a
massive expansion in production over the period, although reliable
figures are hard to acquire. Walter Besant speculated that the reading
public for books grew from a mere 50,000 in 1830 to one hundred and
twenty million in 1890, taking into account the markets opened by
imperial expansion (Sutherland 1976: 64). Wilkie Collins, in his 1859
article on 'The Unknown Public', claimed suddenly to have discovered a
'*monster* audience of at least three million', currently being fobbed off
with penny fiction' that could be taught to read something better
(Brantlinger 1998: 17).

Hardy's novels, however, until the 1890s at least, appear to have
reached only the upper echelons of this potential readership. The first
editions rarely sold their average print run of 1000 copies at the standard
price for the three-decker of a guinea and a half and had often to be
remaindered. *Desperate Remedies*, published at this price in an edition of
500 in March 1871, was by June being offered in their reduced lists for

half a crown and three shillings respectively by Smith's and Mudie's (Purdy 1954: 5). The *Life* records Hardy's devastation on seeing this in Smith's surplus catalogue at Exeter Station 'the day after his birthday' (*Life* 87). The first edition of *Under the Greenwood Tree* in June 1872 appeared in the same miniscule print run although Tinsley also produced a two-shilling edition the following August (presumably designed to undercut the ex-library reductions). For *Far from the Madding Crowd*, which had been so successful in the *Cornhill*, Smith, Elder ran to an additional impression of a mere 500 copies on top of the first edition of 1000.

The pattern seems to have remained the same for all subsequent novels until the 1890s. *The Mayor of Casterbridge* appeared in an even smaller first edition of 758 in May 1886 and yet had even more copies remaindered the following January (Purdy 1954: 53). Of the first edition of 1000 copies of *The Woodlanders* which appeared in March 1887, 170 were remaindered in June (57). Only with *Tess* did the picture change, 17,000 copies of the one-volume edition, the so-called 'Fifth Edition', published at six shillings in September, selling before the end of the year. *Jude* appeared at the same price to similar commercial success as the eighth volume in Osgood, McIlvaine's edition of the Wessex Novels (91). Hardy had already negotiated with Macmillan for them to publish the Colonial Edition of his works (all except *Under the Greenwood Tree*, whose copyright had passed from the bankrupt Tinsleys to Chatto & Windus) although this was 'intended for circulation only in India and the British Colonies' (*Letters* II 58–9, Joshi 1998: 219). Only 3000 copies were printed even for *Tess* (Gatrell 1988: 251).

It was the controversy over *Tess*, of course, that made Hardy better known. Mrs Humphry Ward recalls that 'Tess marked the conversion of the larger public, who then began to read all the earlier books, in that curiously changed mood which sets in when a writer is no longer on trial, but has, so to speak, "made good"' (Ward 1918: 359). When Osgood, McIlvaine were absorbed by Harpers in 1900, however, Hardy's new publishers sought to increase the sale of his most popular fiction by publishing paperback editions of *Tess* and *Far from the Madding Crowd*, at sixpence each (Millgate 1982: 404). A list of sales for these editions in the first twelve months shows that *Tess* sold 100,000 and *Far from the Madding Crowd* over 45,000, figures which Hardy was not slow in quoting to Macmillan in his negotiation with them for their Uniform Edition of 1902 (*Letters* III 14). The situation in the United States, of course, was more complicated, especially before the International Copyright Act of 1891. Prior to that, pirated editions circulated at very low prices. Richard Altick has traced at least five unauthorised editions of *The Mayor of Casterbridge*, costing from one dollar down to twenty cents (Altick 1989: 221). The United States Book Company of New York beat the new copyright law by publishing 13 titles by Hardy in 1890 at prices ranging from ten to fifty cents (Weber 1946: 287). But in the United Kingdom up to the turn of the century the price of his books remained sufficiently expensive for only the reasonably well off to afford.

It was well into the twentieth century, in fact, before Hardy began to be regarded as a 'great' writer, a novelist whom any literate person ought to have read. At the annual dinners of the Royal Literary Fund through the 1880s and 1890s, at which it was customary to lament the decline of literature in general and the absence of great novelists in particular, 'no one even alluded to the work of Meredith, Hardy, Gissing, James and Conrad' (Cross 1985). Hardy, who attended the dinner in 1893, thought it rather tactless of A. J. Balfour to dwell with so 'much emphasis on the decline of the literary art, and on his opinion that there were no writers of high rank living in these days. We hid our diminished heads, and buttoned our pockets' (*Life* 269). The award of the Order of Merit in 1910, however, followed by the production of the Wessex Edition of 1912, appear significantly to have altered Hardy's status. Even then, according to Frank Swinnerton in his account of *The Georgian Literary Scene*, 'his reputation may be said not to have reached its climax until about 1920' (Swinnerton 1950: 14), a judgement confirmed by the figures for the printing of the Pocket Edition of his work from 1906, which 'show a curve of demand' for Hardy's writing in the 1920s. Total figures for Hardy's fiction in this edition over successive five-year periods actually dipped from 83,000 for 1906–10 to 69,000 for 1911–15 before rising to 162,650 in 1916–20. They then leapt to 407,200 for the following five years before descending slightly to 351,300 for 1926–30 and then plummeting to 18,000 for 1931–5 (Gatrell 1988: 253). Even these are enormous figures, however, in comparison with those for the first editions.

Somerset Maugham's irreverent account of the sudden growth in reputation of the fictional novelist Edward Driffield, which so upset the widowed Florence Hardy when it first appeared in 1930 (Gittings 1979: 131–3), captures more imaginatively than these figures the nature of this change in what is clearly Hardy's standing:

When he was a young fellow...his position in the world of letters was only respectable; the best judges praised him, but with moderation; the younger men were inclined to be frivolous at his expense. It was agreed that he had talent, but it never occurred to anyone that he was one of the glories of English literature. He celebrated his seventieth birthday... and it grew evident that there had lived among us all these years a great novelist and none of us had suspected it. There was a rush for Driffield's books in the various libraries and a hundred busy pens, in Bloomsbury, in Chelsea, and in other places, wrote appreciations, studies, essays, and works, short and chatty or long and intense, on his novels. These were reprinted, in complete editions, in select editions... His style was analysed, his philosophy was examined, his technique was dissected. At seventy-five everyone agreed that Edward Driffield had genius. At eighty he was the Grand Old Man of English Letters.

(Maugham 1948: 98–9)

Like Swinnerton, in other words, and in line with Macmillan's figures, Maugham dates the zenith of Hardy's fame at 1920.

Prior to becoming rather late beloved Hardy relied primarily upon the circulating libraries for readers of his novels in volume form. These, of course, were dominated by Charles Edward Mudie, a devout nonconformist lay preacher and writer of hymns, who had founded his Select Library in 1840, and W. H. Smith, an evangelical Anglican whose Circulating Library was founded twenty years later. Guinevere Griest in her study of *Mudie's Circulating Library and the Victorian Novel* explains some of the benefits it brought to the ordinary subscriber, who, for the modest outlay of a guinea a year, was given access to the latest fiction. Mudie's would buy large numbers of novels likely to prove popular (over three thousand of *Silas Marner*, for example), dispatching at their height a thousand boxes of books a week all over the world (Griest 1970: 20, 29). *Tinsley's Magazine* in 1872 (the year it began serialising *A Pair of Blue Eyes*) defended the libraries both on the grounds of promoting new writers (by ensuring sales) and on simple economics: six to twelve members of a household, it calculated, could, for two to three guineas, read between two and three hundred pounds worth of books in any one year (162). An article by Alexander Shand in *Blackwood's Magazine* of 1879 made a similar point:

Nowadays a man who can afford a moderate subscription has such opportunities as the richer of our grandfathers never hoped for, and even students in the humblest ranks of society are generally within reach of some literary institute... the volumes from the libraries in the leading cities gradually find their way into the country towns and villages, till...they pass in process of time into the hands of the housemaids. (Brake 1993: 96)

It may be tempting to believe that some of Hardy's volumes completed this long journey but the subscribers would have been solidly middle class.

The circulating libraries, like the monthly magazines, exerted huge power and influence over publishers. The word 'Select' in Mudie's title in effect meant censored: both Mudie and Smith excluded books of which they did not approve on moral or literary grounds. Mudie is quoted in an article in the *Athenaeum* of 1860 unashamedly defending such selection as a means of erecting 'a barrier of some kind' between his respectable subscribers 'and the lower floods of literature' (Flint 1993: 144). William Wallace's review of *The Woodlanders* in the *Academy* (9.4.87) refers somewhat scathingly to 'the ordinary clients of Mr. Mudie, who feel dissatisfied unless Virtue passes a Coercion Bill against Vice at the end of the third volume'. In the debate that raged over what George Moore called 'A New Censorship in Literature' in the *Pall Mall Gazette* in 1884 after two 'ladies in the country' had written to Mudie complaining about scenes in *A Modern Lover*, leading to the withdrawal of that book from his shelves, George Gissing explained that the difficulties lay deeper than the means of distribution: 'If you abolish the library system tomorrow, you are no nearer persuading the "two ladies in the country"... to let this or that work lie on their drawing room tables' (Flint 1993: 145). There was little point, therefore, in raging against it as Moore did the following year in *Literature at Nurse, or Circulating Morals*. The library system simply reflected the wishes of their subscribers: 'The great mass of middle-class readers...objected to dubious topics in books intended for family reading' (Lonoff 1982: 8). They were quite happy for Mudie or Smith to decide for them what was or was not suitable for their daughters. But for writers, as Edmund Gosse explained in the *Contemporary Review* in 1891, it created

the disease which we might call Mudieitis, the inflammation produced by the fear that what you are inspired to say, and know you ought to say, will be unpalatable to the circulating libraries, that 'the wife of a country incumbent,' that terror before which Messrs. Smith fall prone upon their faces, may write up to headquarters and expostulate.

(Brake 1993: 96)

These, of course, are precisely the complaints Hardy had made the previous year in 'Candour in English Fiction'.

To Richard Altick in his pioneering study of *The English Common Reader* it was clear that the great nineteenth-century authors wrote for a 'relatively small, intellectually and socially superior audience' (Altick 1957). Altick noted the massive growth in literacy during the period, rising to 97.2 per cent of the adult male population and 96.8 per cent of the female population respectively (171). He described the developments in education, in particular the institution of the recommendation of the Taunton Commission of 1868–70 that the teaching of English literature should occupy much more time in the curriculum of the Board Schools (182). He also charted the development through the century of such institutions as Mechanics Institutes, Mutual Improvement Societies, Working Men's Colleges, University Extension Lectures, Public Libraries, and the National Home Reading Union. There was clearly a change between *The British Working Class Reader* of the first half of the century, as portrayed by R. K. Webb, and his (or even her) equivalent by its end; 'only in the memoirs of men who had grown up after the middle of the century,' Altick remarks, 'do we find frequent allusions to contemporary authors' (259). Prior to that (and in many cases later still) the working-class autobiographies edited and discussed by historians such as David Vincent show a familiarity only with an extremely limited range of books of the kind that comprise Gabriel Oak's small collection (*FMC* 63): the Bible and such classics of protestant fiction as *Robinson Crusoe* and *Pilgrim's Progress*, in some cases supplemented by the works of Scott and Dickens. An article in the *Nineteenth Century* of 1886 on 'What the Working Classes Read' lamented that they no longer read even the Bible and *Pilgrim's Progress* but only reports of murders in the *News of the World* (Vincent 1989: 179).

Even the growth of public libraries was slow. The Ewart Act of 1850 had permitted boroughs of over 10,000 inhabitants to levy tax for public libraries but by 1860 only twenty authorities had done so, by 1880 ninety-five and by 1896 only 334 (Griest 1970: 80; Altick 1957: 227). These libraries, like those of the Mechanics Institutes earlier in the century, agonised over whether to stock fiction, which was still regarded as uneducational, even demoralising. Thomas Greenwood, for example, in his 1891 history of *Public Libraries*, records complaints from the public that they were full of 'loafing office boys...devouring all the most trivial trash' (Brantlinger 1998: 20). Even in 1924, as Q. D. Leavis records, the battle continued between what the libraries stocked and what people wanted to read: urban public libraries held 63 per cent non-fiction of which only 22 per cent was issued whereas 78 per cent of its limited stock of fiction was issued (Leavis 1932: 4).

More recently, historians of reading such as Jonathan Rose have challenged some of Altick's conclusions, 'Rereading the Common Reader' and encouraging us to find more evidence of working-class reading of high-brow fiction. It was Rose who discovered individuals such as the housemaid Edith Hall reading *Tess* in the 1920s and Emmanuel Shinwell finding copies of Hardy in second-hand bookshops in Glasgow around 1902 (Rose 1992: 62–3). Hardy, however, does not feature among the authors nominated by the first large cohort of 51 Labour MPs elected in 1906 as having had the most influence over them (56). Ruskin, Dickens, Carlyle and Scott (along with the Bible and Shakespeare) are the writers they remember. Ernest Baker, who conducted a survey of 21 public libraries and their holdings the following year, omitted to include Hardy among his list of eleven 'good' as opposed to 'popular' authors (Baker 1907), as did Simon Eliot in his study of public library borrowing figures for 24 authors between 1883 and 1912 (Eliot 1994). It is only in the twentieth century that Jonathan Rose can find evidence of the working classes borrowing classic Victorian fiction from their libraries (Rose 1993: 75–6). Until hard evidence emerges of heavy borrowing of Hardy from earlier periods, it must remain doubtful that Hardy was read in significant numbers outside the middle and upper classes.

Negative evidence, of course, is inconclusive. But none of the working-class autobiographies listed by David Vincent in his bibliography to *Bread, Knowledge and Freedom* refers to Hardy. Only very few of those indexed under reading as one of their leisure activities in the three-volume annotated critical bibliography of *The Autobiography of the Working Class*, which covers people born up to 1945 (Burnett 1984), mention him. Trade union leaders, especially those involved in the plight of agricultural workers, such as Joseph Arch and Thomas Mann, ought to have read Hardy but did not. Part of the problem appears to have been that serious working-class men read serious political writers. 'The earnest worker,' according to David Vincent, read Carlyle and Ruskin, John Stuart Mill and Henry George; Keir Hardie not Thomas Hardy (Vincent 1989: 261–2). Well-meaning educators such as Richard Green Moulton, who followed up his University Extension Lectures in Newcastle in the 1880s by founding the Backworth Classical Novel-Reading Union, based on a mining village between Newcastle and Monkseaton, at which they read a novel a month for four years, lamented that 'although Backworth read fiction, it was not fiction of the best class'. For him, fiction should provide 'a wholesome and educational influence' (Moulton 1895: 18). What this meant in practice was a diet of Scott and Dickens, Kingsley and Eliot, with an emphasis upon historical fiction. No Hardy appears among the list of 25 novels studied. The National Home Reading Union, a development of University Extension lectures designed to make reading 'educational in the broadest sense of the word', to encourage 'recreative and instructive reading among all classes of the community' (Stimpson 2000: 2), if it recommended novels at all, also chose historical novels such as Henry Esmond, or a special course of 1897 on 'History as Taught in Scott's Novels' (52).

Hardy, as well as not being sufficiently historical (*The Trumpet-Major* never appearing on these lists), appears not to have been sufficiently 'wholesome' for general recommendation. This appears to have been the reason why Robert Blatchford, in the list of recommended reading at the back of *Merrie England* (1894), includes Richard Jefferies but not Hardy, along with Dickens, Hugo and Olive Schreiner. *Tess* makes a fleeting appearance in the chapter on realism in his more sustained account of *My Favourite Books* but Robert Louis Stevenson is recommended more enthusiastically as one of those writers 'whose smiles cheer, whose words delight and heal' (Blatchford n.d.: 56). Hardy, it seems, provided insufficient moral uplift. There are records of individual working class readers of Hardy. Jonathan Rose, in his study of *The Intellectual Life of the Working Classes*, produces some nice examples: a Welsh Nonconformist, Thomas Jones (b.1870), hid his copy of *Far From the Madding Crowd*, borrowed from the Rhymney Workmen's Institute Library, under the ledger at the ironworks where he was supposed to be a timekeeper (Rose 2001: 33–4). A. E. Coppard (b.1878), who educated himself at Brighton Public Library, got into similar trouble when his supervisor found *Jude* in his desk. Jack Lawson (b.1881) read his way through the novelists (including Hardy) in the Boldon Miners' Institute Library (51) while Wil Edwards (b.1888) and D. R. Davies (b.1889) befriended the librarian at the Maesteg Miners' Institute Library and procured their copies of Hardy through him (239–43). But Hardy was regarded as a dangerous writer: Mary Bentley (b.1896) had her copy of *Jude* confiscated by her father who worked in a soap factory when she tried to read it at 14, comforting herself with the thought that she 'didn't like it anyhow' nor 'cry over it as I did over Tess' (210). Kathleen Betterton (b.1913), whose father worked as a lift operator in the London Underground, won a scholarship to Christ's Hospital in Hertford only to find that any books dealing remotely with love (including novels by Hardy) were 'jacketed in red calico' in the school library to indicate that only sixth formers could borrow them (143). Perhaps the saddest case is that of a Coventry millworker who found his son 'dead in his room, with a phial of poison beside him and *Jude the Obscure* under his pillow' (399). Such were the consequences of unwholesome reading.

Other readers from working-class backgrounds have registered how they first encountered Hardy. V. S. Pritchett, for example, found a photograph of Hardy and a chapter from *Under the Greenwood Tree* in his father's copy of the *International Library of Famous Literature*, first published in 1899 (Pritchett 1969: 108). Bonar Thompson, an Ulster-man born in 1888 and brought up to think all novels sinful, read journals such as *Good Words* at his aunt's and the *Illustrated London News* in public libraries. He records how, when he was supposed to be fitting brakes for the Great Central Railways in Manchester, he would instead 'lie on the seat of an old railway carriage reading Dickens or Hardy' (Thompson 1934: 70). That this was an unusual habit, however, is clear from the reaction of his workmates: 'when one of them saw me with a book in my hand he would look at the others and touch his forehead significantly' (67). A. L. Rowse has written of the way he 'fell for' Hardy on being introduced to his work by a teacher in his final year at school shortly after the end of the Great War, although *Jude* succeeded only in contributing to his 'growing exasperation with the circum-stances of my home-life, and with the difficulties, indeed the improb-ability, of my getting to Oxford' (Rowse 1942: 207). For Harold Hobson a few years later the novel had the opposite effect (Hobson 1978: 119–20) while another future Fellow of All Souls, E. L. Woodward, discovered Hardy for himself at Streatham Public Library: 'Hardy's name was never even mentioned to me by my schoolmasters' at Merchant Taylors' in the years prior to his going to Oxford in 1908 (Woodward 1942: 33). These, however, are exceptional individuals, hardly representative of their class as a whole.

It is difficult in many of these cases to date the precise moment of these encounters with Hardy. Most appear to have occurred in the first decades of the new century when his work had become both well known and widely available. It was then that Frederick Gould, who ran a Secular Hall Sunday School for adolescents in Leicester, made his class send Hardy a letter of thanks for the experience of reading *Far from the Madding Crowd*. Even he was clearly attempting to impose middle-class values on his charges, on the principle that 'the most powerful way of fighting an inferior taste is to implant a better' (Gould 1923: 98–9). By the 1920s, as we have seen, when Hardy's reputation was at its height and his work more readily available, it would have become more common for keen readers to encounter him. Some of the extracts from letters written by members of the Women's Co-operative in 1927 record at least a desire to read Hardy. 'I am longing to read *Tess*,' writes one, while another claims, 'I am just going to start to read Hardy's *Tess*' (Davies 1977: 115, 118). Three others record actually having read some of Hardy's work (116, 128–9). But even in 1936, when WEA students in the London area were asked to name the 'fiction writers whose novels you read frequently and enjoy,' only 6.7 per cent nominated Hardy in comparison with over 20 per cent for Galsworthy (Rose 2001: 139). There appears to have been a residual whiff of the WEA about Hardy, however, when a later working-class teenager, Roy Hattersley, heard of him through the agent of a Labour candidate who kept 'quoting from the Thomas Hardy's and George Eliots of his WEA past' in the years immediately after the Second World War (Hattersley 1983: 176–7). By then, of course, he had become more widely known through other educational institutions. Before that time, however, and certainly in the nineteenth century, it is safe to assume that his primary audience was almost exclusively upper and middle class. What the next section of this chapter will argue is that he both knew and resented that fact.

Questions of class: resenting 'Hodge'

Hardy learnt by painful experience that he had to temper what he wanted to write to meet at least some of the demands of his audience. All the potentially controversial political ingredients of his rejected first novel *The Poor Man and the Lady* had to be watered down in order to produce the publishable short story 'An Indiscretion in the Life of an Heiress' (Ebbatson 1993: 118–20). All his subsequent work, Eagleton argues, bears the mark of 'his fraught productive relation to the metropolitan audience whose spokesmen rejected his first, abrasively radical work' (Eagleton 1976: 131). This 'fraught' relationship is perhaps best characterised as a form of resentment: the 'imaginary revenge' of the slave 'to whom the real reaction, that of the deed, is denied'. *Ressentiment*, Nietzsche explains in *The Genealogy of Morals*, is the only available means by which 'the downtrodden' can express their hatred of their masters, attacking them '*in effigie*' (Nietzsche 1996:23). Such class resentment is literally enacted in the skimmity-ride in *The Mayor of Casterbridge*, when the effigies of the elegant Lucetta and her former lover are paraded through the streets, illustrating what Farfrae calls the 'tempting prospect of putting to the blush people who stand at the head of affairs – that supreme and piquant enjoyment of those who writhe under the heel of the same' (*MC* 295).

The oppressed, according to Nietzsche, 'suppurate with poisonous and hostile feelings' which find expression in peculiar distorted ways:

> the man of *ressentiment* is neither upright nor naïve in his dealings with others, nor is he open and honest with himself. His soul *squints*; his mind loves bolt-holes, secret paths, back doors, he regards all hidden things as *his* world, *his* security, *his* refreshment; he has a perfect understanding of how to keep silent, how not to forget, how to wait, how to make himself provisionally small and submissive.
>
> (Nietzsche 1996: 24)

Only 'provisionally', of course, since he is clever enough, while accepting their patronage, to gain his revenge through indirect modes of subversion, 'humbly' nailing his admiring audience. It is a model applied by Jameson to Balzac, Gissing and Conrad that can also be applied to Hardy's fiction, produced in the first place to please his literary masters but incorporating within it an increasingly savage critique. His choice of epigraph for his most autobiographical novel, a phrase from Lucretius, *'Vitae post-scenia celant'* ('[they struggle to] hide these backstage bits of life' [*HE* 425]), nicely captures the 'back-door' secrecy to which both he and his heroine Ethelberta are forced to resort. To include his one-time-servant mother's maiden name in the title of *The Hand of Ethelberta*, a revelation so indirect that only a handful of contemporary readers could have understood it, typifies the kind of 'bolt-hole' in which Nietzsche's 'man of *ressentiment*' takes refuge.

Hardy's complex class position as a professional writer who had worked his way out of the skilled 'working class' to which most of his relatives belonged, made him acutely sensitive to the subtlest indications of class, while his liberal politics, respecting the responsibility of individuals for their own destiny, prevented him from espousing the grand narratives of class conflict and liberation being propounded by his contemporaries Marx and Engels. He rejected the very concept of a 'class' of people, preferring to deal with 'individuals experiencing "history"' in a manner irreducible to generalisation (Goode 1980: 23). Class in the Marxist sense, as Goode explains, is not merely 'a system of social layers' but 'a manifestation of a set of relations . . . of production':

> although this sense of *class* enters the language dramatically in the critical period between the first reform act and the repeal of the corn laws, *class* reverts to something much closer to the eighteenth-century idea of rank at around the time of the second reform bill.

This allowed liberals such as Hardy, writing in the decades immediately after this second significant extension of the franchise, to support reforms which enabled individual social mobility and to be alert to any resistance to such mobility based merely on rank rather than merit without campaigning for radical alteration to the basic economic structure of society. Hardy himself became one of Arnold's class 'aliens', intellectuals who had risen above their original class interests to promote a broader concept of culture (27).

From a Marxist perspective, however, Hardy provides a classic example of alienated labour. The way the *Life* refers disparagingly to novel-writing as a 'trade' into which he was forced for commercial reasons and which he abandoned for poetry, his true love, when he could afford to do so, fits precisely Marx's analysis of labour as a commodity, an alien object from which the producer feels strangely distant (Marx 1977: 78). Hardy's encounter with the Victorian literary marketplace, I would suggest – the compromises he was forced to make in order to meet the demands of his editors and publishers – accounts at least in part for the sense of alienation from his work which the *Life* displays. The *Life* also reveals a contradictory sense of class in the sense of rank, mixing

> the inverted snobbery of the insecure parvenu in its passing comments on Hardy's lack of 'social ambition' (15), his shrinking from 'the business of social advancement' (53), his dislike of 'the fashionable throng' (266)...with an exhaustive...catalogue of his hobnobbings, from the 1890s onwards, with the great and the good of English society.
>
> (Widdowson 1997: xxvi)

The account in the *Life* of Hardy's 'voluntary' suppression of 'The Poor Man and the Lady' is revealing in this respect. 'The story', we are told, was, among other things, 'a sweeping dramatic satire of the squirearchy and nobility, London society, the vulgarity of the middle class' while 'the author's views' were 'those of many a young man before and after him, the tendency of the writing being socialistic, not to say revolutionary'. Meredith, the reader for Chapman & Hall, advised him 'not to "nail his colours to the mast" so definitely in a first book' since 'he would be attacked on all sides by the conventional reviewers, and his future injured'. Hardy flatters later readers of the *Life* by acknowledging that 'the novel might have been accepted calmly enough by the reviewers and public in these days' while insisting that 'in genteel mid-Victorian

1869 it would no doubt have incurred, as Meredith judged, severe strictures which might have handicapped a young writer for a long time' (*Life* 62–4).

Hardy's submission to the necessities of mid-Victorian publishing, however, was by no means complete. He also employed his fiction to challenge or subvert some of the assumptions of his middle-class metropolitan audience, especially their complicity in the myth of 'Hodge', the archetypal 'peasant'. Introducing Stephen Smith's stonemason father to readers of *A Pair of Blue Eyes*, he insists,

> In common with most rural mechanics, he had too much individuality to be a typical 'working-man' – the result of that constant pebble-like attrition with his kind only to be experienced in large towns, which metamorphoses the unit Self into a fraction of the unit Class.
>
> (*PBE* 89)

The *Life* expresses real fears about the urban working class, that 'monster whose body had four million heads and eight million eyes' (*Life* 141). But Hardy was determined to prevent his audience from lumping the rural proletariat together as peasants. This was the main point of his essay for *Longman's Magazine* of 1883, 'The Dorsetshire Labourer', which begins by confronting the inadequacy of the conventional view of Hodge as 'a degraded being of uncouth manner and aspect' who 'hangs his head or looks sheepish when spoken to, and thinks Lunnon a place paved with gold' (*PW* 168–9). Hardy then invites one of his metropolitan readers to pay an extended visit to Dorset. After six months' residence in a labourer's cottage he imagines 'our gentleman' leaving Dorset with his image of 'Hodge, the dull unvarying, joyless one ... disintegrated into a number of dissimilar fellow-creatures, men of many minds, infinite in difference' (170). He concedes that things may be different in towns, where labour can be alienating and destructive, but in the country, he claims, a healthier environment produces happier results (171). He continues to challenge his readers, however, satirising upper-class 'philosophers who look down upon that class from the Olympian heights of society' and philanthropic 'ladies' who take an untidy cottage to be 'a frightful example of the misery of the labouring classes' (172). The first requirement for an informed discussion of the plight of rural labour, in other words, is an accurate knowledge of their real conditions.

Many of the arguments (and some of the same words) of this essay reappear in Hardy's novels along with the same ambivalence towards his audience. Angel Clare, like the 'gentleman' of the essay, is made to spend six months on a farm during which time his perceptions are radically altered:

> The conventional farm-folk of his imagination – personified in the newspaper-press by the pitiable dummy known as Hodge – were obliterated after a few days' residence. At close quarters no Hodge was to be seen... His host and his host's household, his men and his maids, as they became intimately known to Clare, began to differentiate themselves as in a chemical process.... The typical and unvarying Hodge ceased to exist. He had been disintegrated into a number of varied fellow-creatures – beings of many minds, beings infinite in difference...
>
> (*T* 117–18)

These words were recycled in one of the many interviews collected in Hardy's Scrapbook of 'Personal Reviews', 'Hodge as I Know Him', from the *Pall Mall Gazette* of 1892, in which he attributed the unpopularity of the parson not only to his outmoded theology but to his friendship with the squire. He also contrasted rural labourers, who were 'full of character' with 'the strained, calculating, unromantic middle classes' (DCM 6447 f. 17). A similar contrast between rural labourers, full of an individuality belied by the stereotypical Hodge, and 'the calculating, unromantic middle-classes' appeared in another press interview of that year, 'A Chat with the Author of *Tess*' in *Black and White* in August 1892 (f. 29; cf. Lerner 1968: 90–7). Hodge would continue to make satirical appearances in Hardy's work, most poignantly perhaps when he serves as a drummer in the Boer War, dying for a cause of which he has no understanding (*CP* 83). By the 1890s, as we shall see, his fiction too had become more outspoken about class issues, prepared more openly to challenge his readers.

Hardy's sensitivity to the stereotype Hodge is matched by his reaction to the word 'peasant', a label which Merryn and Raymond Williams have called 'the class language of another class' (Williams 1980: 34). It is the word used by Parson Swancourt on discovering that the man he has been encouraging to court his daughter on the mistaken belief that he was a 'gentleman' was in fact 'the son of one of my village peasants' (*PBE* 84). Hardy's own father-in-law is said to have referred to him as the 'low-born churl who has presumed to marry into *my* family' (Millgate 1982: 142–3) while Emma herself, speaking of her husband's family, is reported to have 'declared that the less one had to do with "the peasant class" the better' (355). The *Life* famously engages in extraordinary 'genealogical gymnastics' to disguise 'just how humble' Hardy's origins were. The 1851 census describes his father as a 'bricklayer' (Gibson 1996: 30). When Charles Kegan Paul, however, in a sympathetic article on 'Mr Hardy's Novels' in 1881, described him as 'sprung of a race of labouring men', Hardy wrote at great length to insist that his father's family, for at least the last four generations, had been 'master-masons, with a set of journeymen masons under them: though they have never risen above this level, they have *never* sunk below it – i.e. they have never been journeymen themselves'. He even suggested that they may have come 'from Jersey in the 14th century, like the other Dorset Hardies' (*Letters* I 89).

Hardy's father may have been a master-mason but his brother (Hardy's uncle) John was 'an ordinary labourer who married a labourer's daughter and had seven children. His mother, herself the daughter of a servant, George Hand, had been a cook and a ladies' maid, and was one of seven pauper children brought up on parish relief' (Widdowson 1989: 131). The wider family included a variety of labourers, cobblers, bricklayers and servants, none of whom appears in the *Life* (Gittings 1978: 18). His own rise into respectability, first as an architect and then as a writer, took him into very different circles. When he and Emma moved to Wimborne in 1881, for example, they mixed (however uncomfortably) with generals and judges at local Shakespeare readings and even attended a ball given by Lord and Lady Wimborne (Millgate 1982: 222). Max Gate, however, as Millgate suggests, represents more accurately what he had become: 'not a landowning "gentleman", but ... a man of the professional middle class' (261). It was accordingly sneered at by social superiors such as A. C. Benson as 'a structure at once mean and pretentious', the sort of building to be expected of an *arriviste* (259). Hardy himself, Katharine Adams reported to Sir Sydney Cockerell in 1920, changed dramatically. Thirty years earlier, when they had first met, he had struck her as 'a rough-looking man ... with ... a decided accent', very different from the 'refined, fragile, gentle little old gentleman, with ... polished manners' that he had become (Meynell 1956: 25).

The fashionable London social circles in which Hardy later moved was, according to Raymond Williams, 'a world' to which 'he should never have got near; never have let himself be exposed', one in which men like Somerset Maugham would patronise him as 'a little man with an earthy face' and 'a strange look of the soil' (Williams 1970: 99). His 'apparent weakness for London "society"', however, was 'to a large extent professionally orientated' (Millgate 1982: 265). He needed to maintain contacts with literary people, to broaden his social range and to understand his audience, the people who actually read his work.

It was a constant complaint of reviewers that Hardy could only write about peasants. Even friends such as J. M. Barrie and Edmund Gosse told him to stick with what he knew (Cox 1970: 159, 269). The constant critical carping about his depiction of the 'upper classes', according to Wotton,

> is itself an interesting reflection on the class orientation of the dis-
> course of aesthetic ideology; for well over half a century the produc-
> tion of 'Thomas Hardy' was in the hands of the distinctly definable
> group – the metropolitan intelligentzia.
>
> (Wotton 1985: 150)

Virginia Woolf, complaining that Hardy could become 'lumpish and dull and inexpressive' when he left 'the yeoman or farmer to describe the class above theirs in the social scale' (McNeillie 1966: I 262), exemplifies this tendency precisely.

Hardy's comments, on the other hand, in his own copies of the critical works published in his own lifetime, express his side of the relationship, revealing the anger such comments provoked in him. Annie Macdonell's suggestion in 1894 that 'only a little portion of his life has been spent away' from the neighbourhood of Dorchester is subjected to the cryptic correction 'nearly half at this date' (Macdonell 1894: 33). Among the many corrections in Hardy's copy of F. A. Hedgcock's *Thomas Hardy: Penseur et Artiste* are his objection to being deemed lacking in education, which he calls 'misleading – He learnt Latin at school from his 12th year and had at home the usual Latin classics' (Hedgcock 1911: 17). Latin, of course, was the mark of a 'gentleman', so Hardy calls Hedgcock's suggestion that he drew on his own experience to portray Stephen Smith's attempts to make good his deficiencies in this regard not only 'misleading' but 'invidious and mostly incorrect'. Hedgcock's reference to '*notre jeune campagnard*' provokes the somewhat fanciful comment, 'So little of a rustic was he that he was taken everywhere as a long-time London resident!' (27). More supposed similarities between Smith and Hardy call forth further expostulations: 'S. S.'s father is not at all like T. H.'s (who was not a journeyman)' (31). Nor will Hardy allow similarities between himself and Clym Yeobright (33). He objects to the notion of an abyss suddenly opening between his life in London and 'le simple milieu de son enfance': 'but he had lived at Mr Hicks's in Dorch[este]r for some time' (35). The angry dialogue between Hardy and the well-meaning Hedgcock in the pages of this volume dramatises the class tensions that soured Hardy's relationship with the majority of his readers.

Hardy would subject similar suggestions in the work of the American critics Samuel Chew and Ernest Brennecke to equally severe marginal correction. In rebuttal of Chew's critique of the 'feeble satiric sketches in the London portions of *A Pair of Blue Eyes* and in *The Hand of Ethelberta* Hardy claims, 'Eveline 5th Countess of Portsmouth obtained an introduction to the author because this novel was the only one she had lately met with "which showed society people exactly as they were"'' (Chew 1921: 25). Many of these points are reiterated in the 'Notes on Professor Chew's Book' compiled by Florence Hardy presumably from the margins of the book (*Letters* VI 154–7). Hardy's comments in the margins of his copy of Ernest Brennecke's *Life of Thomas Hardy* of 1925 are briefer, often reduced to single-word cries of 'false', 'garbled' and 'incorrect'. Again, however, the image of Hardy scribbling furiously into the margins of these volumes represents all too clearly his continuing resentment of all references to his supposed class origins.

The image of himself that Hardy attempted to build for his readers through newspapers and later in the *Life* was very different. One of the earliest of the articles in his 'personal' scrapbook, for example, is a potted biography produced at the request of the Boston *Literary World* in 1878, 'written out in Emma's hand' but 'clearly Hardy's own work, embodying the professional self-image he wished to project' (Millgate 1982: 195). This somewhat exaggerated the formality of his 'higher education', which was reportedly conducted by 'an able classical scholar and Fellow of Queen's College, Cambridge', the misplaced apostrophe in the title of the college somewhat undermining Hardy's attempt to invest Horace Moule's role as mentor with a more official status than it merited (DCM 6447 f. 5). In the 1890s, when the controversy over *Tess* made him the target for interviews and other articles in the new crop of papers catering for literary gossip, he tried once more to convey an image of urbanity in every sense. An interview for *Cassell's Saturday Journal* of January 1892 in a series entitled 'Representative Men at Home' has him confiding, 'Originally, you know, I was inclined for the Church, but somehow I abandoned that'. The 'somehow' here conceals the fact that his father could not possibly have supported him through the necessary training. The anonymous interviewer not only describes Hardy as 'a Dorsetshire man by birth and breeding' (with all the gentlemanly associations of those two nouns) but proceeds dutifully to mention the Elizabethan and Napoleonic Hardies. The Dorset Hardies of later generations, he continues, may have been 'landless, as Mr Hardy smilingly says,' but they were not to be seen as peasants. Hardy insists that he is 'much more of a town bird than many of his readers may think'; he comes up to his 'West-End flat' for 'every season' and can even boast a 'town paleness'. He refuses to see himself as 'the novelist of the agricultural labourer' but does accept that he writes 'from the point of view of the village people themselves instead of from the Hall or Parsonage'. The former, he claims, have 'so much more dramatic interest in their lives' and their 'passions are franker' (DCM 6447 ff. 12–13). This is the image Hardy wants to project, that of a man about town (at least some of the time) who chooses to write about rural life not because it is all he knows but because it is intrinsically interesting.

A similar image is presented in the interview in *Black and White* of August in the same year, 'A Chat with the Author of *Tess*', in which it is again only too apparent to what extent the interviewer has been fed (both by Hardy and by Emma) with material designed to alter their public image:

> He is regarded by the public at large as a hermit ever brooding in the far-off seclusion of a west country village. A fond delusion, which is disproved by the fact that he is almost more frequently to be seen in a London drawing room, or a continental hotel, than in the quiet old-world lanes of rural Dorsetshire. His wife, some few years younger than himself, is so particularly bright, so thoroughly *au courant du jour*, so evidently a citizen of the wide world, that the, at first, unmistakable reminiscence that there is in her of Anglican ecclesiasticism is curiously puzzling and inexplicable to the stranger, until the information is vouchsafed that she is intimately and closely connected with what the late Lord Shaftesbury would term 'the higher order of the clergy'. (f. 29)

The sheer transparency of these efforts at public relations indicates the extent to which he and Emma resented being seen as country bumpkins.

Some of the interviews recorded in Hardy's personal scrapbook attempt different strategies. One in a series of 'Personal Sketches' in the *Literary World* of March 1903, for example, makes a virtue of the fact that 'he was not put through the routine educational mill of public school and university, and so probably retains more humanity and originality than most men of his class'. This interview ends by attacking the urban middle classes for their lack of interest in Hardy and his acknowledged rural subjects:

The comparative unpopularity of Mr. Hardy is due to the fact that the great Middle Class, with its suburban villas and its music halls, is not interested in the peasant; to them there is no magic in the woods and heaths, no romance in agricultural labourers who are at once real and idyllic. (f. 51)

It is more difficult in this interview to identify how much of this has been orchestrated by Hardy himself but it appears in the scrapbook without any angry denials, in contrast with other interviews which are peppered with marginal comments: 'lies', 'inventions' or 'not spoken by him'.

One of the articles on which Hardy did write 'Lies' and to which he attached a copy of a letter to the editor complaining about the 'largely false' character of its 'impertinent statements' appeared under the name of Constance Smedley in *T. P.'s Weekly* in January 1910. Hardy clearly resented its reference to his 'peasant stock', his 'kinsmen' who 'still ply humble trades round Dorchester', and its claims that Hardy felt lost outside his home town and had nothing to say in London in 'the artificial atmosphere of drawing rooms, and clubs and restaurants'. It also portrays him as 'very shy and very simple – an extraordinarily nebulous individual' who retreated behind a 'shell of silence' (ff. 105–6). Hardy's letter to the editor, T. P. O'Connor, objected not only to the contents of this article but to the fact that its author gained admission to Max Gate 'on the pretence of paying a friendly call, so that no suspicion of the woman's purpose was entertained' (*Letters* IV 71). He became much more guarded about giving interviews and receiving visitors, continuing to bridle at any account of his origins which employed the term 'peasant' (*Letters* VI 182–4). That resentment, I suggest, can be found in all his work, often more cunningly disguised but indisputably part of his fraught relationship with his readers.

Questions of gender: 'how does a female reader... read Hardy?'

This is the question put by Judith Mitchell at the start of her essay on 'Hardy's Female Reader' (Mitchell 1993: 172). The question of gender is linked to class; both, as Kirstin Brady notes, serve to 'exclude an author or character from the privileges attached to the life of a gentleman' (Brady 1999: 100–1). There is also an 'eroticization of class difference' brought about by Hardy's perennial interest in 'cross-class romance', the perpetual hankering of the 'Poor Man' for 'the Lady', which also politicizes the love relationship, installing 'antagonisms and rivalries of class...at the heart of desire' (Boumelha 1982: 199: 132).

Hardy appears to have believed that his audience was predominantly male and that many women readers disliked his work because of its unflattering depiction of them. When Ruth Head approached him in 1921 for advice on her plan for a selection of his writings for use in educational establishments, he replied that his writings were 'more for men than for women, if I may believe what people say'; 'though what a woman reader likes,' he explained, ' a man may usually like, what a man likes most is what a woman does not like at all. And this especially with my writings' (*Letters* VI 95–6). He may well have gained this view of his audience from his friend Edmund Gosse, who attempted in 1890 to explain the 'curious phenomenon' of 'the unpopularity of Mr. Hardy's novels among women':

> It is not merely that the mass of girls who let down their back-hair to have a long cry over Edna Lyall or Miss Florence Warden do not appreciate his books, but that even educated women approach him with hesitation and prejudice. This is owing to no obvious error on the novelist's part; he has never attacked the sex, or offended its proprieties. But there is something in his conception of feminine character which is not well received.
>
> (Cox 1970: 169)

Later in the same article Gosse attributed this 'unpopularity' to Hardy's women being 'moulded of the same flesh as his men', not always 'quite nice' and sometimes even 'of a coming-on disposition' (170). His 1892 article on 'The Tyranny of the Novel' claimed, 'Men have made Mr. Thomas Hardy, who owes nothing to the fair sex; if women read him now, it is because the men have told them they must' (Gosse 1893: 14). This was, in fact, the case with Cynthia Asquith, who was told by her literary mentor, Charles Whibley, that she should read Hardy (Beaman 1987: 202). But Hardy had a number of society women on his side, including Lady Jeune, to whom he turned when the morality of his work came under attack in 1894 (*Letters* II 56).

Hardy's scrapbooks, however, confirm that Gosse's views on this matter were quite widely shared. In 1886 the *World* was confidently declaring that 'his books are written with an eye to a masculine rather than a feminine audience, and to middle-age [sic] women rather than girls in their teens'. Among the 'extraordinary letters from strangers' that Hardy was in the habit of receiving, it is asserted (presumably on the authority of the author himself), were some 'letters from ladies, charging him with holding a rather low estimate of womankind in general, and with failing to appreciate the excellences of the sex' (DCM 6647, f. 8). A series of 'Letters to Living Authors' in *Wit and Wisdom* told Hardy in 1889,

> I understand you are no favourite with the young lady who patronises the circulating libraries. She is in the habit of making marginal notes in your books which are sometimes more entertaining than complimentary...she considers herself slandered in your female characters, so she calls you 'that horrid man Hardy'.
>
> (DCM 6647, f. 14)

An article on Hardy in the *Speaker* the following year (attributed by Gerber and Davis to Gosse) compared him with Meredith in this respect: 'Neither has the great novel-reading public with him, each enlists the bulk of his readers from the class of adult male persons' (f. 12). The *National Observer* of 2 February 1891 depicted Hardy as 'somewhat cynical' in his portrait of women while the *Spectator* of August that year also complained that it was 'the low view of women pervading all of Hardy's novels' that robbed him of 'the full sympathy of his readers' (p.163).

Some women reviewers such as Janetta Newton-Robinson of the *Westminster Review* praised Hardy's ability to portray women as 'passion-led, against their better judgment' (137 (1892) 153–64). Hardy himself told an interviewer in *Black and White* who had questioned the likelihood of all the dairymaids falling in love with Angel Clare, 'all my men correspondents condemn that as impossible; all my women friends say it is exactly what would have happened'. He also claimed to detect in 'women of position...the same transparency of passions...the same gentle candid femininity that you meet with in dairymaids' (DCM 6447 f. 30). It was only the middle classes who had forgotten how to feel. The argument over Hardy's portrait of women and sexuality, which was to reach a crescendo after the publication of *Jude*, would continue for many years afterwards. An unsigned article on 'Men's Women in Fiction' in the *Westminster Review* of 1898 asked, 'Does not Mr. Hardy know any "nice" women? Or is it only the "nasty" ones that are interesting?' (571–7). The *Literary World* (26.9.02) quotes the article on 'Thomas Hardy' in the new volume of the *Encyclopaedia Britannica* describing his view of women as 'more French than English; it is subtle, a little cruel, not as tolerant as it seems, thoroughly a man's point of view' (DCM 6447, f. 46).

Grace Alexander, writing in the *New York Times* (13.6.05) would defend him as 'A Portrait Painter of Real Women' (f. 67). It is clear, however, from some of these complaints, repeated in reviews of individual novels to be considered later in this book, that his portrait of feminine passion offended many of his more moralistic contemporary reviewers.

More serious problems for a more liberated woman who reads Hardy are 'the blatantly sexist remarks that are scattered throughout his oeuvre like some kind of sexist graffiti' (Mitchell 1993: 172). Judith Mitchell has also drawn attention to the 'implied reader's masculinity', identifying more subtle ways in which the novels appear to 'invite male partnership on the part of the reader', who is asked to 'share a gaze that is ineluctably male' (Mitchell 1994: 156–7). If she were simply to accept what Hardy's generalising narrators tell her, a female reader would surely have to identify him as one more androcentric writer 'not worth saving' from the patriarchal wreckage (Flynn 1986: xvii–xviii). Virginia Woolf, in her obituary of Hardy, argued that she had to go beneath the surface of the text, to those 'moments of vision' produced by the kind of 'unconscious writer' he was:

> It is as if Hardy himself were not quite aware of what he did, as if his consciousness held more than he could produce, and he left it for his readers to make out his full meaning and to supplement it from their own experience.
>
> (McNeillie 1986: IV 510)

This is certainly what recent feminist critics have done, focusing like Penny Boumelha on the places at which explicitly patriarchal attitudes towards women are fractured within the texts, identifying with Rosemarie Morgan the multiple narrative voices and perspectives to be found within the novels, or recognising with Patricia Ingham that there is a massive gap between what the narrator tells us (the diegesis) and what is represented in character, action and dialogue (the mimesis).

The woman reader, of course, should not be identified simply by biological differences. It is not that the actual experience of 'real' (biological) women does not count, but that 'the terms in which femininity is publicly formulated dictate the way in which it is experienced' (Poovey 1984: 10). *Gendering the Reader*, as Sara Mills has shown, is a matter of historical and cultural construction, 'shifting and contextual' rather than stable and essential (Mills 1994: 32). In a patriarchal society, for instance, 'everyone, men and women alike, is taught initially to read like a man; that is, to adopt the androcentric perspective that pervades the most authoritative texts of the culture' (Flynn and Schweickart 1986: xv). Judith Fetterley's 'resisting' female reader, however, refuses to become the male 'implied reader', resisting the perspective offered by many nineteenth-century texts. Hardy, I will suggest, while at times constructing a male implied reader, also provides resistant female readers with much material on which to construct alternative positions.

Perhaps the most sustained historical examination of nineteenth-century discourses about gender can be found in Kate Flint's study of *The Woman Reader, 1837–1914*, which is based upon an impressive range of sources:

> articles in newspapers and periodicals; medical and psychological texts; advice manuals for young girls, wives, servants, governesses; educational and religious works; autobiographies; letters, journals, fiction; and verse, as well as paintings, photographs, and graphic art.
>
> (Flint 1993: 4)

In an attempt to identify key historical moments in the development of gendered reading, she pays particular attention to the debates about the two genres that spanned Hardy's career as a novelist: the controversies over Sensation Fiction in the 1860s and discussions of the New Woman fiction in the 1890s. Women, of course, have always been considered the prime audience of the novel in general (Lovell 1987: 8–10). Flint quotes an article of 1842 which claimed that the 'great bulk of novel readers' continued to be' female' and another of 1859 arguing that 'novels constitute a principle part of the reading of women' (Flint 1993: 9, 12). The vogue for Sensation Fiction appears to have exacerbated this tendency, expressing 'a wide range of suppressed female emotions' in a manner which went well beyond 'many of the premises of the traditional "feminine" novel' (35). By the 1860s and 1870s sensation fiction had become so much associated with women, as Gaye Tuchman showns in her analysis of the Macmillan archives, that men submitting fiction were more likely to assume a female pseudonym than the other way round (Tuchman 1989).

Another historical development relevant to the fashioning of the female reader was the growth of 'English Literature' as an academic subject, both at schools and universities. Dorothea Beale, headmistress of Cheltenham School for Girls, was critical of the force-feeding that characterised the teaching of English to girls in board schools in the later years of the nineteenth century, leading a campaign against annotating literature texts with critical notes and parallel passages, wanting to preserve her charges from the hard mental discipline characteristic of the sciences, to enable them 'to consider literature, ultimately, as something, inspiring, beautiful, and...transcending rational explanation' (Flint 1993: 125). Even in the late nineteenth century, in other words, the reading of English was associated primarily with women, who were deemed to possess appropriately delicate minds for the task. Such delicacy, as we shall see, would be easily affronted by the 'coarseness' of Hardy's work.

Hardy's women seemed to bother both male and female readers. The novelist Katherine Macquoid, for example, wrote to complain of Bathsheba, wanting her 'to have a soul which is not entirely governed by her body' (DCM 4152). Male and female reviewers were increasingly outraged by what Mowbray Morris was to call the 'succulence' of Hardy's female characters, who were quite obviously sexual beings. Hardy clearly challenged Victorian notions of ladylike behaviour in this respect, which is one reason why women readers of a later era have valued his work. As Horace Moule told him with reference of Elfride in *A Pair of Blue Eyes*, 'You understand the *woman* infinitely better than the *lady*' (DCM 4475), a remark which reflected his assumptions about class as much as gender, illustrating precisely the kind of tension in the relationship Hardy had with his readers which it is the purpose of this book to explore.

2
'Breaking into Fiction': the Tinsley Novels

Finding a name: *Desperate Remedies*

Breaking into fiction, as John Sutherland has shown, was no easy matter for Hardy (Sutherland 1976). His failure to persuade publishers such as Chapman and Macmillan to publish his first novel forced him to turn to the less prestigious William Tinsley for his second. Tinsley, sole proprietor of the family firm after the death of his more businesslike brother in 1866, did not move in the same social circles or belong to the same literary establishment as the Macmillans. George Moore wrote of him as 'a dear kind soul' who both dressed and traded sloppily: 'quite witless and quite h-less' (Downey 1905: 9). The son of a Hertfordshire gamekeeper, he retained both his country accent and his imperfect grammar, making money by selling in bulk to the circulating libraries (Sutherland 1991: 299–300). The *Life* captures both accent and grammar in an exchange in the Strand when Hardy told Tinsley that the failure of *Desperate Remedies* had forced him to focus again on his career as an architect, receiving the reply, 'Damned if that isn't what I thought you wos!' When Hardy dared to complain about the arrangements for publishing that novel, he insisted, 'you wouldn't have got another man in London to print it . . . 'twas a blood-curdling story' (*Life* 90–1).

The Tinsleys, in fact, could be said to have specialised in 'blood-curdling stories', having published two of the most successful examples of sensation fiction: Mary Braddon's *Lady Audley's Secret* in 1862 and Wilkie Collins's *The Moonstone* in 1868. Collins explained to Tinsley in a letter of July 1868 that he aimed to appeal over the heads of the reviewers and professional publishers' readers to 'the general public' (Blain 1998: vii–viii). It was Collins who provided the model for the kind of plot-centred novel advised by George Meredith, who had read the manuscript of *The Poor Man and the Lady* for Chapman & Hall (*Life* 62–3). William Rutland claims that Hardy cynically went out and bought *The Woman in White*, 'made a close study of it, and produced a much inferior, but quite recognizable, imitation of this famous "mystery novel"' (Rutland 1938: 50). This, of course, is an oversimplification but Hardy's characteristically ambiguous account in the *Life* blames the 'wildly melodramatic situations' in what was 'admittedly an extremely clever novel' on his adopting 'a style which was quite against his natural grain, through too crude an interpretation of Mr Meredith's advice' (*Life* 87).

Desperate Remedies has been almost universally regarded as 'a disaster'. Contemporaries 'deplored its raw sexuality' while later critics 'have dismissed the novel as bombastic, syntactically awkward, wordy, thickly plotted' and, at the same time, so packed with highbrow allusions as to comprise a kind of 'cultural name-dropping' (Moore 1982: 42). 'Nothing of importance in the book either anticipates the later novels,' according to Lerner and Holmstrom, 'or suggests a writer of genius' (Lerner 1968: 14). Irving Howe claims only that it is 'one of the most interesting bad novels in the English language, bad with verve, bad with passion, bad...with distinction' (Howe 1968: 34). More recent critics have been able to discover some elements of the later Hardy in the novel although Joe Fisher argues that it remains 'a joke; a sustained, contrived jest by the narrator at the expense of the buyer, a literary Trojan horse', concealing within its conventional surface dangerously subversive elements which undermine Victorian attitudes towards class and gender (Fisher 1992: 21–1).

Hardy had been aware from the outset that any criticism of his society would need to be 'inserted edgewise' into his fiction, to employ the phrase from the letter he sent to Macmillan accompanying the manuscript of *The Poor Man and the Lady* (*Letters* I 7). What he was to learn from Alexander Macmillan, relaying the comments of his reader John Morley, was the unacceptability even of this kind of critique:

> Your pictures of character among...the upper classes, are sharp, clear, incisive, and in many respects true, but they are wholly dark – not a ray of light visible to relieve the darkness, and therefore exaggerated and untrue in their results.
>
> (Morgan 1943: 91).

Morley's report on *Desperate Remedies* was even more outspoken in its outrage at the sexual elements in the novel, not only the 'highly extravagant' bed scene between mistress and maid but 'the disgusting and absurd outrage which is the key to the mystery', the 'violation of a young lady at an evening party, and the subsequent birth of a child' (93–4). Such an incident, Alexander Macmillan told Hardy, would 'greatly endanger the success of any novel' (DCM 27). So Miss Aldclyffe's 'secret', when it finally emerges in her dying confession to Cytherea towards the end of the first edition, becomes vaguer and less shocking (though bad enough for a lady), her illegitimate son revised to become the result of being more vaguely if still 'cruelly betrayed by her cousin' (*DR* 397).

Macmillan's advice to tone down the satirical elements in his work, as we have seen, had been reinforced by Meredith, who had himself suffered ten years earlier from the hostile reception of *The Ordeal of Richard Feverel*, held back from his subscribers by the overprotective Mudie. Meredith saw that *The Poor Man and the Lady* as it stood would have been 'attacked on all sides by the conventional reviewers, and his future injured'. He therefore advised Hardy to 'rewrite the story, softening it down considerably' or to 'attempt a novel with a purely artistic purpose, giving it a more complicated "plot"' (*Life* 62–4). What Hardy appears to have done, having tried the manuscript on two more publishers, Smith, Elder and the Tinsleys, is a combination of both these plans. The first two volumes of *Desperate Remedies*, as Pamela Dalziel has shown, incorporate significant elements of his first novel, passages shared with 'An Indiscretion in the Life of an Heiress', while the third volume, in which there are no shared passages, centres entirely on the unravelling of the complicated plot (Dalziel 1995: 220–32). The final form of *Desperate Remedies*, in other words, bears the imprint of what John Sutherland somewhat euphemistically calls Hardy's 'education' at the hands of his all-powerful publishers and their readers. His fiction had to be 'decontaminated' of its 'dangerous' qualities and refashioned on the model of such proven authors as Collins (Sutherland 1976: 224). What remained of satire or social criticism had to be smuggled in.

Even Tinsley, in spite of his connections with Bohemian authors and radical working-class writers (Cross 1985: 96–7), required some changes to the manuscript of *Desperate Remedies*. His reader on this occasion, William Faux, who was in charge of W. H. Smith's library department (and could therefore be relied upon to recognise what was unacceptable to them) apparently wrote a 'glowing report' on *Desperate Remedies* (Downey 1905: 22) but found 'strong reasons why the book should not be published without some alterations', one of which involved the omission of the word 'mistress' originally used of the woman who masquerades as Manston's wife (Purdy 1954: 4–5). The American publisher Henry Holt, who included the novel in his 'Leisure Hour' series in 1874, required even more changes: Miss Aldclyffe's conception had to be made legitimate, the result of a secret marriage with a military officer who turns out to be a criminal (*DR* xlv). George Smith advised Hardy not to reprint *Desperate Remedies* in 1875, since it was 'not... nearly equal to your other books published just now' (DCM 5239), advice which Hardy presumably remembered in telling Ward & Downey in 1884 that he had 'decided to let *Desperate Remedies* stay out of print for the present' (*Letters* I 186). When he did grant them a five-year lease of the novel in 1889, they appear to have insisted on additional changes, removing some of the sexual suggestiveness, not only in Cytherea's 'bosom' but in the metaphorical 'bosom' of the waves (*DR* xlv). Hardy also appended a preface to this edition, explaining that it had been written 'when he was feeling his way to a method, apologising for the extent to which 'mystery, entanglement, surprise, and moral obliquity are depended on for exciting interest'. He decided not to make alterations to the 1896 text, apart from geographical Wessexisation, and left some of the more controversial scenes unaltered, noting somewhat wryly that 'certain characteristics which provoked most discussion in my latest story' (presumably Sue Bridehead's ambiguous sexuality) 'were present in this my first – published in 1871, when there was no French name for them' (448). But he instigated 'some light bowdlerizing of the bed scene between Miss Aldclyffe and Cytherea' for the Wessex Edition of 1912 (xlviii), making the older woman more motherly and less 'sensuous', wanting to 'care' for her younger namesake rather than 'love' her (419). The respectable Grand Old Man appears to have become more self-conscious about his portrait of lesbianism. This novel, in other words, suffered at all stages of its history from the fears at first of its publishers and finally of its author that it might offend its readers.

There were, of course, remarkably few readers of this novel when it was first published. Tinsley sold only 372 copies of their print run of 500, including 92 library copies at knock-down prices to Mudie and Smith (Purdy 1954: 4). It was remaindered after six months, Hardy himself blaming the review in the *Spectator* for having 'snuffed out the book' (*Life* 87). Other reviews were not that bad, although the first, in the *Athenaeum* in April 1871, speculated on the gender of the anonymous author, concluding that 'certain expressions' were 'so remarkably coarse' as to rule out the possibility that 'it should have come from the pen of an English lady'. It found the characterisation good but the story 'disagreeable' in spite of being told 'with considerable artistic power' (Cox 1970: 1). The *Morning Post* (13.4.71) labelled the novel 'semi-sensational', with a clear debt to Wilkie Collins. It was the third review, in the *Spectator* (22.4.71) which denounced its author's 'desperate remedies... for ennui or an emaciated purse'. Not only was the story 'disagreeable' but Miss Aldclyffe 'uninteresting, unnatural, and nasty' (Cox 1970: 3–5). The only other review, by Horace Moule in *the Saturday Review* (30.9.71), praised the novel's characterisation but appeared too late to rescue it from oblivion. Later Victorian references to the novel, as Cox remarks, 'agree in selecting for praise those parts of the novel which point forward to Hardy's most characteristic later work', reserving their censure for its sensational elements (Cox 1970: xv). Charles Kegan Paul in 1881 compared his attempted outdoing of the sensation novelists with Shakespeare's writing *Titus Andronicus* to prove that he could beat contemporary dramatists on their own bloody ground (83). Havelock Ellis found all the notes of Hardy's later work in his first novel apart from his love of nature (108) but J. M. Barrie dismissed it as 'a study in other people's methods' (160). Early twentieth-century American critics such as W. P. Trent and W. L. Phelps found elements to praise in the novel, passages of 'rare descriptive power' and pearls of wisdom which 'no swine save skimming readers can possibly be found to spurn' (222, 297).

Sensation fiction, of course, lent itself both to skimming readers and 'swine in the sewers', revealing aspects of Victorian life normally hidden beneath a surface respectability (Boyle 1989). As well as specialising in 'mystery, secrecy and the resurgence of scandalous effects from the past', sensation fiction enjoyed exploring areas of unorthodox sexuality, 'illegitimacy, bigamy and crimes of passion', presenting 'female characters who are frequently transgressive and complex' (Neale 1993: 116). It made sure that the transgressors were suitably punished in the end, however, thereby reinforcing orthodox moral values.

There are, as Roy Morrell noted, a number of similarities between *Desperate Remedies* and *The Woman in White*, including 'a mistaken identity, a disastrous fire, a guilty secret, an illegitimate child' and finally 'a confession in which obscure points... are clarified'. But there are also 'fundamental differences' between the two writers, most notably the way in which Collins attributes everything to Providence, or 'the hand of God' (Morrell 1965: 46–8). Neither Hardy's narrator nor his characters have much time for so conventional a religious notion. When Mrs Leat piously suggests that 'Providence will settle it all for the best, as he always do', Mrs Cricket replies, 'I have always found Providence a different sort of feller' (161). Her husband is equally sharp with the scullery maid who declares that 'God A'mighty always sends bread as well as children', observing that it is 'bread to one house and the children to another very often' (246). Even in his first published work, in other words, Hardy was prepared to subvert the orthodoxy which Collins took care to appease.

A similar difference can be detected between the fires in *The Woman in White* and in *Desperate Remedies*. Collins's fire is a providential punishment of his villain Sir Percival whereas in Hardy it is the sympathetic Mr Springrove who is brought low as a result of sheer bad luck (a turn in the wind) combined with his own lack of vigilance over the smouldering couch-grass and lack of foresight (failing to renew the insurance). Only a writer of Hardy's deep knowledge and subversive critique of the Bible could have the church bells at midnight ring out over the crackling flames 'the wayward air of the Old Hundred-and-Thirteenth Psalm' (181), which includes among its verses the injunction to praise the Lord who 'raiseth up the poor out of the dunghill' (Springer 1983: 24). Here, of course, he has done precisely the opposite. There are similarly subversive uses of biblical allusion in the way the adulterous Manston is constantly described in terms of the equally bigamous and adulterous David. 'Abigail is lost, but Michal is recovered,' says the steward, planning to pass off his mistress, 'comely as Kedar', as his first wife (291–2). These are the characteristically back-door means by which Hardy marks his difference both from Collins and from religious orthodoxy.

The conventions of sensation fiction, with its interest in madness and abnormality, also allow Hardy to explore his own interest in the uncanny, in borderline areas of the psyche, what the *Life* labels 'a principle [of the universe] for which there is no exact name, lying at the indifference point between rationality and irrationality' (*Life* 332). The *Life* also, as Moore notes (Moore 1982: 32), discusses the possibility of a kind of sensation fiction developing in which 'the sensationalism is not casualty, but evolution; not physical but psychical' (*Life* 213). Cytherea Graye is quite literally psychic, most dramatically in the final chapter of the novel, in which she has a vision of Miss Aldclyffe at the foot of her bed 'looking her in the face with an expression of entreaty beyond the power of words to portray' at the very moment in which she is later found to have died (*DR* 399–400). There are other scenes in the novel that explore psychical phenomena, including an earlier dream of Cytherea's on the night before her marriage in which she is whipped with dry bones suspended on strings by an executioner whose form resembles that of Manston. She wonders whether this is to be understood as a warning from 'Fate', only for the narrator to provide a rational explanation, since the noises of her dream appear to have been caused by the icicle-laden branches of trees beating against her window (242).

Moore argues that the narrator himself has a double voice, one rational, seeking 'scientific' reasons for the events it describes, the other irrational, recording the uncanny effects in the minds of the characters. The point, as in Hardy's own internal conflict between religion and science, emotion and reason, is that 'neither voice alone will suffice' (Moore 1982: 34).

There are, as Todorov has explained (1988: 160), always two stories in detective fiction (which has its roots in sensation fiction), the events as they are originally experienced (vicariously by the reader) and the solution as it is worked out by the detective, in this case, the rational Springrove, assisted by the rector Raunham. Collins may be more skilful than Hardy in the way he narrates novels through the limited point of view of his characters, thereby concealing some of the evidence from his readers. Hardy's omniscient narrator has more clumsily to introduce aporias of knowledge, on two occasions caused by characters failing to hear precisely what others are saying. As in his later fiction, however, Hardy at times employs focalisation for this purpose, sometimes introducing complete strangers such as the local reporter in the epilogue, whose presence strikes a discordant note in the otherwise bland ending.

Perhaps the most significant difference between Hardy and a sensation writer such as Collins, however, lies in their class allegiance. Sensation fiction was 'written for the middle classes, by the middle classes, and about the middle classes' (Ousby 1984: 217). It often centred upon a grand country house and the activities of its insiders, the aristocracy, paying scant attention to outsiders, the remainder of the community whose labour helped to supply and maintain the house and its inhabitants. Lady Audley, for example, is prepared to risk all for her 'fine house and gorgeous furniture' while her creator has little interest in the 'stupid-looking clodhopper' and other rustics who make the briefest of appearances. The plot revolves entirely around the house, 'keeping it in the right hands, and transmitting it smoothly to the next generation' (218). In *Desperate Remedies*, as in *The Woman in White*, there are two houses, Knapwater Park itself and the Old Manor House, but there is also the pub, the Three Tranters, not to mention its neighbouring cottages. If it is to be read as a sensation novel, it is one in which the centre of attention is no longer restricted to the upper-class inhabitants of the country house. Just as *The Poor Man and the Lady* was subtitled *By The Poor Man* (*Life* 58) so Hardy forces readers of *Desperate Remedies* to notice the poor labourers who sustain the lady in her big house. Even the description of the house draws attention to those functional aspects normally concealed from view such as the laundries and stables, however much they are 'half-buried beneath close-set shrubs and trees' (65). Miss Aldclyffe's plan to bring in a new man to superintend the activities of the estate is seen to impinge on the existing steward, who is left to 'suspense, and all the ills that came in its train', including 'sleepless nights, and untasted dinners', while she merely 'looked at her watch and returned to the House' (105). She is seen to be similarly callous and overbearing to her other employees.

It is because Cytherea has not been born into service but forced into it by the financial imprudence of her father that she is so alert to its 'drudgery'. Looking at the various drafts of her advertisement, she cannot see herself in the words 'GOVERNESS or COMPANION' (22–3). She meets her brother's objection to descending still lower and advertising as a 'LADY'S MAID' with the somewhat desperate reply, 'Yes I – who am I?' (53). Her identity, in other words, is bound up with her interpellation into society. She is surprised on entering service to be called 'Mrs Graye', the standard form of address for female servants but one which 'seemed disagreeably like the first slight scar of a brand' (66). She objects also to being summoned by a bell, at having to attend immediately 'whether I want to or no' (69) and quickly bridles on receiving the rough side of her mistress's tongue. Readers are clearly expected to enjoy the comic side of two women denying each other the title 'lady', 'mistress' and 'maid' (77) and of a servant daring to object to the conditions of service. But by placing a well-educated and independent young girl in the unusual position of being at another's beck and call, Hardy defamiliarises the whole nature of service. He also draws attention to the significance of these names.

The man Cytherea falls in love with and eventually marries, Edward Springrove, is also placed in an ambiguous class position similar to Hardy's own. 'He is a man of very humble origin' (toned down in 1889 to 'rather humble origin'), Owen Graye explains to his sister, 'who has made himself' (22, 411). The son of Farmer Springrove, landlord of the Three Tranters, a man whose 'gentleness of disposition' is in pointed contrast to the hard-nosed aloofness of Aeneas Manston, who is 'quite the gentleman', young Edward, always 'one for the prent', trains as an architect (130–1). Hardy even includes a typical 'back-door' reference to his own family in making Miss Aldclyffe's dressing-table the product of 'Mr. James Sparkman, an ingenious joiner and decorator' (70), whose name clearly echoes that of Hardy's cabinet-making uncle, James Sparks. Sparkman disappeared from the text after 1889 (418), presumably because he provided too great a clue to Hardy's own humble class position. There is clearly plenty of autobiographical feeling, however, in

Edward's resentment of Miss Aldclyffe's interference in his personal affairs:

> Miss Aldclyffe, like a good many others in her position, had plainly not realised that a son of her tenant and inferior, could have become an educated man, who had learnt to feel his individuality, to view society from a Bohemian standpoint, far outside the farming grade in Carriford parrish, and that hence he had all a developed man's unorthodox opinion about the subordination of classes. (204)

Miss Aldclyffe pointedly addresses him as 'Mr Edward Springrove' in contrast to her son, who merits an 'Esquire' after his name (209–10). It is significant, however, that the estate finally reverts to the heirs of these two déclassé figures, Cytherea and Edward, who prove worthier to maintain it than the villainous and illegitimate heir of Miss Aldclyffe.

Desperate Remedies exploits the subversive potential of its genre in matters of gender. Cytherea, who displays many of the qualities of Magdalen in Wilkie Collins's *No Name* (1862), in particular a suppleness, elasticity and flexibility of motion (Beatty 1975: 13–14), also experiences some of her disenfranchisement. She has a name but no clear status and no means. She also plans to marry a man she despises before being rewarded for her 'endless deceptions', as Mrs. Oliphant complained of Magdalen, with 'a good husband and a happy home' (Blain 1998: xxi). Hardy also draws his readers' attention to the way his heroine's loss of social status places her at the mercy of all the men she encounters. Once she loses her father's protection the young men of Hocbridge gaze at her 'with a stare unmitigated by any of the respect that had formerly softened it' (19). The narrator adduces a number of quotations illustrative of the standard male chauvinist position, including Terence's belief that women are always contrary (148). With women, says her brother, echoing another Latin *sententia* to be found in Hardy's copy of *Beautiful Thoughts from Latin Authors* (425) ''Tis either love or hate' (78). As so often in Hardy's work, however, the action of the novel undermines these standard sayings, proving them not to be so beautiful in practice.

Hardy's narrator, in fact, finds it hard to decide whether to admire or condemn Cytherea's willingness to submit to marriage to Manston as the only way of attaining sufficient means both to maintain herself and to afford medical care for her brother:

Perhaps the moral compensation for all a woman's petty cleverness under thriving conditions is the real nobility that lies in her extreme foolishness at these other times: her sheer inability to be simply just, her exercise of an illogical power entirely denied to men in general – the power not only of kissing, but of delighting to kiss the rod by a punctilious observance of the self-immolating doctrines in the Sermon on the Mount. (217)

This sentence swerves almost unreadably from complacent chauvinism ('a woman's petty cleverness') to sympathy concealed by irony (her 'foolishness' presumably the sacred folly enjoined by Erasmus) to an undecided ambivalence about Christian self-sacrifice (however much men may like to have their rods kissed). Hardy here conceals his own position behind multiple layers of irony. Similarly, when Cytherea re-solves to abandon Edward, deploring the fact that since his appearance at the wedding, 'she had thought only of him. Owen – her name – her position – future had been as if they did not exist' (252), readers are presumably supposed both to admire her self-sacrifice and to deplore its necessity. Her 'mental agony' on parting from Edward is said to be 'indescribable by men's words' (257), which is partly a tribute to her depth of feeling but also a recognition that a male author can never claim fully to represent women. More dangerously, men's words are seen not only as inadequate but as slanderous. Having been rescued from Manston's clutches only after her wedding to him, Cytherea is left in a 'nameless and unsatisfactory, though innocent state' (297). Local gossip, however, is less generous: 'Utterly fictitious details of the finding of Cytherea and Manston had been invented and circulated, unavoidably reaching her ears' (294), constituting a form of 'defamation' (298), a 'slanderous tale accounting for her seclusion' (301). Hardy does not need to spell out these stories, leaving it to his readers to recognise the villagers' view of her as neither wife nor maid (the acceptable names for a lady).

Another possible name applied by men to women, although not one acceptable to Tinsley, is 'mistress'. Anne Seaway, the woman chosen by Manston to play the role of his missing (or rather murdered) wife, is therefore described by the rector as an 'improper woman' (357). Less censoriously, the narrator suggests that she agrees to her new role since it offers 'a mode of subsistence a degree better than toiling in poverty and alone, after a bustling and somewhat pampered life as a house-keeper in a gay mansion' (356). Mary Rimmer suggests that 'gay' here hints that Anne is a prostitute while the 'bustling life' is 'very likely... that of a brothel' (441). There is a clear irony, however, in Hardy having indirectly to hint at these labels in a novel which has been seen to explore 'the meretricious nature of the available feminine signs' in a patriarchal society, the requirement of women to adjust to 'fit a limited number of ideologically sanctioned subject-positions' (Thomas 1999: 58).

The name 'lesbian', of course, had not yet come into existence since the sexual orientation it represents was unthinkable in a Victorian lady. Swinburne had portrayed lesbian activity unambiguously, as Rimmer remarks, only for Morley to single out both lesbian poems in *Poems and Ballads* for obloquy, comforting himself with the belief that they would 'be unintelligible to many people' (DR 450). The lesbian sexuality in *Desperate Remedies*, according to Joe Fisher, was similarly hidden from many contemporary readers by bourgeois notions of femininity. He imagines such a reader thinking, 'no lady would make love to another lady' so this cannot possibly be what it seems. Hardy, however, by making it obvious that this is precisely what is happening in Cytherea's bedroom, is 'testing the gullibility of the ideology he is expected to reinforce' (Fisher 1992: 27). It is certainly obvious to a modern reader that Miss Aldclyffe's passion for her young namesake blows not so much from Cytherea as from Lesbos. Even in the interview she conducts for the post of maid, much emphasis is given to the 'masculine cast' of the older woman's face, in contrast to the 'girlish-looking' applicant (57) and to Cytherea's success being entirely attributable to her good looks. This last word is one that Miss Aldclyffe, regretting her impulsive appointment, cannot bring herself to pronounce (76). Her feelings for Cytherea are quite literally nameless ('the love that dare not speak its name'). She nevertheless comes to her maid's room in the early hours of the morning, calls her 'darling', embraces her and demands that her kiss be returned (82). In 1912, along with other attempts to play down the sexual nature of the scene, Hardy makes Miss Aldclyffe more maternal, insisting that Cytherea seems like her own child (419). In the first edition, however, Miss Aldclyffe's behaviour is seen as 'the outburst of a strong feeling, long checked' (83).

The fact that one of Cytherea's suitors is a woman certainly complicates the normal plot paradigms of Victorian fiction (Ingham 1989: 33). Miss Aldclyffe, who later turns out to be a more conventionally 'fallen woman', the victim of an unscrupulous cousin, is definitely not a 'lady' in terms which Horace Moule would have recognised. One of the main points of the novel, however, is to question the names that Victorian men gave to their women. That Hardy succeeds in conveying this in a text itself severely restricted in the language open to it is a tribute to the way in which he was already, at the outset of his career, forging strategies by which to overcome the conventions of contemporary fiction and the supposed requirements of his readers.

Playing it safe: *Under the Greenwood Tree*

The *Life* claims that Hardy turned to *Under the Greenwood Tree*, a 'short and quite rustic story' as a result of 'a remark of John Morley's on *The Poor Man and the Lady*, that the country scenes...were the best in the book'. He accordingly 'reintroduced' the 'tranter' of those scenes into his new novel (*Life* 88), which he sent to Macmillan in August 1871 along with a letter explaining that it was 'entirely a story of rural life' written 'humorously' but 'without caricature'. Among the reasons Hardy gave in this letter for turning to pastoral are the reviews of *Desperate Remedies*, which 'made very much of...the rustic characters and scenery'. A second letter enclosing the reviews explained that their difference from each other made them 'useless as guides to me in my second story. It seemed however that upon the whole a pastoral story would be the *safest* venture' (*Letters* I 11–12). At this stage of his career he was clearly aware of the need to play it safe, to provide the reading public with what it appeared to want.

Morley, again employed by Macmillan as their reader for Hardy's third attempt to place a novel with them, found the work 'extremely careful, natural, and delicate' but could not 'prophesy a large market for it, because the work is so delicate as not to hit every taste'. The full version of Morley's report, only selectively quoted in the *Life* (88–9) refers less positively to its 'simple and uneventful sketch of a rural courtship' leading to a 'moderate and reserved climax'. The opening scenes were 'twice as long as they ought to be, because the writer has not sufficient sparkle and humour to pass off such minute and prolonged description of a trifle'. He ended by advising Hardy to study George Sand, the acknowledged model for the prose idyll, to 'shut his ears to the fooleries of critics' and to 'beware of letting *realism* grow out of proportion to his *fancy*' (Morgan 1943: 94–5). In hindsight, it is possible to see that the Victorian prose idyll was precisely 'a reconciliation of the traditional pastoral idyll and the realistic novel', combining the 'charm' and 'quaintness' of the former with at least some of the realism expected of the latter (Jones 1989: 152–3). Contemporary readers, as we shall see, appear to have picked up on the charm while more recent readers have appreciated the more realistic elements, in particular the satire of contemporary attitudes to class and gender. Hardy may later have felt guilty about playing it safe, providing his sophisticated urban readers with amusing sketches of rural life which rather 'burlesqued' the real-life originals (*Life* 17), but he could not avoid building into his version of pastoral at least some subversive elements.

Hardy would later be rather disparaging about this early attempt to charm his audience. In an interview for *Cassell's Saturday Journal* of June 1892, he regretted having 'finished it as I began it' (safely) 'because much more could have been made of the story' (Millgate 1982: 136). His 1896 Preface emphasised its realism, claiming that it was 'a fairly true picture, at first hand, of the personages, ways, and customs which were common among such orchestral bodies in the villages of fifty years ago'. The 'broad humour' of their songs, he noted, had since become 'unquotable'; even their hymns would 'hardly be admitted into such hymn-books as are popular in the churches of fashionable society at the present time' (*UGT* 162). The Uniform Edition of 1902 added the sub-title, *The Mellstock Quire*, focusing attention on this historical dimension, while the topographical revisions of 1896 and 1912, fixing the correspondence between the fictional Mellstock and the real Stinsford more precisely, further shifted the pastoral idyll of 'any rural village' in the direction of history, making the text of 1912 'a substantially different novel from the one that a few hundred people read in 1872' (Gatrell 1988: 176, 128–9). Hardy's 1912 additions to the Preface reiterated his misgivings about having played too 'safe' forty years earlier:

> In rereading the narrative after a long interval there occurs the inevitable reflection that the realities out of which it was spun were material for another kind of study of this little group of church musicians than is found in the chapters here penned so lightly, even so farcically and flippantly at times. But circumstances would have rendered any aim at a deeper, more essential, more transcendent handling unadvisable at the date of writing...
>
> (*UGT* 162–3)

'Circumstances' here, as elsewhere in Hardy, refers primarily to the conditions of publishing, the requirement that his work should amuse rather than challenge his middle-class urban readers.

Again Hardy had difficulty finding a publisher. Macmillan had dragged their heels, fearing that 'the public will find the tale very slight and rather unexciting'. It needed, in their view, considerable cutting and yet it was already 'too small for a circulating library'. To cut the price, however, would require large sales, which they did not anticipate.

The best they could offer, therefore, was for Hardy to resubmit a revised manuscript for possible publication the following spring (Morgan 1943: 99). Tinsley, to whom Hardy next turned after their chance encounter in the Strand, 'knew there was no great money in it' but 'believed' in Hardy, convinced he 'was going to get a grip some day' (Downey 1905: 20). In *Under the Greenwood Tree*, according to Tinsley's *Random Recollections*, 'I felt sure that I had got hold of the best little prose idyll I had ever read'. It was 'little': 'not more than about four or five hours' reading' but it was 'excellent reading':

> I almost raved about the book, and I gave it away wholesale to pressmen and anyone I knew interested in good fiction. But, strange to say, it would not sell. Finding it hung on hand in the original two-volume form, I printed it in a very pretty illustrated one-volume form. That edition was a failure. Then I published it in a two-shilling form, with paper covers, and that edition had a very poor sale indeed; and yet it was one of the best press-noticed books I ever published.
>
> (Tinsley 1900: 127)

It was presumably one of the two-shilling copies in its 'red-and-yellow' paper cover which attracted the attention of Frederick Greenwood, spotting his own name in the title, at a railway bookstall, as he recalled in an article in the *Illustrated London News* in October 1892:

> to all appearance ... my gay bargain was of the refuse order: that is to say, it looked like one of those unhappy tales which, being failures at one vol., 10s. 6d., or two vols., 21s., are stripped of their respectable cloth bindings, hustled into paper covers, and sold on the bookstalls cheap. It was certainly a story that I for one had never heard of, nor on subsequent enquiry could I find anyone who had; but – pleasure of pleasures – dipping into Chapter 1 was like overing a stile into new, unknown, enchanted ground ...
>
> (DCM 6447, f.249)

It was also presumably this 'vile binding of red and yellow' of which Charles Kegan Paul complained in 1881 (Cox 1970: 83) although by then Tinsley had gone bankrupt and sold the copyright to Chatto & Windus, who issued it over their imprint in 1878 (Purdy 1954: 8). Greenwood's delight in his bargain would have important consequences for Hardy's career, since he was then working for Smith, Elder, publishers of the *Cornhill*, and appears to have relayed his enthusiasm to them and

to their editor Leslie Stephen. But it did little for the immediate sales of
Under the Greenwood Tree.

The reviews of the first edition, all four pasted into Hardy's scrapbook,
were encouraging. The *Athenaeum* (15.6.72), after congratulating itself
on having recognised his skilful depiction of West Country rural life in
Desperate Remedies, welcomed the author's abandonment of 'the dark
ways of human crime and folly' for 'that vein of his genius which yields
the best produce'. It also praised the humour in the new novel, complaining only that its rustics 'speak too much like educated people' (Cox
1970: 9–10). That objection was echoed in the *Pall Mall Gazette* (5.7.72),
which praised the novel's 'freshness and originality' but thought its
'humble heroes and heroines' were 'too shrewd' and said 'too many
good things, to be truthful representatives of their prototypes in real
life' (Lerner 1968: 18). Hardy's friend Horace Moule in the *Saturday
Review* (28.9.72) called the novel 'the best prose idyl that we have seen
for a long while', also welcoming Hardy's abandonment of 'the more
conventional, and far less agreeable, field' of sensation fiction. Such was
the 'power and truthfulness' of its depiction of 'the better class of
rustics', according to Moule, that the novel could serve as a 'manual
for any one...desirous to learn something of the inner life of a rural
parish'. The 'love passages' he thought 'unnecessarily prolonged' while
the dialogue displayed 'an occasional tendency' for the rustics 'to express themselves in the language of the author's manner of thought,
rather than in their own', but the book as a whole, 'full of humour and
keen observation', contained 'the genuine air of the country' (19–21).
The *Echo* (11.10.72) too found the novel 'remarkable for quaintness and
originality', altogether 'quite unlike anything we have had for many
seasons'.

Under the Greenwood Tree, however, took some time to attract notice.
Leon Boucher called it 'as welcome as it was picturesque' in his article on
'Le Roman Pastoral en Angleterre' in the *Revue des Deux Mondes* in 1875,
but passed quickly on to a more sustained study of *Far from the Madding
Crowd* (Cox 1970: xviii). A review of *The Return of the Native* in 1879 was
still complaining that both *Under the Greenwood Tree* and *A Pair of Blue
Eyes* had received 'less attention than they deserved' (51). George Fenn
reported to Hardy in March 1880 that he had sung its praises to Tinsley,
'who shrugged his shoulders and said it did not sell' (DCM 2369). The
following year, however, Kegan Paul claimed it had now 'attained that
fatal gift of popularity which makes the book inaccessible in a decent
cover'. It was *Under the Greenwood Tree*, according to Paul, which
'stamped its author as an original and excellent writer' and 'laid down

the lines of his work', demonstrating to its urban audience that 'the country labourer' was neither 'a lout' nor 'stupid' (83–4). Havelock Ellis in 1883 appreciated the 'atmosphere of pure comedy' in the novel (112) while Coventry Patmore in a review of *The Woodlanders* of 1887 found Hardy's best work that in which his focus was confined 'almost exclusively to the manners of the humblest and simplest classes', which he evoked with 'a tenderness, reality and force' matched only by Barnes. Patmore marvelled that a novel whose *dramatis personae* was limited to 'a gamekeeper and his son, the mistress of the village National school, three or four small tradesmen, and a labourer or two', and which could lay claim to no plot, could yet deserve to rank as a prose-idyll with *The Vicar of Wakefield* (147). Two years later J. M. Barrie, while making similar comparisons with Goldsmith, deplored the fact that the novel had made its 'way with the public as slowly as *Lorna Doone*'. It may not have been Hardy's greatest book, but it was 'his most perfect' (160).

By the 1890s, it seems, *Under the Greenwood Tree* had become a firm favourite. W. P. Trent celebrated 'the genial charm of this idyl' in the *Sewanee Review* of 1892 (223). Both monographs of 1894 sang its praises, Annie Macdonell finding in it 'Hardy's surest claim to recognition in another age' (Macdonell 1894: 32). Tim Dolin argues that 'its popularity... grew in proportion as Hardy's later novels alarmed and alienated some readers' (*UGT* xxi). Havelock Ellis, in a review of *Jude the Obscure* in 1896, claimed that no 'fundamental change' had occurred but that the earlier work had avoided morally dangerous areas:

> there really is a large field in which the instincts of human love and human caprice can have free play without too obviously conflicting with established moral codes... It is thus in the most perfect and perhaps the most delightful of Mr. Hardy's early books, *Under the Greenwood Tree*. The free play of Fancy's vagrant heart may be followed in all its little bounds and rebounds, its fanciful ardours and repressions, because she is too young a thing to drink deep of life – and because she is not yet married. It is all very immoral, as Nature is, but it succeeds in avoiding any collision with the rigid constitution of Society. The victim finally takes the white veil and is led to the altar; then a door is closed, and the convent gate of marriage is not again opened to the intrusive novel-reader's eye.
>
> (Cox 1970: 304–5)

There were potentially 'shocking' elements even in this novel, in other words, but Hardy had managed to keep them happily out of sight.

Wilfred Owen, for example, recommended it to his mother as 'a most reposing book' (Owen 1967: 547) while David Cecil called it 'the light-weight among his masterpieces' (Cecil 1943: 31). Most readers seem quite happily to have ignored what Mark Mossman has called the 'underlying issues, lurking just beneath the surface of the happy veneer, on the brink of erupting into the narrative' (Mossman 1998: 21).

Hardy's contemporaries, as we have seen, had little difficulty in identifying *Under the Greenwood Tree* as an example of the 'prose idyl, a recognised although perhaps relatively rarely practised genre', the names of whose more recent practitioners recurred throughout the reviews: Goldsmith, George Eliot and George Sand (Jones 1989: 151). The genre, of course, went back much further than this, to the short Greek pastoral novel of Longus entitled *Daphnis and Chloe*, first translated into English by Angel Day, who, as Paul Turner speculates, may well have lent his surname to Hardy's heroine. There is no external evidence that Hardy read Longus but the number of similarities Turner finds between this novel, regarded by many Victorians as 'obscene', and Hardy's early work supports his suggestion that Horace Moule may have alerted him to it. Longus, who claimed to be telling the story of a painting (a metaphor recycled in Hardy's subtitle), also divided his work into four seasonal books, while his rustic hero Daphnis, like Hardy's, falls in love with the daughter of a rich man. Both authors laugh affectionately at the sexual innocence of their young lovers. In addition, as Turner notes,

> There were precedents in the Greek novel for several other features of the English one: for Dick's blunt approach to Mr. Day... and for her father's feeling that she was too good to marry someone of Dick's class; for the lovers' talk under an apple-tree; for Fancy's bee-sting; for bird-limning as a lover's ploy; and for a wedding-reception associated with animals and snobbery...
>
> (Turner 1998: 30–1)

Given that many of these scenes expanding the love-plot appear to have been added to the manuscript when Hardy returned to it after completing *Desperate Remedies*, Gatrell's suggestion that Hardy, reviewing what he had written earlier, either realised himself that he would have to add romance to the story to interest his 'middle-class female readership' or showed the manuscript to someone else (most likely Moule) fits in well with Turner's identification of the probable source for these additional romantic elements (Gatrell 1988: 8).

That *Under the Greenwood Tree* offers itself primarily as a version of pastoral is abundantly clear. The title and penultimate line advertise the link with *As You Like It*. The subtitle, 'A Rural Painting of the Dutch School', foregrounds the aesthetic, picturesque quality of the writing, also placing Hardy in the more recent tradition of George Eliot, whose manifesto for a more realistic kind of word-painting in chapter seventeen of *Adam Bede*, had also turned to the Dutch school. Contemporary reviewers mentioned Teniers and Hobbema as possible models for Hardy along with English genre painters such as David Wilkie. As Bullen has shown, however, English critics tended to deplore the 'boorishness, bawdiness, and vulgarity' of the Dutch paintings, elements which were 'carefully excluded from the English version of the pastoral' (Bullen 1986: 44). By introducing so much sex and cider into the novel Hardy was cautiously stretching the limits of pastoral as understood in the mid-Victorian period.

The comparison with George Eliot is particularly relevant to Hardy's relationship with his readers. Like her, along with most pastoral writers, Hardy is assuming an urban reader unfamiliar with the rural details he describes, functioning as 'mediator between the world of the text and the world of his assumed (implied) reader' (D'Agnillo 1993: 39). The narrator of *Under the Greenwood Tree*, as Shelagh Hunter has shown, is 'continuously aware of the reader's unfamiliarity' with his world, 'at pains to make the reader *see* the life with which he himself is so familiar' (Hunter 1984: 170, 167). This, as Raymond Williams complained of George Eliot, can cause problems:

> there is a point often reached in George Eliot when the novelist is conscious that the characters she is describing are 'different' from her probable readers; she then offers to know them, and to make them 'knowable', in a deeply inauthentic...way...she works the formula which has been so complacently powerful in English novel-writing: the 'fine old', 'dear old', quaint-talking, honest-living country characters.
>
> (Williams 1975: 208)

A similar 'external observation of customs and quaintness, modulated by a distinctly patronizing affection' reappears, according to Williams, in *Under the Greenwood Tree* (246). As Frank Chapman lamented in *Scrutiny*, 'Hardy cannot stop patronising his rustics', making them 'quaint and picturesque' (Chapman 1934: 31). Geoffrey Grigson would also complain that Hardy's patronising attitude to his peasants, so congenial to his contemporaries, 'distresses the modern reader' (Grigson 1974: 18).

Modern readers also have difficulty, Shelagh Hunter claims, with the sheer emphasis on descriptive detail at the expense of character and plot in the Victorian prose idyll (Hunter 1984: 217). It is 'picturesque' in Lukács' pejorative sense, accumulating pointless detail which tells us nothing of what is 'really' happening. Hardy himself, in an 1879 review of William Barnes' *Poems of Rural Life in the Dorset Dialect*, writing of the poet's exploration of his cottagers' sorrows and joys, was critical as well as appreciative of the 'golden glow...which art can project upon the commonest things' (*PW* 96). Barnes, he later wrote, 'held himself artistically aloof from the ugly side of things – or perhaps shunned it unconsciously; and we escape in his pictures the sordid miseries that are laid bare in Crabbe, often to the destruction of charm'. To this extent 'he does not probe life so deeply' (84), a phrase which connects with the desire expressed in the 1912 Preface to *Under the Greenwood Tree* for 'a deeper, more essential...handling' of the issues involved (*UGT* 163), and with the speech Hardy made at a dramatisation of the novel in 1910, when, after quoting Ruskin's view that 'comedy is tragedy if you only look deeply enough', he said 'tonight, at any rate, we will all be young and not look too deeply' (*Life* 381). I want to suggest, however, that there is a certain melancholy lurking beneath the surface of the comedy in *Under the Greenwood Tree* along the lines of the belief later expressed in 'The Dorsetshire Labourer' that it was in rural communities 'that happiness will find her last refuge on earth, since it is among them that a perfect insight into the conditions of existence will be longest postponed' (*PW* 169). His rustic characters may remain happy but readers 'who look deeply enough' know that their happiness is an illusion.

The surface quaintness of *Under the Greenwood Tree* is also 'shadowed by a pagan and erotic vitality which underwrites the idyll', in which serious questions irreducible to comedy and genuinely earthy elements unacceptable to Victorian taste occasionally break through (Goode 1988: 12–13). In Reuben Dewy's words, 'all true stories have a coarse touch or a bad moral' (*UGT* 46). Among the 'coarse' touches in this novel are the very names of the young lovers, Dick and Fancy, which highlight its central subject (Goode 1988: 12). The novel charts Dick's induction into the opposite sex, firstly at the hands of his father, who advises him to 'take the first respectable body that comes to hand' since 'they be all alike in the groundwork' (*UGT* 85). It is quite literally Fancy's body that Dick has been shown to lust after at the Tranter's party, at which anything that has been in contact with it gains immediately in value: not only her skirt but 'a cat, which had lain unobserved in her lap for several minutes', and 'crept across into his own' (45). Dick marvels that the 'romping girl ... who had not minded the weight of [his] hand upon her waist', who had been 'touchable, pressable – even kissable' all evening, had now retreated into the persona of the village teacher, 'a woman somewhat reserved and of a phlegmatic temperament' (47). There are other lessons which young Dick has to learn about, for instance that she is not as 'good' as he might like, quite capable of encouraging the attentions not only of Farmer Shinar but even Parson Maybold. Both his father and his grandfather make unflattering remarks about 'how a maiden is' (87, 157) while the narrator too suggests that 'those beautiful eyes of hers' might be 'too refined and beautiful for a tranter's wife; but, perhaps, not too good' (151).

Any suggestion of unladylike desire on Fancy's part, however, can only be implied: 'The reader is given virtually no direct representation of any desire, intention, or feeling of Fancy's; all must be inferred from the commentaries and interpretations of (male) others' (Boumelha 1999: 136). Even the words the witch whispers in Fancy's ear are not vouchsafed to (us male) readers; we are simply shown her 'expression of sinister humour' (127). When Fancy sits at her window after eclipsing all the other women at church by her playing and by her costume, her curls and her hat, the narrator himself abandons the question whether she was thinking 'of her lover, or of the sensation she had created at church that day... it is unknown' (135). The final words of the novel express Fancy's resolve to keep her interiority secret.

Some of the difficulties experienced by women are, in fact, allowed to penetrate the fog of male ignorance in the novel. Mrs Brownjohn, we learn in the second chapter, who has buried three of her four children, is pregnant again, despite being 'no more than a maid' herself (12). We later discover that Thomas Leaf's mother has lost all but one of her children (60). The advice Mrs Dewy gives when Fancy is anxious about all aspects of marriage, 'from wedding to churching', is to comfort herself with the cry of resignation, ''Tis to be, and here goes!' (147). These relatively serious and even potentially tragic elements in the novel may sound a quiet note in the overall context of comic pastoral, but they are undoubtedly there, along with other ironic subversions of the supposed joys of marriage. The title of the opening chapter of the final part of the novel, 'The Knot There's No Untying', for example, calls up (again only implicitly, beneath the surface of the text) the rest of Thomas Campbell's sardonic song, which not only contains a clue to the heroine's name ('Love he comes, and Love he tarries,/Just as fate or fancy carries') but to her probable future:

> Can you keep the bee from ranging
> Or the ringdove's neck from changing?
> No! nor fettered love from dying
> In the knot there's no untying. (216)

These submerged elements of the text, present only by allusion, serve at least to suggest a less than happy outcome.

Other tensions that can be said to simmer beneath the surface of this novel involve anxieties and resentment about class. Gatrell identifies some of these elements, again shared with 'An Indiscretion in the Life of an Heiress', which appear to have been rescued from the wreck of *The Poor Man and the Lady* (Gatrell 1988: 13–14). Not only Fancy, for example, but all the wives presented in the novel feel they have married beneath them. The whole social scale of the novel is limited, of course: the lord of the manor is absent while Leaf is the only agricultural labourer represented as an individual. But the 'middling ranks of society', from gentlemen farmers and clergy down to tradesmen, are presented with an insight and an accuracy which matches exactly the evidence of the 1841 census records. Across 'the smooth warp of pastoral,' in other words, 'Hardy weaves a coarser weft of realism' (Howard 1977: 197–8).

'Coarse' is a word often on the lips of Mrs Dewy, who complains that her husband's were always 'a coarse-skinned family', 'sich vulgar perspirers', 'low' talkers (36), with 'low notions' (42):

> Nobody do know the trouble I have to keep that man barely respectable...talking about 'taties' with Michael in such a labourer's way...With our family 'twas never less than 'taters' and very often 'pertatoes' outright; mother was so particular and nice with us girls: there was no family in the parish that kept theirselves up more than we.
>
> (*UGT* 46)

Mrs Dewy clearly puts on a good show for the neighbours at their Christmas Eve party, only 'leaving off the adorned tones she had been bound to use throughout the evening, and returning to the natural marriage voice' once all the guests have left (48). Mrs Day is shown to be equally concerned at the impression Dick may have of their cutlery and tablecloths (79). The pretensions of the lower-middle class, however, are a 'safe' target. When Fancy tells her father not to wipe his mouth with his hand after drinking since this habit was 'decidedly dying out among the upper classes of society' (155) part of the humour comes from the fact that she ranks well beneath these classes.

The desire for upward social mobility, the love of what Fancy in her letter to Maybold calls 'refinement of mind and manners' (142), provides the most significant barrier to the successful resolution of the comedy, first in the form of her father's opposition and secondly her own 'temptation' by the vicar's proposal. Mr Day makes it quite clear to Dick that he is not the husband he had in mind, that Fancy has been educated so that 'any gentleman, who sees her to be his equal in polish, should want to marry her' (123–4). Later editions increased Day's standing in 1896 to 'head gamekeeper' and in 1912 to 'timber-steward' (208). The Wessex Edition also promoted Fancy's mother from 'governess in a county family' to 'teacher in a landed county-family's nursery' (213). Dick's own language was also made less 'educated', more full of dialect in the 1896 edition (203), all these changes increasing the social gap between the two lovers.

Hardy clearly enjoys poking fun at the 'gentlemanly' pretensions of Dick's rival suitors. Farmer Shinar tries to display 'polish' in his accoutrements, his gold shirt studs, his silver watch chain and ring, while Maybold's main claim to Fancy's hand appears to be his umbrella 'of superior silk' (136). He flatters Fancy by offering her a bigger stage for her 'talents' and 'refinement', assuring her, 'you have enough in you for any society, after a few months travel with me' (137–8). Hardy also mocks the deference shown by the choir towards their vicar, from their 'earnest and prolonged wiping of shoes' as they cross his hearth, to their touching of imaginary hats. Maybold himself not only patronises Leaf the labourer, as if his mother's suffering can be made good with half a crown, but reprimands his servant for giving her 'personal opinions' (63–6). This may be satire of a very mild kind but it captures the social hierarchy of the village.

Hardy can indeed be seen to have played 'safe' in his second published novel, toning down the savageness of the satire that had made *The Poor Man and the Lady* unpublishable and maintaining the geniality of tone appropriate to the prose idyll. Nevertheless, the realism which that genre brought to pastoral allowed him to introduce some characteristically subversive elements, rescuing the novel from total blandness.

Reading women: on looking into *A Pair of Blue Eyes*

The eponymous eyes of Hardy's third published novel are described in the opening chapter as 'a misty and a shady blue, that had no beginning or surface, and was looked *into* rather than *at*' (*PBE* 8). What men see when they look into them is shown to bear little relation to their owner, whom they continually misread, projecting onto her their own fantasies. The novel repeatedly employs metaphors of 'reading' character and of 'the heroine as text' (Devereux 1992: 20–2). A man, we are told, recalls a woman's image in 'his mind's eye' or in 'the pages of his memory' (*PBE* 22). The novel also depicts a number of different acts of reading, whether of novels, reviews, notebooks or epitaphs with careful attention to the phenomenological process by which the mind realises or concretises its intentional object, whether text or person, building a complete image from the aspects or stimuli to which it responds.

Hardy himself always retained something of a soft spot for *A Pair of Blue Eyes*, whose opening scenes were based on his own courtship of Emma. The 1895 Preface refers somewhat coyly to the setting as 'pre-eminently (for one person at least) the region of dream and mystery' (*PBE* 390). A letter of 1913 to George Dewar, literary editor of the *Saturday Review*, who had told Hardy that this particular novel 'holds me as much as any of your books' (DCM 2092), acknowledged with unusual frankness that 'the character of the heroine' was 'largely – that of my late wife'. The novel, he boasted, was also the favourite novel of Tennyson and Patmore (*Letters* IV 288). Patmore, in fact, was so enamoured of the novel, his wife explained to Hardy after his death in 1899, that 'from 1875 to 1896 he continually had *A Pair of Blue Eyes* read to him', especially when recovering from illness (DCM 4688). Lord Northcliffe claimed to know it so well he could recite it backwards (*Letters* II 296) while for Proust it was of all Hardy's work 'the one he would himself most gladly have written' (Gibson 1996: 58).

Hardy's predilection for *A Pair of Blue Eyes* is apparent in the special attention he gave it for all the collected editions. He told Henry Macbeth-Raeburn, who supplied the etched frontispiece for each volume of the Wessex novels, that the novel had 'always been a selling book, which is the reason why they want to have it early in the series' (II 65). He was uncertain in which category to place it for the Wessex Edition, first including it among the 'Romances and Fantasies', then moving it to 'Novels of Character and Environment' before returning it to the romances. 'It will come as No.10 just the same,' he told Frederic Macmillan, 'but instead of being the last of the first group it will be the first of the second group' (IV 209). It would not therefore lose its position in the pecking order. It was the only novel which he bothered substantially to revise for the Mellstock Edition of 1920 and when Ernest Rhys asked for just one Hardy novel for the 'Everyman' series in 1923 it was *A Pair of Blue Eyes* that Hardy suggested (VI 181). He urged Madeleine Rolland to translate it since he believed it 'would attract French readers' in particular (VI 61).

To begin with, however, the novel appears to have made little impact. Tinsley failed to supply any figures but called it 'by far the weakest of the three books I published of his' (Purdy 1954: 12). It was, however, the first to appear under Hardy's name as well as the first to be serialised (in *Tinsley's Magazine*). His American publisher, Henry Holt, who arranged for its serialisation, in the *New York Tribune* (Weber 1946: 18) also complained, 'We can't make "Blue Eyes" sell as it ought', a fact he attributed in part to its 'melancholy ending' (DCM 3474). Another American, William Lyon Phelps, recalled being so shocked by the ending that when he 'finished the last page, [he] released a howl like a timber wolf . . . hurled the volume against the wall . . . went to bed and remained there a week' (Dessner 1992:154).

The *Life*, as well as telling the story of Hardy's successful negotiation of a better contract as a result of staying up 'half the night' studying *Copinger on Copyright*, confesses how much of a novice he still was: he had only rough notes of 'the opening chapters and a general outline' when he signed the contract and 'had shaped nothing of what the later chapters were to be like' (*Life* 92–3). He was still telling Tinsley in July 1872 (two months before serialisation began) that the novel required 'a great deal of re-consideration' (17) while in April 1873 (three months before serialisation ended) he announced his intention to make 'several amendments in the early part of the tale' for the three-volume first edition (21). It was 'hurriedly written . . . with inadequate preparation and under constant pressure from the printer', factors which resulted, according to Millgate, in much 'hastily inserted padding and ill-digested autobiography' (Millgate 1971: 67).

The reviews, however, as Hardy's scrapbook attests, were mainly positive. The *Graphic* (12.7.73) felt no qualms in placing its author in 'the first rank of writers of high-class fiction of our day', celebrating the way Hardy had succeeded in freeing his work from 'the trace of sensationalism which somewhat disfigured *Desperate Remedies*' while adding that 'body' to the plot which had been missing from *Under the Greenwood Tree*. John Hutton in the *Spectator* (28.6.73) also welcomed Hardy's discarding of sensationalism and rising above the merely picturesque to demonstrate not only 'quick observation' but 'sparkling humour and true moral instinct'. Both these reviews, along with that in *Pall Mall Gazette* (25.10.73) saw Hardy as rivalling George Eliot in these respects. All three, however, criticised the title, for the *Spectator* 'the weakest point in the book – absolutely injurious to its success'. The *Graphic* called it 'silly and unmeaning', the *Pall Mall Gazette* 'a little weak and sentimental'.

Other reviews supply evidence of contemporary (presumably male) readers being charmed not only by the eyes but by other features of the heroine. The *Athenaeum* (28.6.73) found Elfride 'perilously attractive' while the *Birmingham Daily Gazette* (21.8.77) praised 'the delineation of the character of Elfride . . . with all her sweet virtues, but also with her faults and failings'. *John Bull* (15.9.77) thought her 'a typical woman', *The Times* (9.9.73) 'undoubtedly fickle', full of 'extraordinary folly and extraordinary deceit', and the *Pall Mall Gazette* 'a little petulant' but 'still eminently sweet and docile'. Almost all of the reviews, as Pamela Dalziel notes, sympathised with Knight (*PBE* xxviii). The most notable exception, ironically, appears to have been the *Saturday Review*, written by Horace Moule, Hardy's own friend and mentor, upon whom the character of Knight was based. Moule found Knight 'the least natural character in the book', inclining 'unmistakably to priggishness'. He praised the novel's recognition of 'social barriers', however, before concluding, that 'the author . . . has much to learn, and many faults yet to avoid'. Privately, in a letter to Hardy, Moule complained that his 'slips of taste, every now and then' were 'Tinsleyan' (DCM 4475), itself a nice example of Knightly condescension.

The reviews were divided about the ending. Moule praised its 'tragic power' while the *Pall Mall*, although suggesting that the novel was 'too pathetic', even 'a pain to read', recognised 'the skill and power' of the final scene involving Elfride's three grieving lovers. The *Graphic* felt 'quite injured that the author should be so pitiless to so delightful a heroine' and John Hutton, having publicly celebrated the novel's 'sparkling humour', wrote privately to Hardy to complain that his and his wife's laughter had been undermined by the 'ineffably sad' ending. The 'object of a novel is to relieve and amuse', he reminded Hardy, and to do that it *'should end well'*, avoiding the 'indignant despair' he had experienced (DCM 3350). Hardy must have defended 'the *truth* of her death', which Hutton's next letter accepts while reiterating his view that 'art is produced for – the advantage and recreation of the public' (3531). Their surviving correspondence, one-sided though it is, shows Hardy battling hard with established reviewers to convince them of the tragic potential of the novel.

Later critics found the comic elements more difficult to accept. Havelock Ellis objected to the novel's 'impossible coincidences'. Arnold Bennett found it 'immensely sardonic' (Flower 1932: II 285) but David Cecil disliked the 'practical joke' at the end' (Cecil 1943: 127–8). Richard Carpenter attempted to classify the novel as a 'comitragedy', beginning with comedy and giving way in the end to tragedy (Carpenter 1964: 48). Both terms seemed to Millgate 'unduly grandiose' for a novel with 'persistent alternations of mode' (Millgate 1971: 74–5). Other critics have taken somewhat dangerous refuge in celebrating the novel's incoherence, its refusal to allow readers to impose a pattern upon it (Kincaid 1979: 202), its dazzling unreadability (Ebbatson 1986: 37).

What is evident in *A Pair of Blue Eyes* is Hardy's refusal to gratify his readers. He has been seen to set up two different romantic fantasies both of which are finally subverted: Elfride's elopement with Stephen appears for a moment to fulfil an adolescent dream of passion without guilt or economic responsibility, while her relationship with Knight represents the more bourgeois ideal of union with a dominant male. In the end,

> *A Pair of Blue Eyes* offers none of the satisfactions of the novel that follows it in the Hardy canon. There is no idealized rural community, no one earns anything through self-denial, none of the fantasies that are set up in the story are fulfilled by its pattern, nor do those fantasies have the added resonance of a quasi-mythic dimension... The only defence it offers against the disturbing implications of its patterns is the defence of sardonic humour...
>
> (Steig 1970: 61)

Such humour was not one with which Victorian readers were familiar; they appear to have been simply bewildered by the black comedy of the final chapters, in which the two lovers, sharing their train journey from London with Elfride's coffin, quarrel over the right to call her their 'darling' (*PBE* 372).

The novel to some extent dramatises the difficulties of reading, of attempting to make sense of signs, whether marks on the page or utterances, acts or expressions of the characters. The serial version begins with Elfride 'reading a romance', a novel whose ending is described as 'the saddest *contretemps* that ever lingered in a gentle and responsive reader's mind'. The narrator mocks her passionate involvement in the unfolding plot:

She takes up the third volume and opens it. The list of contents was disclosed, in which the author had, somewhat indiscreetly, too plainly revealed the sorrow that was impending. Elfride was too honest a reader to resolve her suspense into a more endurable certainty by taking a surreptitious glance at the end, yet too much of a woman to be satisfied with going straight on. Her eye strayed to the contents page to scan it, and so help her prognostication.

It becomes clear from these chapter headings that the hero dies at the end, causing Elfride to murmur over a suppressed sigh at her weakness. Never again, we are told, would she weep so much over 'imaginary beings' or allow them so to influence 'her state of mind'. The whole scene functions partly as an index of her character, 'a young creature whose emotions lay very near to the surface' (*PBE* 386–7), partly as a hint to Hardy's own readers about the possible outcome of his own romance, and partly as a self-conscious dramatisation of the extraordinary act of reading, of investing so much emotional energy in the lives of imaginary characters.

This scene was omitted from the first and all subsequent editions of the novel. The first two paragraphs of the first edition, described by the *Spectator* as 'somewhat affected' and subsequently removed from later editions, also refer self-consciously to 'the reader' who, if he 'has taken the trouble to look down the list [of characters] with anything like kindly curiosity', would see that 'three or four of them are capable characters, whose emotional experiences may deserve some record' (7). Hardy appears here to be satirising the likely limitation of his audience's sympathies to the characters identified as lord, clergyman and architect. The fact that he later omitted both this and a similarly direct reference to 'the reader' in chapter four, is in keeping with what Dalziel calls 'the general reduction of self-conscious narration after 1873' (399–400). Other less direct references to the process of reading, however, were allowed to remain.

Elfride's father, for example, reprimands Elfride for worrying about her reception of the expected stranger in the opening chapter, 'You get all kinds of stuff into your head from reading so many of those novels' (10). Knight too rebukes her for asking why he does not write fiction instead of essays: 'It requires a talented omission of your real thoughts to make a novel popular' (158). This may be an indirect expression of Hardy's own resentment at having to disguise his own 'real thoughts' to placate his readers. When Elfride reads Knight's review of her own attempt at fiction, again like her author, she shrinks 'perceptibly smaller', paling before his merciless critique of her 'wearisome' social scenes, her 'analyses of uninteresting character' and 'the unnatural unfoldings of a sensation plot'. Knight, it is clear, shares the criterion of realism advocated by essayists and reviewers such as Leslie Stephen. Just as Stephen in the *Cornhill* lambasted Bulwer Lytton's historical romances and silver-fork novels, so Knight complains of 'the impossible tournaments, towers and escapades' of Elfride's attempts to imitate Scott (148–9).

Knight too is portrayed in the act of reading, firstly of his own work, when he discovers 'how much more his sentences meant than he had felt them to mean when they were written' (189–90) and later of the discarded drafts of Mrs Jethway's letter. 'The abandoned sheets of paper' he somewhat idly scans in her cottage, waiting for Lord Luxellian to return with the doctor after her accident, are clearly 'renounced beginnings' of a final missive which takes on dramatically different significance when he reads it as the addressee (327–30). Stephen too rediscovers the power of letters on rereading Elfride's correspondence, previously 'sealed up, and stowed away in a corner of his leather trunk, while waiting for Knight at their London hotel (354). In the novel's final act of reading both he and Knight feel the power of very simple words as they gaze upon her coffin-plate announcing the bare details of her death in the smithy at Endelstow at the end of the novel: 'They read it, and read it, and read it again . . . as if animated by one soul' (375). It is almost as if Hardy, having committed himself to a career in fiction while writing this novel, is luxuriating in the power this gives him, celebrating the impact of his own words, the whole phenomenon of reading.

There are also several passages in the novel which explore the process of 'reading' people, dramatising and defamiliarising the commonplace metaphor. Elfride laughs in the second chapter at the contrast between 'the reality she beheld before her', the naive, shy, handsome and unthreatening youth, and 'the dark, taciturn, sharp, elderly man of business who had lurked in her imagination – a man with clothes smelling of city smoke, skin sallow from want of sun, and talk flavoured with epigram' (15). Swancourt also 'misreads' Stephen, taking him for a suitably middle-class professional, worthy of his best wine and flattery, only to 're-read' him, when the revelation of his relation to John Smith the mason prompts a total reformulation of his character. Mrs Swancourt expresses complete confidence in her own ability to 'read' faces and to understand other people (138). In 1895 Hardy cut her rather tedious translations of what it is that these faces 'say', which she reads 'as plainly as on a phylactery' (140). He retained, however, her husband's accusation that she is guilty of over-reading, seeing too much in the slightest signs.

One of the difficulties of reading *A Pair of Blue Eyes* is the apparent crudity of the primary narrative voice, which actually conceals a complex range of sometimes contradictory discourses to be found within the text. Radical challenges to Victorian attitudes, to gender for example, are voiced by some of the characters but seemingly undermined by the third-person narrator. This 'dialectic of opposing discourses and discordant voices' is explained by Rosemarie Morgan as one of an array of literary devices for circumnavigating (and presumably confusing) Mrs Grundy (Morgan 1988: xvii, 166). Among these voices, according to Morgan, is the 'moralising, didactic narrator... intrusive, platitudinous, self-righteous, and tonally discordant', who ensures that the challenges to Victorian propriety voiced by some of the characters and implicit in much of the action are softened, prevented from entering 'the Victorian middle-class drawing room without bearing the marks of correction' (10). The apparent contradictions in this novel should therefore be attributed not to the 'faultiness of composition' of which earlier critics complained but to 'a coherent, if complicated, literary stratagem'. Hardy deliberately conceals 'the iconoclastic spirit that must await fame and public recognition before coming out into the open' (28–9).

Hardy's narrative voice, I would suggest, does play with the expectations of his readers but in more complex ways than Morgan indicates. The first of the many examples of dubious narrative generalisations about women cited by Morgan, for example, that they 'accept their destiny more readily than men' (*PBE* 79), is not necessarily pejorative, partially celebrating women's greater adaptability. It may not be altogether flattering to Elfride and it certainly undermines her status as a 'lady' to say that she could 'slough off a sadness and replace it by a hope as easily as a lizard renews a diseased limb' (137) but it is nevertheless a natural quality. Similarly, the second of Morgan's examples appears initially to deplore what is labelled 'Woman's ruling passion to fascinate and influence those more powerful than she'. But in Elfride this desire to earn Knight's 'good opinion' is immediately qualified as 'purposeless':

> in wishing to please the highest class of man she had ever intimately known, there was no disloyalty to Stephen Smith. She could not – and few women can – realise the possible vastness of an issue which has only an insignificant begetting. (192)

Morgan understandably bridles at the narrator's generalisations here, which are 'indefensible' and immediately undermined by 'Hardy's evocation of her [Elfride's] sincerity, her tremulous, fearful heart' (Morgan 1988: 13). The primary purpose of this passage, however, is to enlist his readers' sympathy for his heroine, who is shown to have 'beguiled herself' in seeing her commitment to Stephen as a defence against Knight. Genuinely shocked by the change in Knight, who has returned from Dublin 'feeling less her master', offering the earrings he had previously so scorned and showering her with endearments which she promptly rejects ('Not Elfie to you, Mr. Knight'), she is shown herself to be torn between what she recognises as proper and what her feelings dictate, a contradiction illustrated by her Freudian slip:

> 'I have a reason for not taking them – now.' She kept in the last word for a moment, intending to imply that her refusal was finite, but somehow the word slipped out, and undid all the rest. (194)

The subtlety of Hardy's writing here certainly belies the apparent crudeness of his narrator's initial generalisations. The problem for his readers is how to account for the disparity, whether like Morgan to attribute it to strategy (the deliberate creation of a transparently chauvinistic narrator) or to internal contradiction in Hardy himself, part of whom had not completely escaped widely shared assumptions about women.

Similar complexities are apparent in Morgan's other examples, in which the narrator comments in turn on women's tendency to snub self-effacing men, their secretiveness, their vanity and their fear of losing their beauty (Morgan 1988: 19–22). In some of these cases, it seems at least plausible that the narrator functions primarily to provide male readers with what they are accustomed to hearing while his representation of action and dialogue challenges or undermines those same generalisations. Knight is thus shown to be at least as sensitive about his bald spot and his round shoulders, 'a faint ghastliness discernible in his laugh' (177) as Elfride about her appearance. The narrative comments about Knight are particularly disturbing since they appear to go out of their way to defend him, contradicting what we are actually shown in the action and dialogue. In the scene in which he introduces Stephen to Elfride in the vault of the church, completely oblivious of their feelings and reactions, he first patronises Stephen and then pontificates at length on death, his solemn sentences being interspersed with their terse replies, only for the narrator to dwell on the way 'the thoroughness and integrity of Knight illuminated his features' (262). Even

his 'obtuseness to the cause of her indisposition' is turned to his advantage, 'evidencing his entire freedom from the suspicion of anything
behind the scenes' and his incapacity of deception 'rather than any
inherent dullness in him regarding human nature' (265). It is almost
as if the narrator has to contradict or 'correct' what Hardy realises any
sensitive reader would be bound to think about his behaviour. Similarly,
when he pleads rather absurdly for the privilege of fastening one of the
earrings he has bought Elfride, the narrator intervenes to insist that such
'singular earnestness about a small matter' is only found in deep natures
who have been wholly unused to toying with womankind' (277). Again
the narrator insists, 'Knight was as honourable a man as was ever loved
and deluded by woman' (278) while Elfride voices what any modern
reader must feel about Knight:

> 'I almost wish you were of a grosser nature . . . Ordinary men are not
> so delicate in their tastes as you; and where the lover or husband is
> not so fastidious, and refined, and of a deep nature, things seem to go
> on better . . .' (300)

There is sufficient evidence in the text, in other words, for modern
readers to build a picture of Knight as a victim of mid-Victorian repression, even a closet homosexual, in spite of the narrator's apparent
admiration for him.

The negative reading of Knight, Dalziel insists, is 'a late-twentieth-
century phenomenon' (xxix). What is surprising, however, is how much
there is *in* the text on which to build such a portrait: his pride, for
example, in never having kissed any other woman but his mother, and
his insistence on similarly 'untried lips' (293). And yet, when he fails to
respond to Elfride's desperate pursuit of him to London, allowing her to
return with her father, the narrator continues to come to his defence,
praising his 'moral purity' and 'spirit of self-denial', albeit mixed with 'a
modicum of that wrong-headedness which is mostly found in scrupu-
lously honest people' (341). Again, there is a clear contradiction between what Hardy shows and what his narrator says, a contradiction
perhaps attributable to Hardy's desire not to offend one particular
reader, Horace Moule. That at least may explain why the narrator continues to praise a man who is shown to behave so callously.

It is not merely Knight and the narrator who are prone to chauvinistic
generalisations about women. The novel presents Swancourt pontifi-
cating at some length on the subject. The vicar, in some respects
proud of his daughter, tells Knight rather patronisingly of her prowess

at chess: 'She plays very well for a lady' (167). He also doctors his conversation in accordance with conventional views on what is suitable for both ladies and gentlemen. On their way to church, about to regale Knight with a story which he suddenly realises is unsuited for a Sunday, he substitutes instead 'the story of the Levite who journeyed to Beth-lehem-judah' (180). Mrs Grundy would clearly approve; the Bible is acceptable, not to say obligatory sabbath reading. This story, however, from Judges 19 is one of those *Texts of Terror* which depicts awful female suffering at the hands of brutal men (Trible 1984: 65). The Levite, the purpose of whose journey is to reclaim his concubine, who has 'played the whore against him' and returned to her father's house, follows her there only to find himself 'beset' by 'certain sons of Belial who want to make love to him, to 'know' him in the biblical sense (19:2, 22). The father-in-law promptly gives up his daughter to prevent them doing 'unto this man...so vile a thing', whereupon 'they knew her, and abused her all the night until the morning' (19:25). Finding her body at his door in the morning, the Levite takes it home and cuts it into twelve pieces, which he sends 'into all the coasts of Israel' (19:29). Hardy's implied reader (being, like himself, both knowledgable and critical of the Bible) is clearly supposed to appreciate the irony of Mrs Grundy finding this story acceptable while objecting to the same ingre-dients as they appear in his own novel: a cruel father, repressed homo-eroticism and a female victim whose punishment grossly exceeds her crime.

Swancourt, being classically educated, is able to adduce other respect-able texts to support his view of women. Attempting to assuage his daughter's sense of guilt at betraying her first lover, he embarks on a quotation from Catullus about a 'woman's words to a lover' being 'written only on wind and water' (*PBE* 256). Elfride makes a similarly feeble attempt to draw solace from another of her father's classical authors, a passage in Livy that Knight recognises 'is no defence at all' (275). Knight pours scorn on colleagues of his who build their careers upon 'a few indifferent satires upon women' (305), but his own effu-sions, both in his review of Elfride and in his notebooks, evince similar traits. The review advises her to keep to those areas at which women can excel, the 'murmuring of delicate emotional trifles' and 'matters of domiciliary experience' (148–9). His notebook contrasts the methods of showing off peculiar to the 'Town-bred girl' as opposed to the 'Coun-try Miss' (176). Other examples of Knight's low estimate of women in general include his claim never to have 'met a woman who loves music as do ten or a dozen men I know' (182) and his indulgence of 'a mild infusion of personal vanity' as completing 'the delicate and fascinating dye of the feminine mind' (190). The point, very clearly established in the course of the novel, is that such generalisations about women are rife within the society depicted and that they contribute to the constraints placed upon them.

Hardy's dramatisation of such widespread masculine discourse about women is what opens the novel to the Foucauldian reading given by Jane Thomas, who sees Elfride as 'trapped between the desire to express herself through unfettered movement, speech and writing, and the obligation to be recognised by and within a social order which values stillness, passivity and silence in a woman' (Thomas 1999: 71).

Part of the attraction of the Elfride introduced at the beginning of the novel, according to Thomas, is that she is relatively 'undisciplined' in the Foucauldian sense, allowed by her indulgent father to roam the countryside unchaperoned, to amuse herself by writing his sermons and to behave in a generally 'undomesticated' fashion. Her manner, we are told, 'was childish and scarcely formed... the *monstrare digito* of idle men had not flattered her, and at the age of nineteen or twenty she was no farther on in social consciousness than an urban young lady of fifteen' (*PBE* 8). The Latin tag here, literally 'being pointed at with the finger', provides an appropriate vehicle for the kind of interpellation or 'calling into being' studied by Foucault in *The History of Sexuality*. In the absence of a mother, the normal vehicle for a girl's induction into female propriety, she betrays a refreshing spontaneity towards Stephen, only to be 'warned by womanly instinct, which for the moment her ardour had outrun, that she had been too forward to a comparative stranger'. Later, on entering Stephen's bedroom in the middle of the night in her dressing gown, 'She did not stop to think of the propriety or otherwise' of her action (96). Her domestication, in other words, in terms of expected female behaviour, is incomplete.

Part of the novel's pathos, however, is that her freedom from conventional restraint is shown to be only temporary or illusory. Elfride cannot forever ignore such proprieties or avoid the 'policing' by which feminine sexuality is regulated. In her case, of course, it is Mrs Jethway rather than Mrs Grundy who terrifies her into submission while Knight similarly 'corrects' her attempted transgressions. When she disobeys his warnings and risks falling from the parapet of the tower, his 'correction' is particularly severe, reducing the 'daring equestrienne' (Thomas 1999: 80) to 'a colt in a halter' (*PBE* 167). The words 'fallen' and 'foolish' – the first implied metaphorically here, the second applied literally by Knight – further discipline Elfride, as do the games of chess, in which she is seen to overreach the capacities of her sex, wanting to play by 'club rules' but lacking the strength to do so. After rescuing Knight from the cliff, directed, of course, by his careful instructions about checking the knots and careful to ensure that Knight's end of the rope contains her woollen outer garments – the idea of him 'hurtling down to his death holding her drawers was not to be thought of' (Sutherland 1997: 167) – she allows herself to 'remain passive ... encircled by his arms', luxuriating in the recognition that 'it was infinitely more to be even the slave of the greater than the queen of the less' (*PBE* 220). In this she is entirely conventional. It is the indiscretion of her flying to him unchaperoned that finally proves to Knight that 'the proprieties must be a dead letter with her'. Such 'indifference to decorum', he tells himself, cannot be tolerated even though 'trusting beings like Elfride are the women who fall' (340–1). The irony here, of course, is that Elfride is not a Fallen Woman in the conventional sense, although the spectre of that label, as Thomas argues, pursues her throughout the novel.

The novel thus dramatises the power of male discourse to restrict and finally to destroy women. In a postscript to the Preface added in 1912 Hardy claimed that *A Pair of Blue Eyes* exhibited 'the romantic stage of an idea which was further developed in a later novel' (*PBE* 390). This is normally taken as a reference to *Tess*, who is more explicitly presented as a victim of sexual double standards. At this stage of his career Hardy could not risk such an open challenge to his readers. Nevertheless, there is clearly more to be found beneath the attractive surface of *A Pair of Blue Eyes* than at first appears.

3
The *Cornhill* Stories: 'Healthy Reading for the British Public'?

Celebrating the body: *Far From the Madding Crowd*

'All the world reads the *Cornhill*', insisted Mudie in 1867, putting pressure on its publishers Smith, Elder to reduce the high price of their three-volume novels, for which he claimed there was as a consequence little demand (Huxley 1923: 91). The foundation of the *Cornhill* in 1860 had, according to George Smith, been 'the literary event of the year' (Eddy 1970: 41). He was prepared to offer his editor Thackeray and his contributors lavish terms in order to produce 'the best periodical yet known to English literature' (20). Like other magazines which followed in its wake (*Temple Bar, St James, Belgravia* and *St. Paul's*, all founded in the 1860s) it was named after the part of London in which its offices were located. It adopted a sophisticated tone, both urban and urbane, representing the 'London point of view' in a 'man of the world' manner (Schmidt 1985: 79–80). Its title, Thackeray thought, also had 'a sound of jollity and abundance about it' (Huxley 1923: 95). Its famous yellow covers reinforced the suggestion of good harvests, the four medallions in each corner representing a ploughman, a sower, a reaper and a thresher respectively, offering readers an 'escape from the grime and grind of London' (Eddy 1970: 18). Thackeray's prospectus underlined this wholesome image, instructing contributors, 'we shall suppose the ladies and children always present' (19). He was able to commission fiction from the top-ranking novelists of the day: Trollope, Eliot, Collins, Reade and Meredith. Circulation for the first issue was 120,000, although this had dropped by 1871 to 20,000. For Hardy to appear in such a prestigious magazine, nevertheless, was to have arrived on the London literary scene. It was also, however, to enter a world whose conventions had been firmly established.

No one understood those conventions better than Leslie Stephen, appointed editor early in 1871 in an attempt to boost circulation. 'I have nothing to do,' he told Charles Eliot Norton in January 1872, 'but provide healthy reading for the British public and to be sure that our Magazine may lie on the table of the most refined female without calling a blush to her cheek' (Bicknell 1996: 109). His evangelical upbringing, from which (like Angel Clare) he had emancipated himself theologically but not morally, had prepared him well for this role, leaving him with 'a puritanical obsession about sex' (Gibson 1980: 196). So when Frederick Greenwood, who had acted as sub-editor of the *Cornhill* in the 1860s, alerted him to the qualities to be found in this new anonymous author, qualities which his own reading confirmed, he not only commissioned a new novel from Hardy but took upon himself the task of providing not only 'shrewd advice and warm encouragement' (Millgate 1982: 160) but 'a short sharp course in Grundian conventions' (Morgan 1992: 13).

Some of the evidence necessary for a full understanding of Hardy's relations with Leslie Stephen is lacking. Hardy's side of the story, the pages he contributed to Maitland's *Life and Letters of Leslie Stephen* and the section in his own *Life*, are characteristically reticent. Many of Stephen's letters to Hardy, however, only partially quoted in Maitland and in Purdy (Purdy 1954: 336–9) survive in the Dorset County Museum. The manuscript and proofs of *Far from the Madding Crowd* provide further evidence of his interference. Hardy's 'continuing and often unwitting transgression of social and moral boundaries,' Rosemarie Morgan concludes, 'eventually taxed his editor's patience so sorely that he simply cut and deleted as and when he saw fit, with or without the author's permission'. Stephen's 'slashing editorial pencil' deleted whole passages of Hardy's text, most famously the 'tender delineation in the manuscript of Fanny's last sleep with her stillborn babe in her arms' (*FMC* xix–xx). Further editorial pressure would presumably have been exerted at the many meetings between author and editor at Stephen's house in South Kensington, at which Hardy first called in December 1873, a month before *Far From the Madding Crowd* was due to make its first appearance in the *Cornhill*. The *Life* records how they would over the next few years discuss into the early hours of the morning a range of issues including 'theologies decayed and defunct, the origins of things, the constitution of matter, the unreality of matter and kindred things' (*Life* 109). It is hard to believe that this would not have included the expectations of the reading public and the responsibility of writers and their editors.

Hardy gives a glimpse of the kind of exchange he enjoyed with Stephen in the pages he sent to Maitland, which describe 'an unexpected Grundian cloud' in the shape of three 'respectable ladies and subscribers' who had upbraided Stephen for 'an improper passage' in *Far from the Madding Crowd*. Morgan identifies this as the reference to Bathsheba's father having spiced up his marital sex by getting his wife to remove her wedding ring, giving him at least the illusion of adulterous excitement (Morgan 1992: 105). 'I was struck mute,' Hardy recalls, 'till I said, "Well, if you value the opinion of such people, why didn't you think of them beforehand, and strike out the passage?"' Stephen then emitted 'a half-groan' before acknowledging that his normally acute sensors had for once let him down. When the review of the novel in *The Times* lavished praise on the very paragraph about which the ladies had complained, Hardy could not resist pointing it out to his editor with the comment, 'You cannot say that the *Times* is not respectable'. Stephen was not to be silenced by this, however, and replied, 'I spoke as editor, not as man. You have no more consciousness of these things than a child' (Maitland 1906: 275). He seems genuinely to have 'inferred a simple ignorance of the proprieties in this new and inexperienced novelist' rather than any desire deliberately to subvert them (*FMC* xix).

Stephen's essay on 'Art and Morality' in the *Cornhill* of July 1875, the first month in which *The Hand of Ethelberta* appeared, also gives an insight into the principles on which he operated. The essay is structured almost as a dialogue, with Stephen carefully putting both sides of the debate, that of the artist who resents restrictions on what he can write and that of the critic entrusted with the responsibility of making moral judgements. It is certainly tempting to identify Hardy as the artist in the following passage:

> When a man is accused of writing an immoral book, he has...a number of excuses. One is that the book is perfectly moral; another, that it has nothing to do with morality; a third, that it is not written for children, but for men; a fourth, that if it does not express the morality of Philistines and prudes, it embodies a higher morality.
>
> (Stephen 1875: 91)

Stephen insists, however, that art is wrong if it harms others, emphasising the responsibility artists have to 'their weaker brethren' (92). He again puts the artist's point of view, that he has 'to reflect what he sees around him, that he cannot 'prune and clip human nature' or confine himself to 'writing for schoolgirls' (93). Stephen replies that there are 'passions which ought to be repressed', while to 'the doctrine that novels should be written for men as well as schoolgirls' he counters, they should not be written for 'men...who have ceased to be manly' and become 'beasts'. 'All our great novelists', he insists, 'were moralists' although some, such as Fielding, moralised too explicitly, producing 'little nuggets of moral platitudes' instead of allowing the morality to pervade the whole work. 'A man who encourages the baser sentiments', however, Stephen is convinced, 'is a villain' (94–7). Faced with the suggestion that 'a great writer must necessarily be morbid', he accepts that genius is likely to incur 'some diseases of the mind' but insists on the responsibility of an author to consider the likely effect of a work of art upon its audience. Art has a responsibility to 'purify and sustain the mind', to make its readers 'healthier and happier' (100–1).

As editor of the *Cornhill* Stephen put these principles into rigorous practice. Another contributor, W. E. Norris, recalled,

> More than once he made me re-write whole chapters, and often I was required – a little against the grain I must confess – to strike out passages or incidents which he thought likely to jar upon the susceptibilities of his readers. One's tidyness used to come back scrawled all over with alternatives and emendations in his diminutive script, which was not always over-legible...it was difficult for him to keep his hands off anybody's manuscript.
>
> (Schmidt 1985: 87)

His very first letter to Hardy, introducing himself to 'the author of "Under the Greenwood Tree"' and soliciting a new novel for the *Cornhill*, cannot resist the temptation to observe that

> "Under the Greenwood Tree" is of course not a magazine story. There is too little incident for such purposes; for, though I do not want a murder in every number, it is necessary to catch the attention of readers by some distinct and well arranged plot.
>
> (Purdy 1954: 336)

Hardy appears initially to have been happy to receive advice from someone whose own attempts to 'shock the orthodox' he had read and admired in the *Fortnightly* (Maitland 1906: 272). He expressed willingness 'to give up any points which may be desirable in a story when read as a whole, for the sake of others which shall please those who read it in numbers' (*Letters* I 28). He was clearly keen to impress Stephen with his professionalism, his preparedness to learn the conventions of periodical publication.

Hardy could not, however, have anticipated the extent to which his editor would keep him 'constantly aware of the needs of his middle-class audience' (Morgan 1992: 14). Stephen was particularly sensitive to anything remotely sexual, disapproving of contemporary French novelists because they were 'always hankering and sniffing after sensual motives' (Maitland 1906: 266–7). He would remove at proof stage any references to the 'buttocks' even of sheep and horses he had failed to notice in manuscript (Morgan 1992: 14–16). One of his letters to Hardy begins by acknowledging 'an excessive prudery of wh[ich] I am ashamed' but proceeds to insist that 'Troy's seduction of the young woman will require to be treated in a gingerly fashion'. In similar vein the following month he opined that 'the cause of Fanny's death [her illegitimate child] is unnecessarily emphasized ... I have some doubts whether the baby is necessary at all' (Purdy 1954: 338–9). The *Cornhill* version of the novel thus makes no direct references to the baby as seen by Bathsheba in Fanny's coffin, replacing 'each plural pronoun with the singular' (383). Hardy, who was in no position to resist, did not even replace the excisions in the first edition, as he would later learn to do.

In some respects Stephen's influence may have been beneficial. Millgate claims that Stephen was right to recommend pruning of some of the dialogue involving the rustics: the two Malthouse scenes, the paying scene and the shearing supper all benefit from 'this fining-down process' (Millgate 1971: 81; cp 1982: 160). He also suggests that Stephen 'sometimes used the Grundean threat as a tactful cover for criticism of a more aesthetically significant kind' (82). Gatrell, however, argues the reverse, that 'Stephen used the need for narrative pace as a convenient excuse for censorship' (Gatrell 1988: 17). The cuts to the original shearing supper dialogue, for example, remove the dismissed bailiff Pennyways' account of seeing Fanny Robin 'too well-off to be anything but a ruined woman' (*FMC* 400). Whichever was the dominant motive, it is clear that Stephen resisted all Hardy's attempts to 'stretch to the limit (and sometimes beyond it) what a respectable family magazine of the sort that published and paid for serial fiction felt it could accept on behalf of its readership' (Gatrell 1988: 16).

It is worth dwelling on these battles between Hardy and his first conscientious editor because Stephen, widely recognised as one of the finest Victorian literary critics, was the first reader of the two *Cornhill* novels (after Emma, of course). His reaction can be taken as representative of many of his contemporaries. What he regarded as offensive, as likely to bring a blush to the cheek of a young lady, was no doubt suspect in many Victorian homes. Hardy's attempt to smuggle risky elements past his censorship, on the other hand, helps us appreciate the extent to which he was writing *against* his readership, deliberately attempting to shock and provoke them. Sometimes this battle degenerates into a kind of game, Hardy seeing if he can introduce words such as 'buttocks' into the description of his animals (*FMC 104, 128*) and Stephen carefully removing them. At other times, we can see how Hardy is forced into more subtle manoeuvres to elude the censor but produce the same sense of shock. To portray 'bodily contact between male and female', for example, as Morgan argues, was a flagrant violation of decorum but Hardy engineers an enounter between Bathsheba and Troy in which this is unavoidable, trapping her skirt provocatively in his spurs. He manages later to place his readers in the same position of ignorance of Bathsheba's marriage to Troy as Boldwood so that they overhear with him the shocking invitation she makes to her lover: 'There's not a soul in my house but me to-night . . . so nobody on earth will know of your visit to your lady's bower' (202). The need to circumvent Mrs Grundy, as Stephen Marcus argues, can generate an indirect eroticism of the most ingenious kind (Marcus 1969: 110–11).

Many of the cuts upon which Stephen insisted related to sexual impropriety. Not only the scene at the coffin, but virtually all references to Fanny Robin, had to be toned down. The manuscript, taken by Morgan as the copy-text for her edition of the novel, has Boldwood say of her, 'She has now lost her character – he will never marry her' (*FMC* 100). This was removed for the *Cornhill*, for which Hardy wrote the additional chapter in which Fanny's unmarried status is attributed to her turning up at the wrong church. Morgan accordingly omits this from her edition since 'it was grafted on to the story on proofsheets and does not represent an extant part of the holograph manuscript' (xxxiv). A reference by Liddy to Troy as 'a walking ruin to young girls' was similarly excised for the *Cornhill* (144, 373) while her whisper to her mistress about the coffin that 'there's *two of 'em* in there' (256) had to be made inaudible (Morgan 1992: 63). The lengthy description of Bathsheba gazing at the dead mother and child, as we have seen, stood no chance of survival.

Other cuts to the original manuscript removed any semblance of unladylike behaviour on the part of the heroine herself. The manuscript has Henery, one of the rustics, refer to 'the dare of the woman in general', illustrated by her 'saying a man's Damn to Liddy when the pantry shelf fell down with all the jam-pots upon it' (93). This too had to be removed from the *Cornhill* (Morgan 1992: 118). Hardy managed, however, to smuggle through the description of her face turned defiantly upward on her first visit to the Corn Exchange, suggesting 'that there was depth enough in that lithe piece of humanity for alarming potentialities of exploit, and daring enough carry them out' (*FMC* 80). The Wessex Edition added the two words 'of sex' after 'exploit' just to clarify what it was that he wanted to suggest (NW *FMC* 124). Bathsheba's language had generally to be cleaned up for the *Cornhill*: she was not allowed to call Liddy a 'fool' or a 'hussy', as she does in the manuscript (*FMC* 172, 376), she could not use the word 'wantonness' (221, 380) and she was even made prissily to object, 'don't be improper', to Oak's suggestion that they will put a notice of their babies in the birth columns of the paper (Morgan 1992: 134). In the manuscript she had objected, 'Don't talk so!' (*FMC* 27), which is much more down to earth and even a little flirtatious. Gabriel lists among the qualities that make her worthy of him the fact that she speaks 'like a lady' (29) but Hardy also wanted her to speak like a country woman. As we shall see in the reviews, contemporaries were bothered by Bathsheba's 'unladylike' tendencies, some of which managed to defeat Stephen's 'pruning'. There was a clear conflict between the 'bad girl' who excited Hardy and the 'good girl' his contemporary readers expected (Morgan 1992: 129).

Other characters were also 'improved' for the *Cornhill*: Oak was not allowed to lie about the story of an illegitimate baby belonging to 'another poor girl' (*FMC* 256, 382) although he did still wipe the chalked words 'and child' off the lid of the coffin. Even Troy became less obviously a danger to young girls. Stephen excised not only Liddy's comment to this effect but the narrator's suggestion that 'his sacrifices to Venus... introduced vice, not as a lapse, but as a necessary part of the ceremony' (146, 374). Morgan contends that Hardy's attitude towards Troy became 'increasingly ambivalent', refusing to remain satisfied with the 'restless libertine' of Victorian melodrama (Morgan 1992: 21). The *Cornhill* heightened his class status, Fanny referring to him as 'a nobleman by blood' (*FMC* 367). Liddy calls him 'a doctor's son by name' and 'an earl's son by nature' (373), adding details of the 'romance' attaching to him as the son of a French governess and 'a poor medical man', details further expanded in 1912 when Lord Severn was introduced as Troy's likely father (367–8). These changes, presumably introduced by Hardy himself, heighten the tensions between the classes.

Readers of the *Cornhill* may have welcomed the introduction into the serial of a political element. An article on 'Agricultural Labourers' appeared in its June issue, right in the middle of the novel's serialisation, attacking the 'tendency of the luxurious classes... to invest the labourer with an ideal idyllic grace' and to 'veil the stern reality of the facts'. What they thought of as 'England's true peasantry, loyal, devout, humble to their betters' had in reality disappeared, quite literally abandoning the country for the city or, if they remained, engaged in a political rebellion against 'their existing conditions', a revolt 'conducted with remarkable temper and an absence from violence' (686–7). Their wages may have improved but remained low, in one Dorset village as low as eight shillings a week 'within the last ten years'. The article proceeded to itemise the average weekly expenditure of a farm labourer with a wife and three children, showing that this amounted to much more than this. In addition, many cottages had only one bedroom and no proper sanitation, so 'personal cleanliness' was 'out of the question'. Women too were forced to work, taking their part in 'the coarseness of the fields', which included bad language. The article quoted long passages from representatives of the Agricultural Labourers' Union, including one citing *The Times* on 'the advance of civilization' giving the labourer 'nothing but lucifer matches and the penny post' (two items which would reappear in Hardy's 1895 Preface to the novel). Hardy, it would seem, had read this article and so must many of the first readers of *Far From the Madding Crowd*. They should not therefore have been under any illusions about the 'real' conditions of rural labour or of their idealisation in the novel.

Helen Allingham's illustrations would have added to the 'distortingly idealized' representation of the countryside in the text (Dalziel 1998: 13). Hardy had written to Smith, Elder requesting that his rustics and their equipment be portrayed accurately, that 'the rustics, although *quaint*, be made to appear *intelligent*, and *not boorish*' (*Letters* I 25). He seems to have been pleased with the final result, calling Allingham 'the best illustrator I ever had' (I 181). She herself would go on to become 'the most successful of the... Idyllist school of watercolourists', winning praise for her depiction of 'all that is picturesque' in the country, her brushes happily restoring to cottages that had been modernised their former thatched roofs and lattice windows (Dalziel 1998: 16–17). Her twelve full-page illustrations in the *Cornhill* were reproduced in the first edition of the novel, continuing, in other words, to influence the reception of this novel as a pastoral idyll, a deliberate softening of the reality of rural life.

Far From the Madding Crowd was something of an overnight sensation, at least among the chattering classes who read the *Cornhill*. The *Life* records Thackeray's daughter Anne Ritchie, being 'besieged' with enquiries about the anonymous author and *'its'* gender (*Life* 104). Gosse recalled that Hardy 'became suddenly famous' in mid-January 1874 (Cox 1970: 167) while A. J. Butler, Professor of Italian at University College London, remembered it as the first of Hardy's books to get 'talked about in drawing-rooms' (Cox 1970: 286). Critically, however, the reviews of the first edition were 'markedly *less* enthusiastic' than they had been for *A Pair of Blue Eyes* (Pettit 2000: 4). It was only later in the nineties, according to Lerner, that reviewers looked back with nostalgia to this 'happier' novel, possibly projecting 'their disappointment with later books into a flattering distortion of what they had thought of the earlier one' (Lerner 1968: 42).

Contemporary reviewers had three general complaints about the novel: first that it imitated George Eliot too closely, second that its representation of rustic labourers was unrealistic, and third that its characterisation (of Bathsheba in particular) was confusing and disturbing. The comparison with George Eliot, initiated by R. H. Hutton in the *Spectator's* review of the first *Cornhill* instalment, began as a compliment. 'If "Far from the Madding Crowd" is not written by George Eliot,' Hutton announced, 'then there is a new light among novelists'. The novel, he felt, had both 'the wit and the wisdom' of George Eliot, particularly in its description of natural phenomena (23–4). William Minto, later to become Professor of Logic and Literature at Aberdeen, took up the comparison in the *Examiner* in December 1874, finding a similar 'truth to nature' but also noticing differences in both style and substance. Hardy was less of a master of language but also 'less of a preacher', 'more exclusively dramatic, he is absorbed in delineating character and tracing the workings of passion . . . and does not withdraw from his dramatic work to deliver his soul of pent-up reflections' (24–5). Henry James, writing in the *Nation* on Christmas Eve, stressed the similarities with George Eliot, of which Hardy had produced 'a very fair imitation', catching 'very happily her trick of seeming to humor benignantly her queer people and look down at them from the heights of analytic omniscience' (30). Other critics developed the comparison even less sympathetically: the *Observer* thought it 'a wonderfully clever book' but not in the same league as George Eliot. All it proved was that 'her semi-scientific reflections about nothing' were easily copied (33–4). Frederick Napier Broome in *The Times* also detected an attempt to imitate George Eliot (39) while the *World* (2.12.74) complained of their shared 'stilted pseudo-scientific cant', 'the slang of the laboratory and the jargon of the mechanics institute'. The *Westminster Review*, however, rejected the comparison, finding in Hardy none of Eliot's 'spiritual depths' but much melodrama, which was absent from her work, singling out the sword-exercise scene as 'a piece of extravagance, fit only for the boards of some transpontine theatre' (Cox 1970: 33).

The complaints about the realism of Hardy's depiction of rural characters in the novel also began with Hutton, who claimed in the *Spectator* in December 1874, after the final instalment had appeared, that for any reader acquainted with 'the Dorsetshire labourer, with his average wages, and his average intelligence, a more incredible picture than that of the group of farm labourers as a whole...can hardly be conceived'. Hardy was clearly guilty of investing his 'incredibly amusing' rustics with his own 'subtler thoughts' (Lerner 1968: 26–7). Andrew Lang in the *Academy* (2.1.75) noted that Hardy's peasants had 'not heard of strikes' and seemed to have plenty to eat. He also questioned whether labourers really talked in the manner portrayed in the novel (Cox 1970: 35–7). The *Saturday Review* the following month welcomed Hardy's turning his Boeotians into Athenians, contrasted his rustics with previous depictions of the agricultural labourer as 'an untaught, unreflecting, badly paid, and badly fed animal, ground down by hard and avaricious farmers'. There was surely an element of sarcasm, however, in its praise of 'the flights of abstract reasoning with which Mr. Hardy credits his cider-drinking boors' (Lerner 1968: 38). The *Guardian* in February liked Hardy's labourers but felt that Oak 'rises somewhat too much above the class he lives amongst' (39). Leon Boucher in the *Revue des Deux Mondes* the following year thought that Hardy was rejuvenating the ancient genre of pastoral by injecting it with a '*verité d'observation*' (42).

The third aspect of the novel on which contemporary reviewers focused was the depiction of its heroine. Some liked her. William Minto in the *Examiner* (5.12.74) wrote enthusiastically of her 'shrewdness, strong-minded frankness and courage, and decorous, imperious, wayward womanliness'. Frederick Napier Broome in *The Times* (25.1.75) also found her 'a natural, adorable woman down to her finger-tips...we recognise a certain nobility of nature and largeness of soul underlying her rustic coquetry and arrogance'. *Scribner's Monthly*, however, was less convinced, recognising in Bathsheba 'the completest study of this sort of woman which he has yet given us' but noting that 'the type...seems to have a dangerous fascination for him' (March 1875). Hutton thought both her and Oak 'half-conceived and half-drawn'. He could not 'exactly define' the nature of Bathsheba's 'uninterestingness', suspecting that it might have been a result of her tendency to 'shilly-shally' with Boldwood (Cox 1970: 26). Henry James could not 'either understand or like

Bathsheba' (Lerner 1968: 33). The *Observer*, which could not decide whether Bathsheba was 'intended to be a "lady," or the opposite', could not believe that Oak would accept Troy and Boldwood's 'leavings'. Her behaviour in the first encounter with Troy, altogether lacking in 'modesty and reserve', proved her 'an incorrigible hussy' (35). The *Guardian* called her 'a young woman of manifold attractions but skittish propensities' (39) while the *Westminster Review* thought her selfish, 'wayward and inconstant, ... described with great skill' but 'not to be admired, as he [Hardy] would seem to intimate' (Cox 1970: 34). Andrew Lang could not 'easily pardon Bathsheba ... for losing her heart to Troy's flattery' (38) but the *World* (2.12.24) saw in her final submission 'the old tale of the taming of the shrew'.

All these reviews were presumably written by men, some of whom appear to have been terrified by Bathsheba's overt sexuality. Some contemporary women readers also found her frightening. The novelist Katherine Macquoid, as we saw in Chapter 1, wrote to Hardy in November 1874, admitting that 'her nature is just that of a true woman – because she is centred on self' but questioning whether 'the ordinary type of woman' should be 'idealised into a book heroine'. She would prefer portraits of really good women, not necessarily like Dorothea Brooke and Dinah Morris, who were 'too superhuman', but with 'a soul which is not entirely governed by her body' (DCM 4152). Anne Procter, by contrast, wrote in August to acknowledge 'the pleasure your story gives me', especially the 'shock' of Bathsheba's marriage, which successfully deceived 'such an old novel-reader as myself' (DCM 4826). In September she wrote, 'I am more and more interested in Bathsheba' while also admiring 'the honest way that Troy still cherishes poor Fanny's hair and won't let the woman he loves be despised by the woman that loves him' (DCM 4827). It is somewhat tantalising to have only two immediately contemporary responses from women but even this limited evidence suggests that they, like their masculine counterparts, were divided in their attitude towards Bathsheba.

Two of the three issues that dominated the immediate reception of the novel remained in the foreground of later Victorian references to the novel, although again, critics were divided both about the rustics and about Bathsheba. In his 1881 survey Kegan Paul, who thought *Far From the Madding Crowd* 'not so great a success as his earlier or his later novels', condemned Bathsheba for playing 'fast and loose with her lovers' and being altogether less 'womanly' than his other heroines (Cox 1970: 88). Havelock Ellis, just two years later, called the novel 'perhaps the finest, as it is certainly the most popular, among

Mr. Hardy's novels', lavishing praise both on its treatment of love and on its rustics (114). J. M. Barrie also liked the rustics in this novel, along with Bathsheba (161–4). Edmund Gosse waxed lyrical on the rustics and 'their Shakespearian richness of humour' (169) while William Minto, who returned to the novel in the opening volume of the *Bookman* in 1891, celebrated Hardy as 'the champion of rural character and the noble heart that beats beneath the smock-frock'. In retrospect, he understood how the early chapters could be mistaken for George Eliot's but she 'never had drawn a woman as Mr Hardy draws Bathsheba, in whole-hearted admiration, without the least scratch of disparagement' (172).

The same two issues have dominated more recent consideration of the novel, first the generic question (what kind of pastoral Hardy is writing and how realistic it can be expected to be) and second the representation of Bathsheba as a woman, complete with sexual desire. That Hardy is writing a version of pastoral is evident enough. He celebrates, like the poet Gray, lines from whose elegy provide the title of the novel, the 'moral superiority of a life of rural retirement', appealing to the nostalgia of his sophisticated city readers for a world of lost innocence (Draper 1987: 9). Morgan has demonstrated the way the monthly parts captured for the benefit of city-dwellers the farming activities appropriate to that time of year, lambing being described in the April issue, shearing in May, and the hiving of bees in June, almost in the manner of a modern georgic (Morgan 1992: 16). Hardy delights in explaining for his ignorant urban audience the difference between wheat and straw burning, and how the 'vegetable world' of the countryside 'begins to move and swell and the saps to rise', exerting powerful natural forces 'in comparison with which the powerful tug of cranes and pulleys in a noisy city are but pigmy efforts' (*FMC* 106). 'The citizen's *Then*,' he pronounces, 'is the rustic's *Now*,' since time passes (and things change) so much more slowly in the country (127). He rhapsodises over the 'unadulterated warmth' of newly shorn wool, which will eventually contribute to the 'winter enjoyment of persons unknown and far away, who will . . . never experience . . . the wool as it here exists new and pure' (129). He even draws a series of diagrams of the different hoof-marks made by Bathsheba's increasingly lame horse, illustrating the difference between a gallop, a canter and a trot, diagrams which Stephen insisted on being translated into incomprehensible prose (184–6, 377). The contrast between the rural world he describes and the city world inhabited by the majority of his readers is brought out strongly in each issue.

As many critics have recognised, however, Hardy's rural world is hardly devoid of the 'ignoble strife' from which Gray's 'madding crowd' are supposed to suffer. Michael Squires accordingly adopts the label 'modified pastoral' (Squires 1974: 124) while Ian Gregor and Charles May independently adopt the term 'grotesque' to qualify the generic label. Gregor derives his 'grotesque' from Ruskin, referring to the juxtaposition of incongruous elements involving both the ludicrous and the terrible (Gregor 1974: 60–1) while May draws his term from Wolfgang Hayser's study of *The Grotesque in Literature*, in which a familiar harmonious world is shattered, producing a sense of disorientation and 'estrangement' (May 1974: 150). Squires too notices that Hardy's version of pastoral, while retaining traditional subject-matter (shepherds in love) and even some of the traditional manner (an emphasis on the beauty rather than the harshness of the natural world), excludes 'the falsification and artificiality of traditional pastoral . . . there is no perpetual summer, no frolicking sheep, no piping shepherds who live without care' (Squires 1974: 124). Oak can 'pipe with Arcadian sweetness' (*FMC* 36), tell the time from the stars and pick up the signs of 'Mother nature' but he suffers unarcadian financial difficulties after his sheep are driven to their death and has also to battle against fire, disease and storms. Hardy can therefore be seen to operate within the more realistic tradition of pastoral developed by George Eliot.

Hardy's pastoral, of course, cannot meet strictly realistic standards. Weighed in the balance with the demanding statistics of a social historian's *Annals of the Labouring Poor*, Hardy is found 'unrealistic and evasive', failing to convey the extent of poverty, unemployment and class strife (Snell 1985: 394–5). It is not until the early 1880s, as Millgate recognises, that Hardy's novels began to represent some of the details of 'agricultural distress and discontent' (Millgate 1971: 100). One way of reading the novel, however, as John Goode argues, 'is to see it as a fable of the recuperation of the organic moment of the survival of the values of work and love' in spite of the pressures imposed both by capitalism and romantic love (Goode 1988: 18). The novel emphasises the importance of the physical – what Joseph Poorgrass, celebrating 'victuals and drink' as 'a cheerful thing', calls 'the gospel of the body' (*FMC* 133). That is the significance too of "The Great Barn" celebrated by the narrator in chapter 21, a building contrasted with both the church and the castle in remaining fully functional:

The fact that four centuries had neither proved it to be founded on a mistake, inspired any hatred of its purpose, nor given rise to any reaction that had battered it down, invested this simple grey effort of old minds with a repose if not a grandeur . . . The defence and salvation of the body by daily bread is still a study, a religion, and a desire. (126)

There is an underlying seriousness about the novel's celebration of labour and many minor subversions of orthodox 'spirituality' (Bathsheba's father's pretence of 'committing the seventh', Bathsheba herself using the Bible as a vehicle for discerning her future marriage partner, Joseph swearing over his failure to find Ephesians). The narrator constantly insists on the extent to which 'the soul is the slave of the body, the ethereal spirit dependent for its quality upon the tangible flesh and blood' (310). The stress on buttocks, like the description of the women who 'huddle against the walls like sheep in a storm' after Boldwood's murder of Troy (333), can be seen as part of a materialist celebration of all things physical.

The most interesting aspect of Hardy's emphasis on the body for many readers is his celebration of sexuality. Morgan, for example, dwells on the auto-eroticism of Bathsheba's self-scrutiny in the mirror, in which 'she parted her lips, and smiled' then 'blushed at herself and seeing her reflection blush, blushed the more' (*FMC* 6). She is constantly portrayed outdoors, the natural settings underlying the naturalness of 'her vibrant sexuality' (Morgan 1988: 34–5). She is not content to remain conventionally passive but actively flirts with Oak, placing his head provocatively on her lap after rescuing him in the hut and challenging him to find out more about her. She clearly enjoys being the centre of attention both on her own farm and in the corn exchange, where the focus on her 'red mouth' and 'parted lips', as we have seen, are made to suggest her 'daring' in other 'exploits'.

This is particularly manifest in her relations with Troy. Morgan retells 'indecorously' the scene of their initial encounter, in which 'she feels the heat of his male body' through his clothing, becomes entangled in his spur, her rescue involving much 'touching and handling of his person' and bending over 'for the performance', leaving her so excited that she runs back to the house, arriving flushed and 'panting' before retiring to her bedchamber 'to relish sweet, retrospective frissons of delight' (33). Troy's sword exercise in the suggestive 'hollow amid the ferns', of which Gerard Manley Hopkins wrote excitedly in a letter to Robert Bridges (Abbott 1935: 239), leaves her similarly aroused, 'stinging as if aflame to the very hollows of her feet' (*FMC* 163). Even Oak excites her, particularly in the suggestive scene in which she watches him fling a ewe over 'upon its buttocks' and strip it ('He...opened up the neck and collar...'). Bathsheba notices how the sheep 'blushes at the insult', 'watching the pink flush which arose and overspread the neck and shoulders...a flush which...would have been creditable...to any woman in the world'. Finally the 'clean sleek creature' is portrayed rising from its fleece 'like Aphrodite rising from the foam' before being branded with the initials B.E., confirming that the animal stands in for its watching mistress throughout (128–9). Hardy succeeds here not only in circumventing Mrs Grundy but in generating an eroticism whose power matches the strength of the repression it evades.

Recent women readers emancipated from any Victorian tendency to blushing embarrassment have noted that it is not just Troy who is surrounded by phallic imagery. Oak too possesses a formidable array of tools, from the torchar with which he saves Bathsheba's bloated sheep, a 'holler pipe with a sharp pricker inside', to his ricking-rod, 'a long iron lance, polished by handling' (Beegel 1984: 118–22). These may be post-Freudian readings but it is difficult to imagine that Hardy would not have recognised the sexual significance of these passages. Victorian readers may not always have recognised what we now label Freudian symbolism (although the undefined sense of uneasiness about Bathsheba felt by a critic such as Hutton suggests at least some awareness of this). But they could not have missed the way in which Oak and Bathsheba's heads are made to whirl as they grind shears together. And they would presumably have been more likely than most modern readers to pick up the allusion to the erotic Song of Solomon at the end of the much-quoted final paragraph of the penultimate chapter, in which, after commending the *camaraderie* which had grown up between Oak and Bathsheba, the narrator celebrates 'that love which many waters cannot quench, nor the floods drown' (348). Far from suggesting the abandonment of sexual love, this paragraph appears to confirm that their marriage will be based not only on physical labour but on physical intimacy. The original readers of this novel may have been disturbed by its celebration of the body, especially by its heroine's full-blooded enjoyment of all things physical. But if this made her less of a 'lady' the clear implication is that they should revise their notions of femininity.

Telling stories: *The Hand of Ethelberta*

Leslie Stephen was so pleased with the success of *Far from the Madding Crowd* that he was soon pressing Hardy for 'a new story in the Cornhill about April next [1875]' (DCM 5511). Hardy managed to put off beginning *The Hand of Ethelberta* until July but still felt that he had been

rushed into 'the unfortunate course of hurrying forward a further production before he was aware of what there had been of value in his
previous one'. Angered by the charge of having imitated George Eliot
and determined to avoid 'writing for ever about sheepfarming, as the
reading public was apparently expecting him to do', he sent Stephen the
opening chapters 'of a tale called *The Hand of Ethelberta – A Comedy in
Chapters*, which had nothing in common with anything he had written
before' (*Life* 105). Stephen's initial response to the new story, not mentioned in the *Life* and only partially recorded in the pages Hardy contributed to Maitland (in which Hardy conflates two separate letters written
in May) appeared quite positive: he had 'no criticisms to make of any
importance' and thought 'the "comedy" tone very well preserved'
(DCM 5513). By now, however, Hardy would have learnt to recognise
the significant qualifications: even the inverted commas around the
word 'comedy', for example, would have alerted him to some editorial
anxieties about the genre of the new story, anxieties which surfaced all
too explicitly in the letter which followed:

> I am sorry to have to bother you about a trifle! I fully approved of
> your suggestion for adding to 'Ethelberta's Hand' the descriptive title
> 'A Comedy in Chapters'. I find however from other people that it
> gives rather an unfortunate idea. They understand by Comedy some-
> thing of the farce description, and expect you to be funny after the
> fashion of Mr–, or of some professional joker. This, of course, is
> stupid; but then advertisements are made for stupid people. The
> question is, unluckily, not what they ought to feel but what they do
> feel.
>
> (*Life* 106–7)

The *Life* omits the next sentence, which is underlined in the manuscript:

> and if specimens whom I take to be superior representatives of the
> average reading public imagine that you mean to present yourself as a
> clown with a bell we also may [?] see that it is undesirable that they
> should not be impressed with so silly a notion.
>
> (DCM 5514)

Stephen accordingly advised Hardy to drop the subtitle, adding that he
could restore it when 'the book is reprinted ... because then the illusion
would be immediately dispelled' (*Life* 107). Readers, in other words,
would quickly see that it was not very funny.

As with all their correspondence, it is necessary to read Hardy's reply between the lines to recognise his anger. He is happy, he says, to omit the subtitle 'after your discovery of the effect it would be likely to have', but the term 'comedy' was supposed to imply that

> the story would concern the follies of life rather than the passions, and be told in something of a comedy form, all the people having weaknesses at which the superior lookers-on smile, instead of being ideal characters. I should certainly deplore being thought to have set up in the large joke line.
>
> (*Letters* I 37)

He had intended to include as an epigraph to the serial a long (and slightly modified) quotation from Charles Lamb's essay 'On the Artifical Comedy of the Last Century' in which Lamb confesses to being 'glad for a season to take an airing beyond the diocese of the strict conscience ... now and then, for a dream-while or so, to imagine a world with no meddling restrictions' (*HE* 425). This too was omitted from the *Cornhill* along with the subtitle (which was subsequently restored to the first and all subsequent editions).

Stephen appears to have taken the hint about 'meddling restrictions'. He seems to have interfered much less in *The Hand of Ethelberta* than its predecessor (although there is no manuscript to confirm this). Hardy mentions just three examples of changes insisted upon at proof stage. In the first (May 1875) Stephen wonders 'whether a lady ought to call herself or her writings "amorous." Would not some such word as "sentimental" be strong enough?' (Maitland 1906: 276). Hardy accordingly made Ethelberta call her work 'tender and gay', only to restore 'amatory' in the Wessex Edition (*HE* 437). The second example is more substantial, referring to a scene in which it is clear in the proofs that the petals spread suggestively over Neigh's waistcoat and Ethelberta's 'bosom' are the result of a passionate embrace between them. 'I may be over particular,' begins Stephen, in characteristically ominous fashion, 'but I don't quite like the suggestion of the very close embrace in the London churchyard' (Maitland 1906: 276). Hardy accordingly revised the scene so that Ethelberta merely gives her admirer some petals from her flower which he secretes in a pocket-book (*HE* 201–4). In case readers should wonder why Neigh is made to apologise so profusely for this (205), they are told in the following chapter that, in taking Ethelberta's petals, he 'pressed her fingers more warmly than she thought she had given him warrant for' (209). Stephen wrote in October to express gratitude for these changes and to remind him, 'Remember the country parson's daughters' (Maitland 1906: 276). A year later he was to thank Hardy again for 'the kindness with which you accept my criticisms' (290). It is difficult, however, to believe that Hardy's feelings were altogether 'kind' towards his editor. The novel itself, as we shall see, attacks Stephen's rather limited notions of realism, albeit indirectly, through the heroine's admiration in Defoe of precisely the 'insincerity' and 'deceit' of which Stephen accused him. Lying and art, the novel will suggest, are necessary defences against disempowerment.

Hardy's battles with his editor would be repeated with his public. The *Life* begins its account of the reception of *The Hand of Ethelberta* positively enough, claiming that it 'was received in a friendly spirit and even with admiration in some quarters – more, indeed, than Hardy had expected'. He quotes one critic praising it in public as 'the finest ideal comedy since the days of Shakespeare' while begging privately to meet 'the lady in the flesh'. The mood then darkens:

> It did not however win the cordiality that had greeted its two forerunners, the chief objection being that it was 'impossible'. It was, in fact, thirty years too soon for a Comedy of Society of that kind – just as *The Poor Man and the Lady* had been too soon for a socialist story...The most impossible situation in it was said to be that of the heroine sitting at table at a dinner party of 'the best people', at which her father was present by the sideboard as butler. Yet a similar situation has been applauded in a play in recent years by Mr Bernard Shaw, without any sense of improbability.
>
> (*Life* 111–12)

Hardy had made the same point in a postscript to the Preface added in 1912. The Preface itself of 1895 explained to readers that 'this somewhat frivolous narrative' had been 'given the sub-title of a comedy' to reduce their expectations of 'probability' while indicating that 'there was expected of the reader a certain lightness of mood'. Hardy also took the opportunity afforded by this Preface to rail against critical complaints of 'unexpectedness...that unforgivable sin in the critic's sight – the immediate precursor of "Ethelberta" having been a purely rural tale'. Finally, 'readers even of the finer crusted kind' were asked 'to pardon a writer' for presenting the children of servants 'as beings who come within the scope of a genial regard' (*HE* 3). The bitterness apparent in the Preface also surfaces in the *Life* as Hardy blames his audience for approaching this novel full of prejudice about its author:

Had this very clever satire been discovered to come from the hands of a man about town, its author would have been proclaimed as worthy of a place beside Congreve and Sheridan; indeed, such had been hinted before its authorship was well known. But rumours that he had passed all his life in a hermitage smote like an east wind upon all appreciation of the tale. That the stories of his seclusion were untrue, that Hardy had been living in London for many years in the best of all situations for observing manners, was of course unknown.

(*Life* 112)

His anger at the response to this novel clearly rankled over forty years after its publication.

Hardy may in fact have been remembering and resenting later attitudes than those evinced by its first readers. As Michael Millgate points out, the initial reviewers 'wrote about the book enthusiastically and even perceptively' (Millgate 1971: 116). The highest praise came in the *Examiner* (13.5.76), whose editor William Minto wrote privately to Hardy in November 1875 to express his admiration of Ethelberta, whom he found 'even more daring and finer than Bathsheba' (DCM 2338). He was presumably the critic referred to in the *Life* as enamoured not only of the 'ideal comedy' in the novel but of its heroine. His review began with a summary of what he deemed to have been the general view of the novel:

If you asked anybody, during the progress of Mr. Hardy's novel through the *Cornhill*, how they liked the story, you generally received an uncertain and qualified answer. All admitted that it was very clever and original, not like any other novel they had ever read, but most people added that they thought the character of the lady as well as her adventures too improbable.

He conceded the 'accusation of improbability' himself. As an 'ideal comedy' of the kind written by Shakespeare, however, its claim to acceptance lay in being 'full of life and spirit' as well as 'very subtle and intricate in its psychology'. Hardy's art did not 'lie on the surface' but in the way he traced 'motives with a much more perfect concealment of the process' than could be found in George Eliot. His reliance upon striking visual effects might impose 'too constant a strain on the pictorial faculty of the reader' and for this reason, the review concluded, the author 'must reconcile himself' to this novel not achieving 'the popular interest of some of Mr. Hardy's previous novels...but it is more masterly as a work of art'. Minto anticipated later reception theory in recognising the need to probe beneath the surface of Ethelberta's apparent coldness in order fully to comprehend her.

The *Athenaeum* (15.4.76) also noted Hardy's reliance upon the reader to supply what was only implicit in the text. Ethelberta, for example, was obviously supposed to be 'exceedingly beautiful' but this

> Mr. Hardy, with a reticence which cannot be sufficiently com-
> mended, leaves the reader to gather from the remarks of other per-
> sonages. It is easy enough to describe a beautiful woman, but it is far
> better to leave each reader to fill in the general outline for himself.

She thus became much more interesting than 'the familiar lady of *Punch*' suggested by du Maurier's illustrations. Her fate too threatened to descend deeper, but 'Mr. Hardy, after leaving his readers on the verge of tragedy, kindly lifts the curtain, and shows that it is not to be much worse than comedy after all'. The *Morning Post* (5.8.76) also praised Hardy's 'novel and unconventional' characterisation.

There were less positive reviews. R. H. Hutton in the *Spectator* (22.4.76) found Ethelberta 'a riddle ... from beginning to end', refusing to believe 'that she would sell herself to a disreputable, sly old nobleman like Lord Mountclere, with no more of repulsion and inward conflict than she actually exhibits'. George Saintsbury in the *Academy* (13.5.76) preferred the mild and conventional Picotee to her calculating and inscrutable sister. He also complained of the novel's 'laboured eccentricity'. The *Graphic* (29.4.76), which lamented the novel's 'extravagantly improb-able' situations and 'unreal beings', criticised Hardy for abandoning 'that rustic life which few can portray as he can'. A brief review in the *Guardian* (19.7.76) complained of a certain 'stage trickiness' and 'strain-ings after unnatural effects' while a similarly short notice in the *World* (19.4.76) accused him of attempting to throw 'a glamour of verisimili-tude over the blankly impossible'. *Harper's Magazine* found the novel undemanding and its heroine neither 'intriguing enough to disgust nor unselfish enough to attract' (Cox 1970: xx).

The first edition of *The Hand of Ethelberta* sold reasonably well, only 61 copies out of the print run of 1000 needing to be remaindered, but the one-volume edition of 1877 was less successful, more than half of its thousand copies being remaindered to Sampson Low, Marston & Com-pany for their cheap single-volume reprints of Hardy's work in 1882 (*Letters* VII 94–5; Purdy 1954: 23). A review of the 1877 edition in *London* (29.9.77) called *The Hand of Ethelberta* 'with all its cleverness, about as bad a novel as one would care to see'. Mrs Sutherland Orr, in her survey of Hardy's work in the *New Quarterly Review* of October 1879 also saw it as a 'fantastic interlude to his more serious work' (Cox 1970: 67). Kegan Paul, however, who had commissioned that survey, thought it 'one of the most striking works of English fiction' (88). Havelock Ellis argued that 'readers who came to it fresh from the perusal' of *Far from the Madding Crowd* had been 'disappointed' with its 'too facile . . . brilliance'. He nevertheless expected Hardy's career to continue 'the vein of comedy which began' in this novel and was 'the most characteristic outcome of his genius' (132). Less positive responses came from Coventry Patmore, who thought *Ethelberta* 'signally below his true mark' (148), J. M. Barrie, for whom it brought 'a disappointment of a double kind. It is not a comedy, and its London life is preposterous' (159), and Edmund Gosse, who counted this among Hardy's 'partial failures' (168). This became the critical consensus. Among the litany of disparaging remarks cited by Clarice Short in her pioneering 'Defense of *Ethelberta*' (Short 1958: 48–9) are a number which lament his ill-conceived attempt to 'write outside his range' (Cecil 1943: 121). Later critics would be even more outspoken. Irving Howe dismissed it as 'execrable trash' (Howe 1968: 38, 69), Gittings referred to it as a 'manufactured and cryptic book', of interest mainly for its 'typically devious' mode of autobiography (Gittings 1978: 293, 290) and Martin Seymour-Smith called it an experiment which 'fails in the reading' (Seymour-Smith 1994: 211–12).

The novel is very self-conscious, continuing the debate between Hardy and Stephen over art, morality and truth. Hardy's editor even enters the text when the narrator, after commending Ethelberta's ability to make fiction 'seem like truth', refers to a 'modern critic' who 'has well observed of Defoe that he had the most amazing talent for telling lies' (*HE* 119). Stephen's article on 'De Foe's Novels' of 1868, had attacked Defoe for insincerity and dishonesty, particularly in pamphlets such as *The Shortest Way with the Dissenters*, written from a supposedly Tory perspective to satirise their bigotry. Stephen objected in principle not only to such authorial subterfuge, 'exploiting conventions of verisimilitude to pass off flagrant untruths', but to his characters, who were 'neither properly moral nor immoral, but acted according to need or convenience' (xxx). The essay on 'Art and Morality' discussed above, which appeared in the same issue of the *Cornhill* as the opening chapters of *Ethelberta*, enlarged upon what he saw as the moral responsibility of novelists to be both truthful and realistic. These issues of truth, sincerity and verisimilitude are made central to this novel, which subtly undermines most of Stephen's cherished principles.

The character of Neigh has been seen in some respects as a caricature of Stephen, swearing under his breath and saying 'nay' to everything, knackering his poor hacks (Fisher 1992: 67). More seriously, Christopher Julian is represented as a naive reader in the Stephen mould when he interrupts Ethelberta practising her art to a family audience in the woods and mistakes her fictional adventure as real, forcing her to explain to him the difference between historical truth and fictional verisimilitude. She also expounds the conventions of first person narrative employed by her model Defoe and by 'the professional storytellers of Eastern countries'. Defoe's colloquial style, she insists, although 'somewhat out of place on paper in these days', is entirely appropriate for a live performance of the kind she intends, since they 'have a wonderful power in making narrative seem real' (*HE* 105–7). The seeming (Stephen, please note) is all: not to appreciate the difference between a literary device and a moral principle is to confuse art and life. Questions of realism and truth are again prominent in the chapter describing Ethelberta's first public performance. Her plan is 'to tell her pretended history and adventures while sitting in a chair – as if she were at her own fireside, surrounded by a circle of friends', this 'touch of domesticity' giving 'a great appearance of truth and naturalness'. Her tale, the narrator observes, may have had its defects but possessed 'the one pre-eminent merit of seeming like truth' (118–19). Hardy even anticipates reviews of his own novel by including several mock reviews of Ethelberta's performance, including a complaint about the insincerity and improbability of its artifice (123).

The performance of Ethelberta's to which most coverage is given in the novel, however, is when she plays the 'last card' mentioned to Christopher, 'the tale of my own life' (106). This occurs at Lychworth Court, when she recounts, 'as if they were her own, the strange dreams and ambitious longings' which Lord Mountclere soon recognises actually to be hers. It is a strange form of double-bluff and, as with the novel in which this story occurs, the audience is 'perplexed' at what is 'not at all the kind of story that they had expected' (299–300). Peter Widdowson has analysed this passage in some detail, enumerating the many respects in which Ethelberta's story reflects Hardy's own, telling under the guise of fiction the 'truth' about her contradictory class position (Widdowson 1989: 156–7). He argues that the device of defamiliarisation or 'making strange' both prevents readers from identifying with her and dramatises the alienation (in a Marxist sense) from which she suffers as a result of the constant repression of her true feelings (162, 190).

Equally significant in any consideration of this novel is its self-con-
sciousness about the kinds of story available to women. For *The Hand of
Ethelberta*, as Penny Boumelha has observed, exposes the 'double bind' of
traditional romantic fiction, in which 'the achieving of marriage...is to
be the primary concern of women's lives, and yet it is to be brought about
apparently without intention, without consciousness' (Boumelha 1993:
246). Austen, for example, makes Miss Bingley and Mrs Bennet appear
ridiculous because they make their matrimonial intentions so obvious.
Elizabeth Bennet, in contrast, only confesses, as a joke, that her changed
feelings towards Darcy stem from the time she first saw his estate. Ethelberta totally rejects this convention, making research trips to the estates
of her prospective husbands. There appears even to be an element of
Austen pastiche in her confessing about her richest suitor, 'His staircase
alone is worth my hand!' (296).

Ethelberta, as Tim Dolin has remarked, belongs to a long line of
'performers of femininity' in English fiction, beginning with Defoe's
adventuresses, Roxana and Moll Flanders, so morally objectionable to
Stephen (xxii). Her story, however, has been seen to exceed all 'the
central plot paradigms of the nineteenth-century heroine'. She is, by
the end of the first paragraph, an 'ex-virgin, ex-governess, ex-wife', well
'beyond the orthodox array of endings for the narrated woman of
Victorian fiction' (Boumelha 1993: 251). As with Elfride, the metaphor
of reading is frequently employed of her, as if she were herself a book.
Christopher Julian, who dwells on her as 'a romance...fitted out with
circumstance, crisis, and catastrophe, in the regular way' (*HE* 47–8), is
later portrayed 'regarding her as a stall-reader regards the brilliant book
he cannot afford to buy' (312).

The Hand of Ethelberta, like *A Pair of Blue Eyes*, portrays several acts of
reading. The second chapter begins with Christopher Julian trying to
make sense of Ethelberta's volume of poetry, 'a series of playful defences
of the supposed strategy of womankind'. He is particularly intrigued by
the final poem 'Cancelled Words', in which he recognises himself as the
addressee, and asks his sister for her opinion, only to lecture her on the
difference between the implied author, the persona of the poems, and
the actual author when she speculates on the impulsiveness it evinces
(25–7). This volume of poetry is the subject of much critical discussion
in the first part of the novel, for example by the Doncastles and their
guests at a dinner party in chapter seven, during which Ladywell
defends them on the somewhat dubious ground that they reflect 'a
society where no woman says what she means or does what she says'
(60). They are also discussed by the Belmaines and their guests in

chapter ten, during which Mrs Napper is made (in the 1896 edition at least) to confess that 'they are not quite virginibus puerisque' (436). These scenes allow Hardy to satirise the assumptions of his own readers and critics, some of whose complaints are echoed all too clearly in the drawing-room chatter of his characters.

As a woman writing within literary traditions largely dominated by men, Ethelberta has to fall back upon male role models whether of fiction (Defoe) or epic (Milton). Given access to the libraries of grand houses by the back door, through her father serving 'as a footman' or in some other servile capacity (299), she makes use of their resources to create a space for herself, a room of her own, in which she can find at least some form of expression. As Jane Thomas explains, this dramatises the way in which women, with no language of their own and 'no place from which to speak,' are forced to work with male discourse (Thomas 1999: 86–7). Ethelberta attempts to train Picotee in the strategies women have devised to overcome such disempowerment, the first principle being never to tell men the truth. When her naive sister objects, 'I thought honesty was the best policy', Ethelberta warns her not to believe in such sayings, which are 'all made by men, for their own advantages' (*HE* 145). She even turns for support to the ancient Christian 'doctrine of reserve' to prove (*contra* Stephen) that 'lying is no sin' (289). Hardy clearly expects his readers to enjoy the spectacle of his heroine being forced deeper and deeper into subterfuge and having to discover more and more outrageous contrivances in order to extricate herself and her family from these entanglements.

Ethelberta, of course, tells stories in more than one sense. She is shown right at the outset of the novel to be economical with the truth, failing to tell the whole story both to Christopher (about her status as a widow) and to her mother-in-law (about her encounter with him). Such subterfuge was her undoing with some readers. Anne Procter, for example, asked Hardy 'why Christopher, who is so honest and straightforward, is not more surprised and more angry when he found his love had lied in telling him she was the daughter of a bishop' (DCM 4828). Christopher actually reads this in a newspaper, but Ethelberta, it is true, makes no attempt to contradict it. She begins to write a letter confessing the truth about her father but the first draft of this goes into the fire, to be supplanted by a less frank communication. Throughout the novel we see her honesty 'making war upon her manoeuvres' (298) in a manner which is clearly meant to amuse.

The problem was that many of Hardy's readers, like Stephen, seem not to have found the novel funny. The whole tradition of English comedy from the Restoration to the eighteenth century on which it draws was regarded as suspect. Denounced by Macaulay in the 1840s, it had been only partially defended by Thackeray in the 1850s and by Meredith in the 1870s. Leslie Stephen would himself attack Congreve and Wycherley in an article on 'The Moral Element in Literature 'in the *Cornhill* in 1881. To present a promiscuous maid named Menlove 'in a night forage after lovers' (*HE* 20) in the opening chapter is to give a clear generic signal while to have suitors called Neigh and Ladywell is to continue in this vein. Not only in its 'allegorical nomenclature', however, but in other elements noted by Taylor, its 'episodic structure' and 'farcical convolutions of plot', the novel is 'very much a latter-day Restoration comedy' (Taylor 1982: 59). The chapter titles also reinforce the suggestion of the subtitle that this is a theatrical performance transferred to prose. The scene is thus set for each episode as in the opening chapter: 'A Street in Anglebury – A Heath near – Inside the "Old Fox Inn"'. Theatrical references abound in the narrative: Christopher, for example, is described as feeling 'like a man in a legitimate drama' after kissing Picotee's hand in mistake for her sister's (159–60). Legitimate drama was the term employed for the kinds of 'proper' play performed by patent theatres such as Covent Garden. Many of the scenes in *Ethelberta* could come straight out of such theatre, most obviously that in Rouen where all three of her suitors converge on her hotel.

One of the positive aspects of Restoration drama to which Meredith pointed in his 1877 *Essay on Comedy* was its role in raising the status of women (Boumelha 1993: 248–9). He held up Congreve's Millamant in *The Way of the World* as an example of 'an admirable, almost a lovable, heroine' who resents the slurs of 'horrid' men (Meredith 1978: 102). It may therefore be more than coincidence that Hardy makes Ethelberta describe Neigh as 'one of those horrid men who love with their eyes, the remainder part of him objecting all the time to the feeling' (*HE* 232). One criticism that Hardy had of Meredith, however, was 'he would not, or could not – at any rate did not – when aiming to represent the "Comic Spirit", let himself discover the tragedy that always underlies Comedy if you only scratch it deep enough' (*Letters* VII 38). Whether or not he encountered the essay before its publication or even discussed the subject with Meredith, this novel shares similar views both on comedy and on class.

The English class-system was also a favourite subject for du Maurier, illustrator for *Punch* and for the serial of *The Hand of Ethelberta*. Every page of the novel, as Widdowson has shown, bears witness not only to its heroine's but to its author's 'extreme sensitiveness to the nuances of class position' (Widdowson 1989: 183–4). The personal animus driving this hostility to the English class system may still have been unclear to most of Hardy's contemporary readers, encrypted as it was in the Hand of the title. Other details in the novel were equally personal: Ethelberta's maiden name is derived from Chickerell, a village near Weymouth where Hardy walked with Tryphena Sparks; her sister Martha had married a butler while their brother James, like Ethelberta's brother Sol, was a radical carpenter; even the emigration to Queensland at the end of the novel of two of Ethelberta's maidservants echoes that of Martha and her butler-husband. 'Hardy was so involved with secret family history', Gittings claims, that he included all these details gratuitously (Gittings 1978: 292). Like Ethelberta herself, entertaining Mountclere's guests to the story of her own life disguised as fiction, Hardy expressed his resentment of his readers in back-door fashion, providing them with the 'truth' of his own class origins in a form they could not possibly decode.

The class position of every single character in the novel is registered with similar attention to detail, whether of clothing, furniture, voice or manner. Ethelberta herself, having experienced the full range of the class system, is minutely sensitive to the slightest hint of snobbery. When Mrs Belmaine criticises other members of the aristocracy for 'petting' and trying to educate her servants, she suggests that someone should write a pamphlet along Defoe's lines on 'The Shortest Way with the Servants' (*HE* 80–1). She continues to feel 'an outsider' in the company of the Belmaines, unable to discern whether their professed enthusiasm at the proposed visit to Cripplegate Church is mere politeness, 'so perfectly were they practised in sustaining that complete divorce between thinking and saying which is the hallmark of high civilisation' (198). The novel is punctuated throughout with similar outbursts of sarcasm from Ethelberta and from her creator, both of whom find it hard to suffer rich fools gladly. When the visit to Milton's tomb takes place, for example, Hardy cannot resist the remark that it is right for her to read the poet's work aloud, being 'the only one present who could properly manage blank verse' (200).

Hardy's anger at the ill-warranted sense of superiority exhibited by the upper classes breaks through in a number of narrative comments whose savageness of tone reveals all too clearly the tragedy underlying this comedy. On one of these occasions, the narrator intrudes with aggressive irony on Ethelberta's sensitivity to her humble origins:

> It might be a pleasant surprise to many a modern gentleman of birth to find himself allied with a lady none of whose ancestors had ever

pandered to a court, lost an army, taken a bribe, oppressed a community, or broken a bank; but the added disclosure that, in avoiding these normal stains, her kindred had worked and continued to work with their hands for bread, might lead such an one to consider that the novelty was dearly purchased by a mover in circles from which the greatest ostraciser of all is servitude. (210)

At other times Ethelberta's embarrassment over her father being 'still in harness' is itself treated ironically; she dreams of some vocation with 'a more dignified sound' such as library caretaker, stationer or registrar of births and deaths in spite of 'the unmanageable fact that her father was serenely happy and comfortable as a butler', a profession in which 'the remuneration was actually greater than in professions ten times as stately in name' (211). Like her creator, in other words, she is not herself without the social snobbery which exacerbates her embarrassment.

Ethelberta's complex feelings on this score are most powerfully represented in the scene in which she joins Lord Mountclere and other members of the Imperial Archaeological Association on a visit to Coomb Castle. Travelling in the interests of economy on an ass, which she abandons on the lower slopes of the castle grounds, she becomes an object of great interest to the other archaeologists, who gaze at her as one of the three sorts of women allowed to 'move abroad unchaperoned... the famous, the ministering, and the improper', clearly uncertain to which of these groups she belongs. It soon becomes apparent, however, that her qualities are 'the subversive Mephistolian endowment, brains' rather than 'the select and sequent gifts of heaven, blood and acres' (241). She finally suffers the humiliation of having to deny all connection with the donkey as Peter denied his working-class Lord, himself quite content with this form of transport.

The class frictions characteristic of English society play a prominent role in the final part of the novel as Mountclere's brother forms an uneasy alliance with Ethelberta's family to prevent the proposed wedding. He is studiously ignored by Sol Chickerel and his fellow-carpenters when he calls at their yard:

> the texture of that salmon-coloured skin could be seen to be aristocratic without a microscope, and the exceptional artisan has an off-hand way when contrasts are made painfully strong by an idler of this kind coming, gloved and brushed, into the very den where he is sweating and muddling in his shirtsleeves. (328)

It is Sol who expresses the radical point of view in the novel. Thrusting his misshapen hand before his sister, he accuses her of being a 'deserter' of her own class, 'creeping up among the useless lumber of our nation', a backslider from the girl who refused to drop curtseys to the local aristocracy (376–7). His resentment at his sister's alliance with the idle rich does not, however, prevent him accepting her loan to set up as a builder in London, although he insists on paying interest on it.

The novel ends with comic irony rather than social anger and indignation. Hardy is content to 'punish' Ethelberta by making her entirely successful in all of her goals except perhaps the one that matters more than all others, personal happiness. She is also, we are told, 'occasionally too severe with the servants' (403). D. H. Lawrence wrote acerbically about this ending that it was 'the end of the happy endings', involving 'the hard, resistant, ironical announcement of personal failure' and 'the zenith of a certain feeling in the Wessex novels that the best thing to do is to kick out the craving for "Love" and substitute commonsense' (Lawrence 1978: 169). It is, however, more open than this, leaving readers free to decide whether or not this is 'the best thing' for Ethelberta.

Readers of this novel are made to work very hard, never allowed to settle into a comfortable passivity. They are also constantly reminded of the many injustices in their society. It should not be a matter of surprise, therefore, that so few of them have recorded enjoying it.

4

'Middling Hardy': Reconsidering His Readers

The Return of the Native: mapping the human condition

'Middling Hardy' is a term applied to that 'stretch of six rather lost years in Hardy's creative life from 1879 to 1884 ... a period which falls into the middle of Hardy's fictional career', when he might have been expected to produce his best work, but instead wrote many of the novels which have come to be regarded as mediocre (Gatrell 1986a: 70–1). I have included *The Return of the Native* in this category partly because it was so spectacularly unsuccessful at the time, both critically and commercially, and partly because it was the critical onslaught on this novel that forced Hardy into a reconsideration of his work, turning away from tragic and artistic intensity to a style intended to be more 'reader friendly'. Most accounts of his career present the three novels which followed *The Return of the Native* as a 'relapse' (to use the term employed by Beach for the middle section of his book) or as a 'recession' (the title Millgate gives to the middle part of his account of Hardy's career). My own focus will be on the changed attitude these novels display towards his readers. For the two novels which followed his 'failure' at tragedy Hardy attempted to provide his readers with the gentle amusement they appeared to crave. In the third, however, he took his revenge, playing with them in a manner that can only be called mischievous.

The Return of the Native is probably Hardy's most ambitious book, the most difficult and demanding for readers. Hardy put an extraordinary amount of energy into its planning, its writing, its revision and its marketing. He had taken a 'sabbatical' year from writing after *The Hand of Ethelberta* precisely in order to 'improve' himself, a project on which he consulted Leslie Stephen, who advised him not to spend time on literary criticism, which might endanger that 'fresh and original vein' of writing which was his strength, and cause him to become 'self-conscious and cramped'. He would do better to read 'the great writers' such as Shakespeare, Goethe and Scott. If he must consult critics, Sainte-Beuve and Matthew Arnold 'were the only modern critics...worth reading' (Maitland 1906: 290–1). Hardy duly set himself to read and make notes from a range of writers (*LN* I xxi), determined to make his next novel 'an unmistakable work of art, not just another run-of-the-mill serial' (Millgate 1982: 198).

Hardy however, had some doubts about his new style. He sent the first fifteen chapters not only to Leslie Stephen but to George Smith, asking him to 'tell me if you think it a kind of story likely to create a demand in the market' (*Letters* I 47). Smith was happy enough to publish the three-volume edition but Stephen feared that the triangular relationship outlined at the start 'might develop into something "dangerous" for a family magazine' and demanded to see the whole manuscript before making a decision (Purdy 1954: 27). John Blackwood, to whom Hardy next turned, while finding the tale 'excessively clever', doubted 'whether you are right to occupy so large a portion at the beginning of your story without a thread of light to throw an interest round the rugged figures you so vividly paint'. There was 'hardly anything like what is called Novel interest' in these opening chapters (Gatrell 1986b: xi). Hardy next tried George Bentley of *Temple Bar* before turning to Chatto & Windus, new owners of *Belgravia*, with whom he negotiated a much worse deal (£20 per month) than he had managed to obtain for *The Hand of Ethelberta*.

Belgravia, subtitled 'A Magazine of Fashion and Amusement', was a much less prestigious magazine than the *Cornhill*. Founded in 1866 by the publisher John Maxwell as a vehicle for the sensation fiction of his partner Mary Elizabeth Braddon, the magazine had 'developed a rather low-brow reputation, closely associated with hers' (Nash 2001: 56). Both had been attacked for blasphemy and obscenity while Mrs Oliphant had been unimpressed by the kind of heroine they offered:

Women driven wild with love for the man who leads them on to desperation...women who marry their grooms in fits of sensual passion; women who pray their lovers to carry them off from their husbands and homes they hate...the dreaming maiden [who] waits now for strong arms that seize her, and warm breath that thrills her through, and a host of other physical attractions which she indicates to the world with a charming frankness... (*RN* xli)

Eustacia Vye may seem not altogether out of place among these inhabitants of *Belgravia* but that this magazine was a distinctly down-market step for Hardy to take is registered in the *Life* by his embarrassed reference to publishing his new attempt at high art 'in (of all places) *Belgravia*' (*Life* 120).

The original version of the novel, according to John Paterson, was even more morally dubious than the final manuscript sent to *Belgravia*. Initially, in an episode echoing Cytherea's predicament in *Desperate Remedies* and foreshadowing a similar trick played upon Tess in the *Graphic*, Thomasin was to have been the victim of a fake marriage, the invalidity of which she only discovers after a week (Paterson 1960a: 10–12). The original Eustacia (then named Avice) appears to have been a more 'satanic' figure (20–1). Paterson suggests that Hardy's increasing sympathy towards his heroine led to the 'suppression of the diabolical Eustacia Vye and the emergence of the romantic heroine' whose Promethean rebellion against Fate and the gods is underscored by the array of classical references with which she is surrounded (29–30). The original Eustacia not only lacked 'much love for my fellow creatures' and 'disliked English Sundays' but expressed positive 'hate' for both (81). Her language was still being toned down in the proof-sheets of the serial version: no longer does the thought of Budmouth drive her to blasphemy ('Ah God, Budmouth!') but to the more sedate, 'Ah, my soul, Budmouth!' (89).

Hardy's conception of Eustacia continued to develop. A number of revisions in 1895 made explicit what was only suggested, or even left open, earlier. It was only then that she told Wildeve, 'I won't give myself to you any more', which is considerably more explicit than her original refusal to 'encourage' him (406). She also became more exotic in her ancestry, her father changing from the Belgian of *Belgravia* and the bandmaster of unspecified nationality in the first edition to 'a Corfiote by birth, and a fine musician' in 1895 (407). Her maternal ancestry also improved in rank, the outright denial of any aristocratic links of the first edition being reversed in 1895 with the hint that her dignity might derive 'from Fitzalan or De Vere, her maternal grandfather having had a cousin in the peerage' (407–8). It becomes much more possible that she might elope with Wildeve, a step she only rejects because it would smack of 'humiliation': 'He's not *great* enough for me to give myself to'. Only 'a Saul or a Napoleon', she feels, would 'suffice for my desire' (424). Even whether she commits suicide becomes more open by Hardy's changing her 'plunge' of the manuscript to a 'fall' (425).

An important factor in the way readers of *Belgravia* would have seen Eustacia was the way she was drawn by Arthur Hopkins, who was given the unenviable task of attempting to capture her 'deep Pagan eyes', her quivering lips and 'a profile suggesting both Marie Antoinette and Lord Byron' (Dalziel 1996: 92). Not surprisingly, Hardy was disappointed with the dumpy figure Hopkins produced for the February instalment, who reflects the artist's moral disapproval more than the writer's excited desire. He told Hopkins that 'Eustacia should have been represented as more youthful in face, supple in figure, and, in general, with a little more roundness and softness than have been given her' (*Letters* I 52). Even Hardy accepted that 'Eustacia in boy's clothes, though pleasant enough to the imagination, would perhaps be unsafe as a picture' (54) and he was much happier with her depiction in the August issue, which was 'just what I imagined her to be', combining charm with 'rebellious-ness' (*Letters* I 59). The October issue portrayed her in Pre-Raphaelite pose, dreamily ignoring Charley's proffered cup, 'her expressive eyes, her melancholy expression, and a languorous posture displaying to full advantage her immaculate dress and "perfect" figure' (Dalziel 1996:103). In the final issue, however, Hopkins rendered her dead body 'as undesirable as possible, with a grotesquely clawlike hand...and impossibly contorted upper body' (104). The illustrations, in other words, hardly matched Hardy's exotic word-painting and were accordingly dropped from the first edition.

The reviewers appear to have made a coordinated attempt to put Hardy in his place. It may simply be that they shared assumptions about fiction which Hardy had violated; they probably read each other's reviews. But it is difficult not to suspect that conversations in London clubs contributed to the similarity of their complaints. Britten in the *Athenaeum* (23.11.78) called it 'distinctly inferior to anything of his which we have yet read'. Its characters talked 'as no people ever talk now' while the book as a whole was both pretentious, 'packed with 'forced allusions and images', and immoral, about 'a man who is in love with two women, and a woman who is in love with two men' (Lerner 1968: 44). Hardy defended himself against the charge of failing realistically to represent the language of his rustics in a letter to the *Athenaeum* published the following week (44–5). This, however, was not the most important complaint. A review in *London* (23.11.78) attacked what it labelled Hardy's 'Victor-Hugoism': a combination of the same descriptive power with 'the same aptitude to spoil...the effect aimed at...by the introduction of exaggerated circumstances, of an offensive personality'. Hardy's, the reviewer continued, was an 'intellectual and not an emotional sympathy...you never cry over him and you seldom laugh. You read and think'. This might not be bad in itself were it not for the degree to which he manipulated the plot: 'is it possible to be in sympathy with a writer who goes so far out of his way as this to make his creatures hopeless and his readers miserable? Is not life wretched enough as it is...?'

Some of these complaints were echoed in the four reviews which appeared on 30 November 1878, all carefully pasted into Hardy's scrapbook. W. E. Henley in the *Academy* also noted 'a certain Hugoesque quality of insincerity' in Hardy's work and complained of 'affectation' in the writing. He too detected an 'intellectual' rather than 'emotional' sympathy on Hardy's part and found the tragedy 'arbitrary and accidental rather than heroic and inevitable'. Henley blamed Hardy's character: 'rare artist as he is, there is something wanting in his personality, and he is not quite a great man' (Cox 1970: 48–50). The *Examiner*, which had been so positive about *The Hand of Ethelberta*, complained of the 'verbose eccentricity' of the opening chapters of the new novel. It too found 'obvious imitations of Victor Hugo', complained of its improbable characterisation, and felt that the ending left readers 'disgusted...and disappointed'. *Vanity Fair* repeated the charge that Hardy was 'purely intellectual': he 'rarely gets at our emotions' and the book is ultimately 'cruel'. *John Bull* complained of 'a palpable striving after effect' in the author, and 'heartlessness' as well as 'a want of true wifely feeling' in his heroine.

The critical onslaught continued. The *Telegraph* of 3 December joked about the need to skip Hardy's long descriptive passages while *The Times* of the same date regretted that no one in the novel came 'nearer the station of a gentleman than Yeobright, the ex-Parisian shopman'. It acknowledged that Hardy had a talent for 'word-painting...in the Grosvenor Gallery style' but his descriptions were the only part of the novel worth reading. The *Graphic* (7.12.78) too praised his 'word-pictures' as did the *Illustrated London News* (14.12.78), which found 'the personages uninteresting, the action poor and the conclusion flat' (Cox 1970: xxi). The *Saturday Review* (4.1.79) returned to the issue of the responsibility of novelists to amuse their readers, citing Hardy as one of those writers 'who seem to construct their fictions for themselves rather than for other people'. It also complained of his style as 'intensely artificial', that of 'a literary gymnast who is always striving after sensation in the form of some *tour de force*'. The *Observer* (5.1.79) felt that readers who skipped such passages were 'scarcely to be blamed; for *The Return of the Native* is for the most part written in a style almost ostenta-

tiously disdainful of any effort to secure popularity'. Its 'sham profund-
ity' and 'pretentious nonsense' undermined its 'shrewd touches', 'genuine dramatic force' and 'psychological discernment'. The latest of the
reviews in Hardy's scrapbook, that of the *Spectator* (8.2.79), recognised
the 'singular power and interest' of the story but thought this was
undermined by the unreality of his peasants and by his pessimism,
which reduced tragedy to mere 'dreariness' and the characters to
'puppets of a sort of fate' (Cox 1970: 55–9).

The reviews in the monthlies were no more encouraging (though by
this time Hardy had given up collecting them). The *Contemporary Review*
noted the unevenness of Hardy's work: 'Where else are we to look for
anything like the same amount of rugged and fantastic power' mixed
with equally evident weaknesses (XXXIV 205–6)? Innes Shand in *Blackwood's Edinburgh Magazine* complained both of his pseudo-
Shakespearean peasants and of a 'labouring after originality which has
rather the air of affectation' (CXXV 338). It was left to Charles Kegan
Paul to come to the novel's defence in his *New Quarterly Magazine*,
celebrating the details of its Dorset landscape and calling it 'a tragedy
of no common power and sadness' (I 237–9). He also commissioned
Mrs Sutherland Orr to write a survey of 'Mr Hardy's Novels' in which she
recognised that *The Return of the Native* represented 'a new phase, and
perhaps a new departure in the development of Mr Hardy's genius'; it
was 'a more serious work than any of its predecessors' and 'generally
considered to be in every sense "stronger"' (at least in *New Quarterly*
circles):

> The present writer does not, however, share this opinion, and for the
> following reason. If *The Return of the Native* is more earnest than *A Pair
> of Blue Eyes* or *Far from the Madding Crowd*, it is also less spontaneous.
> It suggests a more definite intention on the author's part, but also,
> dramatically, though not otherwise, a less equal inspiration. In his
> earlier works character is developed by circumstance; we cannot
> predict what is coming, and when the end comes, we can imagine
> no other to have been possible. In the present work the characters are
> defined from the first, the action soon becomes transparent, and the
> catastrophe nevertheless brings a kind of shock in which there is a
> decided element of objection.

Mrs Yeobright's death in particular she found insufficiently 'rooted in
the facts of the story'. She also objected to the positivist tendencies all
too observable both in Clym and his creator (Cox 1970: 67–70).

American reviews of *The Return of the Native*, as Joan Pinck has shown, were rather more positive. Both the *Literary World* (1.2.79) and the *Atlantic Monthly* (April 1879) carped over the book's title, apparently chosen from a list offered by Hardy to Henry Harper on a bench in Green Park (Weber 1946: 41). The *Literary World*, however, enthused over 'the incomparable Eustacia' who was 'drawn with fire and dash' (X 37) while Harriet Preston in the *Atlantic* admired his delineation of the heath and of 'the crushing tyranny of circumstance' (XLIII 500–3). In a later essay for the *Atlantic Monthly* (November 1879) she called it the finest of Hardy's novels to date, particularly admiring the 'evident charity' with which he treated Eustacia (XLIV 672–4). The *Nation* (February 1879) found 'much genuine pathos' in the death of Mrs Yeobright and much to admire in Eustacia, 'a woman of extreme beauty, of a certain sinister sort' (XXVIII 155). The New York *Eclectic*, however, thought Eustacia a 'thoroughly selfish, cruel, unprincipled, and despicable woman' who spoilt an otherwise splendid novel (XXIX 378). There was a positive review in the *New York Independent* (6.3.79) but *Scribner's Monthly* complained of the amount of 'padding' in the novel (XVIII 910–11).

Commercially, the book was a disaster. Four years after publication of the first edition of 1000 copies, there were still '100 quires and 22 copies in cloth to be remaindered' (Purdy 1954: 27). Some individuals wrote to Hardy praising it, the most notable being Walter Besant, who invited him to join the Rabelais Club in 1879 as 'the creator of the Native...the most original, the most virile and most humorous of all modern novels' (DCM 1038). Kegan Paul continued to back the novel, publishing a one-volume edition in 1880 and trumpeting its merits in his survey of Hardy's work the following year. As a fellow-sympathiser with the Religion of Humanity, he thought the novel offered 'a sustained philosophy, a grasp of the problems of life, a clear conception of human duty'. He particularly appreciated the concluding portrait of Clym, than whom there was no 'more noble, more pathetic figure' (Cox 1970: 89). Havelock Ellis praised its 'freshness of vision' (119) while J. A. Symonds, whose discussion of the Greek tragedians in *Studies of the Greek Poets* Hardy annotated in preparation for the novel (*LN* I 267), wrote in 1889 to praise 'its vigour and its freshness and its charm' (DCM 5419), eliciting from Hardy a long letter on the difficulties he had had in keeping the 'tragical conditions of life imperfectly denoted' in the novel out of his work (*Letters* I 190).

Gradually the book appears to have won more admirers. Gosse in 1890 called it one of his 'two masterpieces' (Cox 1970: 168) while

W. P. Trent in 1892 put it in third place, judging it 'not a thoroughly artistic success' because of 'the repulsiveness of many of his characters' and the pessimism to which its author had fallen victim (226–7). Laurence Lerner cites Lionel Johnson as the only critic to have 'considered *The Return of the Native* Hardy's best novel' (Lerner 1968: 47) but George Douglas claimed it was 'the finest novel in the language, . . . the most artistically perfect' (Douglas 1900: 111) and W. L. Phelps thought it 'perhaps his greatest contribution to literature . . . a masterpiece of despair' (Cox 1970: 398–9). Charles Whibley was equally enthusiastic about 'that great masterpiece' (413). While Evelyn Sharp told Hardy at a garden party in Max Gate in 1907 that she was rereading *The Return of the Native* 'and still liked it best of all his novels' (Sharp 1933: 98). The 'scholars', it seems, came to appreciate the self-conscious literary qualities with which Hardy had been so careful to endow it, and the novel has duly taken its place among Hardy's 'major' novels, its multiple classical allusions and universal tragic message to be dutifully noted by generations of students.

This, in a sense, is what Hardy had aimed at all along. The map he drew for the first edition may, when turned from vertical to horizontal, be recognisable as the heath adjoining Bocklington (Millgate 1971: 124) but the inner space it represents is no less than the whole human condition. The map of Egdon, in editions after 1880, would be replaced by the map of Wessex but the point remains the same. Hillis Miller writes of the way all novels 'tend in fact to be mapped, at least implicitly, in the mind of the reader as he [*sic*] makes his way through the text of the novel' (Miller 1981: 119–20). Having carefully studied the sociology and anthropology of his own time, Hardy creates an imaginative space which represents nothing less than that of the tragic human predicament as registered in the religions and culture of the western world. The biblical and classical allusions should not therefore be seen as mere ornamentation but as deliberate attempt (along the lines suggested by Leslie Stephen) to broaden his range and to tackle universal issues.

Some of Hardy's reading in preparation for the writing of *The Return of the Native* can be traced in the *Literary Notebooks*. Among the most relevant entries are those on Greek tragedy, taken from the second series of J. A. Symonds' *Studies of the Greek Poets*. This charted a development from Aeschylus through Sophocles to Euripedes in relation to divine justice, which the first accepted, the second showed dignity in the face of and the third dared to challenge (Goode 1988: 53). The self-improving novelist made notes under headings such as *'What is fatality'* and *'Greek philosophy of life'*. Under the latter he recorded Clough's account of the 'Stoic-Epicurean acceptance' of the world (I 65). The novel itself would refer to Clym as 'an absolute stoic' in his acceptance of his blindness (*RN* 245) while this affliction itself appears to have been suggested by another passage copied from Symonds:

> *Greek morality*... leaned on a faith or belief in the order of the universe... Man was answerable only to its order for his conduct... If disease and affliction fall upon us we must remember that we are the limbs and organs of the whole, and that our suffering is necessary for its well-being.... Nature [man's] with all its imperfections in the physical and moral orders,... must be accepted as the best possible, as that which was intended so to be.
>
> (*LN* I 65)

A little later, a further annotation from Symonds considers some of differences between the Greek and Christian views of life, along with the desirability of a synthesis of the two, 'to combine both the Hellenic and Xtian conceptions in a third, which shall be more solid and more rational than either' (I 65–6).

Hardy's annotations from Symonds, which include a fleeting reference to Calypso as '*Not woman* but Goddess', suggestive of the famous description of Eustacia possessing 'the passions and instincts which make a model goddess... not quite a model woman' (*RN* 68), gradually give way to excerpts from the recently translated *Social Dynamics* of Auguste Comte, the third volume of the *System of Positive Polity*, which attempted a similar Hegelian synthesis of religion on scientific principles. The whole point of Comte's three stages of human development, as Hardy realised, was that the Theological phase (first fetishistic, then polytheistic and finally monotheistic) gave way initially to the Metaphysical (the negative critique of theology) before giving rise to the Positive, embodied in the Religion of Humanity, founded upon scientific law and merely human morality (Wright 1986: 202–17). The detailed notes Hardy made from both Symonds and Comte in 1876, I suggest, help to explain some of the elements of *The Return of the Native* which baffled its first readers: why the heath is personified so fully in the opening chapter and why to 'an emotional listener's fetishistic mood' the spirit of the heath can be heard blowing through the heath-bells (*RN* 56), why Clym ends up preaching a humanitarian creed based upon 'ethical systems popular at the time' in Paris (172) and why Hardy's readers at the beginning of 'Book Third' are treated to a long disquisition on Clym's face as 'the typical countenance of the future', suggesting that 'view of life as a thing to be put up with, replacing that zest for existence which was so intense in the early civilisations' so that even 'our nursery children' now feel what Aeschylus imagined 'as we uncover the defects of natural laws' (167).

All this is a lot to read into a face. It was certainly too much for contemporary readers used to skipping these descriptive and philosophical passages in order to follow the story. Hardy's many allusions, as Ian Gregor argued, force readers to slow down, keeping them moving 'from a dramatic to a contemplative mood, and then back again' (Gregor 1974: 89). This novel, to use a phrase from another of Hardy's favourite thinkers, T. H. Huxley, is about nothing less than *Man's Place in Nature* (Goode 1988: 45). It also echoes the concerns of contemporary anthropologists about *Primitive Culture* and *The Origins of Civilisation*, the survival of primitive ideas 'rooted in our minds, as fossils imbedded in the soil' (O'Hara 1997: 155). Hence its description of bonfires as 'the lineal descendants from jumbled Druidical rites and Saxon ceremonies' (*RN* 20), of mumming as 'a fossilized survival' from past times rather than a revival (122), and of maypole dancing as the expression of the 'instincts of merry England' in which 'homage to nature' and 'fragments of Teutonic rites to divinities whose names are forgotten' are seen to have 'survived medieval doctrine' (376).

The last word of this last sentence had in the manuscript been 'Christianity', the change presumably designed to soften the possible offence to believing readers. Similarly, the manuscript's original description of the dance at East Egdon, at which Wildeve and Eustacia renew their acquaintance, had been even more explicitly anti-Christian in both manuscript and serial as 'Christianity was eclipsed in their hearts' and 'they adored themselves and their own natural instincts' (Paterson 1959: 111). It is clearly significant that Eustacia, surrounded as she is by references to pagan goddesses (*RN* 55), plays the part of an infidel knight murdered by St George while Clym, likened by her to St Paul and by the narrator to John the Baptist, ends the novel preaching a new Sermon on the Mount. Eustacia not only has 'Pagan eyes, full of nocturnal mysteries' but prefers the names of Saul and Sisera to the more orthodox Jacob or David and wonders 'if Pontius Pilate were as handsome as he was frank and fair' (72). The manuscript and serial version of this passage proceed to identify her 'chief priest' as Byron and 'her antichrist a well-meaning preacher at Budmouth, of the name Slatters' (Paterson 1959: 112). Hardy thus goes out of his way to identify her as an opponent of the Christian faith. He also christens the weakest character in the book Christian, making him mumble ineffectual prayers rather than join in the demoniac dance around the fire. In writing a novel so openly attempting to map the human condition in a manner offensive to many of his readers, Hardy clearly laid himself open to the outrage and animosity evident in the contemporary reviews.

Hardy's sympathetic portrait of Eustacia was also designed to offend contemporary morality. In the conventional terms which Hardy himself employed for the benefit of his illustrator Hopkins, 'Thomasin . . . is the *good* heroine' who 'lives happily' and Eustacia 'the wayward and erring heroine' who 'is unhappy and dies' (*Letters* I 53). The wickedness of which Eustacia is supposed to be guilty can only, of course, be implied. As Hillis Miller points out, 'the wild love-making of Wildeve and Eustacia on the heath' precedes the action of the novel and is not therefore 'described directly. It remains a blank space in the narrative' (Miller 1981: 132) which the reader has to supply. When Eustacia tells Wildeve, 'We have been hot lovers in our time' (*RN 278*), she is referring to events preceding the action of the novel itself. Literal-minded critics have even questioned (on the basis of lack of opportunity) whether Eustacia could ever have been Wildeve's mistress in the full sexual sense:

> After all, Wildeve was never asked into the house by his proud though condescending mistress' (I, 11). It is difficult to imagine Eustacia's visiting Wildeve at his inn. That leaves only the out-of-doors, the 'heathy, furzy, briery wilderness' (I, 1), where there are bushes but no trees, where there are brambles that are regularly mentioned, where the 'heath-croppers' (wild ponies) seem always likely to gallop up disturbingly, where adders apparently abound, and where the weather seems to alternate between blazing heat and furious storms.
>
> (Heilman 1979: 87)

Hardy, however, needs only to hint at the 'secret recesses of sensuousness' (*RN 96*) within his heroine and leave such practical problems to the imagination of his readers.

Hardy's sympathy for his 'erring heroine' is evident enough, especially when she asks, 'do I desire unreasonably much in wanting what is called life – music, poetry, passion, war, and all that is going on in the great arteries of the world?' (*RN 276*). But it is limited. He has been seen to invest her with nearly all the dubious 'feminine' qualities noted by Herbert Spencer in *The Study of Sociology* of 1873: capriciousness, love of admiration, inability to see beyond the moment, lack of a sense of justice, absence of sound intellect and so on (Ingham 1989: 25). According to Judith Mitchell, he has sufficient sympathy with his 'bad girl' to empathise with her sufferings; he even comes close to investing her with a genuine 'sexual subjectivity'. But she is presented most of the time as the object of male desire, her female gaze (as she looks for Wildeve through her telescope) quickly framed in terms of her own appearance as she does so (Mitchell 1994: 176–7). Hardy thus forges a masculine bond of 'wry superiority' between narrator and reader who are both fascinated but ultimately repelled by her (182–7).

As with the proprietary narrator in *A Pair of Blue Eyes*, however, it can be argued that Hardy satirises contemporary moral attitudes. The figure of the reddleman has been seen as a 'moral watchdog', a 'furtive stalker' who tracks her down and tries 'catch her out in actions he disapproves'. This, Morgan argues, exposes the 'Grundyan overseer, for the malevolent bully he is'. Reddle, she points out, is smeared on the belly of rams in order to indicate the ewes with whom they have mated (Morgan 1988: 67, 179). Employed by Wessex mothers as a bugbear for naughty children, the reddleman serves, in Morgan's reading, as symbol of the world of 'self-interested, joyless, punitive men' (70).

Hardy was himself unhappy with the ending of the novel, which allows his 'good' heroine Thomasin to marry his 'moral watchdog' Diggory Venn, adding a footnote to the penultimate chapter of the Wessex Edition stating that 'the original conception of the story did not design' a marriage between the two but 'certain circumstances of serial publication led to a change of intent'. Readers were invited to choose between two endings, the one in the original text and another suggested in the footnote in which Venn 'retained his isolated and weird character to the last', disappearing 'mysteriously from the heath', while Thomasin remained a widow: 'those with an austere artistic code can assume the more consistent conclusion to be the true one' (*RN* 427). The implication is that he was forced to compromise with the wishes of his original readers and create the kind of romantic ending they craved. It is yet one more example of Hardy looking back at those readers and the compromises they forced upon his work with less than affection.

The Trumpet-Major: reading history

The Trumpet-Major, which was popular with Victorian readers, has since suffered a long period of disparagement and neglect from admirers of the tragic novels, who have found it 'the most difficult of Hardy's books to take seriously' (Morrell 1976: 60–1). Hardy himself, in his later years, tended to play down its significance, presenting it as a forerunner to the more ambitious verse play *The Dynasts*, which dealt more directly with some of the main events of the Napoleonic Wars. His preface to *The Dynasts* refers to 'the first published result' of his interest in the period as having merely 'touched the fringe of a vast international tragedy without being able, through limits of plan, knowledge, and opportunity, to enter further into its events' (*PW* 40–1). A letter of 1907 to the biographer of Napoleon, Alexander Broadley, was equally dismissive of a story written 'from hand to mouth as it were, for a periodical merely' (*Letters* III 286). Hardy's lifelong fascination with the Napoleonic wars is well documented in the *Life*, which records his first reading his grandfather's battered copy of *A History of the Wars*, with its 'melodramatic prints of serried ranks, crossed bayonets, huge knapsacks, and dead bodies' (*Life* 21). This early reading was bolstered by research at the British Museum, begun in the spring of 1878, when he copied details of the period from newspapers and other sources into his 'Trumpet-Major' Notebook (*PN* xxi–iii). The imaginative leap from the page to the age, from historical records to attempted reconstruction of the 'reality' behind them, is one of the main preoccupations of Hardy's historical novel, which foregrounds the whole question of reading and interpretation (Cunningham 1994: 98).

The critical and commercial failure of *The Return of the Native* caused Hardy some difficulty in placing its successor. He had moved to London in March 1878 precisely to further 'the practical side of his vocation' (*Life* 121), quickly falling 'into line as a London man again' by dining with publishers, editors and reviewers (125). In a letter of August to George Bentley, editor of *Temple Bar*, in August, offering 'a new story... to begin as a serial about next May', Hardy was able to suggest a meeting at the Savile Club, to which he had just been elected (*Letters* I 59). When nothing came of this he turned once more to Leslie Stephen, who was again non-committal, wanting 'to see your story when further advanced', but happy to reply to Hardy's query whether or not he should include actual historical figures. Stephen was against the idea: 'a historical character in a novel is almost always a nuisance; but I like to have a bit of history in the background, so to speak: to feel that George III is just round the corner though he does not present himself in full front' (DCM 5517). Hardy decided in the end to give George III a number of brief appearances, otherwise following Stephen's advice to keep him and the grand events of history very much in the background.

In May, giving up on the *Cornhill* (there is no written evidence of a rejection), Hardy tried Macmillan once more, again promising a 'cheerful' tale in which 'everything winds up well and happily' (*Letters* VII 91). This too must have failed to produce a contract, for in June he approached John Blackwood, yet again vowing that his new venture, unlike his last, would be 'a cheerful story, without views or opinions', a promise he repeated to the American publisher J. B. Lippincott in July (I 65). It must presumably have been a fairly desperate Hardy who in July closed with William Isbister, proprietor of *Good Words*, for the serial publication of *The Trumpet-Major* to begin the following January (VII 92). In August he was arranging to meet the editor of the magazine, the Very Reverend Donald Macleod (I 66), a minister of the Church of Scotland who was later to become Moderator of its General Assembly, to clarify the 'rules' his new novel would have to obey.

Good Words was by no means 'a negligible or poor placement'. Founded by the philanthropic Alexander Strahan in the 1860s as part of an ongoing campaign to educate the masses and transform society, it had quickly become 'the best-selling magazine in the English-speaking world', publishing a range of material, from sermons to essays to fiction, directed at a wide middle-class, non-sectarian but religious readership (*T-M* 342–3). Its first editor, Dr Norman Macleod, one of the Queen's Chaplains, prided himself on the fact that 'no infidel, no immoral man or woman . . . will ever be permitted to write in the pages of *Good Words*' (Altick 1957: 125–6). His brother Donald clearly shared these values, quickly letting Hardy know that 'all our stories should be . . . free . . . from anything – direct or indirect – which a healthy Parson like myself would not care to read to his bairns at the fireside'. Humour was welcome, along with 'as much manly bracing fresh air – as much honest love-making and stirring incident as you like,' but nothing 'likely to offend the susceptibilities of honestly religious and domestic souls' (DCM 2625). The word 'manly' would recur in many of the reviews, suggesting that in the portrait of the trumpet-major Hardy provided exactly what Macleod and his readers wanted. After the debacle of his previous novel, Hardy appears to have been genuinely keen to please them. He promised a Mrs Franklyn, who had written to complain about Eustacia, that the '*good* woman' she demanded would appear in his next novel, 'and I hope that you and my other lady readers will like her' (*Letters* I 64).

Hardy's account of his relations with his editor in a letter to Macleod's biographer Sydney Smith in 1925, suggests that they were fairly amicable. He could only remember two of the 'small literary points' they discussed 'whenever he came to London':

that he asked me to make a lover's meeting, which I had fixed for a Sunday afternoon, take place on a Saturday, and that swear-words should be avoided – in both which requests I readily acquiesced, as I restored my own readings when the novel came out as a book.

(Letters VI 333)

This appears to have been the first occasion on which Hardy adopted what was to become his normal practice, restoring to the first edition what had been modified to suit the requirements of serial readers. Smith suggests that Macleod took up Hardy's invitation to alter for himself 'any passages out of keeping with the general tone of the magazine' (Smith 1926: 113) but these unauthorised changes, according to Hardy, were of 'infinitesimal proportions' (*Letters* VI 333). Comparing the text of *Good Words* against surviving copies of the American serial version in *Desmorest's Monthly Magazine*, Gatrell has discovered the deletion of a passage on 'the value of diluted spirits in restoring good-humour..., a passionate embrace in the rain, and a description of how Anne's waist was encircled by Bob's arm' (Gatrell 1988: 55). Hardy appears to have attempted to 'slide incidents and phrases' past him (as he had with Stephen), failing, for example, with a late manuscript addition to chapter 18, restored to the first edition, in which John Loveday reveals Matilda's acquaintance with a suspicious number of Dragoons. Macleod, like Stephen, removed all references he noticed not only to 'kissing' but even to 'armpits' as too 'coarse' for the delicate consciences of his readers (56).

In some respects, notably that of class, the serial was more radical than later versions of the novel, suggesting that Hardy was playing to the prejudices of the solidly middle-class readers of *Good Words*. At the end of chapter 11 in the serial, for example, Anne is shown to have 'a romantic interest in court people and pageantry' which emerges in her imagining specks on the distant down as coaches 'full of ladies of resplendent charms' and 'rattling dots of horsemen' as 'gallant nobles and knights', only for her dreams to be undermined by the revelation that these coaches contained an unprepossessing collection of countesses 'of placid nature, plain features, and dowdy dress', a 'virtuous and homely' lady and a 'strange-tempered Marchioness' while the horsemen were a 'puffy, red-faced, General...a couple of grey and bald-headed colonels, a diminutive diplomatist, and numbers of commonplace attendants on the court' (*T-M* 316). The removal of this passage in the first edition is also in keeping both with other revisions reducing the amount of irony directed at Anne but

Hardy seems to have gone through the manuscript systematically pointing up 'class' aspects of the book. Late insertions of this kind include many of the direct or indirect expressions of Anne's feeling that the Lovedays are socially her inferiors, as well as those opening paragraphs of chapter 2 which roundly declare the essential sturdiness of the Lovedays' unaristocratic pedigree.

(Millgate 1971: 150)

His insistence on the importance of the miller and his family to 'the unwritten history of England' (*T-M* 18) would also have gone down well with the readers of *Good Words*.

Perhaps the most significant change in the first edition of the novel was the darkening of the ending. The serial ending is unexpected enough, causing Leslie Stephen to complain that the heroine married the wrong man. 'When Hardy objected that they mostly did, Stephen retorted: "Not in magazines"' (Millgate 1982: 211). But the first edition not only makes John Loveday depart to 'blow his trumpet over the bloody battle-fields of Spain' as he does in the serial (John Collier producing a nice illustration of him waving goodbye for the final instalment) but adds the chilling final words 'till silenced for ever upon one of the bloody battle-fields of Spain' (*T-M* 301). There are a number of similar references scattered through the novel to the fate awaiting many of the soldiers: Sergeant Stanner's satirical song about Napoleon, for example, is interrupted by a note that the sergeant was 'mortally wounded and trampled down by a French Hussar' only 'a few years after this pleasantly spent summer at Weymouth' (37). The description of the King's review of his glorious troops is brought similarly down to earth by a reference to their now 'lying scattered about the world as military and royal dust' (92). Hardy may give his readers some episodes of picturesque militaristic 'flag-waving' (Neill 1999: 33), which would have been reinforced by some of Collier's otherwise disappointing illustrations, but he also reminds them of the grim realities of war.

The novel was a tremendous success with reviewers, although at least some of its critical acclaim can probably be attributed to Hardy's careful cultivation of their acquaintance in the Savile and other clubs. Having ganged up on the 'pretensions' of his previous novel, they appear to have decided that he had now learned his lesson and deserved their support. Britten, in the *Athenaeum* (20.11.80), while continuing his private argument with Hardy about the language of his rustics, went out of his way to commend the 'Rabelaisian' descriptive profusion of the novel and called John Loveday 'the best character that Mr Hardy has drawn' (Cox 1970: 71–2). Julian Hawthorne in the *Spectator* (18.12.80) found both the hero and the author 'masculine and shy'. The novel's subservience to conventional gender stereotypes was for Hawthorne very much to be commended: 'his heroines are profoundly feminine; his heroes thoroughly, and at times comically, masculine' (74). Like many of Hardy's contemporaries, Hawthorne found Anne 'personally lovely and attractive...amiable, innocent, generous, and tender-hearted'. He even found Uncle Benjy and Festus funny, advising Hardy to avoid tragedy since his voice 'breaks when strained at more powerful notes' (75–6).

Other reviewers echoed the view that Anne was 'one of the author's sweetest conceptions' (*Daily News* 18.11.80) and John 'a fine manly true-hearted fellow (*Scotsman* 19.11.80), a 'true soldier and gentleman', full of 'healthy and simple manliness' (*Graphic* 27.11.80), 'a really fine fellow (*Whitehall Review* 3.2.81), 'a straightforward, self-sacrificing, humble-minded English soldier' (*John Bull* 13.11.80). The *Saturday Review* (6.11.80) also enthused over his 'simple and noble nature', calling the scenes in which Festus chases after Anne 'capital'. You can almost hear the slapping of thighs throughout clubland in these adjectives. The *Queen* rejoiced at the fact that Hardy had abandoned the 'semi-scientific' nonsense of his previous novel for a simpler style 'told in choice and wholesome English' that made for 'good reading' (13.11.80). The *Morning Post* also celebrated the fact that it was undemanding, 'a novel to be read through at a sitting' (21.12.80). *The Times* too found fewer 'mannerisms and affectations' and less striving after effect (1.2.81) while the *Westminster Review* called it 'decidedly the best story' he had yet produced (CXV 327). George Saintsbury in the *Academy* (11.12.80, the identification in Hardy's hand in his scrapbook) noted the novel's 'deliberately subdued' manner, its 'delicate...and carefully elaborated grace'. The *Pall Mall Gazette* (23.11.80) also appreciated the 'quiet and effective pathos' of a novel which did not, like its predecessor, 'rely for its effect on purple patches'.

Other reviewers had their reservations. *Vanity Fair* (27.11.80) thought Hardy had sacrificed 'power' to 'charm'. The *Court Journal* (20.11.80) detected signs of Hardy holding himself back, which resulted in 'a second-rate work from a first-rate author'. The *British Quarterly Review* (LXXIII 116–17) also felt that Hardy did not 'aim high enough' in this novel. The New York *Nation* (XXXII 16–17) complained of his style but the Boston *Literary World* (XII 25) thought the novel not only as original as *The Return of the Native* but 'to our taste a more pleasing story'. Private responses to the novel, moreover, at least when reported in letters addressed to the author, were even more flattering. Walter Besant found the opening chapters 'perfectly delightful' (DCM 1040); the novel as a whole 'only had one fault – it was too short' (DCM 1042). Edmund

Gosse recorded having read its first volume 'with great relish', ranking it 'with the very cream of your writing' and going into rhapsodies over the scarlet uniforms, 'deep green landscape', 'darling' heroine and 'delight-ful' mother (DCM 2709).

Hardy was puzzled by the fact that such high praise had led to such low sales, only 750 copies of the first edition of a thousand being sold (Cox 1970: xxiii). Besant later told him that circulating libraries had purchased volumes bound from the serial instalments of his 1883 *Good Words* novel *All in a Garden Fair* 'earlier and at a much cheaper price...in preference to the book itself', leading Hardy to suspect that the same had happened to his novel (*Letters* VII 99). Two New York magazines had also serialised the novel, not only *Demorest's Monthly Magazine* but a 'short-lived pirated reprint of the London *Fortnightly Review*' (*T-M* xlvi). So there would have been even more readers than purchasers of the novel than normal; the disappointing sales should not be read as a lack of success with the public.

That *The Trumpet-Major* was popular with contemporary readers is attested by a number of Hardy's admirers who were not themselves enamoured of his departure from the greater ambition of its predecessor. Kegan Paul confessed, 'we care less' for *The Trumpet-Major* but acknow-ledged that 'the mere novel-reader will probably like it better' (Cox 1970: 90). Havelock Ellis saw that 'forsaking for a while the carefully elaborated method of *The Return of the Native*' had resulted in a 'slighter and less powerful' novel whose 'fresh and careless vivacity' were 'foreign to Mr Hardy's genius' (122–3). But W. P. Trent called it 'the most charming of Mr Hardy's stories' (228–9) and even Emma dubbed it 'one of the pretty ones!' (Taylor 1982: 82). Later critics such as Charles Whibley and Harold Williams also found it 'delightful' (Cox 1970: 430). R. B. Cunningham Graham enthused privately to Hardy over 'the sailing of the Victory scene' (DCM 2657), which George Dewar also thought 'one of the most moving things I know in fiction' (DCM 2088). There may sometimes have been ulterior motives behind this flattery: Ellen Terry thought it 'would make a *perfect play*' (DCM 5542) while Sir George Forrest, historian of India and friend of Anne Procter, who had read the novel when it came out 'in a tent on the sandy plains of Gujerat', thought on rereading in 1925 that he recognised his friend in the heroine (DCM 2444), an identification partially confirmed by Hardy himself (*Letters* VI 315). He had not only turned readers into friends but friends into characters.

The very qualities which pleased his contemporaries, however, would themselves grow out of fashion, bringing this novel with them into disrepute. Virginia Woolf complained in her diary of its 'flatness, tedium and complete absence of gift' (Bell 1977: 4–5), finding it 'a refuge in time of headache' but otherwise 'the worst book in the language' (Nicholson 1975: VI 4). Arnold Bennett grumbled at its 'excessively slow method of narration' and 'old-fashioned...humour' (Flower 1932: I 28). Of 'some twenty commentaries on Hardy's novels published between the wars,' laments H. A. T. Johnson in 'In Defence of *The Trumpet-Major*', 'only two or three make more than glancing references' to it. Even these damn it with faint praise, Rutland calling it a 'slight' if 'charming' book (Johnson 1976: 41), Grimsditch 'a light and pleasant story' (Grimsditch 1925: 167). From the 1940s the comments start to become more acid: Guerard attributes its popularity to the Victorians 'naturally' preferring Hardy's 'worst books', Hawkins laments that it was 'written to a box-office formula', Howe complains that it appealed to the 'beef-and-ale critics of an earlier generation' and Stewart calls it 'antiquarian rather than historical' (Johnson 1976: 42–5). 'This novel has never stirred readers deeply,' claims Carl Weber inaccurately, 'and it never will' (Weber 1965: 118). Even Richard Taylor, attempting to see as much virtue as possible in the neglected novels, concludes that it fails to hold the reader's interest, lacks emotional crises and degenerates into episodic tedium (Taylor 1982: 94). Marxist critics have been particularly scathing about its failure to live up to Lukács's ideal of the historical novel; the novel's history, according to John Goode, is at best 'only local colour – at worst it imparts a coy tone of quaintness' (Goode 1988: 66).

It is certainly the case that Hardy did not share the Hegelian view of history that lies behind Marx. Hegel's *Lectures on the Philosophy of History*, which had been translated into English in 1878, declared history to be the unfolding of Spirit, which was not 'tossed to and fro amid the superficial play of accidents' but remained 'entirely unmoved by contingencies' (Sanders 1978: 1–2). Hardy's view of history was more humble, certainly more open to contingency, and altogether less purposeful. Reading Hegel in the British Museum in 1886, he would complain of the way these 'venerable philosophers...cannot get away from a prepossession that the world must somehow have been made to be a comfortable place for man' (*Life* 185). Two years earlier he questioned all teleological views of history:

> Is not the present quasi-scientific system of writing history mere charlatanism? Events and tendencies are traced as if they were rivers of voluntary activity, and courses reasoned out from the circumstances in which natures, religions, or what-not, have found them-

selves. But are they not in the main the outcome of *passivity* – acted upon by unconscious propensity? (175)

Another note from this period make it even clearer that Hardy can see in history 'nothing organic' or 'systematic':

It flows on like a thunderstorm-rill by a road side; now a straw turns it this way, now a tiny barrier of sand that. The offhand decision of some commonplace mind high in office at a critical moment influences the course of events for a hundred years. (179)

These passages, although written after the novel, clearly illustrate Hardy's adamantly non-teleological view of history.

This sense of history as lacking in direction and purpose clearly informs *The Trumpet-Major*. When Anne sees the King in Weymouth, for example, and for a moment feels herself 'close to and looking into the stream of recorded history, within whose banks the littlest things are great, and outside which she and the general bulk of the human race were content to live on as an unreckoned, unheeded superfluity' (*T-M* 93), she is shown to be doubly mistaken: first in thinking that history flows ever onwards to some great goal, and secondly in thinking that people such as her and the Lovedays are unimportant. It is their 'unwritten history' (18) which Hardy wants to recreate and to celebrate. Again, in chapter 34, when she actually meets the King, for a time succumbing to her mother's belief that Bob and John are 'both instruments in the hands of Providence, chosen to chastise that Corsican ogre' (246), she has the momentary illusion that her mentioning of Bob's name to the kindly old monarch will make a dramatic difference. But since 'she was not a girl who indulged in extravagant fancies long' she accepts that 'the King had probably forgotten her... and her troubles, and her lover's name' by the time she reached home (255). There is similar bathos in the chapter in which the Garlands, the Lovedays and half the village of Overcombe wait half the night for a glimpse of the King and his retinue on their route to Weymouth. The whole novel, in fact, could be called an exercise in disappointment, at least for those who are expecting great events. If *The Trumpet-Major* can be read as an historical novel at all, it is only in the sense of its contribution to *Kulturgeschichte*, the attempted recreation of the life of a period (Fleishman 1971: 186). It is the ordinary soldiers and their wives whom Anne finds interesting, wanting to invite one of the camp-followers into their house 'to acquire some of that practical knowledge of the history of England which the lady possessed, and which could not be got from books' (*T-M* 23–4). Only in this respect could the novel be aligned with Lukács, who claimed that the French Revolution and the rise and fall of Napoleon 'for the first time made history a *mass* experience', giving people an opportunity 'to comprehend their own experience as something historically conditioned, for them to see in history something which deeply affects their daily lives and immediately concerns them' (Ebbatson 1993: 47).

It is to two later theorists of history that Roger Ebbatson turns to make sense of *The Trumpet-Major*: Foucault is sceptical about history as 'that which transforms *documents* into *monuments*', holding out the illusory but ever-to-be-sought 'promise that one day the subject – in the form of historical consciousness – will once again be able to appropriate' such records and make sense of them (Ebbatson 1993: 49–50). Hardy's 1895 preface to the novel also recognises the difficulty of attempting 'to construct a coherent narrative of past times from the fragmentary information furnished by survivors' (*T-M* 3). Hayden White in *Metahistory* sees comedy as a mode of maintaining hope 'for the temporary triumph of man over his world by the prospect of occasional *reconciliations* of the forces at play' in history, reconciliations which are 'symbolised in the festive occasions' which terminate 'dramatic accounts of change and transformation: weddings, celebrations of triumphs in battle and so on' (Ebbatson 1993: 48). Hardy too focuses on the festivities of the Lovedays as 'occasional reconciliations' of this kind. He makes no attempt to fit history into a grander narrative.

As in his earlier novels, the reading of documents, as Valentine Cunningham has shown, occupies a significant part of this novel. The characters are 'all constantly engaged in acts of reading: literal reading of books and newspapers and letters and other publications' as well as metaphorical reading, trying to make sense of what they see (Cunningham 1994: 98). The 'delightful privilege of reading history in long columns' (*T-M* 41), of inheriting the newspaper which Squire Derriman buys, has to be earned by Anne reading it to him. The subsequent fate of the paper is an extraordinary history in itself, as it is passed on from the Garlands 'to the miller, the miller to the grinder, and the grinder to the grinder's boy', ending 'its career as a paper cap, a flagon-bung, or a wrapper for his bread and cheese' (42). Other documents which are the source of much complicated deciphering include Bob's letters, his marriage licence, in which he finds 'beautiful language' but in which his father cannot 'see the real meaning' (153), the genuinely historical 'Address to All Rank and Descriptions of Englishmen', reproduced in its entirety (165–6), and the 'final and revised list of killed and wounded' on board the *Victory*. This, however, is dismissed as a 'useless' sheet 'since it includes only officers, the friends of ordinary seamen and marines being on that occasion left to discover their losses as best they might' (257).

Other texts read or performed in the course of the novel include the ballads sung at the miller's party, the play seen at Weymouth, the despatches read by the King at that performance, a verse of Psalm 107, begun by Anne and completed by John (*T-M* 253), the Burial of the Dead at Sea (for a while Anne's favourite reading), and the deeds to Overcombe Hall (one of the many documents hidden in boxes, their secrets requiring to be unlocked). References in the novel to other literary texts include the Bible, Shakespeare, Tennyson and a variety of eighteenth-century plays and novels which help to establish its period feel (xxiv). The opening sentence, with its reference to 'the days of high-waisted and muslin-gowned women' and 'two ladies of good report, though . . . limited means' (11) immediately conjures up the world of Jane Austen (Millgate 1971: 149) while the novel can be said to self-consciously rewrite *Persuasion*, whose heroine also waits patiently (if somewhat more constantly) for the return of the sailor she loves (*T-M* xxxi). Hardy reread Smollett while preparing for *The Trumpet-Major*, reproducing in his own novel the sardonic style of chapter-heading to be found in a novel such as *Sir Lancelot Greaves*. Anne Garland has been seen to bear a resemblance to Sophia in *Tom Jones*, especially in her baiting of Festus and theft of his horse, while Matilda is reminiscent of Mrs Waters (Johnson 1976: 48–9). Hardy's 'Trumpet-Major' Notebook includes an impressive list of over thirty eighteenth-century plays, at least some of which he appears either to have read or seen performed (taking advantage of his move to London) in preparation for the writing of this novel (*PN* 161–2). Festus should thus be seen as a character out of Goldsmith's *She Stoops to Conquer* (Turner 1998: 71). The list of similarities and borrowings could no doubt be longer but the point remains the same. *The Trumpet-Major* may 'appear artless enough at a first reading' but much of the success of the novel (and perhaps some of its failure) results from precisely what the reviewers of *The Return of the Native* had called for, 'an art that conceals art' (Sanders 1978: 247). Hardy's contemporaries may have found Festus and Benjy more amusing than modern readers can. But, as with his earlier attempts at pastoral, to the reader-friendly qualities of which he was self-consciously returning, there is more going on beneath its bland surface than at first meets the eye.

A Laodicean: penetrating Paula, or the will to power

A Laodicean is widely considered to be Hardy's worst novel, 'in the opinion of most critics – a fairly disastrous failure' (Millgate 1971: 166). Most of the novel was dictated from his sick-bed to Emma, whose involvement in the very act of writing may have cramped his style (Taylor 1982: 99). But Hardy began the project with confidence, demanding and receiving £100 per number from *Harper's New Monthly Magazine*, who wanted something special for the first issue of their new European Edition. *Harper's Monthly* could offer many advantages, including a circulation of 10,000 (Brake 1994: 107), although, as Henry Harper explained to Howells, there were some subjects 'at any approach to which' the censor 'rang a little bell', a bell to whose 'tinkle' authors learnt to attune (Harper 1912: 321–2). 'I am not quite sure at present,' Hardy declared, 'whether the story will conveniently run to thirteen numbers, but if it can be made to do so without prejudice to the narrative I will thus arrange it' (*Letters* I 75). He fell ill after only thirteen chapters, however, and although he remained 'determined to finish the novel, at whatever stress to himself' (*Life* 150), appears not to have been able to maintain the ambition of the opening chapters – the large issues they introduce.

Florence Henniker must have remarked on the quality of the opening chapters when she read them in 1893, eliciting from Hardy the reply, 'Yes: the opening of "A Laodicean" is generally considered good. But think how I was handicapped afterwards' (*Letters* II 25). He claimed in a note in her copy of the novel that 'the original conception was but partially carried out' (Millgate 1971: 165). 'It was an awful job', he later confided to Edmund Gosse (*Letters* V 237) but this should be read with reference to the process rather than the product. There is at least a good phenomenological answer to the question adapted from Thurber, which Millgate poses to Paula, 'What do you want to be inscrutable *for*?' (Millgate 1971: 166). Paula provides a fascinating example of Hardy's tendency to characterise *from the outside*, to present his heroines in particular through the eyes of the other characters, leaving his readers alternately puzzled, provoked, fascinated, and even titillated by their mysterious interiority. The main point of the novel, as some contemporary reviewers recognised, is to explore the constantly frustrated desire (both of readers and of characters) to penetrate the mystery that is Paula. The novel also raises questions of power arising both from her gender and her ambiguous class position as the daughter of a self-made man, a member of the aristocracy of talent rather than birth.

These subtleties do not appear to have carried much weight with Hardy's publishers. As a result of a conversation with Henry Holt, in whose Leisure Hour series the novel was to appear, the *New York Tribune* announced,

> The hero of the "Laodicean" is flat, the heroine is a bundle of inso-lent caprices, and the men and women who surround them are alike tame or disagreeable. It only adds to the injury Mr. Hardy has in-flicted upon his readers that he has cleverly compelled them to take an interest in the final stupidities of two most uninteresting people.
>
> (Weiner 1978: 151).

Holt subsequently promised to 'say no more concerning "A Laodicean" to anyone' (151) but Henry Alden, editor of *Harper's Magazine*, shared his low opinion of the novel, acknowledging only a month after the serial had ended,

> Mr. Hardy has pitched his new romance, *A Laodicean*, on a lower and feebler key than usual. Compared with the best of his former novels, its movement is languid, its actors tame and colourless, and its plot and incidents hackneyed. Hitherto one of the most unconventional of modern novelists, in this story he rivals the most conventional.

Hardy's admirers would look in vain, Alden warned, for 'the powerful scenic and dramatic effects' or for 'the intensely realistic delineations of picturesque aspects of common life among the agricultural labourers ...and the vivid descriptions of heath and fen and moorland scenery that have characterized the strongest of his previous performances' (Weber 1946: 46–7). Holt and Alden had clearly expected (and paid for) another *Return of the Native*. What they got, as the *Observer* (2.11.82) pointed out, was more akin to *The Hand of Ethelberta*.

Hardy worked hard on revising the serial for the first edition, the version which would be reviewed. Some of the dramatic endings of separate instalments of the serial, often blatant examples of the artificial creation of suspense to induce readers to stay with the story, were smoothed over by being placed halfway through chapters of the first edition. Part Six of the serial, for example, ends with the porter's an-nouncement of Havill's wife's death, whose relative unimportance for the development of the novel as a whole is more suitably reduced to mid-chapter in the first edition (Vann 1985: 15). There are other less obvious examples of Hardy moving chapter divisions in order to avoid artificial

climaxes created solely for the serial version (85–6). He also made significant if small changes to his presentation of Paula, telling Mrs Orr, who
wrote to congratulate him on the serial, 'If you should ever have time to
look into the library form of the book you will find that some crudities in
Paula's character etc. (which invariably occur in writing from month to
month) have been smoothed out – I hope to her advantage' (*Letters* VII
94). He would later claim in a 1912 postscript to the Preface,

> the character of Paula, who on renewed acquaintance, leads me to
> think her individualized with some clearness, and really lovable, . . . is
> of that reserved disposition which is the most difficult of all dispos-
> itions to depict, and tantalized the writer by eluding his grasp for
> some time.
>
> (*AL* 380–1)

It may be a characteristic of modernity to strive after certain knowledge,
to want to 'grasp' the whole truth, but Hardy's otherwise ultra-modern
heroine is supposed to tantalise readers too by her impenetrable reticence.

The smoothing out of Paula's 'crudities', making her 'less dominant',
'more restrained in her physical movements' and 'less sensual or sexual-
ized' was presumably designed to 'avoid the censure of the critics' (*AL*
xxxv–vi). The serial has her challenge her lesbian friend Charlotte, 'Is
not that pretty?' as she performs her acrobatics in the gym. This is toned
down in the first edition: 'Is not that shocking to your nerves?' (Hardy
1975: 18). Among other examples of the greater focus on her sexual
allure in the serial are the description of 'the red line of her lips . . .
a scarlet thread upon the white skin around' as she hovers at the edge
of the baptismal pool (*AL* 385) and Somerset's imagining that 'her daily
vocabulary might include (mentally at least) such words as flirtation,
polka-mazurka, true-lover's knot, meet-me-by-moonlight alone' (386).
In similar vein he observes 'two or three pairs of silk stockings' (388) –
fodder for hours of fetishistic meditation – scattered carelessly on the
floor of her room only in the serial version. Paula herself behaves in a
more come-hither fashion in the serial, displaying 'archness' and
'bestowing on him a smiling look of recognition' (392–3). She not
only provokes 'rose-coloured thoughts' in him (393) but colours herself
in 'nameless sympathy with his feelings' (394). The word 'flirtation' by
which Somerset himself characterises their relationship in the serial
(395) is toned down to 'community of interest' in the first edition (76)
while her 'bottomless eyes' lose their 'seductive' quality in the first

edition (395). The flower on her bosom no longer excites Somerset by rising and falling 'like a boat on a tideway' (397) but only 'somewhat more than usual' in the first edition (97). All these changes reveal Hardy deliberately subduing Paula's sexual provocativeness.

Paula continued to evolve textually, becoming more emotional (and more easily readable) in 1882 with the addition of 'tears in her eyes for one gone', which reveal her underlying feelings for Somerset. In 1896 she becomes more outspoken about the 'idea of his dancing with a woman of that description' when she finally catches up with him in Entretat (414). Further additions in 1912 make her abandon herself to 'long and silent tears' (411) and speak 'in a perceptibly husky note' indicative of suppressed emotion (414). Hardy thus establishes her motives without making her too transparent. It is a difficult balancing act: she has to be mysterious and enigmatic in order to offer a challenge to her suitors (and her readers) but she cannot afford to be too inscrutable or they will abandon the quest altogether.

Paula's provocative impenetrability presented a particularly difficult challenge to the illustrator of the serial, George du Maurier, to whom Hardy only turned after Helen Allingham and Frank Dicksen declined the invitation (Jackson 1982: 48). Du Maurier complained to friends about the way Hardy 'gave him the points minutely', wanting to read the relevant passages to him aloud and to monitor every stage of the drawing (50–2). The resultant portraits of Paula vary considerably from 'the almost disembodied candidate for baptism' of the first instalment to 'the curvaceous drawing-room hostess' who appears in later months (*AL* 419). Du Maurier pressed Hardy to let him know 'by what feelings all the guests are animated toward each other' at the luncheon party in the second instalment (DCM 2254). Having made his name in *Punch* with satirical portraits of 'English Society at Home', he seems to have been happier with crowded scenes than with individual portraits. He certainly complained of having too few figures to work on in the third instalment (2257), pleading with Hardy to 'Think of the poor artist' and provide him with 'a [dramatic] scene in every number' (Jackson 1981: 52). The most forceful presence in many of his illustrations is not Paula but Sir William de Stancy, which may explain why Mrs Orr, writing to Hardy after reading the final number, felt that de Stancy 'seemed intrinsically as suitable a husband as the other man' (DCM 4647). Hardy claimed to be 'much pleased' by her view that 'poetic justice did not demand Somerset's success too exclusively' (*Letters* VII 93), but she seems to have missed the point, that the aristocracy of talent should replace that of birth.

The earliest reviews unsurprisingly focused on the novel's enigmatic heroine. Britten in the *Athenaeum* (31.12.81) thought Paula 'the most charming of Mr. Hardy's heroines' although he complained about the author's continued insistence on 'the physical charms of women' (Cox 1970: 95). Arthur Barker in the *Academy* (7.1.82) also feared that the novel would appeal to 'coarser and vulgar natures' (xxiii–iv). The *Saturday Review* (14.1.82) felt that Hardy 'has not sufficiently explained his heroine's character'. It recognised that not all readers would welcome the new direction in which Hardy had turned, missing 'the accustomed rustic flavour', but the novelist 'cannot be expected to go on for ever turning precisely the same kind of work which first made him famous'. The *Morning Post* (19.1.82) welcomed this 'entirely new direction', which proved that he could deal with characters 'from the higher walks of life' not simply with 'rustic subjects'. The *Court Circular* (28.1.82) thought it ranked 'with the best works of English fiction', the *Daily News* of the same date praised its 'subtle and minute study of character', while the *Globe* (17.2.82) found 'real grandeur' and commendable idealism in its heroine.

Not all the reviews were enamoured with Paula. The New York *Critic* (25.2.82) called her an 'unworthy heroine'. The *Spectator* (4.3.82), while (pruriently?) praising Hardy's ability to create female characters who 'stand out prominently in the minds of readers', thought she displayed 'a want of natural refinement and touch of vulgarity... in keeping with her plebeian origin' and was 'sometimes as puzzling to the reader as she was to her lovers'. It was left to the *Observer* (2.4.82) to explain that this was the point: 'it is evidently part of Mr. Hardy's plan... to leave her incomprehensible'. Havelock Ellis also saw Hardy's narrative method as the key to understanding the novel. Abjuring 'the subjective method' which dealt 'directly with mental phenomena', Hardy confined himself exclusively to external observation. He never penetrated Paula's inner thoughts, which is why she remained 'an enigma for us as she is for Somerset'. This insistence that his readers work out for themselves what was taking place in his characters was for Ellis 'a distinct note of Mr. Hardy's art' (Cox 1970: 124–7).

Ellis's view of Hardy, however, pleasing as it was to Hardy himself (DCM 2284), was by no means common among his contemporaries. The novel did not sell well and was remaindered to Mudie within two months of publication (Purdy 1954: 40). It continued to baffle critics. J. M. Barrie thought both of Hardy's 'Society novels', *A Laodicean* and *Two on a Tower*, not only 'dull' but 'nasty' (159). W. P. Trent felt 'the story as a whole... not representative of him at his best'. Both monographs of

1894 lambasted it, Annie Macdonell criticising its style and Lionel Johnson calling it 'annoying' and 'distasteful' (Johnson 1923: 55–6). Abercrombie found 'less of the Hardy that matters in *A Laodicean* than in any other of his books (Abercrombie 1912: 69) while Beach too complained that there was 'not enough of Wessex' and 'too much of smart life' in it (Beach 1922: 118).

The chorus of critical disapproval has continued: for David Cecil it was Hardy's 'worst work' (Cecil 1943: 142), for Carl Weber 'the poorest novel he had ever written' (Weber 1965: 127), and for J. I. M. Stewart 'Hardy's only unredeeemed failure' (Stewart 1963: 37). Norman Page laughed at its 'clumsy' and often 'downright ludicrous' vocabulary' (Page 1977: 110). Even critics who discuss the serious issues the novel raises, Bullen, for example, bringing out the Arnoldian and Ruskinian debates underlying Hardy's exploration of the modern condition, feel the need to acknowledge a failure not only of resolution but of imagination (Bullen 1986: 118). Valentine Cunningham commends Hardy's even-handed representation of nonconformity at the start of the novel, but acknowledges 'its degeneration into one of Hardy's worst novels' (Cunningham 1975: 15). Jay Clayton, while enjoying the novel's creation of a 'queer space' in which Hardy is allowed to play with lesbian elements in Paula's temperament, has to admit an 'uncertainty of tone' which detracts from the 'fascinating touches' to be found within it (Clayton 1997: 219). The plot, in Barbara Hardy's words, is 'ludicrously implausible' (Hardy 1975: 23), irrecuperable in terms of the tragic realist Hardy of widespread critical acclaim (Fisher 1992: 99). But there are a number of aspects worthy of closer attention, not the least of which are its phenomenological and political concerns, its exploration of the processes of perception, and its awareness of the modern 'fluctuation' of classes as well as creeds. The novel can be said to dramatise the will to power both in terms of interpretive and of political mastery.

It is unlikely, as Schad admits, that Hardy would have been familiar with Nietzsche's discussion of the will to power, which started to enter his work later in the 1880s. So it may simply be coincidence therefore that two of the villains in this novel are called Will and the object of their desire Power (*AL* xxviii). Paula's impenetrability, however, has been seen to expose as unrealistic the 'phenomenological assumption about reading' that it is possible fully to recover or recreate the original object intended by the text. The 'happy and passive reading' described by Poulet 'does not work in *A Laodicean*' (Austin 1989: 211–12) There is no hidden secret or truth beneath the signs that constitute Paula's character, 'no hidden signifieds' waiting for us to grasp (218), merely a blank surface upon which readers and suitors alike attempt to inscribe meaning.

In dramatising the absence of a solid, fixed or stable centre of meaning in his gymnastic heroine Hardy can be seen to anticipate postmodern scepticism about identity. It may bother Charlotte de Stancy that appearances are deceptive, that Dare can so doctor a photograph of Somerset that he can appear drunk, 'as if God's sun should bear false witness' (*AL* 335), but Paula seems well aware of the extent to which 'reality and truth' about the self are 'discursively produced' or performed (Thomas 1999: 96). From the moment that Somerset's expectations about what will be taking place inside the Baptist chapel are so dramatically disrupted in the second chapter of the novel, the novel stages the 'persistent misreading of appearances' on the part of its protagonists (*AL* 101). Somerset wonders what kind of man will have 'wrestled with himself' and 'worked up his courage' for such a trying ceremony, only to discover that the initiand is in fact a woman. Since he cannot see her face, 'His imagination, stimulated by this beginning, set about filling in the meagre outline with most attractive details' (10–11). Finally vouchsafed a view of her face, Somerset claims to detect 'a clandestine, stealthy inner life which had very little to do with her present outward one' (12). Like any reader of fiction, in terms of Iser's description of the phenomenology of reading, he quickly builds a picture of Paula, filling in any missing details with the help of his own imagination.

What Paula really wants, what her inner thoughts are, is the subject of continual speculation throughout the novel, with the narrator refusing to grant his readers any greater insight than his characters. We see only what they see. Like Somerset, we are given a number of clues by the reading matter distributed around her room, by what Charlotte tells him and by the way in which she does so, blushing 'as if the person spoken of had been a lover rather than friend' (29). The landlord also describes the two friends as 'more like lovers than girl and girl' (42). Somerset's own sexual orientation, it should be recognised, is no more clear-cut; not only is Paula called 'more woman than Miss de Stancy, but more woman than Somerset was man' (57). The serial version of the novel claims that 'girls of sixteen would have pronounced him a man complete' (384), in contrast to Captain de Stancy, 'who would have been called interesting by women well out of their teens' (132). Manhood, for de Stancy, requires the regular consumption of alcohol and women, his resumption of interest in both causing him to rejoice that he has become 'a man again after eighteen years' (158). But then men, according to Paula, are 'a dreadfully encroaching sex' and 'being in the army makes them worse' (174).

Somerset's not being very much of a man appears almost to be an advantage in his pursuit of the Laodicean heroine, who is lukewarm not only in religion but in sexual orientation. He in turn appears unfazed, even positively attracted by her sexual ambivalence. Far from being dismayed by the closeness of the friendship between Paula and her companion, the way in which 'she clasped her fingers behind Charlotte's neck, and smiled tenderly in her face' (72) excites him almost as much as seeing her draw her 'forefinger across the marble face of the effigy' of a 'beautifully preserved... recumbent lady' who resembles Charlotte in the castle chapel (95). When she performs her gymnastics, her maid reports, 'she wears such a pretty boy's costume, and is so charming in her movements, that you think she is a lovely youth and not a girl at all' (149). Readers, like Somerset, uncertain of what she really thinks or wants, are also expected to find this tantalising.

Part of Paula's motivation in being so inscrutable, as she explains to Somerset on a number of occasions, is strategic: women's minds cannot afford to be as 'transparent' as their dresses (100). 'There are genuine reasons for women's conduct in these matters,' she tells Somerset, 'though it is sometimes supposed to be regulated entirely by caprice' (212). She resists his demands for a kiss just as Sue Bridehead retains control over when she sleeps with Jude, insisting, 'I don't want to go so far, and I will not' (213). Hardy continues to tantalise his readers as Paula does Somerset, holding out just enough hope for them both to continue. As she admits in one of her many letters to Somerset, 'a woman who is *only* a compound of evasions, disguises, and caprices, is very disagreeable' (235). She cannot, however, reveal her hand completely, as she explains in another letter (in a passage deleted in 1882): 'a declaration of love is always a mortifying circumstance to us' (239). Similarly, when her aunt suggests she could ease Somerset's mind by letting him know how she feels, she resists 'showing what I would rather conceal' (355). The joke in the final book is that the tables are finally turned, reversing the pattern of the previous books, in which Somerset has had to pursue her all over the continent. When she finally catches up with him, after finally revealing her feelings in 'roguish' manner, she vows never to run after him again, 'for it is not the woman's part' (366–7). The conventional models of masculine and feminine behaviour, however, have been sufficiently destablised for the final union of the two lovers to be left in doubt until the very end.

It is the fact that she is rich, of course, that gives Paula so much power. As Somerset ruefully remarks, 'She can afford to be saucy... considering the power that wealth gives her to pick and choose almost where she will' (241). De Stancy, whose castle she has inherited from her engineering father, dubs her 'Miss Steam-Power' (134), an aristocratic sneer at the source of her wealth. The original Laodiceans in the Book of Revelation, as Paula is told by her minister (14), made the mistake of thinking that their wealth was everything, unaware that they were really 'wretched, and miserable, and poor, and blind, and naked' (Rev 3:16–17). Not that Hardy is particularly reverential towards the minister, later to be described by John Masefield as 'the old geezer' who gets his 'clothes wet for nothing' (Lamont 1979: 102). He gives Paula weightier reasons than wealth for refusing to immerse herself in her father's faith, including an Arnoldian sense characteristic of the 'modern spirit' that the institutions she has inherited, the system of beliefs, 'by no means corresponds exactly with the wants of their actual life'. These words, from Arnold's essay on Heine, along with other passages from him that Hardy copied in his *Literary Notebooks* (Thomas 1999: 103–4), introduce into the novel large religious and political issues.

Somerset too is stimulated to ponder these great themes after following the telegraph wires he encounters, symbolic of modern technological progress, to their source in the medieval castle inhabited by Paula:

> There was a certain unexpectedness in the fact that the hoary memorial of a stolid antagonism to the interchange of ideas, the monument of hard distinctions in blood and race, of deadly mistrust of one's neighbour in spite of the Church's teaching, and of a sublime unconsciousness of any other force than a brute one, should be the goal of a machine which beyond everything may be said to symbolise cosmopolitan views and the intellectual and moral kinship of all mankind. (*AL* 18)

Somerset proceeds to marvel that the two daughters of 'antipodean families', Charlotte, whose father has been reduced from aristocratic splendour to 'roadside respectability' (36) and Paula, the offspring of a successful engineer, 'had broken down a barrier which men thrice their age and repute would probably have felt it imperative to maintain' (33), proving that class prejudice can be overcome. He preaches to Paula, who still hankers after external marks of power and prestige, about 'that other nobility – the nobility of talent and enterprise' to which she can genuinely lay claim (96). At the end of the novel, while bemoaning the burning of her castle, she too quotes Arnold on being 'a perfect representative of "the modern spirit" ' (379) having given Charlotte the surviving works of art as a gift 'from a representative of the old aristocracy of internationality to a representative of the old aristocracy of exclusiveness' (376). Her plan to rebuild on the old site suggests at least the possible replacement of the old class system by a more meritocratic social order.

It is significant, however, that these passages come from the beginning and end of the novel, written before and after the debilitating illness during which Hardy wrote the middle sections, which at times degenerate into travelogues. There are flashes of class feeling to be found after chapter 13 (the last to be written before the illness), for instance when the guests at Paula's garden party are 'so madly devoted to lawn-tennis that they had set about it like day-labourers at the moment of their arrival' (100) or when Somerset feels as much 'an outsider still' at the theatricals as he had at the Hunt Ball (204). There are undeniable *longueurs* to be endured, however, before the de Stancy family is finally displaced by the Arnoldian heroine, the embodiment of 'sweetness and light'. Paula herself meanwhile continues both to resist interpretation and to tantalise readers with the dream of ultimate possession.

Two on a Tower: playing games with readers

When Virginia Woolf read *Two on a Tower* in Italy in 1908 in order to decide whether Hardy was truly to be numbered 'among the Classics', her reaction was ambivalent. She could recognise 'a certain gaunt honesty in his way of setting to work', building a tower, putting an astronomer upon it and setting a beautiful lady in his way as a kind of experiment. Hardy's sincerity, his determination to observe 'certain aspects' of human nature and of the universe 'unflinchingly', command her respect. The story, however, she found 'fantastic', full of absurd complications, and Hardy himself, as always, uncomfortable 'with ladies who live in drawing rooms; his boots creak and he does not know where to put his hat'. This, she felt, endangered his status as a 'classic' in spite of the intensity and originality of his vision (Woolf 1990: 387). David Cecil would be even more blunt about Hardy's inability to portray a 'lady', numbering Lady Constantine among his 'stuffed dummies of high life' (Cecil 1943: 122).

It was to the writing of *Two on a Tower*, however, that Hardy would later date the beginning of his campaign to demolish 'the doll of English fiction' in order make room for the 'development of a more virile type of novel' (*Letters* I 250). He had been delighted to be asked to contribute a story to the *Atlantic Monthly*, a magazine for which he claimed to have 'long had a great liking and respect' (I 102). Under the editorship of

Thomas Aldrich, who had succeeded Howells in February 1881, 'Maga' gained the reputation of being 'the best edited magazine in the English language' (How 1919: 85). It also insisted on 'exclusive publication', so the novel 'stands alone' among his novels as 'one which was prepared by him with an American audience in mind from the start' (Weber 1946: 72, 76). The *Life* claims that Hardy invented the alliterative title, which he afterwards came to dislike, 'off-hand' (*Life* 155). But Aldrich, initially at least, appeared to approve. 'The title is striking,' he wrote on the arrival of the first instalment in March 1882, 'the story opens admirably, and I promise myself great pleasure for the months to come' (DCM 816). He was happy to give the novel 'the place of honour in the magazine – that is to say the opening pages' (817).

Hardy's honeymoon period with Aldrich, however, as with so many of his editors, was shortlived. Having initially admired 'the daring of the story', Aldrich was later to complain that he had asked for 'a family story' only to receive 'a story in the family way' (Rideing 1912: 286). The novel's concluding chapters, he told Hardy, had been 'not quite in the line of the *Atlantic*'. Not only had the whole situation been 'a little *risqué*' but the bishop was 'very unfairly used by your heroine'. If they were to accept any more of Hardy's work in their magazine therefore he would need to see the whole manuscript 'before beginning it' (818). Like Stephen before him, Aldrich, for whom 'reading proof was a sacrament' and whom later contributors came to regard as 'something of a martinet' (How 1919: 85–6), resented the way Hardy had deliberately smuggled past his censoring gaze material of an obscene and blasphemous nature.

R. B. Marston of Sampson Low, Marston, Searle & Rivington, the publishers of the first edition in England, claimed to have enjoyed the jarring quality of the novel: 'it was like getting a chilled shot (hard as steel) crashing into a favourite old double tooth when eating a delicious bit of pheasant – I mean when the sweetest and most womanly heroine of late years bolts that old Bishop'. Even he questioned Viviette's dying of happiness, however, thinking suicide might have been a more appropriate means of disposing of her. He was also puzzled by the discrepancy between the positive response of readers and the hysteria of some of the reviews, blaming Mudie and Smith for buying only half the numbers really required and thus 'putting the subscribers off until the first rush is over' (DCM 4198). But the novel quickly went into a 'second edition' in one volume as well as being widely pirated in the States (Purdy 1954: 47). Weber claims that at least twenty different American editions appeared before the end of the century (Weber 1946: 76).

The friends to whom Hardy sent advance copies made the usual approving noises. Kegan Paul enthused:

> You seem to have created several wholly new types of character, Swithin and Viviette especially, and it is no common tour de force that you enable the reader to retain his sympathy with the woman who perpetuates such a fraud on her husband. You introduce a marvellously comic touch in making the victim a Bishop.
>
> (DCM 4701)

Edmund Gosse also praised the novel. He had been expected to 'perceive, if nobody else does, what I have aimed at – to make science, not the mere padding of a romance, but the actual vehicle of romance' (*Letters* I 110). 'The plan of the story was carefully thought out', Hardy told him, although the actual writing had been 'lamentably hurried' and it would 'have been rewritten for the book form if I had not played truant and gone off to Paris' (I 114). Hardy expressed his usual amazement that anyone could find the novel objectionable:

> I get most extraordinary criticisms of T. on a T. Eminent critics write and tell me that it is the most original thing I have done – that the affair of the Bishop is a triumph of tragi-comedy... while other eminent critics *print* the most cutting rebukes you can conceive – show me (to my amazement) that I am quite an immoral person: till I conclude that we are never again to be allowed to laugh... (I 110).

To Anne Procter he distinguished between the response of the critics, who had been 'quite acid', and the public, who, 'by their buying, and enthusiastic letter-writing to me on the subject, show that their interest in it is greater than in anything I have done latterly' (I 114). What evidence he had for this is unclear: there is only one surviving letter of praise, apart from those of his friends Kegan Paul and Gosse (DCM 2033).

The critics, in fact, had not all been acid. The earliest review, in the *Daily News* (12.11.82), praised the 'artistic dexterity' with which Hardy had handled his limited cast of characters. It particularly liked the portrait of the two lovers, Swithin, 'the ardent young pursuer of science', and Viviette, 'whose nature swings like a pendulum between human passion and religion'. The *Athenaeum* (18.11.82) too admired the novel's 'ingenuity', claiming it was the first 'astronomical novel' ever to be published. It laughed at the 'impossible names' of the characters and at the alliterative title but praised the skilful manner in which Hardy trod his morally 'hazardous ground'. The *Saturday Review* of the same date objected in particular to the passing off onto the Bishop of the heroine's illegitimate child: 'a most repellent incident' (Cox 1970: 97–100). The *Pall Mall Gazette* (16.12.82) complained about the 'exasperating' quality of the novel while the *Morning Post* (28.12.82) laughed at the novel's 'quaint and fanciful title' and found its hero 'a rather improbable character'.

It was the review in the *St James Gazette* (16.1.83) which raised the temperature of the discussion. After outlining a number of positive qualities possessed by Hardy, including the ability to portray scenes and characters in vivid detail, and to create lively and credible dialogue, it deplored the 'disregard...of all moral purpose' apparent in creating 'a series of events which are more likely, on the whole, to shock than to please the majority of his readers'. The choice of a bishop to be the victim of Viviette's trick, it felt, had 'a suspicion of burlesque about it' and might 'even be regarded in certain quarters as a studied and gratuitous insult aimed at the Church'. If Hardy wanted to demonstrate 'the inexpediency of a love affair between a very young man and a woman some years his senior' he could have done so 'in a less repulsive way'.

Hardy chose to focus on the accusation of ecclesiastical burlesque, sending to the *St James Gazette* on 18 January perhaps the least credible of all his disclaimers of mischief:

> Will you allow me to state that...no thought of such an insult [to the Church] was present to my mind in contriving the situation. Purely artistic conditions necessitated an episcopal position for the character alluded to, as will be apparent to those readers who are at all experienced in the story-telling trade. Indeed, that no *arrière-pensée* of the sort suggested had existence should be sufficiently clear to everybody from the circumstance that one of the most honourable characters in the book, and the hero's friend, is a clergyman, and that the heroine's most tender qualities are woven in with her religious feelings.
>
> (Taylor 1982: 132)

It does not, however, take a particularly incisive reader to see that the Bishop is the butt of some almost blasphemous biblical citations while the 'honourable' clergyman is also the subject of much satire. Hardy's attempts to mystify the business of reading and telling stories add this letter to the many games that he would play with his readers not only in the text itself but in its margins, in letters, prefaces and later revisions.

Worse reviews were still to appear. Harry Quilter in the *Spectator* (3.2.83) gave an absurd account of a plot he pronounced 'as unpleasant as it is practically impossible', mingling 'passion, religion, and false self-sacrifice' in a 'repulsive' manner. The book was altogether 'bad, – the worst the author has written...It is melodramatic without strength, extravagant without object, and objectionable without truth' (Cox 1970: 101–2). The American response was no more positive. The *Nation* (11.1.83) puzzled over Hardy's intentions in producing this 'strange mixture of love and astronomy' while even Harriet Preston in the *Century,* normally a staunch admirer of Hardy, found the element of 'intrigue...insufferably low' and the character of its heroine 'a pathological study' (Weber 1965: 135).

The 1895 Preface to the novel quotes some of the most offensive phrases from these reviews, deliberately refuting two views of the book expressed on its publication:

first, that the novel was an 'improper' one in its morals, and, secondly, that it was intended to be a satire on the Established Church of this country. I was made to suffer in consequence from several eminent pens, such warm epithets as 'hazardous', 'repulsive', 'little short of revolting', 'a studied and gratuitous insult', being flung at the precarious volumes.

These quotations were dropped in 1902 but all versions of the Preface retain the claim that

those who care to read the story now will be quite astonished at the scrupulous propriety observed therein on the relations of the sexes; for though there may be frivolous, and even grotesque touches on occasion, there is hardly a single caress in the book outside legal matrimony, or what was intended so to be.

Hardy is again being disingenuous, deliberately misleading: there only needs to be a 'single caress' for a child to be conceived and he had actually revised this edition to identify explicitly when it takes place. There is even a suggestiveness about the claim in the Preface, that 'the Bishop is every inch a gentlemen' while it is simply untrue that 'the parish priest who figures in the narrative is one of its most estimable characters' (*TT* 289).

The games Hardy plays with his readers over the exact date of the conception of Viviette's illegitimate child are particularly devious in this 1895 edition of the novel. The first edition had specified only the date of the child's birth, 10 April. The one-volume edition of 1883 added the date of the final meeting between the two lovers, 7 July. These dates alone gave a fairly clear indication of the child's provenance. But

> in 1895, to make it entirely clear that the child was conceived on this occasion, Hardy introduces in the same chapter [36] the explicit information that 'Viviette yielded to all the passion of her first union with him,' and in Chapter 40 he adds this sentence to Viviette's letter to Swithin: 'I ought not to have consented to that last interview; all was well till then!'
>
> (Taylor 1982: 134)

The Wessex Edition continues the game, making Parson Torkingham tell Swithin on his return from Africa that her child is 'remarkably fine' for 'a seven-months' baby' (xxxvii).

It was with this novel, Havelock Ellis acknowledged in 1896, that 'the general public...began to suspect that in reading Mr. Hardy's books it was not treading on the firm rock of convention' (Cox 1970: 304). 'Disagreeable' and 'nasty' were two of the adjectives applied to it (153). Mrs Oliphant wrote in 1892 of its 'grotesque and indecent dishonesty' (203) while W. P. Trent complained of its 'repulsiveness' (230). Andrew Lang objected both to 'the practical joke on the clergyman' and the 'warmth' of the widow so 'conspicuously dwelt upon' (241). Lionel Johnson, while sympathising with the 'sentimental pleasure' Lady Constantine found in her young lover, convicted her of 'indiscretion' (Johnson 1923: 198). Lascelles Abercrombie admired the 'exquisite melancholy' to be found in this novel (Abercrombie 1912: 91) but Charles Whibley the following year found a real 'spirit of mischief' in its writing (Cox 1970: 418).

Hardy's claim that no satire against the Church was intended rings particularly hollow in the face of the sustained subversion of conventional Christianity provided by the novel. Not only are all the clergy presented satirically as struggling unsuccessfully to impose middle-class values upon their reluctant and often rebellious parishioners but biblical references are employed subversively throughout the novel. Swithin's father is the first clergyman in this novel to find the call of nature stronger than his vocation, suffering social ostracism for marrying a farmer's daughter, 'a playward piece o'flesh' to whom 'the toppermost folk wouldn't speak'. Then, in Amos Fry's account,

> he dropped a cuss or two, and said he'd no longer get his living by curing their twopenny souls o' such nonsense as that ... and he took to farming straightway, and then 'a dropped down dead in a nor'west thunder-storm, it being said hee-hee! – that Master God was in tantrums wi'en for leaving his service. (*TT* 14)

Amos himself, in spite of his prophetic name, retains no more belief in 'such trumpery about folks in the sky, nor anything else that's said on 'em, good or bad' (14), than his creator.

Parson Torkingham, the supposedly 'estimable' clergyman in the novel, is little more effective, especially in his role as choirmaster. The first edition portrays him singing 'Onward, Christian Soldiers' (altered in 1912 to Psalm 53) 'in notes of rigid cheerfulness' (18, 265). The Psalm is particularly appropriate, since it involves the Lord looking 'down from Heav'n's high tower/The sons of men to view', only to discover that 'they are altogether become filthy' (Psalm 53:3). Mr Torkingham at this stage in the novel merely discovers his choir's 'defective ... pronunciation' and succeeds only in eliciting from them an exaggerated echo of his own upper-class vowels, a subservience which he rewards with approval 'in the strenuously sanguine tones of a man who got his living by discovering a bright side in things where it was not very perceptible to other people' (*TT* 19). He succeeds in striking fear into the heart of Lady Constantine by reciting the 'Commination, or Denouncing of God's Anger and Judgements against Sinners' assigned by the Book of Common Prayer to Ash Wednesday, the climax of which invokes a curse upon all fornicators and adulterers. She is made to feel even more guilty when she reads 'the portion of the eastern wall whereon the ten commandments were inscribed' (77). The Church continues to play a somewhat farcical role in her life when the stand-in clergyman deputed to marry her fails to appear and is found wandering around the churchyard under the misconception that he is supposed to be conducting a funeral. The clerk proceeds to explain that they could only obtain 'a weak-talented man or none' to deputise for the regular incumbent because 'the best men goes into the brewing, or into the shipping now-a-days ... doctrines being rather shaddery at present' (126).

Hardy conjures up an astonishing array of recondite biblical allusions in this novel, nearly all of which, directly or indirectly, undermine the

Church's teaching on sexual matters. Swithin's hut, for example, in which the love-making takes place, is as 'small as the prophet's chamber provided by the Shunamite' (*TT* 123). In II Kings 4, the Shunamite who prepares a small chamber for the prophet Elisha is rewarded by conceiving a son, despite her advanced age. For the unmarried Lady Constantine, however, to conceive a child is hardly a reward. A less obscure biblical reference to a hero seduced by a woman occurs later in the novel when Swithin, like Samson, breaks the trap set for him by Louis (184). More controversially, Hardy likens Viviette's 'despising the shame' of bearing an illegitimate child (235) to Christ's submitting to crucifixion in Hebrews 12:2. Later, sensing possible salvation in marriage to the Bishop, the narrator blasphemously transfers to her the biblical words used of Abraham's discovery of a ram as a vicarious substitute for his son: 'behold – here was a way!' (242)

The treatment of the Bishop, who cuts an absurd figure throughout the novel, is clearly designed to offend Hardy's more orthodox readers. When he arrives at Welland to conduct the confirmation service, it is clear that his interest in Lady Constantine is far from spiritual. He comically misreads her calm and relaxed demeanour, a result of her 'recently gratified affection' for Swithin, as 'a sweet serenity, a truly Christian contentment, which puzzled the learned Bishop exceedingly to find in a warm young widow' (149). The Bishop, like his vicar, struggles to appear different from other people, so when Lady Constantine fails to appear at dinner that evening, he endeavours 'to mould into the form of episcopal serenity an expression which was really one of common human disappointment' (152). Swithin, who sees him as 'an opinionated old fogey' (190), marvels at his nerve: 'to lecture me, and love you, all in one breath' (207–8). His hesitation before risking a second proposal is seen to disclose a mind motivated merely by 'fear of danger to its own dignity' (255). He emerges from this renewed proposal, in which he had 'a pleader on his side whom he knew little of', pompously celebrating both 'the persuasive force of trained logical reasoning' and the wisdom that taught his wife not 'to despise Heaven's gift' (260–1). The final lines of the novel comprise a pastiche of melodrama (in which the erring woman is always punished): 'Viviette was dead. The Bishop was avenged' (281). This cannot, however, be taken at face value as the conclusion of a novel in which the Bishop and his Church have been represented throughout as vengeful (thundering Comminations against sinners), hypocritical (pretending to a difference from the rest of humanity which they do not display), interfering (in other people's private affairs) and destructive (attempting to separate those who truly love each other). Only a malevolent religion, it is implied, could regard the heroine's death as a form of divine punishment.

The sexual longings of Lady Constantine, as of Lawrence's Lady Constance, are portrayed sympathetically throughout the novel. There are in fact, as Roger Ebbatson has observed, several similarities between this novel and *Lady Chatterley's Lover*: both heroines languish of ennui, neglected or abandoned by their husbands. The 'symbolic configurations of landscape' in the two stories are also similar: 'the great, gloomy house, the park, and the woods, with the "sanctuary" of tower or cottage' and the adjacent huts in which the heroines escape from their cold and hostile external world to a warm, idyllic sexual interior (Ebbatson 1977: 89, 93). The tower, dominating the landscape at which the bored Lady Constantine stares, is an unambiguous phallic symbol, 'erected as the most conspicuous and ineffaceable reminder of a man that could be thought of' (*TT* 6). The eyes of Viviette and her servant (whose very name is Nobbs) are portrayed in the second paragraph as 'bent...upon this object' (5) in a manner similar to that in which Arabella and Jude regard the fragment of pig hanging from the bridge in the first edition of *Jude the Obscure* (*JO* 40). The narrator, as in Lawrence, dwells on the beauty of the 'erection' (*TT* 4) as a thing not to be ashamed of, the lower part being surrounded by firs while the upper part 'rose into the sky a bright and cheerful thing, unimpeded, clean, and flushed with sunlight' (7). It is difficult not to suspect here as much a desire to shock and as strong a resentment of the Church's denial of sexuality as in Lawrence.

Equally shocking to Hardy's contemporaries would have been the way Hardy plays with Swithin's sexual 'awakening' like Shakespeare with the young man of his affection whose 'darling buds' are shaken by 'rough winds' in Sonnet 18. In spite of the 'tardiness of his awakening,' we are told of Swithin, 'like a spring bud hard in bursting, the delay was compensated by after speed' (84). Viviette's age, which brings 'superiority of experience and ripeness of emotion', becomes the object of 'peculiar fascination over him as over other young men in their first ventures in this kind'. The narrator again turns to Shakespeare, this time to Sonnet 115, which advocates the immediate consummation of love, to convey Swithin's eagerness 'to register his assertion in her heart before any of those accidents which "creep in 'twixt vows, and change decrees of kings"' (85). As with his biblical allusions, Hardy employs the 'respectable' Shakespeare to circumvent Mrs Grundy, subtly celebrating the introduction of a young man to the delights of sexuality.

Swithin himself is the vehicle for a more direct attack on the metaphysical beliefs of the Church. Havelock Ellis picked up the novel's many echoes of Richard Proctor, author of some seventy books on astronomy (Cox 1970: 125). What more recent critics have noticed, however, is the manner in which Hardy transforms this material. For while Proctor sought to illustrate 'the wonders of God's universe' and 'to reconcile his belief in God's goodness with evidence of planetary extinction', Hardy abandons Proctor's increasingly 'desperate attempts at comfort, to offer a far bleaker vision of the cosmos' (*TT* xxi). Swithin clearly takes a certain gruesome delight in acquainting Lady Constantine with the terrifying discoveries of astronomy until she begs him to stop: 'It makes me feel that it is not worth while to live – it quite annihilates me' (32–3). It is difficult not to see behind the beautiful young Swithin lecturing his enamoured Viviette, the stern Hardy browbeating his readers into abandoning their false and shallow optimism.

There is an additional irony in the way Viviette at first insists that the subject of Swithin's lecture has 'completely crushed' the love she came to talk to him about (35). For one of the purposes of this novel, according to the opening paragraph of its 1895 Preface, is 'to set the emotional history of two infinitesimal lives against the stupendous background of the stellar universe, and to impart to readers the sentiment that of these contrasting magnitudes the smaller might be the greater to them as men' (289). Hardy, like Swithin, may wish to bludgeon any lingering theological belief out of his audience but retains a humanism which continues to place a high value on the feelings and emotions of which individuals are capable, a Comtean suspicion of the dangers of reason alone unalleviated by the 'affective faculties' (xxii). This may help to explain at least in part the dynamics of the relationship between Swithin and Viviette. He teaches her the rudiments of astronomy while she attempts to impart to him the importance of the feelings, the beauty of 'the better heaven beneath' (88).

Hardy, it may be objected, wants to have it both ways, to bully his readers into a recognition that neither the universe nor the accidents of our life within it are ordered for human ends, and to illustrate, through the actions of his tragic heroine, that human beings are nevertheless capable of the highest altruism and love. There is no logical contradiction between these two beliefs, of course. But in terms of the response expected from his readers to the ending which he provides, he does appear to want them at the same time to laugh sardonically at the limitations of his characters (particularly Swithin and the Bishop) and to sympathise fully with his tragic heroine as she dies from joy at her lover's change of heart. Gatrell claims that 'it is the most generous ending that Hardy could conceive' (Gatrell 1986a: 89). But Hardy succeeds not only in killing off his heroine but in satirising both the Bishop (in the mock-Gothic final phrase) and Swithin, whose gaze cannot help alighting, even as his former love lies dying at his feet, upon Tabitha Lark, 'skirting the field with a bounding tread' (262).

Not only the Bishop therefore but the beautiful young hero are found finally to be unworthy of Lady Constantine. The sexual fulfilment of the lovers, like the happiness that the young heroine of his next novel can expect, is shown to have been merely a brief 'episode in a general drama of pain' (*MC* 322). Even the moments of comedy in the novel are of a very black kind, temporary escapes from the bleakness and absurdity of the human condition. It is scarcely surprising therefore that Hardy's contemporary readers found so much to dislike in the mischievous and subversive games he played with them.

5
'*Graphic* Tragedies:
Writing for Two Audiences'

The Mayor of Casterbridge: from melodrama to tragedy

Hardy's return to his native roots in the summer of 1883 is often seen as the most significant factor behind his writing of the four great tragic novels in the decade beginning in 1886 with *The Mayor of Casterbridge* (Millgate 1982: 249). It was not only to Wessex, however, that he owed this development but to his reading of contemporary debates about the novel, debates, as we shall see, in some of which his own work came under discussion. It was in the *The Mayor of Casterbridge* that he first adopted the practice of dividing his novels into two versions: one for a crude magazine readership wanting mere entertainment and the other aimed at a more sophisticated literary audience. Finally recognising the incompatibility of these two audiences, Hardy resolved no longer to compromise but to provide them with significantly different products.

Perhaps the most surprising feature of Hardy's work from 1883 to 1891 is that most of it appeared in the pages of the London *Graphic*, a weekly newspaper with a good reputation for illustrations but no great claim to 'literature'. It had been founded in 1869 as one of a new breed of newspapers benefiting from advances in the technology of wood engraving to make the news more accessible to a broader market of readers by providing illustrations of prominent events and personalities. Its 'ideology of production', according to Feltes, can be characterised as 'brevity and personality', reducing the most complex of issues to 'easily digestible portions' under headings such as 'Topics of the Week', 'Pastimes', 'Home', 'Foreign', 'The Court' and 'New Novels' (Feltes 1986: 67–8). The principle of brevity also governed its fiction, of which it began to include about two pages a week in 1873. Perhaps the most noticeable feature of its contents is the fascination with royalty: the silver wedding of the Prince and Princess Christian of Schleswig-Holstein and the marriage of the Princess Louise altogether displaced *Tess* from what should have been its second instalment (11.7.91) while the fiftieth birthday of the Prince of Wales caused a second gap in the sequence (7.11.91). But it also displayed an interest in the plight of the agricultural labourer, the front page of the issue which contained the sixth instalment of *The Mayor of Casterbridge* depicting a number of radical MPs such as Joseph Arch and Jesse Collings together with snippets of their speeches demanding improvements in their conditions (6.2.86). It had quickly become popular, its regular issues reaching a circulation of a quarter of a million while its special Christmas issues of 1881 and 1882 each sold over half a million copies (Law 2000: 133). It was clearly aimed at both genders, combining updates on sporting and military campaigns with a regular column entitled 'Place Aux Dames' introduced in 1891. Its advertisements juxtaposed 'Advice to Mothers' with 'Mexican Hair Renewer' (22.8.91).

As a 'family' newspaper the *Graphic* prided itself on its 'decency' and 'respectability'. It had become embroiled in a much-publicised dispute with Wilkie Collins in 1875 after contravening the terms of their agreement for *The Law and the Lady*, which contained a clause forbidding them to alter the text submitted by the author. Forced to reprint the sentence they had bowdlerised, describing a woman's attempted resistance to an unwanted embrace, the *Graphic* added a paragraph explaining that the story was 'not one which we should have voluntarily selected to place before our readers'. Collins in turn protested at this latest outrage perpetrated by 'that British Domestic Inquisition, otherwise known as the family circle' which the *Graphic* were so anxious not to offend (Collins 1992: 415–18). It was this anxiety and the desire to avoid similar embarrassments which dictated their insistence on an unusually long period of time between the submission of an author's manuscript and its appearance in print. Hardy, for example, had finished the manuscript of *The Mayor of Casterbridge* in April 1885, over eight months before it started to appear in the pages of the *Graphic*, and there would be a similar gap with *Tess* (Gatrell 1988: 76).

Hardy had first turned to the *Graphic* for 'The Romantic Adventures of a Milkmaid', 'a short hastily written novel' designed for their 'Summer Number' (*Life* 163), where it had been beautifully presented, the title appearing in a large Gothic typeface and each chapter beginning with ornate initial letters, as in an illuminated manuscript. Hardy's own attitude to this 'arrant pot-boiler', which went through multiple pirated editions in the United States, some selling for as little as three cents

(Weber 1946: 49), is clear from his refusal to publish it in volume form until 1913, when it appeared in the Wessex Edition of *A Changed Man* with the disclaimer that it had been 'written only with a view to a fleeting life in a periodical, and...was not deemed worth reprinting' (Purdy 1954: 49).

The Mayor of Casterbridge appears initially to have been designed for the same undiscerning audience, which would explain why Hardy again chose the *Graphic* alongside *Harper's Weekly* in the United States. Henry Alden, who had graduated from managing editor of *Harper's Weekly* to editor of *Harper's Magazine* in 1869, certainly believed that Hardy had begun *The Mayor of Casterbridge* with the intention of a producing 'a merely adventurous tale' such as that of the milkmaid but that 'the work had grown under his hand' into something greater (Cox 1970: xxv). The *Life* calls it

a story which Hardy fancied he had damaged more recklessly as an artistic whole, in the interest of the newspaper in which it appeared serially, than perhaps any other of his novels, his aiming to get an incident into almost every week's part causing him in his own judgment to add events to the narrative somewhat too freely.

(*Life* 185)

Since each instalment occupied just two pages of the paper, albeit in three columns of small print, its maximum length was three chapters, often ending mid-chapter. Hardy's diary entry for the day of the first issue attempted to allay fears that it would 'not be so good as I meant' by arguing that 'it is not improbabilities of incident but improbabilities of character that matter' (183). The *Life* maintains that 'at this time he called his novel-writing "mere journeywork",' caring 'little about it as art' although 'others' (among whom he includes Robert Louis Stevenson) 'thought better of it than he did'. He records as an example of 'mid-Victorian taste' the fact that he had 'some difficulty in getting it issued in volume-form, Mr James Payn the publishers' reader having reported to Mr Smith that the lack of gentry among the characters made it uninteresting'. Payn, himself a writer of sensation fiction, had no problem with the number of melodramatic incidents in the novel but Hardy can be seen still wrestling with the fear that they had fatally compromised the claims this novel could make to the status of art (186).

The Mayor of Casterbridge, even in its final form, retains many elements characteristic of sensation fiction:

excitement, suspense, surprises, mysteries, instalment closings known as 'curtains,' strongly delineated characters, numerous coincidences, disguises, misdirected letters, overheard conversations, bigamous or secret marriages, and illegitimacy.

(Allingham 2001: 41)

The serial version, however, as it appeared in the *Graphic* from January to May 1886, was even more obviously geared towards the sensational taste of what Mary Ellen Chase called 'the magazine public' as opposed to 'the Hardy reader' (Chase 1927: 26). In the serial, for example, Lucetta, rather than nursing Henchard through one of his 'gloomy fits' of depression (*MC* 77), rescues him from drowning after he falls out of a boat in the harbour. She then marries him, having had 'a foolish liking for him for more than five years'. In the book, by contrast, Henchard recounts how she 'got to have a foolish liking for him' after nursing him back to health, her warmth of feeling and disregard for appearances giving rise to 'a terrible scandal' (*MC* 77). On his first wife's reappearance, Henchard dispatches Farfrae to meet Lucetta at Budmouth, where, because she is seasick, she receives the letter incognito: 'a white hand and arm...stretched out from behind a red curtain' (*Graphic* 1886: 134–5). The serial version even manages to engineer a meeting between Henchard's two wives, the Mayor observing Susan seated on a bench beside 'a lady closely veiled, of graceful figure, wearing a Paisley shawl' (Chase 1927: 28). It had been her 'red Paisley shawl', along with her black veil, bonnet and dress, which had helped the reader to identify the wicked Miss Gwilt in Wilkie Collins's *Armadale* (Collins 1989: 125). Here it enables Henchard to recognise his first wife sitting with his second, as a result of which he looks understandably 'thunderstruck' (Chase 1927: 28).

The serial also milks the scene in which Lucetta meets Henchard in the Ring to beg for the return of her letters for all the melodrama, mystery and suspense that it can yield. In the book, in order to display how much she has suffered, Lucetta merely omits her customary toilette; the fact that she has not 'slept all the previous night' gives to her 'naturally pretty though slightly worn features the aspect of a countenance ageing prematurely from extreme sorrow' (*MC* 246–7). In the serial, however, she obtains 'disfiguring ointments' from a chemist to produce 'a countenance withering, ageing, sickly' and 'a head of hair with a few incipient grey threads'. The sight of her transformed self in a mirror is enough to elicit from her 'a shudder, almost...a terror'. The serial creates additional suspense by having Farfrae encounter them in the amphitheatre where he fails to recognise his wife in her uncharacteristic guise (Chase 1927: 37–40).

Another example of the serial's maximisation of all opportunities for melodrama occurs in the bull episode, which is given three times the space it occupies in the novel. In the serial the 'lily-white' Lucetta exclaims, 'It is all over with us now!' while Elizabeth-Jane grabs the staff attached to the bull's nose, 'the hot air from her antagonist's nostrils blowing over her like a sirocco' (32–3). Hardy clearly decided that the final version of the novel could do without such sensational touches. He also altered psychologically implausible elements in the serial, such as Elizabeth-Jane happily continuing to live with Henchard while regularly meeting with her biological father on the Budmouth Road. The characterisation of Elizabeth-Jane is altogether more developed in the book, in which she has knowledge, 'the result of great natural insight', though 'learning, accomplishments – those, alas, she had not' (*MC* 84). In the serial she lacks all three and only supplements this lack with a dictionary and a grammar; in the book she reads 'omnivorously' (127), learns Latin (131) and has an abundance of books around her room as a sign of 'her endeavours for improvement' (143). She is no longer simply pious as in the serial but 'subtle-souled . . . asking herself why she was born . . . why things around her had taken the shape they wore' and other difficult questions (116).

The *Graphic* placed a great deal of importance on its illustrations, which provided an acceptable reason for their requiring their manuscripts well in advance of publication. Robert Barnes's illustrations for *The Mayor of Casterbridge*, praised by Arlene Jackson both for their 'exceptional quality' (Jackson 1982: 55) and for their faithfulness to Hardy's text (105), drew attention not so much to its sensational elements as to its powerful depiction of character. Barnes's strength, according to Forrest Reid, lay in his ability to reproduce the robust solidity of 'the well-to-do farming class (Reid 1928: 256). He seems deliberately to have avoided direct depiction of the most melodramatic scenes: the wife-sale, the hand through the curtain, Farfrae meeting Henchard and Lucetta in the Ring, the bull-fight, and the Skimmington ride. Instead he chose to focus on Farfrae *telling* Lucetta about his encounter with Henchard and companion, Elizabeth-Jane meeting Farfrae *after* the bull has been brought under control and Lucetta and Elizabeth-Jane observing the spectacle of the ride. Perhaps the only melodramatic moment Barnes depicts is Henchard wrestling with Farfrae and exclaiming 'between his gasps, "Your life is in my hands."' (*MC* 270). Most of the illustrations, as Jackson remarks, 'are carefully linked to character revelation'. The portraits of Henchard capture his emotional path 'from haughtiness to anger and, finally, to despair' (Jackson 1981: 100) while Elizabeth-Jane, who appears in more illustrations than any other character in the novel (11 out of the 20), achieves a greater importance than she occupies in the text.

The book, published in an unfashionable two-volume format priced at a guinea by Smith, Elder in May 1886, sold badly, 150 copies of its small print run of 758 being remaindered to Sampson Low in January 1887 for the grand total of seven guineas (Cox 1970: xxiv, Purdy 1954: 53). It received a mauling from the critics. The earliest review, in the *Globe* (14.5.86) made fun of its original place of publication and genre, finding its 'graphic and vivid narrative' as full of incident and 'movement as a story of Charles Reade'. The *Athenaeum* (29.5.86) praised Hardy's 'wonderful knowledge of the minds of men and women, particularly those belonging to a class which better-educated people are often disposed to imagine has no mind' but rated this novel lower than *The Trumpet-Major* because it recounted the tragedy of 'a self-willed instead of an unselfish hero' (Cox 1970: 133). The *Saturday Review* of the same date (probably George Saintsbury) found it 'very slight and singularly devoid of interest', lacking 'a single character capable of arousing a passing interest in his or her welfare' (134–6). This came as no surprise, Hardy told Stevenson, since 'the Saturday man' always said 'my stories are dull' (*Letters* I 147). *John Bull* (19.6.86) found the novel 'too full of mannerisms', labelling Hardy 'an accomplished literary craftsman' rather than 'an artist of a higher type of genius'. The *World* (23.6.86) found the novel 'unpleasant, painful, oppressive', disliking its exclusive focus on the 'lower classes', while the High Church *Guardian* (28.7.86) took issue with the 'elaborately pessimistic' and 'unpleasantly cold-blooded' view of life expressed at the end of the book through Elizabeth-Jane. *Vanity Fair* (4.9.86) thought the book 'dull'.

Many of the reviews, however, picked up on the subtitle of the first edition: 'The Life and Death of a Man of Character'. Even the *Globe* recognised that this was 'precisely its subject' and that Henchard was 'a figure...likely to remain in the memory'. The *Whitehall Review* (20.5.86), the *State* (27.5.86) and the *Daily Telegraph* of the same date, all praised Hardy's portrait of Henchard. R. H. Hutton in the *Spectator* (5.6.86) probed the etymology of the word 'character' (from the Greek for something carved, cut or engraved):

Properly speaking, character is the stamp graven on a man, and character therefore, like anything which can be graven, and which,

when graven, remains, is a word much more applicable to that which
has fixity and permanence, than to that which is fitful and change-
ful...a man of character ought to suggest a man of steady and
unvarying character...But the essence of Michael Henchard is that
he is a man of large nature and depth of passion, who is yet subject to
the most fitful influences...

(Cox 1970: 137)

Hutton praised the vividness of Hardy's portrait of Henchard, however,
and the 'gentleness and wisdom' to be found in Elizabeth-Jane, in spite
of her 'fashionable pessimism' (138–9). Other reviews to focus on
Henchard included the *Scotsman* (24.6.86), who liked his 'manliness'
and 'grandeur' and the *Guardian*, who recognised in him 'the most
powerful and original portrait of a man' while objecting that he had
'character and nothing more – neither faith, nor principle, nor social
tradition – to shape his life'. The *Daily News* (30.9.86) also praised
Hardy's ability 'to reveal the inner nature of his imaginary folk', not
only Henchard but also 'the sweet, unselfish, and, though untaught,
essentially refined Elizabeth-Jane'. Other contemporary readers of the
novel testified to its power: Robert Louis Stevenson told Hardy Henchard was 'a great fellow' (*Life* 186) while Morley Roberts wrote to Gissing
from British Columbia, admitting that he had 'nearly snivelled' over
Henchard's will (Mattheissen 1990: III 42). The misogynistic Gerard
Manley Hopkins loved 'the wife-sale' (Abbott 1935: 239), though
W. D. Howells thought this a rather 'old-fashioned way' of attempting
to seize the attention of readers. Like Alden, Howells felt that 'Hardy
seems to have started with an intention of merely adventurous fiction';
when he 'found himself in possession of something so much more
important...we could fancy him almost regretting the appeal first
made to the reader's wonder' rather than from 'some fact more com-
monly within the range of experience' (Howells 1993: II 38).

The reception of this novel generally in the United States appears to
have been mixed. The Boston *Literary World* (12.6.86) praised what it
called 'a bold charcoal drawing from the hand of a master'. Six weeks
later it was reporting in 'A Letter from London' that there had been 'an
unhappy pause, a hiatus in Hardy's fame' but with his most recent novel
he 'had again made a striking success' (Gerber 1973: 40). W. M. Payne in
the *Dial* (VII 67–8) also praised the 'acuteness' of Hardy's observation
but claimed that his characters were 'essentially unreal': they 'excite the
curiosity, but rarely the sympathy of the reader'. In New York the *Critic*
(3.7.86) found 'much human nature' in this 'entertaining story' but the

Nation (XLIII 142) complained that it had 'too many catastrophes in it, whether deaths or deliverances'. The *Book Buyer* (III 243), however, thought it 'a fine story' and Henchard 'one of the most powerful and most interesting of Mr. Hardy's creations'.

Critical comments on *The Mayor of Casterbridge* continued to combine admiration for its powerful characterisation with scorn for its melodrama. J. M. Barrie in 1889 thought it 'in some ways the most dramatic and powerful' of Hardy's novels (Cox 1970: 166) but the following year Edmund Gosse put it behind nearly all Hardy's other work (168). In 1892 W. P. Trent claimed that in this novel 'the sun of Mr. Hardy's genius seems almost sunk from sight' (230). For Lionel Johnson, however, Henchard illustrated 'the immitigable strength of Hardy at its best', perfectly fulfilling Aristotle's conception of tragedy: 'for good and bad, Henchard is his own fate' (Johnson 1923: 179,188). Later critics such as Beach would still complain of 'a story dealing in incidents of more than usual strangeness and improbability' (Beach 1922: 134–5) but Virginia Woolf placed it among the truly 'great' works of literature:

> if you think of these books, you do at once think of some character who has seemed to you so real (I do not by that mean so lifelike) that it has the power to make you think not merely of itself, but of all sorts of things through its eyes – of religion, of love, of war, of peace, of family life, of bulls in country towns...through some character. Otherwise they would not be novelists; but poets, historians, or pamphleteers.
>
> (McNeillie 1986: III 428)

It started to appear in Higher School Certificate papers in 1926 and quickly became one of the three novels widely thought to 'constitute "Hardy" in school education', providing material for endless questions on character, fate and tragedy (Widdowson 1989: 80–3).

A focus on the question of character may help to explain how a novel which started as melodrama could develop into one of the greatest examples of tragedy in English fiction. Characterisation had been much debated in highbrow periodicals of the early 1880s, with Howells and Stevenson (disparager and admirer respectively of the *Mayor*) on opposite sides of the debate. It was Howells, in an essay on 'Henry James' in the *Century Magazine* of 1882, who appears to have started the discussion, contrasting the subtle analysis of character of the new American school with the old-fashioned focus on the 'moving accident' of the kind he later found in the *Mayor* (Graham 1965: 108). Stevenson rallied to the defence of the romance, arguing that incidents were necessary to excite and involve readers (109). An essay on 'The New School of Fiction' by Arthur Tilley in 1883 located the difference largely 'in the elaborate analysis of character, in the absence of plot, in the sparing use of incident', all of which were anathema to 'a novel reader of the old-fashioned type, who likes a thrilling story, ... who fidgets and finally skips if the story stands still' (Olmsted 1979: 255–6).

The discussion continued in a series of lectures on 'The Art of Fiction' by Walter Besant, Henry James and Robert Louis Stevenson, published in *Longman's Magazine* in 1884. Stevenson distinguished between the 'novel of adventure' characteristic of Sir Walter Scott, the 'novel of character' produced by James, and the 'dramatic novel', of which he adduced *A Pair of Blue Eyes* was an example, 'founded on one of the passionate *cruces* of life, where duty and inclination come nobly to the grapple'. This was in direct contrast with a writer such as James, who focused on 'the statics of character, studying it at rest or only gently moved' (347). The debate became quite heated, with the American vice of analysis being attacked not only as 'a violation ... of literary good breeding' but as one of the 'plagues' sent by the New World with the Colorado beetle (Graham 1965: 104–7). Both Stevenson and Howells placed Hardy on the English side of the ocean as a writer high on incident and low on analysis. His presentation of character in *The Mayor of Casterbridge*, however, can be seen to bridge the gap, even to span the Atlantic.

Hardy had clearly followed at least some of these debates. He copied passages from Vernon Lee's 'A Dialogue on Novels' from the *Contemporary Review* into his *Literary Notebooks*, including one on 'the fatality of heredity', the way in which

> a human being contains within himself a number of different tendencies ... ready to respond to its special stimulus ... there must be, in all of us ... tendencies which ... may be lying unsuspected, at the very bottom of our nature, far below the level of consciousness; but which, on the approach of the specific stimulus ... will suddenly come to the surface.
>
> (*LN* I 165)

Lee went on to observe (and Hardy to note) that a 'substitution of psychological sympathetic interest for the comic interest of former days has certainly taken place in the novel' (I 166). Hardy's notes from this period also contain passages from Anthony Trollope's *An Autobiography* on the superiority as an artist of the writer 'who can deal adequately with tragic elements' and on the need for the reader to 'sympathise [underlined three times] with the characters.... The novelist must make his char[acter]s living creatures to the reader... (I 164). All this advice appears to have contributed to Hardy's attempt to 'modernise' his work in accordance with the 'New School of Fiction', in particular in terms of characterisation.

Hardy's presentation of Henchard at the beginning of *The Mayor of Casterbridge* begins with external details, marking 'the shape of his face, the occasional clench of his mouth, and the fiery spark of his dark eye', but these details are soon related to deeper characteristics, revealing how he becomes 'overbearing – even brilliantly quarrelsome' after alcohol (*MC* 8). Similarly, when Susan and Elizabeth-Jane catch up with Henchard after a gap of nearly twenty years, the narrator dwells on the quality of the mayor's laugh, which 'was not encouraging to strangers', falling in 'well with the conjectures of a temperament which would have no pity for weakness' and the conclusion that its 'producer's personal goodness, if he had any, would be of a very fitful cast – an occasional oppressive generosity rather than a mild and constant kindness' (32). Hardy does not tell us, as a matter of omniscient narrative 'truth', that Henchard *was* like this: he presents Susan's observation of the man and develops a hypothetical reading which is not even identified as hers – the passage falling some way short of free indirect speech. Readers are thus involved from the outset in the phenomenological process of constructing character, building an interpretation or *Gestalt* of Henchard on the 'aspects' of his character made available to them.

Henchard's character is gradually substantiated in the course of the narrative by means of external observation, dialogue, and comments made both by other characters and by the narrator. The mayor tells Farfrae, for example, that he is 'a rule o' thumb sort of man', not given to recording his transactions on paper (48). Susan observes to her daughter that his 'sudden liking for that young man' is consistent with his character when he was younger: 'He was always so' (58). It is clear from the way Henchard behaves, for example his blunt acknowledgement, 'hang it, Farfrae, I like thee well!', that he is what the narrator calls a 'man of strong impulses' (63–4). Farfrae too labels his new patron 'a man who knew no moderation in his requests and impulses' (75), a diagnosis confirmed when Henchard tells him about his earlier lover nursing him though one of his 'gloomy fits' (77). Hardy has his narrator tell readers much more about Henchard than about earlier characters, for instance that 'there was still the same unruly volcanic stuff beneath the rind of

Michael Henchard as when he had sold his wife at Weydon Fair' (110). He likens Henchard to Faust as 'a vehement gloomy being, who had quitted the ways of vulgar men without light to guide him on a better way' (112), one of a number of self-consciously literary passages added to the first edition in order to appeal to the more up-market readers of the book (342).

The point is that Henchard is presented both dramatically, in Stevenson's terms, revealing inner character in a series of striking incidents, the *cruces* of his life (the encounter with the royal personage, the visit to the conjuror, the fight with Farfrae, the impulsive lie to Newson, the return to the wedding and the writing of his will) and through a more explicit narrative analysis than had appeared before in Hardy's work. The result, as contemporary reviewers and later critics have recognised, is the most convincing portrait of 'a Man of Character' that he had yet achieved, a portrait which Rosemary Sumner has shown to contain 'all the main elements [of] the aggressive personality as analysed and defined by twentieth-century psychologists' (Sumner 1981: 72). To the external observation characteristic of his earlier work Hardy adds a more sustained use of metaphor, to capture the 'fire' burning beneath the surface, and a more explicit mode of analysis borrowed at least in part from the 'new school of fiction'.

A similar development is observable in the characterisation of Elizabeth-Jane. The early scenes establish her seriousness, her reiterated sense of what is 'respectable' (24, 39). The people of Casterbridge see that she is 'sober and discreet' and also that 'she seemed to be occupied with an inner chamber of ideas' (*MC* 93). Henchard, as we have seen, is given some insight into her inner character by the increased range of the books that the first edition makes her read. But Hardy also takes his readers into her consciousness,

> all this while the subtle-souled girl asking herself why she was born, why sitting in a room and blinking at the candle; why things around her had taken the shape they wore in preference to every other possible shape. Why they stared at her so helplessly, as if waiting for the touch of some wand that should release them from terrestrial constraint; what that chaos called consciousness, which spun in her at this moment like a top, tended to, and began in. (116)

This is a very different mode of characterisation than that of Hardy's earlier work, more analytic in the manner of the new 'American' school. There are a number of similar moments in the novel, most notably in its final pages, where Elizabeth-Jane is again called upon to philosophise. These passages all illustrate new elements in Hardy, an increased commitment to what his characters think and feel.

The whole question of character, of identity, of giving coherence and a name to the 'chaos called consciousness', is crucial to this novel, which explores the continuities and discontinuities of personality at a number of different levels, not all of them that serious. Lucetta, for example, complains about the difficulty of choosing between the two new outfits laid out on her bed: ' "You are that person" (pointing to one of the arrangements), "or you are *that* totally different person" (pointing to the other) "for the whole of the coming spring" . . . '. She finally opts for the 'cherry-coloured person' (166) who will be so easily identified in the Skimmington Ride. There is a deleted passage in the manuscript even more satirical of the manufacture of a lady of fashion in which Lucetta, asked by Elizabeth-Jane how she became fashionable, explains that she went into a Paris shop and 'said "Make me fashionable," holding out some banknotes'. As a result, 'Four women hovered round me, fixed me on a pedestal like an image, and arranged me and pinned me and stitched me and padded me' (Bullen 1986: 149). Such radical subversion of the construction of the feminine was presumably cut on the grounds that it risked alienating at least half his audience. The problematic nature of identity provides a somewhat specious defence for Lucetta when, under pressure from Henchard to honour their agreement to marry, she claims that her altered social status releases her from any such obligation: 'I was a poor girl then; and now my circumstances have altered, so I am hardly the same person' (196). Henchard in turn tells the returned Newson that the drunk man who sold his wife was a different person: 'I cannot even allow that I'm the man you met then. I was not in my senses, and a man's senses are himself' (287). His impulsiveness, however, is seen to be part of his character still, causing him in 'the impulse of a moment' to lie to Newson's face and claim that his daughter is dead. There is, as Elizabeth-Jane recognises when reading his will, a clear continuity between the various Henchards of the story, so that this act can be seen as 'a piece of the same stuff that his whole life was made of' (321). Not only, in other words, does *The Mayor of Casterbridge* reveal a new mode of characterisation in Hardy; it also explores the very nature of character, those elements 'lying unsuspected at the very bottom of our nature, far below the level of consciousness' of which Vernon Lee had written.

At least part of the tragedy of this novel is caused by the sheer force of Henchard's character. He is 'a character', a strong personality, in the sense of which John Stuart Mill wrote in the chapter 'On Individuality' in one of Hardy's favourite books, *On Liberty*: 'A person whose desires and impulses are his own – are the expression of his own nature, as it has been developed and modified by his own culture – is said to have a character'. Society, according to Mill, finds it hard to accept such power-ful characters and therefore attempts to control and discipline them (Gatrell 1993: 85–6). Casterbridge at least is shown to prefer the more manageable personality of the good-humoured but shallow Farfrae. John Goode accordingly reads the novel as a degeneration myth in which 'unitary being of character' of the kind displayed by Henchard is superseded by the 'compartmentalised personality' of a man such as Farfrae (Goode 1988: 89).

The connection between tragedy and character is emphasised by Hardy, in a note of November 1885: 'a tragedy exhibits a state of things in the life of an individual which unavoidably causes some natural aim or desire of his to end in a catastrophe when carried out' (*Life* 182). A later note of October 1892 argues that the 'best tragedy' involves 'that of the WORTHY encompassed by the INEVITABLE' (265). *The Mayor of Casterbridge* can be seen to slide from the first definition to the second. Both recognise character as crucial: the first, however, is more Aristotel-ian in locating a basic flaw or *hamartia* in the otherwise noble protagon-ist who is thus to some extent responsible for the fate which overtakes him or her. Hegel developed this notion further, locating the site of tragedy in

> a conflict between two incompatible but equally valid laws, em-bodied in two individuals or in the collision between what the prot-agonist has 'knowingly done... [and] what he was fated by the gods to do and actually did unconsciously and without having willed it'.
>
> (Lothe 1999: 120)

Critics of this novel have tended to divide between those who regard Henchard as responsible for his fate, guilty of violating a moral order in the world, and those who see him as an essentially good man destroyed by the chance forces of a morally indifferent world (Schweik 1975: 133). Schweik argues that the novel itself moves from the first position to the second, gradually moving its readers from the 'socially orthodox, famil-iar, and comforting' view that there is justice in the world (and that Henchard brings his sufferings on himself) to the 'less immediately acceptable' and altogether bleaker view that much of our suffering is the product of chance:

Henchard's first downfall is the product of a variety of interconnected causes, some related to character (as he is variously prompted by instinctive antagonism, superstitiousness, Southern doggedness, disappointment, unconscious cravings, rashness, rivalry in love) and some more clearly matters of chance (coincidental discoveries, inopportune revelations, the vagaries of the weather)...(147)

The quotation from Novalis, 'Character is Fate' (*MC* 112), along with allusions to Sophocles and Shakespeare, serve initially to place Hardy's novel within the acceptable horizon of Aristotelian tragedy. Later events, however, such as the foiling by Jopp of Henchard's intention to return Lucetta's letters, cannot be blamed on him. The novel turns into a different kind of tragedy, the punishment meted upon the outcast Cain-figure that he becomes revealing 'a kind of excess which makes claims upon our sympathy' (Schweik 1975: 144). Arthur Locker, editor of the *Graphic*, certainly felt Henchard had been 'almost too severely dealt with', even 'his good deeds, as with Claudius, producing evil' (DCM 2628). Elizabeth-Jane is thus left to meditate on the fact that the world can be a harsh place in which no 'human being deserved less than was given' while 'there were others receiving less who had deserved more' (*MC* 322).

Another significant difference between Aristotelian tragedy and that produced by Hardy, as some of his contemporary critics complained, is that the protagonist in this novel is not noble in rank but decidedly bourgeois. Hardy presents the commercial and emotional battles of his modern Wessex polis as worthy of tragic treatment (Moses 2000: 180–1). Hardy has been seen to hang 'the trappings of Greek tragedy' upon his mayor, superimposing 'the story of Oedipus on that of Henchard as an ideological feint', overlaying 'the contradictions of bourgeois existence', the difficulties of reconciling commerce and friendship, 'with the aura of Greek myth' (192). Hardy makes his novel acceptable to his middle-class audience, full though it is of the kind of sensational incidents necessary for its success as a serial, by presenting it as a tragedy of Sophoclean and Shakespearean proportions. His hero thus combines some of the qualities of Oedipus (unable to escape the consequences of an early impulsive deed and driven eventually into voluntary exile) with those of Lear (the caged bird a final attempt at reconciliation with his daughter) and Timon (his misanthropic final testament). He also insists that the sufferings of corn-merchants are at least as heroic as those conventionally seen as 'noble' and therefore 'worthy' of the status of tragedy.

A novel which appears to have begun as a straightforward melodrama, full of 'graphic' incidents, seems to have developed in the course of writing, partly as a result of Hardy's reading of high-brow debates about the novel, into a fully-fledged tragedy. It is not so much the literary allusions that convince readers of this transformation as the depth of characterisation, the creation of a world viewed through the eyes of one man.

The Woodlanders: for 'souls' and 'machines'

The Woodlanders has been seen to display a conflict between Hardy's 'continuing economic need to write for a magazine public and the growing urgency of his need as an artist' to give expression to 'his disturbing vision of the human condition' (Millgate 1971: 260). The *Life* registers at this point in his career a 'resignation to novel-writing as a trade' about whose 'business' he went 'mechanically' (*Life* 189). A note from his diary written shortly after finishing the novel in February divides not only his audience but people generally into two groups: 'souls', a 'certain small minority who have sensitive souls', and 'machines', the majority, 'the mentally unquickened, mechanical, soulless' (192). The writing of this novel about 'tree and machine', the life principle celebrated by the Romantics, and its betrayal by the 'modern' sensibility, appears to have brought home to Hardy the reality of his dual audience, the realisation that he was doomed to continue to satisfy the demands of the majority for profusion of incident while aiming simultaneously to produce work that would appeal to more 'sensitive souls'. *The Woodlanders* itself hinges upon a heroine suspended 'as it were in mid-air between two stories [*sic*] of society' (*W* 216) who betrays her natural instincts at the end of the novel by returning to her cultured, upper-middle-class but faithless husband. As in the 1887 poem 'In a Wood', subtitled 'From "The Woodlanders"', in which the persona retires 'City-opprest' to the woods in hope of rest and peace, only to find even there the marks of violence and competition, 'no grace.../ Taught me of trees', so in the novel there is little consolation Hardy can supply to his 'sensitive' readers in a post-Darwinian world of struggle for survival but the occasional 'good deed' (*CP* 56–7).

Macmillan's Magazine, which commissioned a novel in twelve parts from Hardy in the summer of 1884 before he had any idea of what its subject would be, was intellectually more up-market than the *Graphic*. It disdained illustrations, providing a serious monthly diet which had remained unchanged from its foundation in 1859: 'Each issue usually contained a political article, a serial, a literary or philosophical article, a history or travel article, and a poem or short story' (Sullivan 1984: 216). The fiction in *Macmillan's* was not initially as distinguished as that in the *Cornhill*, founded two months later (Houghton 1966: I 554–5). Under its first editor David Masson, it had tended to stick with house authors such as Tom Hughes and the Kingsley brothers (Sutherland 1989: 401) but it had taken *The Portrait of a Lady* in 1880–1 and was clearly seen by Hardy as a good place to publish (especially if, as eventually transpired, the volume too came out with Macmillan). 'I am very anxious,' he told Frederick Macmillan in November 1885, 'that the story may be in every way worthy of the high character of the magazine' (*Letters* I 139).

Under Morley (whose editorship lasted from May 1883 to September 1885) the main focus of *Macmillan's* had reverted to politics but his successor Mowbray Morris gave greater prominence to fiction. An article expressing 'Some Thoughts about Novels' appeared in the magazine while *The Woodlanders* was running, deploring the low taste of the new generation of novel-readers:

> In former times, when the body of readers was much smaller...the public asked for what they were assured was the best. But now, I suspect the booksellers and the libraries are really the arbiters of taste, and the good patient public take whatever is offered them across the counter.

The article took up Rider Haggard's complaint (in the February issue of the *Contemporary Review)* that novelists were 'at the mercy of the "Young Person"', that all fiction was judged by its suitability for a girl of sixteen. Haggard himself, it suspected, along with Stevenson and Blackmore, appealed mainly to women. The reason why 'men hardly ever read a novel', it claimed, was that, 'in ninety-nine cases out of a hundred, it is utterly false as a picture of life'. What was needed to raise the status of the novel in the literary world was 'a higher ideal, and more freedom to work it out' (*Macmillan Magazine* LV 360–3).

The magazine's editorial practice, however, continued to place severe limits on this freedom. Mowbray Morris, 'a conservative mind dealing with an age of transition' (Sullivan 1984: 218), soon registered his alarm at the dangerous direction Hardy's novel appeared to be taking, dropping a 'gentle hint' on 'the affair between Miss Damson and the Doctor'. His 'queer public: pious Scottish souls who take offence wondrous easily', would object if Hardy brought 'the fair Miss Suke to too open shame' (DCM 4403). Frederick Macmillan had promised not 'to "edit" your work in any impertinent way' (4088). But Morris could soon point to a letter from an aggrieved reader expressing

> the regret felt by myself and other mothers that you should have admitted such a story as *The Woodlanders* into your *Magazine*. We have hitherto felt that *Macmillan's* might be put without any hesitation into the hands of our daughters . . .
>
> A story which can hinge on conjugal infidelity, can describe coarse flirtations, and can end in pronouncing a married woman's avowed lover to be a 'good man who did good things', is certainly not fit to be printed in a high-toned periodical and to be put into the hands of pure-minded English girls.
>
> (Nowell-Smith 1967: 130–1)

He would reject Hardy's next novel out of hand rather than risk further maternal wrath.

Macmillan's appear to have been more relaxed than the *Graphic*, however, in terms of the timetable it imposed upon its authors, allowing Hardy to revert to the hand-to-mouth existence characteristic of his earlier serials (Gatrell 1988: 77). He only began work on *The Woodlanders* in November 1885, returning to the 'original plot' first conceived a decade earlier (*Life* 105, 182). He managed to put back the starting date from January to May 1886, allowing 'a longer time for incubation' (*Letters* I 139) but Frederick Macmillan only saw the first instalment of the manuscript at the end of March 1886, when he opted for *The Woodlanders* rather than 'Fitzpiers at Hintock', the alternative title Hardy offered (DCM 4088). Hardy completed the manuscript the following February, two months before the final instalment was due to appear and only six weeks before the first edition was published. Agreement to publish in book form was only reached in the middle of that month. Hardy had to admit that 'my last story did not sell so largely as it might have done – owing, I was told, to the plot not being romantic, nor the accessories rural'. The new story, however, met both these conditions (*Letters* I 161). He had also experienced difficulties in disposing of the serial rights in America. Both the *Independent* and the *Atlantic Monthly* turned it down, in spite of his assuring the former that 'the moral tone will be unexceptionable' (I 137–8). He had even offered them to Macmillan, insisting 'my works are in large demand in America' (I 140). They were eventually taken up by *Harper's Bazaar*, who published the novel in weekly parts from mid-May 1886. But it is clear that Hardy's reputation for being morally 'exceptionable' was as bad in

America as it was in Britain. The number of pirated editions of *The Woodlanders* published in the States confirms his appeal to the wider American public (Kramer 1981: 30) but editors of family magazines remained wary.

The manuscript of *The Woodlanders* reveals the extent to which it was originally designed as a serial, the twelve parts being carefully marked and sent to the firm in separate packets (8). When Morris could not adhere to the divisions indicated by Hardy, as in January 1886, he let him know (DCM 4403). Each part, as Jacobus has shown, was 'carefully plotted to maximise the opportunities for suspended action and ironic reversal provided by part-publication', the whole novel being structured in three blocks of four, each block 'comprising a crucial phase in Grace's marital adventures'. The careful introduction into each instalment of a new twist of fate, 'a chain of circumstances working against the characters' natural alignments', served to heighten the frustration which is both the theme of the novel and the experience of its readers (Jacobus 1979: 122–3).

The manuscript of the novel also bears evidence of much revision, which it is not always possible to date. Sometimes it is clear, as in the suggestive final line of chapter 20, which leaves the lovers in their hayfield until 'daybreak'. Here the manuscript has the clear instruction 'omit for mag.' (Kramer 1981: 142), although it was deemed printable by *Harper's Bazaar* (32). A similar concern not to offend keeps Suke and Felice out of the marital bedroom when they come to see how the wounded doctor is progressing (45, n.37). For the English first edition, Kramer claims, 'the text of the novel was revised more extensively than for any other printed text' of Hardy's. Some of these changes involved merely 'deleting explanatory or bridging passages which had been helpful to readers of a novel appearing at month-long intervals' (37–8). Others appear to have been the result of Hardy's reconceiving the central characters after finishing the serial. Giles, who had been 'a forceful, critical, and almost bitter man' in the early instalments of the serial, expressing resentment towards Grace, her clothing and fine manners, becomes in the first edition more gentle and self-deprecating, consistent with his later preparedness to sacrifice his life to her honour. The serial calls him 'a trifle cynical, for that strand was wound into him with the rest' (35, n.3); it also refers to the 'grimness . . . in his character' (113, n.46). He responds to Grace 'with some causticity of humour' (55, n.14), sighing 'with mock awe' at her literary references (67, n.9). In the serial 'he is coolly objective and even somewhat scornful in his opinion of her' (38), treating Melbury's warnings about the sophisticated critical eye she is likely to cast over his clothing first with 'misgiving; then with indifference' (35, n.4), as if it is her problem if she judges him by externals. He resolves to be 'not altogether her fool' even when driving to meet her at Sherton-Abbas (36, n.1) while later, once her interest in the doctor becomes apparent, he leaves her in no doubt about his 'silent, almost sarcastic, criticism' of her (150, n.33). After her marriage, he is less 'ardent' in his love (258, n.10), 'without the embarrassment' that had marked him when they met (259, n.23) and more 'critical' (261, n.35). This causticity and detachment disappeared in the first edition, where Grace also changes in response to the softer Giles, becoming 'more encouraging and seductive' (39). These changes are not necessarily attributable to the different audience Hardy expected for the first edition so much as to his rethinking of their characters after completing the novel. Having written his 'tragic' ending, he had to create a more 'worthy' hero.

The novel continued to evolve. Its sexual dimension was made more explicit in the Osgood, McIlvaine edition of 1896, when the storm over *Tess* had made Hardy 'combative and defiant' towards the public. The narrator now refers explicitly to 'the intimacy established in the hayfield' between Fitzpiers and Suke (implying that it continued afterwards). Grace now exclaims, 'He's had you', in response to Felice's confession (228) and invites both of her husband's other lovers, 'Wives all,' to visit him in the marital bedroom (242). The hut she shares with Giles at the end is significantly reduced from two rooms to one (287). Her father can therefore complain of her living 'with him' and even 'giving up yourself to him' (298, 300). 'Let her take him back to her bed if she will,' he now says of her return to Fitzpiers, 'But let her bear in mind that the woman walks and laughs somewhere at this very moment whose neck he'll be coling next year as he does hers tonight' (335).

These changes, although introduced partly to annoy Hardy's moralistic readers, can be seen simply to make explicit what was implicit in the first edition. Hardy told two adaptors of the novel for the stage in 1889,

> You have probably observed that the ending of the story – hinted rather than stated – is that the heroine is doomed to an unhappy life with an inconstant husband. I could not accentuate this strongly in the book, by reason of the conventions of the libraries, etc....it is therefore a question for you whether you will accent this ending; or prefer to obscure it.
>
> (*Life* 230; *Letters* I 195).

The dramatisers (J. T. Grein and C. W. Jarvis) seem to have opted for a more explicit ending. Jarvis, at least, in his reply to Hardy, quoted their projected ending in which Fitzpiers would ask Grace, 'You will come back to me?' only for her to reply, 'What else can I do? My father says so, he tells me, every body tells me – to be unhappy?' (Millgate 1971: 399). A century later, having filmed a relatively faithful ending which had to be discarded after test screenings in America, Phil Agland would make his Grace answer a slightly different question from Fitzpiers, 'What do you feel for me?' with the more assertive 'Nothing', before striding purposefully into her independent future (Woof 2002). By deliberately *obscuring* his ending, in other words, making its full meaning apparent only to 'sensitive souls', who would see through the superficial 'reconciliation' to the grimmer reality beneath, Hardy appears to have baffled more mechanical readers.

One of the 'sensitive souls' who appreciated the subtlety of Hardy's ending was Lord Lytton, who wrote at length in July 1887:

> The idea of closing the story with the picture of the heroine's foreseen reconciliation with the husband after her passionate, and well justified, love for the dead lover, is – to me at least – a complete novelty in fiction. The effect of it is singularly successful but the success implies extraordinary skill in the construction of the story and the delineation of character. For though this denouement is boldly true to life and nature I do not think its truth could have so completely reconciled to such a reconciliation a reader accustomed to the conventions of the ordinary novel had there been one false note in the delicate process that leads up to it. When I came to the end of the book – a light not new but intensified seemed thrown by it over all the previous pages – and I then recalled with increased appreciation the... subtlety of numerous touches in your first delineation and subsequent development of the heroine's character.
>
> (DCM 3967)

Lytton captures the way in which readers are forced to revise their earlier impressions of character, discovering in Grace those aspects of her character (conformity, desire for acceptance, enjoyment of the physical side of marriage as well as the refinements brought by her husband's social status) which make this ending plausible.

Most reviewers of the first edition (of which Hardy's scrapbook contains an unusual range, many supplied by Macmillan) failed to see this. The earliest, Britten in the *Athenaeum* (26.3.87), singled out the ending

as 'unsatisfactory', complaining that Fitzpiers was not 'adequately punished' and that Grace 'forgives and forgets on very slight inducement'
(Cox 1970: 141–2). The *Yorkshire Post* (27.4.87) also complained that 'the
good people suffered more than their deserts' while 'the sinners too
easily atone by a late repentance'. R. H. Hutton in the *Spectator*
(26.3.87) launched a savage attack on the immorality of a book that
could portray 'shameless falsehood, levity and infidelity... crowned at
the end with perfect success'. Hutton worked himself into a fury at
Fitzpiers, 'this mendacious, easy-going, conscienceless, passionate
young doctor, ... this sensual and selfish liar' (142–3). Coventry Patmore
in the *St. James Gazette* (2.4.87) also found Fitzpiers and Felice 'throughout repulsive' (148) while the *Dublin Evening Mail* (30.3.87) saw an
'unusual indelicacy' in the episode involving Fitzpiers and Suke
Damson.

Edmund Gosse attempted to come to the novel's rescue with what he
himself described as 'an arrant piece of log-rolling' (DCM 2712) in the
Saturday Review (2.4.87), praising 'the richness and humanity of the
book' along with its rendering of the beauty of the landscape (Cox
1970: 152). But the complaints quickly resumed, first in the *Globe*
(5.4.87), which thought the novel 'not quite worthy of Mr. Hardy's
powers' and then from William Wallace (Professor of Moral Philosophy
at Oxford since 1882) in the *Academy* (9.4.87), who thought it powerful
but 'disagreeable' (Cox 1970: 153–4). The *Daily Telegraph* (12.4.87)
praised the novel, which *The Times* (27.4.87) called 'a credit to English
literature'. The *World* (20.4.87), however, brought the discussion back to
morality, describing Fitzpiers as 'one of the most contemptible and
offensive characters in fiction'; the novel might rank as 'literature' but
was 'not a good book nor a pleasant one'. *John Bull* (7.5.87) too thought
Fitzpiers 'a most offensive... specimen of humanity', detecting suspiciously 'French' elements in the plot. Hardy, it suspected, had 'gone out
of his way to bring in episodes calculated to offend'.

Not all the reviews focused on the moral issue. The *Sphinx* (13.5.87),
while feeling that 'a few passages might have been omitted with advantage, enjoyed both Hardy's humour and his 'sympathetic study of the
better side of country character'. The *Pall Mall Gazette* (19.5.87) recognised the novel's pervasive 'tone of sadness' but thought it left 'a more
pleasing impression' than its predecessor. Neither of the two leading
female characters, it thought, 'succeeds in winning the sympathies of
the reader'. The *Leeds Mercury* (25.5.87) found Grace 'a little insipid' and
Felice 'a little too hysterical' while the *Daily News* (28.5.87) felt the
'depressing' tone of resignation would 'consort more with the mood of

the middle-aged than with the sanguine spirit of...younger readers'. The reader craving poetic justice would certainly need to 'look elsewhere'.

The monthlies appear to have been divided between literary appreciation and moral disapproval (sometimes in the same review). The *Westminster Review* welcomed what it called 'a treat for all lovers of imaginative literature of a high order' (CXXVIII 384) but the *London Quarterly* thought 'the moral of the story...very bad' (LXVIII 382). In the States, the Boston *Literary World* (5.4.87) recognised 'the touch of a master's hand' but deplored the novel's pessimism, which left the reader 'baffled, stupified, cast down'. It failed to understand how Hardy could appear to demand sympathy for 'a clever trickster and a heartless libertine'. The *Nation* (19.5.87) felt that Grace 'affects us unpleasantly' while the *Dial* thought the story 'tragic enough' but lacking in seriousness. Henry Alden in *Harper's Monthly* described the novel as a strange mixture of George Eliot and Charles Reade, subtle psychological analysis being applied incongruously to sensational material (LXXV 317–18).

The novel sold reasonably well. Of the first edition of 860 copies 170 were remaindered after three months but Macmillan reissued it in a one-volume format in September 1887 in two impressions of 2000 copies each (Purdy 1954: 57). Some of Hardy's admirers were disappointed. George Gissing, who had 'shouted with joy' on reading the *Athenaeum's* comment that it was 'not a book for the young person' (Mattheissen 1990: III 100) and initially expressed 'much delight' at its 'exquisite woodland painting', found 'the human part on the whole painfully unsatisfactory' (Coustillas 1970: 24). J. M. Barrie detected in it 'a falling away' (Cox 1970: 166) while Gosse placed it among the 'second class' of Hardy's novels, along with *A Laodicean* and *A Pair of Blue Eyes* (168). W. P. Trent thought it displayed Hardy's genius 'rising slowly' from the depths of his previous novel though 'the total impression produced by the book' was 'painful' (231). Annie Macdonell placed it 'just after' the 'greater novels', disliking 'the taint of fineladyism' in Grace (Macdonell 1894: 54–5), but Lionel Johnson rated it highly, regarding Winterbourne as an example of 'Hardy at his best' (Johnson 1923: 181–2). A. J. Butler in 1896 thought it 'perhaps the most powerful' of Hardy's books (Cox 1970: 287) but Edward Wright in 1904 was still irritated by its combination of 'a matchless story of rustic life' with 'inferior work' (356). The sensitive 'soul' can be seen here to resent Hardy's continuing to service the 'machines'.

It was Hardy's own reassessment of the novel on rereading it for the Wessex Edition in 1912 that seems to have triggered a more widespread recognition of the 'greatness' of this novel. 'I like it *as a story*,' he confessed to Florence Dugdale, 'the best of all' (*Letters* IV 212). 'In after years,' Florence added to the *Life*, 'he often said that in some respects *The Woodlanders* was his best novel' (*Life* 510). Perhaps taking their cue from the Preface to the Wessex Edition, where it is included with the 'Novels of Character and Environment', subsequent critics write of the way in which 'the villagers are drencht [*sic*] by the subtle influence of their surrounding woods' (Abercrombie 1912: 120). Arnold Bennett, who recommended it to his niece as one of Hardy's 'two best' (Hepburn 1966: IV 351–2), went on to call it 'the finest English novel' (Lodge 1981: 79). For Siegfried Sassoon in Egypt in 1918 (Hart-Davis 1983: 230) and for E. M. Forster in India it represented rural England: 'Trees, trees, undergrowth, English trees! How that book rustles with them,' exclaimed Forster (Lodge 1981: 80). 'Here is the reign of trees, who are like sacred beings,' enthused J. W. Beach (Beach 1922: 162). Some of the 'sensitive souls' seem to have been so moved by the trees that they missed the Darwinian aspects of the wood.

The Woodlanders, however, as John Peck observed, has always had a 'curious reputation'; it is one of the big six, acknowledged as a 'major' novel, but it has been 'nearly always the least admired, and by far the least discussed' (Peck 1981: 147). Unlike its predecessor and in spite of its opening chapter's claim to 'dramas of a grandeur and unity truly Sophoclean' (*W* 8), it resists being read as a tragedy, perhaps because the narrative focus is spread across a number of the characters. Hardy apparently told his American friend Rebekah Owen that Grace might have taken the role of tragic heroine: 'If she would have done a really self-abandoned impassioned thing (gone off with Giles), he could have made a fine tragic ending of the book, but she was too commonplace and too straitlaced, and he could not make her' (Bayley 1987: 7). She is 'by far the most important character in the novel' and yet tends to provoke only 'the reader's chagrin, in that he [*sic*] expects a heroine and gets somebody disconcertingly less' (Gregor 1974: 155). More recent critics have reacted uncertainly to the novel's 'unnerving oscillations between knockabout farce and tragic pathos', most notable in 'the elaborate measures taken by Grace and Giles to avoid sleeping together' at the end (Radford 2001: 30). There is 'an unsettling generic ranging across social comedy, tragedy, and melodrama' in the novel (Boumelha 1999: 140), which retains a surprising number of sensational elements for a work written so late in Hardy's career: a 'profusion of mysteries, liaisons, infidelities, secret meetings, and mistaken identies' (Millgate 1971: 249). It remains ultimately unreadable by the 'rules' of any single literary genre.

The safest option, given the detailed description not only of the woods themselves but of the activities of its inhabitants – planting trees, making spars, stripping bark, pressing apples and so on – is to label it pastoral. Other pastoral motifs include the theme of dispossession, the celebration of the spurned but faithful lover, the elegy to him at the end, the intrusion of idle urban characters who violate the purity of the countryside, and the celebration of chastity. All these conventions, however, are developed in ways that go far beyond Hardy's earlier attempts at pastoral. The motif of 'cross-eyed Cupid', for example, apparent in the way that Marty loves Giles who loves Grace who loves Fitzpiers who loves Felice, is linked to Hardy's particular concern with class, so that the lovers span the whole social spectrum, increasing in wealth and sophistication. Not only this, but 'the novel's moral hierarchy is inversely related to class structure' (Squires 1974: 161). The wealthy Felice, who dispossesses Marty of her hair, Giles of his hut and Grace of her husband, is clearly the most wicked, closely followed by the philandering Fitzpiers. The society composed of the woodlanders is one ridden with class feeling and exploitation, Melbury being as ridiculous in his ambitions for his daughter as Fitzpiers and Felice in their claims to superiority of rank. Fitzpiers bases his sense of entitlement to the body parts of his neighbours on his supposedly belonging to 'the oldest, ancientest family in the country' – in 1912 it is stipulated that he is descended through his mother from the Lord Baxbys of Sherton' (*W* xl–xlii) – while Mrs Charmond turns out to be a retired actress who gained her wealth by marrying 'a rich man engaged in the iron trade . . . twenty or thirty years older than she' (227).

Other pastoral elements are also transformed. The hut in the woods in which the lovers meet is no *locus amoenus* but rather 'a chamber of sickness and death . . . of abortive, disappointed love' (Squires 1974: 170). Even the woods themselves are described in terms which undermine the normal conventions of pastoral. Chapter 4, for example, begins with an astonishingly bleak description of 'a sunless winter day' emerging 'like a dead-born child' before dwelling on the violence of nature, the owls 'catching mice in the outhouses' and the stoats 'sucking the blood of the rabbits' (23). The plant world too is engaged in a continuing struggle for survival in which 'the Unfulfilled Intention' is

as obvious as it could be among the depraved crowds of a city slum. The leaf was deformed, the curve was crippled, the taper was interrupted; the lichen ate the vigour of the stalk, and the ivy slowly strangled to death the promising sapling. (52)

Later in the novel the trees are seen 'wrestling for existence, their branches disfigured with wounds resulting from their mutual rubbings and blows' (311). These passages have been compared with Darwin's description in *The Origin of Species* of the struggle between 'the several kinds of trees' in American forests (Lodge 1981: 88). This struggle to survive finally extends to the different classes of society, Giles resenting Grace calling out to him while he is 'moiling and muddling for his daily bread' (177).

Hardy's sympathies, as Casagrande recognises, continue to lie with Giles and Marty, representatives of a way of life in harmony with nature. But he can no longer believe in the 'romantic naturalism' characteristic of earlier strands of pastoral (Casagrande 1971: 112). The 'conventions of realism' (the duty to describe the world as the best available evidence shows it to be) displace the 'conventions of pastoral', which lie 'mainly on the periphery of the work, or beneath its surface, in allusion, metaphor and suggestion' (Lodge 1981: 93). As with the conventions of tragedy in his previous novel, Hardy can be seen to draw readers into his work under the impression that they are encountering something familiar only to shock them all the more by altering the rules, producing something very different from what they had expected. The ending of the novel in this respect continues the Darwinian theme: 'Fitzpiers survives because he is fitter, not better than Giles – fitter to survive in a "modern" age' while Grace chooses an unfaithful man 'with the future in his bones' over an honest one whose death 'symbolises an old order passing' (87). Conventional pastoral morality no longer applies. The 'machines' are left simply to deplore what the 'sensitive souls' will find tragic.

Tess of the D'Urbervilles: 'sincere' work for 'adult readers'

The controversy surrounding *Tess* brought Hardy to the attention of a much wider reading public than he had previously attracted. The *Life* talks of his having 'apparently not foreseen' the attention it would attract (*Life* 255) but Hardy did everything he could to generate it. His essay on 'Candour in English Fiction' of 1890, as we shall see, functioned not only as an attack on the inhibiting conditions of publishing but as a trailer for the novel. The subtitle, *A Pure Woman/Faithfully Presented*, added as the first edition was going to press, drew attention to the novel's challenge to conventional notions of purity. The text itself, in John Goode's graphic phrase, '*puts the reader through*' the appalling experiences of a protagonist doubly disadvantaged by being both female and working class (Goode 1988: 131). Its very language is violent, expressing not only Hardy's rage against an unjust class-ridden society but the 'becoming violent' of language itself as the opposing discourses of rural working-class England are invaded and finally suppressed by the discourse of the dominant upper classes. The position of the heroine, as Lecercle has observed, brought into 'subjection' by the languages available to her, reflects the struggle of Hardy himself to find a personal voice within the conventions afforded by the literary establishment of his day (Lecercle 1993: 148–53).

A novel which ends with 'the execution of the female protagonist, who has already been raped' (Goode 1988: 137), is clearly not designed to be read for pleasure. Hardy's ostensible reason for inflicting such pain upon his readers was that, however offensive it might be, the 'truth' had to be told. The final chapter of the version of *Tess* which appeared in the *Sydney Mail* (under the title *A Daughter of the D'Urbervilles*) began with a paragraph omitted from the *Graphic* and from all other editions (except the *Nottinghamshire Guardian*, also based on unrevised proofs of the *Graphic*) insisting that 'the humble delineator of human character and human contingencies... must primarily and above all things be sincere' (Gatrell 1983: 540). Hardy may have decided to omit this paragraph from the *Graphic* as 'inappropriate' in the mutilated version he was offering its readers (Laird 1980: 423). It was then rendered redundant by the 'Explanatory Note' appended to the first edition of the novel in 1891, which sent the story out 'in all sincerity of purpose, as representing on the whole a true sequence of things'. Any 'too genteel reader who cannot endure to have it said what everybody thinks and feels' was asked to remember St. Jerome's saying, 'If an offence come out of the truth, better is it that the offence come than that the truth be concealed'. Hardy also used this note to explain that 'the main portion of the story appeared – with slight modifications – in the *Graphic*' while 'other chapters, more especially addressed to adult readers' had been distributed elsewhere. He tendered 'thanks' to 'the editors and proprietors of those periodicals for enabling me now to piece the trunk and limbs of the novel together, and print it complete, as originally written two years ago' (*T* [3]).

This account is itself somewhat economical with the truth, suggesting that Hardy had completed the novel as he would have liked to publish it as early as November 1889 and had then to revise it to make it acceptable for the magazines. As we shall see, Hardy discovered in 1889 that no magazine would accept what he had by then written (up to Tess's return from Trantridge) and wrote the rest of the novel with an acute awareness of the limitations of what in England was regarded as publishable. He had in 1889 signed the plea for the release from gaol of the publisher Henry Vizetelly, found guilty of obscenity for publishing an English translation of *Abbé Mouret's Transgression*, which he read shortly before beginning work on *Tess* (*LN* I 404). Zola's novel has been shown to anticipate many of the themes and even some of the events to be found in *Tess*, charting as it does the rejection of a naturally sensual country girl by a frigid, moralistic man who at one point has to carry her over a flooded path (Mason 1991: 89–102). There are similarities too between Hardy's novel and another work by Zola, *La Bête Humaine*, published in book form in March 1890, in which a bloodstain is seen to spread across a ceiling (Ebbatson 1997: 83). Hardy clearly knew Zola's work and resented the fact that such writing was regarded as a criminal offence in England.

Hardy's anger at 'the conditions under which our popular fiction is produced' (*PW* 126) found immediate expression in his contribution to a symposium on 'Candour in English Fiction' published in the *New Review* in January 1890, which begins by claiming that 'the great bulk of English fiction of the present day is characterized by its lack of sincerity' (126). The kind of fiction which could 'excite a reflective and abiding interest in the minds of thoughtful readers of mature age' is simply not encouraged by the magazine and circulating library which are both geared towards 'household reading'. The editors of these magazines 'rigorously exclude from the pages they regulate' anything involving the very subject which has stimulated the best literature of the past, the passions and the relations of the sexes. The 'crash of broken commandments', they proclaim, particularly the ones relating to adultery, 'shall not be heard' (127–9). Hardy proceeds to an example which applies precisely to *Tess:*

> The opening scenes of the would-be great story may, in a rash moment, have been printed in some popular magazine before the remainder is written; as it advances month by month the situations develop, and the writer asks himself, what will his characters do next? What would probably happen to them, given such beginnings? On his life and conscience, though he had not foreseen the thing, only one event could possibly happen, and that therefore he should narrate, as he calls himself a faithful artist.

If this event, however, involves one of those 'issues which are not be mentioned in respectable magazines and select libraries', what the author often does is to belie his literary conscience ... by arranging a denouement which he knows to be indescribably unreal and meretricious, but dear to the Grundyist and subscriber. If the true artist ever weeps it probably is then, when he first discovers the fearful price he has to pay for the privilege of writing in the English language – no less a price than the extinction, in the mind of every mature and penetrating reader, of sympathetic belief in his personages. (129–30)

This, as we shall see, is precisely what happened to *Tess*, whose central 'event' (Tess's rape/seduction) had to be 'extinguished' along with the credibility of its characters.

Quite why Hardy reverted to the *Graphic* as the vehicle for this novel is difficult to explain. The *Life* puts it down to financial necessity: 'Hardy would now have much preferred to finish the story and bring it out in volume form only, but there were reasons why he could not afford to do this' (*Life* 232). Arthur Locker, editor of the *Graphic*, had been pressing him unsuccessfully for a serial novel since October 1887 (*Letters* I 170, 173–4). Hardy had accepted (after a delay of three months) an offer of March 1887 from W. F. Tillotson, for whom he had already written three short stories (Purdy 1954: 341), to produce an as yet untitled story of 'the same length as *The Woodlanders*' for a thousand guineas, having been 'much struck with the straightforward sincerity of his character' (*Letters* I 188). Unfortunately, by August 1889, when Hardy submitted the first part of the manuscript of what was now called 'Too Late Beloved', including the seduction, birth and midnight baptism, Tillotson himself was dead. His successor William Brimelow objected to the material at proof stage but Hardy refused to alter it and the contract was cancelled (Purdy 1954: 72). Hardy then offered the novel to *Murray's Magazine*, only for them to reject it 'on the score of its improper explicitness' (*Life* 232). Its editor Edward Arnold acknowledged that 'these tragedies are being played out every day in our midst' but argued that 'the less publicity they have the better' (DCM 4416).

Presumably anticipating this rejection, Hardy had already offered the *Graphic* 'a serial story' (*Letters* I 202–3), a proposal its editor accepted on 21 October. By this time, however, Hardy had already sent the manuscript to *Macmillan's Magazine*, whose editor Mowbray Morris wrote at length to report that, although he had 'read it always with interest and often with pleasure' and found no 'theological offence' in such scenes as the 'amateur baptism' since 'poor Tess was obviously in very sober earnestness', there were 'other things' to which he did object:

It is obvious from the first what is to be Tess's fate at Trantridge; it is apparently obvious also to the mother, who does not seem to mind, consoling herself with the somewhat cynical reflection that she may be made a lady *after* if not *before*. All the first part therefore is a sort of prologue to the girl's seduction which is hardly ever, and can hardly ever be out of the reader's mind. Even Angel Clare, who seems inclined to 'make an honest woman' of Tess, has not as yet got beyond a purely sensuous admiration for her person. Tess herself does not appear to have any feelings of this sort about her; but her capacity for stirring and by implication gratifying these feelings for others is pressed rather more frequently and elaborately than strikes me as altogether convenient, at any rate for my magazine.

(DCM 4404)

The impression left on Morris by the story 'so far as it has gone' was of 'rather too much succulence', a phrase which would return in his review of the published novel.

Hardy seems therefore to have had no option but to accept the only offer that he had so far received, which was from the *Graphic* for serial rights only, and to look elsewhere than Macmillan for volume publication. The new firm of Osgood, McIlvaine and Co., established in April 1890 as a 'semi-autonomous' London subsidiary of Harpers (Millgate 1982: 308), agreed to publish both *Tess* and *A Group of Noble Dames*, a collection of short stories designed for the Christmas number of the *Graphic*. Hardy was also able to arrange American serial publication in *Harper's Bazaar*, whose subtitle *A Repository of Fashion, Pleasure, and Instruction* confirms its orientation towards 'a relatively sophisticated adult, and exclusively female, readership' (Gatrell 1983: 38).

That the *Graphic* would prove resistant to much of the material in the original manuscript of *Tess* should have been obvious to Hardy from the difficulties he had experienced with them over *A Group of Noble Dames*. The six stories of which this book was originally comprised were published in *Harper's Weekly* 'as originally written' (Purdy 1954: 63), but Hardy was summoned to the *Graphic* office by its editor Arthur Locker in June 1890 to be told that the directors of the magazine objected to them (*Life* 236–7). When Hardy presumably resisted this interference, the editor's son William appears to have been deputed to read them. It was he, at least, who reported on 25 June:

I have now read 'Group of Noble Dames' and am sorry to say that in the main I agree with our Directors' opinion. In the matter of tone they seem to me to be too much in keeping with the supposed circumstances of their narration – in other words to be very suitable and entirely harmless to the robust minds of a Club smoking-room; but not at all suitable for the more delicate imaginations of young girls. Many fathers are accustomed to read or to have read in their family circles the stories in the *Graphic*; and I cannot think that they would approve for this purpose a series of tales almost every one of which turns upon questions of childbirth, and those relations between the sexes over which conventionality is accustomed (wisely or unwisely) to draw a veil.

(DCM 2629)

The letter proceeds to go through each story in turn explaining what needs changing for 'a paper with the peculiar clientele of the *Graphic*'. Hardy's manuscript registers his powerless resentment at his 'lines being deleted against the author's wish, by compulsion of Mrs. Grundy' (Purdy 1954: 65). His revisions, while dutifully removing all references to extra-marital sex, made a nonsense of some of the stories, displaying in the process 'a minimal regard for the seriousness or intelligence of the readers of the *Graphic*' (Gatrell 1988: 90).

Hardy's problems with *A Group of Noble Dames* clearly impacted upon his writing of *Tess*, causing him not only to dismember and bowdlerise what he had already written but to write the remainder of the novel with the *Graphic's* requirements unavoidably present in his mind (Gatrell 1983: 11). The *Life* claims that he 'carried out this unceremonious concession to conventionality without compunction and with cynical amusement' (*Life* 232). The cynicism is apparent in the text, perhaps most obviously in the substitution of a mock marriage staged by Alec before a fake registrar for the manuscript's rape/seduction:

What the readership of the *Graphic* thought of a story in which the whole of a girl's future happiness is made to depend upon her inability to tell a real registrar from a man made up as one is hard to say. At this moment in his career Hardy probably imagined that they were incapable of thinking about it at all.

(Gatrell 1988: 95)

He explained to friends who were following the novel in the *Graphic* that the mock marriage had been 'substituted for the seduction pure and simple of the original MS...for the sake of the Young Girl. The true reading will be restored in the volumes' (*Letters* I 245–6). Tess's speech explaining Alec's trick to her mother in the *Graphic*, which is as mechanical as the readers for whom it was written, insists that as soon as she discovered what had happened she 'came away from Trantridge instantly' (80). Her prompt return, of course, rescues her 'honour' in the eyes of readers of the *Graphic*, but makes Clare's rejection of her even less plausible. Even in *Harper's Bazaar* she is made to shoulder some of the responsibility by 'staying on at Trantridge' until 'I at last felt it was wrong, and would do so no longer' (Gatrell 1983: 115). Hardy also 'rewrote for the *Bazaar* an account of the seduction of Tess and the birth and death of her child' demonstrating a certain faith in their 'relatively liberal outlook' (38)

The changes introduced for the serial were clearly intended to be temporary, the manuscript often distinguishing between his two audiences by marking in blue ink and crayon the 'changes to be made in serial form only' (Gatrell 1983: 36). The best known example of a passage Hardy was forced to change is the scene in which Clare carries the dairymaids across the flooded lane. The *Life* explains, in lines which J. M. Barrie advised Florence to add, that the editor of the *Graphic* 'suggested that it would be more decorous and suitable for the pages of a periodical intended for family reading if the damsels were wheeled across the lane in a wheelbarrow' (*Life* 511, 536). It is tempting to think that Hardy would have had the last laugh here, however, since he must have known that the wheelbarrow in French signified an unorthodox (or at least non-missionary) sexual position. It was a joke exploited in his friend and illustrator George du Maurier's novel *Peter Ibbetson*, also of 1891 (Hall 2001). Hardy appears here to be doing metaphorically to the readers of the *Graphic* what Clare does metonymically to the dairymaids.

Hardy himself appears to have had no involvement in the 24 illustrations for the *Graphic*, 11 of which appeared in *Harper's Bazaar* and in the first American edition published by Harper in January 1892, demonstrating the extent to which the novel was mediated to much of its original audience by factors beyond Hardy's control. Sir Hubert Herkomer was an obvious choice as principal illustrator, since he 'specialized in rural or proletarian subjects charged with human suffering' (*T* 481). His double-page illustration for the opening instalment, however introducing the heroine in resplendent and virginal white in the doorway of the family cottage, while also drawing attention to her mother's wholesome labour at the washtub and the 'togetherness in the family grouping', all of which make 'a calculated appeal to an audience looking for a "family" novel' (Jackson: 1981: 106), runs counter to the text's emphasis on the 'unspeakable dreariness' of the scene (*T* 20). His illustration for 29 August, which depicts Dairyman Crick straightening up from the task of searching in the meadow for the butter-tainting garlic, also runs counter to Hardy's avowed aim of destroying the popular image of 'Hodge' (Feltes 1986: 70). Again, while the text emphasises the harshness of labour at Flintcomb Ash, Daniel Wehrschmidt's illustration for that episode (21.11.91) depicts a Tess whose 'respectable costume seems at odds with her status as a mere labourer' (Allingham 1998: 8). Tess, in fact, appears immaculately dressed in all the illustrations. Even when she discovers Alec preaching in the barn (14.11.91), she is 'surprisingly well-turned-out' for someone 'who has been trudging the roads to and from Emminster for several days' (14). Other illustrations emphasis melodramatic features to be found in the text itself, most notably Herkomer's depiction of the diabolic Alec (albeit with shovel rather than fork) threatening a terrified Tess. Here the *Graphic* highlights elements of the novel which were clearly designed for the 'mechanical' audience which Hardy now claimed to despise.

Hardy's attempt to distinguish clearly between his two audiences and to avoid the changes he had to make for the serial from contaminating the 'true' version of the novel was ultimately unsustainable. Some individual passages could be marked 'for serial only' but larger questions of characterisation and interpretation could not be so easily ringfenced. Gatrell and Grindle, for example, attribute 'the increased combativeness of Hardy's defence of his heroine to his indignant 'sense of the fiction-reading public and its self-appointed guardians' (Gatrell 1983: 12). This sustained 'campaign to purify Tess' involved the removal of 'the greater degree of intimacy permitted by the Ur-Tess' (Jacobus 1975: 327), who responded to Angel's embrace with 'lips parted', panting and 'burst into a succession of ecstatic sobs' (330). This campaign also involved a demonisation of Alec, who had been less of a caricature in the earliest layers of the manuscript. Angel too had been a more sympathetic figure, more passionate, full of 'a growing madness of passion for the seductive Tess' (Gatrell 1983: 28–31). The first edition cannot therefore be said to represent 'exactly what [Hardy] had in mind when the manuscript was completed'. It was an amalgamation of the *Graphic* proofs with passages from the original manuscript which could now be restored alongside new revisions introduced at this stage (Gatrell 1983: 40–1).

The first edition, published in three volumes in November 1891, was unambiguous about Tess's drug-induced rape. It also included a paragraph commenting explicitly on the irony that 'the sons of the forest' stirring from their slumbers at the moment of rape were unable to help, having not 'the least inkling that their sister was in the hands of the spoiler' (74). This 'event', however, was made much more complex and unclear in the 'Fifth Edition' (in one volume) of 1892, when the draught of cordial Alec had administered to his victim was removed along with the paragraph about 'the hands of the spoiler'. At the same time, however, as if to restore at least some suggestion of rape, Hardy added the comment made by one of the harvesting women as Tess feeds her baby at Marlott: 'A little more than persuading had to do wi' the coming o't, I reckon…and it mid ha' gone hard wi' a certain party if folks had come along' (45–6). There are other significant differences between the 1891 and 1892 editions. After the rape in 1891 Tess wanders 'desultorily around the grounds of the Slopes 'eating in an abstracted half-hypnotized state whatever d'Urberville offered her'; in 1892 she remains uncertain but more positively acquiescent, wandering round in a 'half-pleased, half-reluctant state'. In 1891 both Tess and the narrator claim that she had never really loved Alec: 'She had dreaded him, winced before him, succumbed to him, and that was all.' In 1892, however, she acknowledges, 'My eyes were dazed by you for a little', and the narrator confirms that she had been 'temporarily blinded by his ardent manners' (*T* lvi–ii). Hardy, who had played similar games with his readers in *Two on a Tower*, appears deliberately to have complicated the whole question of Tess's 'purity' on which the first edition had been so outspoken. Having forced readers to sympathise with the guiltless Tess of 1891, he appears deliberately to have muddied the waters in 1892.

There are other significant differences between 1891 and 1892, for instance in the depiction of the relationship between Tess and Angel Clare. In 1891, Tess is consistently subservient to Angel, lowering her eyes in his presence and calling him 'Mr Clare'. Angel himself, as Tim Dolin remarks, is 'less likable in the 1891 *Tess* than in any other edition: he is more priggish, and he reacts more savagely to Tess's confession'. In 1892 Hardy added a passage expressing Clare's acknowledgement of his own 'parochialism'. He also added a number of endearments and a much less confident mode of expression to his speech, especially in his reaction to Tess's confession, revisions which 'undo the hardening of Angel's character that was the result of the 1891 changes' (*T* lviii–lx). Alec meanwhile became rather more embarrassed about his conversion, coming in 1892 to recognise that it might appear 'ridiculous' (Gatrell 1983: 47). Hardy continued to tinker with the text in all subsequent editions, adding such details as Marian 'shrieking with laughter' at the phallic shapes of the flints in 1895 (50), making Alec even less serious about his conversion in 1902, finally restoring the Chaseborough Dance in 1912 and making further minor changes in the Mellstock Edition of

1920. In discussing readers of *Tess*, in other words, it is important to recognise that they were not all responding to the same text.

All editions of *Tess* sold well. Osgood, McIlvaine, who had printed the usual thousand copies of the first edition, rushed through three additional impressions of 500 copies each in the first three months of 1892. The one-volume 'Fifth Edition' produced in September of that year went through five impressions totalling 17,000 copies by the end of the year (Purdy 1954: 73–7). Hardy benefited in addition from the International Copyright Law of 1891, which finally outlawed piracy in the United States. In 1900, in fact, before relinquishing Hardy to Macmillan, Harper experimented with a paperback edition priced only at 6d, which sold 100,000 copies (Gatrell 1988: 241). Macmillan in turn printed 27,000 copies of their 1902 Uniform Edition and 190,900 of their 1906 Pocket Edition between 1902 and 1929 (251). In terms of sheer sales *Tess* turned Hardy into a 'major' writer.

Critical recognition, however, was slower to arrive. Hardy's account of 'The Reception of the Book' in the *Life* claims that 'an endeavour was made by some critics' to represent the 'great popularity' of the book as a 'scandalous notoriety' (*Life* 255). But there can be little doubt that it was the controversy over the novel which stimulated its high sales. Only the first few of over fifty reviews which appeared before the end of 1892 focused on the novel's literary merits rather than the cause it espoused. The earliest, by the novelist Richard Le Gallienne in the *Star* (23.12.81), welcomed what it called 'one of Mr. Hardy's best novels – perhaps his very best' but acknowledged some 'jarring...defects' of style which made one 'grind one's teeth, like "sand in honey"' (Cox 1970: 178–80). The *Speaker* (26.12.91) was also confident that *Tess* would 'take rank with the best productions of his pen' although it made the usual complaint about Hardy restricting his scope to 'the lives of the toilers' (Lerner 1968: 59–61). The *Daily Chronicle* (28.12.91) found *Tess* as pitiless and tragic...as the old Greek dramas' (62–3) while the *Pall Mall Gazette* (31.12.91) also thought the novel 'a grim Christmas gift' (Cox 1970:180).

The New Year brought more enthusiastic reviews. The *St James Gazette* (7.1.92) hailed *Tess* as 'one of those books which burn themselves in upon the soul'. The *Athenaeum* (9.1.92) also thought it 'a great novel'; its only reservations were about Clare, who was 'too perfect', and the ambiguity caused by the gaps in the narrative (Cox 1970: 185). All these early reviews were sympathetic, supporting Hardy in his battle against the censors. The novelist Clementina Black, for example, in the *Illustrated London News* (9.1.92) praised Hardy's 'open challenge' to the 'conventional reader' who 'detests unhappy endings' and any questioning of the 'traditional pattern of right and wrong'. *Tess* in her view demonstrated 'the ironic truth . . . that the richest kind of womanly nature, the most direct, sincere, and passionate, is the most liable to that sort of pitfall which social convention stamps as an irretrievable disgrace' (Harvey 2000: 15) No less an authority than *The Times* (13.1.92) declared Hardy's last novel to be 'his greatest . . . daring in its treatment of conventional ideas, pathetic in its sadness, and profoundly stirring by its tragic power'.

The backlash began in the *Saturday Review* (16.1.92), which detected 'not one single touch of nature . . . in any . . . character in the book. All are stagey, and some are farcical'. It also complained of the focus on Tess's physical attributes: 'Most people can fill in the blanks for themselves, without its being necessary to put the dots on the i's so very plainly'. It concluded with an attack on 'the terrible dreariness of this tale': 'Hardy . . . tells an unpleasant story in a very unpleasant way' (Lerner 1968: 66–8). Hardy, who claimed such critical *animus* had 'never before come within my experience' (*Letters* I 253), turned for the identity of this critic to Gosse, who suspected 'one of the horrid women that live about the Albany'. Hardy could not believe the writer to be a woman, however, since he had received 'numerous communications from mothers (who tell me they are putting "Tess" into their daughters' hands to safeguard their future) and from other women of society who say that my courage has done the whole sex a service (!)' His prime suspect was George Saintsbury. He also expected an onslaught from the *Spectator* (I 255), although R. H. Hutton (23.1.82) actually began by calling *Tess* 'one of his most powerful novels'. He had found the novel 'very difficult to read', however, 'because in every page the mind . . . shrinks from the untrue picture of a universe so blank and godless' (Lerner 1968: 69–71).

Tess continued, however, to receive glowing reviews, for instance from the poet William Watson in the *Academy* (6.2.82), who called it 'a tragic masterpiece' (75). Even *Punch* (27.2.82) called *Tess* 'a striking work of fiction' full of 'graphic descriptions' of nature, the only 'blot' being its 'absurdly melodramatic villain' (83–4). *Tess*, according to the *Bookman* for February 1892, was 'capable of dividing families and of severing long-standing friendships' (73). The *Life* claims that the Duchess of Abercorn's guests had been 'almost fighting across her dinner-table over Tess's character', a problem only solved by her seating supporters of Tess well away from those who believed the 'little harlot' should have been hanged. 'Hanged?', snapped 'a well-known beauty' at another 'large dinner-party', 'They ought all to have been hanged' (*Life* 258).

Andrew Lang, whom Hardy accused of having 'a hollow place where his heart should be' (*Letters* I 257), raised the temperature of the discussion still further by his facetious account of the plot in the February *New Review*, characterising Alec as 'a Bounder' and Angel as 'a prig'. He also objected to the idea of 'the President of the Immortals' sporting with Tess (*T* 397). 'If there be a God,' asked Lang, 'who can seriously think of him as a malicious fiend?' (Lerner 1968: 72). The Preface to the 'Fifth Edition' of the novel would refer scathingly to 'a gentleman who turned Christian for half-an-hour the better to express his grief that a disrespectful phrase about the immortals should have been used' (462–3). Lang in turn issued a not altogether ingenuous rejoinder in his regular feature in *Longman's*, where he confessed to being 'in an insignificant minority' in not liking the novel: 'On all sides ... one learns that *Tess* is a masterpiece' (Cox 1970: 238–44).

Among the other monthlies, the *Westminster Review* came down firmly on Hardy's side not only in Janetta Newton-Robinson's 'Study of Thomas Hardy' in the February issue praising Hardy's treatment of women in general and *Tess* in particular, but in the 'Belles Lettres' section in March. In December D. F. Hannigan attacked 'the hackneyed moralizing of such critics as Mr Andrew Lang' (Cox 1970: 244–8). Hannigan would continue his defence of *Tess* against 'idiotic' critics in the *Westminster* the following August and yet again the following year, celebrating Tess's 'rich, voluptuous, daring, downright nature' (*WR* CXXXIX 136). Further support came from Alfred Austin in the *National Review* in February (Cox 1970: xxix), from the *Book Buyer* in March (Gerber 1973: 57) and from the *National Observer* in April, which found Hardy 'not guilty' of the 'fin-de-siècle foolishness and abomination' of which he stood accused (52). James Little wrote strongly in support of the novel both in the *Literary World* and in the *Library Review* (54). Hardy was clearly grateful for all this support (*Letters* I 258, 277).

Other prominent critics, however, continued to issue broadsides against *Tess*. Margaret Oliphant in the March issue of *Blackwood's* attacked Hardy's morals and his characterisation. She found both Clare's rejection of Tess and her return to Alec implausible, a product of Hardy's anger with God 'for not existing' (Cox 1970: 203–14). Mowbray Morris in the April *Quarterly* also criticised Clare's refusal to forgive Tess, agreeing with Lang that Hardy had 'told an already disagreeable story in an extremely disagreeable manner'. He particularly resented Hardy's coarse manner of parading Tess's 'sensual qualifications' with the relish of 'a horse-dealer egging on some wavering customer to a deal, or a slave-dealer appraising his wares to some full-blooded pasha' (214–21). Hardy, who admitted that

Morris's attack was 'amusing and smart' (*Letters* I 264–5), attempted to reply to some of these attacks through the *Bookman*, to whom he gave a not entirely satisfactory interview in April, his own copy of which is scribbled over in red pen denying having said some of the things attributed to him. His reply to the question 'why he gave "Tess" so sad an ending', however, is unmarked and more likely therefore to be accurate:

> 'For the simple reason,' he replied, 'that I could not help myself. I hate the optimistic grin which ends a story happily, merely to suit conventional ideas. It raises a far greater horror in me than the honest sadness that comes after tragedy. Many people wrote to me begging to end it well. One old gentleman of eighty implored me to reconcile Tess and Angel. But I could not. They would never have lived happily. Angel was far too fastidious and particular. He would inevitably have thrown her fall in her face. But indeed I had little or nothing to do with it. When I got to the middle of the story, the characters took their fates into their own hands, and I literally had no power.'

Similar comments, this time divided between Hardy and his wife, would appear in 'A Chat with Thomas Hardy' in *Black and White* in August (Lerner 1968: 92), by which time there had been a further attack on the novel by Francis Adams in the *Fortnightly* (1.7.82) criticising its 'not infrequent lapses into the cheapest conventional style of the average popular novelist' (Lerner 1968: 87–8). The *Gentleman's Magazine* also decided in September that *Tess* was 'not a great novel', being too strongly influenced by French realism (Gerber 1973: 58).

America had its own debate about *Tess* along similar lines to that which was raging in England. The New York *Review of Reviews* of February recognised the strong influence of French realism 'for good and ill' on a work whose 'Zolaesque' qualities were 'likely to alienate not a few well-meaning persons' (Lerner 1968: 74–5). The Boston *Literary World* lamented its 'unpleasantness' and immorality (Cox 1970: xxxi) while W. M. Payne in the *Dial* in April noted its many melodramatic elements (Gerber 1973: 57). The *Nation* proceeded to call the novel 'as profoundly immoral and dangerous a book as a young person can read' (57). Thomas Page, editor of *Harper's Monthly*, also attacked its immorality. But there were defences from William Sharp in *Book News Monthly* (57–8), C. T. Copeland in the *Atlantic Monthly* (51) and the New York *Critic* (Cox 1970: xxxi).

Hardy followed these debates closely, bracing himself in June 1893 at the news that 'a lady-critic is going to drag me over the coals in next month's *Century* for the way in which I spoilt "Tess"' (*Letters* II 13). This was Harriet Waters Preston, whose article on 'Thomas Hardy' ran enthusiastically through his career until this last novel, in which she thought he had made the mistake of adopting 'a cause'. The novel itself she found convincing up to the point of Tess's yielding for a second time to 'her now doubly repulsive suitor', at which the story degenerated into 'mere vulgar horrors, gratuitously insulting to the already outraged feelings of the deeply disappointed reader' (Gerber 1973: 60–1). Hardy's former editor Henry Alden, however, came to his defence in *Harper's Weekly* the following December, claiming that Hardy was simply presenting the truth as he saw it, convinced as he was of 'the grimness of the general human situation' (61–2).

Other contemporary reactions were equally violent, whether for or against the novel. Kegan Paul wrote on Christmas Day 1891 to congratulate Hardy on his 'really great novel . . . at once Aeschylean and Dantesque, yet intensely modern with its dread background of Heredity' (DCM 4703). Rival novelists were less generous. 'Something whispers to me,' reported George Gissing in January 1892 to his brother Algernon, 'that the praise it receives is exaggerated' (Mattheissen 1990: V 7). Henry James expressed similar doubts about a novel which was 'chock full of faults and falsity and yet has a singular beauty and charm'. Stevenson's reply lambasted *Tess* as 'one of the worst, weakest, least sane, most *voulu* books I have yet read . . . *Not alive, not true*, was my continual comment as I read; and at last – *not even honest!*' It was in reply to this that James made the comment that so upset Hardy: 'oh yes, dear Louis, she's vile. The pretence of "sexuality" is only equalled by the absence of it, and the abomination of the language by the author's reputation for style' (*Life* 259–60). Stevenson boasted to Sidney Colvin, 'If ever I do a rape . . . you would hear a noise about my rape, and it should be a man that did it' (Booth 1995: VII 284). Some of these comments, of course, can be put down to professional jealousy. But Stevenson's term *voulu* may register a genuine suspicion that Hardy was pandering to his readers by providing them with at least a hint of the sexuality they wanted, while the accusation of dishonesty 'at last' presumably refers to the fact that Tess is finally punished for her crime in the manner expected of all 'fallen women'.

Critics remained divided about the novel, sometimes ambivalent within themselves. Annie Macdonell, for example, while calling it Hardy's 'greatest book . . . a tragedy of force enough to drive complacency out of the smuggest', acknowledged that it had many 'improbabilities'. Had Hardy 'omitted the violent acts of the end,' she thought, 'and made claims for Tess's lovableness, not for her virtue, he might have carried all his readers with him'. But 'he preferred to make war' (Macdonell 1894: 56–8). Lionel Johnson, who claimed to have read the novel 'some eight or ten times' (Johnson 1923: 227), was critical of Hardy's continual narrative intrusions and could not see the victimisation of Tess ('All this passion, sorrow, and death, inevitable and sure, to come upon one poor girl') as genuinely tragic rather than 'an excuse for setting up a scarecrow God, upon whom to vent our spleen' (244–5). Another admirer of Hardy's earlier work, Havelock Ellis, regretted the fact that Hardy had become 'a popular novelist', swelling the 'crowd' of his admirers by 'illustrating a fashionable sentimental moral' (Cox 1970: 301–5).

Perhaps *because* of its commercial success, *Tess* continued to attract the disapproval of 'serious' critics. Edward Wright, for example, surveying 'The Novels of Thomas Hardy' in the *Quarterly Review* in 1904, complained that 'too much machinery' was employed in *Tess* 'to bring about the catastrophe' and to enforce its predetermined moral:

> Having conceived a strangely immaculate heroine, who, from no impulse of her own, proceeded from fornication to adultery, and ended in murder, he had first to make her life such a succession of unmerited troubles, misfortunes and disasters, as dispels the credulity of the most sympathetic reader; and next to encompass her about with so many persons of nefarious or brutal, weak, or scornful natures ... that verisimilitude in the characterization, as well as verisimilitude in the fable, is sacrificed to pathetic effect. (361)

Critics such as Phelps (401) and Abercrombie continued to praise the novel's tragic power' (Abercrombie 1912: 137) but even reviewers of the Wessex Edition were by no means sure that Hardy's last novels had been his best (Cox 1970: 408–10, 432–3).

Both Virginia Woolf and Arnold Bennett agonised over the novel's status. In her journal of 1903 (when she was 21) Woolf recorded that Hardy had 'taken a grim subject and stuck to it till the bitter end', portraying 'with an almost savage insistence' how 'the judgment of a brutal world' can descend upon an innocent girl and destroy her. He was 'so sternly determined that we shall see the brutality of certain social conventions,' she felt, 'that he tends to spoil his novel as a novel'. She came to the conclusion nevertheless that it was 'an impressive piece of work' (Woolf 1990: 205–6). Arnold Bennett confessed in his hastily written obituary of Hardy for the *Evening Standard* that he found *Tess* 'terribly uneven' in spite of its marvellous pages' (Mylett 1974: 117). Unhappy with this judgement, however, he proceeded to reread the novel and write another article on 'The Weakness and Greatness of *Tess*' in which he concluded that although it was indeed uneven, at times 'sentimental' and even 'maladroit...I had not gone far in it before I began to be convinced afresh that I was in the presence of greatness' (123–4).

Literary critics, however, would remain doubtful about the novel's supposed greatness for some time. One of the first 'Revaluations' of literary reputations in the early issues of *Scrutiny* argued that *Tess* was 'grossly theatrical', full of 'Victorian journalese' and 'tedious and unconvincing' philosophy (Chapman 1934: 27–33). Even the academic recognition Hardy received on the centenary of his birth was couched in somewhat patronising terms, presenting him as a primitive representative of an old oral tradition, who 'introduced into the novel the typical seductions, rapes, murders, and lusty love-makings' of the ballad (Davidson 1940: 172–3). David Cecil's 1942 Clark Lectures celebrated Hardy as a brooding, peasant-Shakespeare in whose work 'the reader' was always 'liable to knock up against these crude pieces of machinery', clumsy plots, full of improbabilities and stylistic lapses (Cecil 1943: 116). Examination questions on *Tess*, as Widdowson has shown, would exhibit a persistent tendency to set 'questions which seek to circumscribe Hardy's "artistic achievement"', asking students to discuss whether the novel is 'melodramatic rather than tragic' or 'full of faults, but a very great novel' (Widdowson 1989: 86–7). This, however, is not to be attributed simply to middle-class academic patronage. *Tess*, like all of Hardy's work for the *Graphic*, addressed itself in part to this 'mechanical' audience.

What is extraordinary about this novel, as John Paul Riquelme notes in his survey of the novel's 'critical history', is its openness to such variant readings. One biographer presents its author as a voyeur, fascinated with his heroine as a sexual object, while another emphasises the narrator's 'advocacy of the heroine's case' (Riquelme 1998: 390–1). John Holloway presents Hardy as a determinist, only for Roy Morrell to demonstrate his belief in character as fate (392–3). The novel is 'discursively *overdetermined*', the product of competing generic and ideological codes which cannot be reconciled (Silverman 1993: 138). It is on one level a confession novel in the tradition of Wilkie Collins's *The New Magdalen* and George Gissing's *The Unclassed* (Shumaker 1994: 445–6) but Tess's confession, as George Moore complained (Moore 1936: 81), is never vouchsafed to readers. It can also be read as 'foundling romance' but proceeds to attack not only the class system but the cruel behaviour of the aristocracy towards peasants and animals (Garson 1991: 132–4). If, as Hillis Miller suggests, the novel poses the question, 'Why does Tess suffer so?', the implied answers provided by critics have been many and various:

> Tess has been described as the victim of social changes in nineteenth-century England, or of her own personality, or of her inherited nature, or of physical or biological forces, or of Alec and Angel as different embodiments of man's inhumanity to woman. She has been explained in terms of mythical prototypes, as a Victorian fertility goddess, or as the hapless embodiment of the Immanent Will, or as a victim of unhappy coincidence, sheer hazard, or happenstance, or as the puppet of Hardy's deliberate or unconscious manipulations.
>
> (Miller 1982: 140–1)

The text 'provides evidence to support any or all of these interpretations'. Even the central 'event' of the novel, which Miller calls her 'violation' (to avoid deciding between rape and seduction), 'exists in the text only as a blank space, like Tess's "beautiful feminine tissue... practically blank as snow", on which Alec traces such a coarse pattern'. This metaphor belongs to 'a chain of figures of speech in the novel, a chain that includes the tracing of a pattern, the making of a mark, the carving of a line or sign, and the act of writing' (116–18). The whole point about the many gaps in the narrative, Hardy's refusal to provide any direct representation of so many of its key events, is that it forces readers to provide their own interpretations, to make good the textual absence. Perhaps this is what Hardy meant in the Preface to the 'Fifth Edition' when he thanked readers for having 'repaired my defects of narration by their own imaginative intuition' (*T* 462). This novel more than most requires the reader to impose his or her own meaning upon it.

There is a sense (picked up by contemporary reviewers such as Mowbray Morris) in which the reader is constructed as a voyeur, even a kind of tourist, enticed into the text to enjoy the beauties that Wessex can offer, beauties which include not only its landscape but its unspoilt inhabitants. The second chapter describes the entry into the Blackmoor Vale from the perspective of a 'traveller from the coast, who, after plodding northward for a score of miles... is surprised and delighted to behold, extending like a map beneath him, a country differing absolutely from that which he has passed through' (12). Clare himself, along with his brothers, is precisely one of these tourists, his attention captured like other passing strangers by the sight of 'a fine and picturesque country girl' (16). There is, as many feminist critics have complained, a great deal of masculine gazing in this 'scopophiliac pastoral':

> The novel casts all aspects of the 'most finely-drawn figure of them all' as *aspects*; it makes everything about her available for viewing – not just the 'flower-like mouth,' the 'colour of her cheeks,' 'the 'hundred' shades of her 'large tender eyes,' but also all kinds of things that are normally invisible. Tess's voice, her past, her psyche ...
>
> (Nunokawa 1992: 72)

If these 'aspects' of Tess are understood in a phenomenological fashion, as the only parts of the 'object' available to us (as readers and especially as men) then Hardy's reticence is surely defensible. He draws back from the attempt fully to represent a woman, aware that the languages available to her are mostly provided by men (Higonnet 1993: 17).

In the end it remains impossible to establish the 'truth' of Tess, not just what 'actually' happened to her in the Chase but her 'essential' personality. There can be no doubt that this novel, with all its contradictions and confusions, partly the result of countless revision and rewriting, engages in a sustained attack on many of the most prized beliefs of its contemporary readers, beliefs about morality and religion, about gender and class, and about the freedom of the individual to control her own destiny. But it is the enigmatic and ultimately undecidable quality of Tess herself which continues to challenge and provoke its readers.

6

'Phase the Last: Farewell to Fiction'

Jude the Obscure: 'an act of literary suicide'

'An act of literary suicide' was the verdict of one of the reviews on the pig-killing chapter of *Jude the Obscure* (Lerner 1968: 113). The novel itself developed from an idea for a short story about a young man 'who could not to go to Oxford' whose struggles ended in suicide (*Life* 216). *Jude*, I want to suggest, was a deliberate farewell to the whole business of writing fiction. The 'Postscript' to the Wessex Edition of the novel refers to the violent attacks from which it suffered as 'completely curing me of further interest in novel-writing' (*JO* 466). The *Life* too places the decision to abandon fiction *after* the critical 'misrepresentations' from which *Jude* suffered (*Life* 309). Having finally established himself as 'the leading English novelist of the day', however, with *Jude* itself joining the first collected edition of his work, the decision, as Millgate argues, probably preceded its composition. The Preface casts 'a retrospective and suspiciously valedictory glance...over his past career' while 'the very forcefulness of the social criticism suggests that he knew the novel was to be his last and deliberately incorporated views and feelings which had been largely suppressed' in his earlier work (Millgate 1971: 340–1). He would still revise his 1892 serial 'The Pursuit of the Well-Beloved' for its publication in book form but he would embark upon no more full-length fiction. There was no financial need for continuing to seek a compromise between what he wanted to write and what would please his readers.

The Preface explains that the 'scheme' for the novel 'was jotted down in 1890, from notes made in 1887 onwards, some of the circumstances being suggested by the death of a woman in the former year' (*JO* 3). This woman, of course, was Hardy's cousin, Tryphena Sparks, who had undergone like Sue Bridehead the rigours of a Teacher's Training College while the notes have been identified as his jottings from a newspaper report of John Morley's 1887 address to University Extension students 'On the Study of Literature'. 'It is true,' Morley told them, that their lectures could not supply 'the indefinable charm that haunts the grey and venerable quadrangles of Oxford and Cambridge' or surround them 'with all those elevated memorials and sanctifying associations of scholars and poets, of saints and sages, that march in glorious procession through the ages' (Kearney 1987: 499; cf. *LN* I 178). They could, however, gain an insight into literature: 'all the books – and they were not so very many – in which moral truth & human passion were touched with largeness', books which 'explored the impulses of the human heart . . . & the shifting fortunes of great conceptions of truth & virtue' (*LN* I 178). Hardy, it seems, wanted his last novel to be precisely such a book, concerned not only with working-class intellectual aspirations (Morley's first issue) but with his second, questions of 'truth and value' in relation to 'the strongest passion known to humanity' (*JO* 3).

The two issues are connected in the novel. Sue seems from the start to have been associated with Jude's longing for Christminster. The earliest strands of the manuscript have her being adopted after the death of her natural father by the provost of a college (Ingham 1976: 163). The surviving manuscript of *Jude* has a number of passages in which the attack on marriage and the religious system that supports it is so strong as not to have found its way into any published version of the novel. These include Sue's definition of marriage as manufactured 'by chaining people together' and her condemnation of living in intimacy without love as 'adultery', alongside Jude's denunciation of what he calls 'legalized prostitution' and the 'code which makes *cruelty* a part of its system'. Jude also denounces Sue's 'senseless mysticism': 'Supernaturalism, supernaturalism,' he exclaims at one point, 'what vices and crimes you've got to answer for' (*JO* xxxvii–viii). He also complains to the Widow Edlin about 'the barbarism, cruelty and suspicion of the times in which we have the unhappiness to live' (Ingham 1976: 37). Even without these passages, of course, *Jude* constitutes a severe critique of late Victorian ideology, a direct challenge to his readers.

Hardy's approach to the writing of *Jude* was significantly different. He chose not to show it to Emma, normally his first reader; when Alfred Sutro dared to praise it on a visit to Max Gate shortly after its publication, she said that had she read it, 'it would *not* have been published, or at least, not without considerable emendation' (Millgate 1982: 380). Ford Madox Ford even claimed that she called upon Richard Garnett

at the British Museum 'to beg, implore, command, threaten, anathema-
tize her husband until he should be persuaded or coerced into burning
the manuscript' (Ford 1938: 128). Neither the *Graphic*, the main outlet
for his previous serials, nor the *Illustrated London News*, which had
published the serial version of 'The Pursuit of the Well-Beloved', would
take it, so he turned to Harper's, the parent company of Osgood, McIlvaine and Company, who were publishing *Jude* as part of their complete
edition of his work, for the serial too. Hardy met Henry Harper in
October 'on business' in October 1894 (*Life* 283), presumably to clarify
the emendations that would be required for *Harper's Monthly*, which had
omitted a whole chapter of Henry James's translation of a Daudet novel
because there were 'passages in the chapter which would give offence to
a large number of our Christian readers' (Harper 1912: 620). This hardly
boded well for a novel designed to do precisely that.

Henry Alden, aware that 'a number of anxious mothers had written in
protest at the publication of *Tess*' (Harper 1934: 164), warned Hardy that
his new novel should be 'in every respect suitable for a family magazine',
receiving the usual bland assurance that 'it would be a tale that could
not offend the most fastidious maiden' (Harper 1912: 529–30). Before
long, however, Hardy was reporting that 'the characters had taken
things into their own hands' (Harper 1934: 164–5) and that 'the development of the story was carrying him into unexpected fields'. Alden had
to write in protest about unacceptable elements in the second instalment, whereupon Hardy (following the pattern established with *Tess*)
offered to cancel the agreement and 'discontinue the story', or alterna-
tively to allow Harper to 'make any changes in the serial form that we
might deem desirable'. Alden explained once more the rules for publication in the *Monthly*, that it should 'contain nothing which could not
be read aloud in any family circle' (Harper 1912: 530). He personally
delighted in all the scenes he was obliged to cut or change, especially the
'artfulness of Arabella herself and even the pig-killing'. Hardy in turn
'rewrote one of the chapters' and allowed other changes to be made
'without any expression of irritation' (530–1).

Hardy may have expressed no public anger. He even wrote to the
Morning Chronicle in September 1895 to assure readers that 'little or
nothing has been omitted or modified without my knowledge'. He
admitted, however, that he 'failed to see the necessity for some of the
alterations, if for any'. His letter distinguishes diplomatically between
the novel as 'abridged in the magazine', which remained 'a not uninteresting one for the general family circle', and ' the novel as originally
written, addressed mainly to middle-aged readers, and of less inter-

est . . . to those young ladies for whose innocence we are all so solicitous' (Purdy 1954: 305). The different titles also indicated different products designed for different audiences. Privately too he distinguished between the 'real copy of the story' and the magazine version, for which 'I have been obliged to make many changes, omissions, and glosses' (*Letters* II 68–70).

The serial version of *Jude*, 'Hearts Insurgent', was 'ludicrously watered down' (Millgate 1982: 349), 'so watered down . . . that the anti-Victorian elements in the story were almost all washed away' (Slack 1957: 262). Many of the details of Arabella's seduction of Jude disappeared completely: she no longer pretends to be pregnant but invents an additional lover to provoke his jealousy. Sue and Jude never cohabit or pretend to be married: he remains 'a companion', always takes lodgings at a respectable distance and even when he greets her for breakfast does not go beyond shaking her hand (146). Sue accordingly never becomes pregnant, leaving readers somewhat baffled by the mysterious appearance of a child in the October instalment (Purdy 1954: 88). Other scenes absent from the serial include the pig-killing, the killing of the children and the biblical pastiche, for example description of Father Time as the Suffering Servant of Isaiah: 'For the rashness of those parents he had groaned, for their ill-assortment he had quaked, and for the misfortunes of these he had died' (Chase 1927: 157). The ending too is deprived of the passages from the Book of Job interspersed with the hurrahs from the regatta and the final words of Arabella, echoing the ending of *Oedipus Rex:* 'call no man happy, ere he shall have crossed the boundary of life' (Millgate 1971: 324). Any challenge to Victorian optimism, any hint of blasphemy, had to go (Marsh 1998: 271–2).

It was 'Hearts Insurgent', however, that many contemporaries would have read. The first instalment had been entitled 'The Simpletons', which was changed in the second to avoid the similarity with Charles Reade's *A Simpleton*. Hardy had yet another change of mind, suggesting the alternative title 'The Recalcitrants' just too late for the January number (Purdy 1954: 87). Occasionally it achieves effects lost in the volume, for instance the way one of Arabella's friends echoes the title at the end of the first instalment, exclaiming 'He's as simple as a child' and laughing at their courting on the bridge, 'wi' the piece o' pig hanging between ye' (XXIX 81). This powerful image of the temptations of the flesh 'hanging' between the lovers would be removed in 1903 and remain absent from all subsequent English versions based on the Wessex Edition.

The illustrations provided by William Hatherell for the serial and reproduced in the American edition of the novel were also powerful.

They too suffered from an internalised form of censorship: Hatherell went to extraordinary lengths to 'avoid depicting Jude and Sue alone with each other', providing 'a companion or chaperone' for all but one of the illustrations in which they both appear (the one in which Jude is sick). But he employed the newly developed half-tone process to create a 'dominant gray tone', which reflects the bleak atmosphere of the novel (Jackson 1981: 117, 114). Hardy himself was delighted with them; 'Jude at the Milestone', he wrote, was 'a tragedy in itself...I do not remember ever before having an artist who grasped a situation so thoroughly' (*Letters* II 94). He eventually had the entire set framed and hung in his study (Jackson 1981: 60).

The publication of 'Hearts Insurgent', unusually for a serial, was itself the subject of much speculation and comment in the press, presumably because the controversy over *Tess* made anything produced by Hardy newsworthy. *Life's Little Ironies*, published in February 1894, had also caused something of a stir: a cutting in Hardy's 'Personal' Scrapbook relates how it was boycotted by W. H. Smith after William Archer remarked that it was 'less calculated than *Esther Waters* to discourage *unlicensed* manifestations of the sexual impulse' (*Daily Chronicle* 6.5.94). It is difficult not to think that this may contribute to Sue's attack on marriage as a 'licence' to love (*JO* 204). Henry Alden helped to fan the flames of interest in the new serial by writing a defence of 'Hearts Insurgent' in *Harper's Weekly* before it had even had a chance to be attacked (Lerner 1968: 104–7). Other periodicals followed the progress of the serial month by month, quick to spot the dangers lurking in Arabella, described by the *Guardian* (12.12.94) as 'a pig-breeder's strapping if coquettish daughter' and by the *Illustrated London News* (15.12.94) as the usual 'young woman of Wessex with the coming-on disposition'. The reviewer of the first instalment in the New York *Critic* (28.12.95) felt that young people needed protecting from 'contamination' by the 'morbid animality' of the story. Its regular feature 'The Lounger' the following week noted the adverse reception it had been receiving, while the week after that it contained two letters and an editorial comment on the provenance of Sue's children (Gerber 1973: 68–9). The *Literary World* reported in September 1895 that Hardy was again suffering the 'indignity' of being bowdlerised for American readers although he could 'console himself with the thought that the process may increase sales of the unexpurgated version when it appears in book form' (71).

The first edition of *Jude the Obscure*, published in England on 1 November, was indeed a '*succès de scandale*' (Cox 1970: xxviii) and could boast of having sold 20,000 by mid-February (Purdy 1954: 91). It did not matter that the critics had been almost universal in their condemnation of what the *Daily Telegraph* on the day of publication called its 'prevailing gloom' and 'audacious breaches of laws and conventions which civilised society has generally accepted for its governance'. Other reviews were equally damning. The *Morning Post* (7.11.95) objected to having to read over 500 pages of 'unmitigated wretchedness', sneering at Jude as 'a most promising subject for University extension lectures' and at Sue as uncommonly well-read 'for a shop-girl of 19 or 20' (Lerner 1968: 107-9). Even Edmund Gosse in the *St James Gazette* (8.11.95) called the novel 'very gloomy' and 'grimy', dragging its readers through 'the sordid phases of failure' until they were 'stunned with a sense of the hollowness of existence'. Gosse, like all these early reviewers, lamented the absence of Hardy's 'delicious bucolic humour'.

'The Reviews begin to howl at Jude,' Hardy noted in his diary for 8 November (*Life* 287). Gosse's, he wrote rather sadly on the 10th, was 'the most discriminating that has yet appeared' (*Letters* II 93). Worse were to follow. Under the title 'Jude the Obscene' the *Pall Mall Gazette* (12.11.95) gave an absurd summary of a plot in which all the characters 'lived unhappily ever after, except Jude, who spat blood and died'. It proceeded to label the novel 'a book...of dirt, drivel, and damnation... shaped indeed by the hand of a master, but of a master in a nightmare' (Lerner 1968:109-11). The High Anglican *Guardian* (13.11.95) also found itself 'very much offended by the whole book', warning readers that 'a great many insulting things are said about marriage, religion, and all the obligations and relations of life which most people hold sacred' (111-12). Another denunciation appeared in the *World* on the same day under the title 'Hardy the Degenerate'. 'None but a writer of exceptional talent,' it acknowledged, 'could have produced so gruesome and gloomy a book; but that is the mischief of it' (113).

Hardy continued to be 'called by the most opprobrious names' (*Life* 287). *Queen, the Lady's Newspaper* (16.11.95) complained that Sue was 'unbalanced' and 'unhinged', swept from one wave of feeling to another until her final 'hopeless wreck'. The *Spectator* (23.11.95) thought *Jude* 'too deplorable a falling-off from Mr. Hardy's former achievements to be reckoned with at all'. The *Athenaeum* (23.11.95) called it 'a titanically bad book' which merely created 'antipathy in the reader' (Cox 1970: 249-50). *The Times* (8.12.95) pronounced it 'dull' and 'sketchy' with too many 'triumphs over good taste' and as much 'purpose...as if it were a tract or a pamphlet'. *Punch* (14.12.95) produced a parody entitled 'Dude the Diffuse', focusing in particular on the hero's autodidactic inventory:

'I have translated HOMER's *Odyssey* into Aztec; I know all the *Iliad* by heart; I have done the *Treaty of Shimonoseki* and *Ruff's Guide* into Greek iambics...I can repeat from memory any chapter of the *Decline and Fall*...I could tell EUCLID a thing or two were he alive. My leisure moments – if I have any – are filled in by researches into Esoteric Buddhism. But all this is nothing...in comparison with what I intend to accomplish'.

(Watts 1999: 459–60)

The *Yorkshire Post* (30.12.95) also derided the prophetic ambitions of both hero and author.

Hardy received some support: William Archer in the *Daily Chronicle* (1.1.96) chose *Jude* as 'the book of the year', the 'first sustained and deliberate utterance of philosophic pessimism in English fiction'. The *Bookman* for January contained an article by Sir George Douglas 'On Some Critics of *Jude the Obscure*' and a review by Annie Macdonell calling it 'a work of the intensest human interest', although even she complained of Sue's 'shilly-shallying' and the amount of 'downright propaganda' in the novel (Lerner 1968: 130–2). Further support came from Edmund Gosse, who wrote a second review of the novel for the January issue of the new magazine *Cosmopolis*. But even this remained ambivalent, claiming merely that to 'tell so squalid and so abnormal a story in an interesting way' was 'in itself a feat' while Sue Bridehead, 'a terrible study in pathology', was drawn with 'sustained intellectual force'. Gosse too could not resist a sneer at the 'University Extension jargon' with which his characters spoke and warned Hardy 'to struggle against the jarring note of rebellion which seems growing upon him', to stop shaking his fist at his Creator and to return to 'the singing of the heather' (Cox 1970: 262–70). It is difficult not to detect some sarcasm in Hardy's thanking Gosse 'for the generous view you take of the book' (*Life* 515).

In comparison with other reviews, however, Gosse could be called generous. For the *Illustrated London News* (11.1.96), which could not accept that 'baby Schopenhauers' were 'coming into the world in shoals', the death of the children proved the 'snapping point'. It remained the case that *Jude* was 'manifestly a work of genius', with passages of 'extraordinary power and even beauty' but Hardy needed to treat his readers a little more gently if they were to take his work seriously (Lerner 1968: 124–6). Perhaps the most outspoken attack came in an article on 'The Anti-Marriage League' by Mrs Oliphant in *Blackwood's Magazine* (January 1896). 'I do not know...for what audience Mr. Hardy intends his last work,' she asserted, but 'nothing so coarsely indecent...has ever been put in English print . . . from the hands of a Master'. Far from keeping to the conventions of pastoral in which Hardy had first made his name, *Jude* was 'more brutal in depravity than anything which the darkest slums could bring forth'. 'Is it possible,' she asked, 'that there are readers in England to whom this infamy can be palatable?'. What most annoyed Hardy about Mrs Oliphant's review (to which he appended the comment that she 'had novels of her own to sell to magazines') was the accusation that he had engineered a 'double profit', toning down his material for the serial audience before trading 'the viler wares under another name, with all the suppressed passages restored' (Cox 1970: 256–62).

Some of those who had rallied to the defence of *Tess* also found things to admire in *Jude*. D. F. Hannigan in the *Westminster Review* (January 1896) noted Hardy's affinities with the French naturalists but insisted that there was 'nothing prurient' in Hardy's latest work, which would rise above 'the mosquito-like criticism of the day' (Cox 1970: 270–4). Less predictable was the appreciation the novel received from the *Saturday Review* (8.2.96) at the anonymous hands of the young H. G. Wells, who had read the serial instalments eagerly and would reproduce some of its elements in his own novel *The Wheels of Chance* (Gittings 1980: 110–11). It was *Jude's* misfortune, Wells thought, to have appeared just after the collapse of the public taste for 'New Woman' fiction. Hardy had thus become the victim of a witch-hunt against the slightest hint of impropriety. The sexual theme of the book, however, 'the destructive influence of a vein of sensuality upon an ambitious working-man' was only secondary, subservient to its main theme . . . the fascination Christminster (Oxford) exercises upon his rustic imagination'. Wells celebrated Hardy's vivid depiction of Jude's struggles to educate himself, his slow accumulation of books, his subsequent exclusion from a university restricted to the middle class. 'For the first time in English literature,' Wells claimed, 'the almost intolerable difficulties that beset an ambitious man of the working class . . . receive adequate treatment'. (Cox 1970: 279–83).

Further praise of the novel came from another novelist, Richard Le Gallienne, in the *Idler* in February, who pronounced *Jude* 'the most powerful moving picture of human life which Mr. Hardy has given us', not an attack upon marriage so much as on 'the laws of the universe' (Lerner 1968: 137). John Allen in the *Academy* (15.2.96) doubted whether Hardy had in fact overstepped the limits of realism, while A. J. Butler in the May *National Review* suspected that 'his fame has probably always been greater among his brethren of letters than among the mass of novel-readers'. Even he thought *Jude* unbalanced, presenting

life as 'all squalid, unredeemed tragedy' and at times defying Mrs Grundy
just for the sake of it (Cox 1970: 284–91). R. Y. Tyrrell in the June
Fortnightly suspected that Hardy was not in fact as 'very angry as
he would wish to appear' but conceived himself 'to be in a position in
which he may flout his readers' (291–9).

By now the controversy over the novel had been reawakened by the
widely reported burning of a copy of the book by the Bishop of Wakefield, William Walsham How. Hardy's scrapbook contains an article in
the *Westminster Gazette* (9.6.96) reporting the worthy prelate's letter to
the *Yorkshire Post* in which he claimed to have been so disgusted with the
'insolence and indecency' of 'one of Mr. Hardy's novels' passed on to
him by his son that he 'threw it into the fire'. Hardy's 'Postscript' to the
Wessex Edition of the novel attributes How's action to 'his despair at not
being able to burn me' (*JO* 466). The *Life*, bearing in mind 'the difficulty
of burning a thick book even in a good fire,' is 'mildly sceptical of the
literal truth of the bishop's story', expressing more concern at his persuading Smith's to withdraw it from their library (*Life* 294).

The American press expressed similar outrage. The earliest review, by
W. D. Howells in *Harper's Weekly* (7.12.95) had been measured and
respectful, treating *Jude* as a modern form of tragedy, replacing the
'august figures of Greek fable' with the 'modern English lower-middle-
class'. The novel might be 'almost unrelieved by the humorous touch
which the poet is master of' but it was 'sublime' (Lerner 1968: 115–17).
The mood changed with the review by Jeanette Gilder in the New York
World the following day, which began by asking, 'What has happened to
Thomas Hardy?' Gilder called *Jude* 'almost the worst book I have ever
read'. Her review, which was divided into subheadings such as 'Coarseness and Brutality', 'Love and Pig-Sticking', and 'Too Filthy to Print',
ended famously opening the window and thanking God 'for Kipling and
Stevenson, Barrie and Mrs. Humphry Ward...four great writers who
have never trailed their talents in the dirt'. Hardy wrote to Harper's
claiming to have been taken aback by 'the nature of the attack in the
N.Y.*World*' and offering to withdraw the novel rather than 'offend the
tastes of the American public' (*Letters* II 103). Harper's, of course, refused
to accept his offer but the American public continued to express its sense
of outrage. The New York *Sun* complained of the novel's 'sordid...
unrelieved...gloom' and its coarseness (Lerner 1968: 114). The Boston
Literary World (11.1.96) found it powerful, often too powerful, but unfit
for 'general reading' (Gerber 1973: 75) while Harry Peck in the New York
Bookman called it 'A Novel of Lubricity', an 'improbable' story told with
'extraordinary lack of reticence', a novel in which its author was clearly

'speculating in smut' (Lerner 1968: 132–3). W. M. Payne in the Chicago *Dial* (1.2.96) read it as a 'bitter tirade against the fundamental institutions of society' which fell well short of the Aristotelian model of tragedy (Gerber: 1973: 77). The *Nation* (6.2.96) noted the 'clamor of disapproval' the novel had raised, finding it 'a less immoral book than *Tess*, but...slightly coarser, many degrees colder' (Lerner 1968: 133–5).

American disapproval of *Jude* appears to have lingered on into the next century. The novelist Sherwood Anderson recalls in his *Memoirs* that both it and *Tess* and were 'spoken of as vulgar books at certain literary gatherings' in Ohio in the early years of the twentieth century (Casagrande 1987: 176). In England too it remained controversial. Hardy claimed to friends such as Florence Henniker that letters of support 'continue to flow in', that 'the only people who faint and blush over it are fast men at clubs'. London society, he told Sir George Douglas, was 'not at all represented by the shocked critics' (*Letters* II 100). Letters of enthusiastic support for the novel came from fellow-novelists 'John Oliver Hobbes' (Pearl Craigie) and 'George Egerton' (Mary Clairmonte), who called Sue 'a marvellously true psychological study of a temperament less rare than the ordinary male observer supposes' (22.11.95, DCM). Ellen Terry feared that it was '"coarser" now and again in *expression* than it had *need* to be...but oh, it's *far finer* than your *finest*...As for "Sue" – never was there drawn a more life-like true picture of a woman' (DCM 5543).

Other friends were less supportive. Hardy could still recall after an interval of fifteen years that the only time Edmund Gosse had made him 'really angry' was when he 'said to my face at the lunch-table at the Savile that Jude was the most indecent novel ever written' (*Letters* IV 33). Gissing, with whom Hardy appears to have discussed some of the problems he experienced in writing the novel, in particular 'the difficulty he had in describing in decent language' the scene involving the pig's pizzle, recorded in his diary that 'Thomas', as well as being 'vastly the intellectual inferior of Meredith', had 'a good deal of coarseness in his nature' (Coustillas 1978: 387–8). 'This is a sad book,' he reported to his brother:

> For one thing, Thomas has absolutely lost his saving Humour – not a trace of it. The bitterness which has taken its place is often wonderfully effective...But the book as a whole is wearisome. The talk often outrageous in its lack of verisimilitude.
>
> (Mattheissen 1990: VI 49)

He told another friend, 'Poor Thomas is utterly on the wrong tack... At his age a habit of railing at the universe is not overcome' (VI 62). He was still complaining in 1902 to his French mistress Gabrielle Fleury how 'lamentable' it was 'that Thomas Hardy should become known in France by such a book as *Jude the Obscure*' (VIII 105). It was the hanging scene that annoyed Gissing most (IX 278), an irritation later shared by George Orwell, who also hated the 'preposterous incident where the eldest child hangs the two younger ones' (Orwell 1968: IV 510). Arnold Bennett too saw in *Jude* 'something of a falling off from the best of Hardy's earlier work' (Hepburn 1966: II 29).

There were contemporary readers, however, who recognised in *Jude* a new departure in English fiction. Two sexual gurus of the period welcomed its insight into complex sexual questions. Edward Carpenter, writing in March 1896 to his bisexual friend Kate Salt, called it a 'wonderful piece of work' finding both Arabella and Sue

> marvelously [*sic*] drawn – both so true to life, Arabella not an uncommon character, Sue less common and more difficult to delineate, and yet she is so clearly shown. Arabella's sex instincts are so keen that she sees some things in Sue's character wh. Sue herself hardly perceives. Hardy's clear impartial handling is very remarkable – but I think he is *wickedly* tantalising and cruel in his plots. I suppose he wd. say, so is life.
>
> (Greenslade 1987: 37–8)

Havelock Ellis, in an article 'Concerning *Jude the Obscure*' in the October *Savoy Magazine*, called it 'the greatest novel written in England for years'. He recognised that many readers preferred the 'romantic charm' of Hardy's earlier heroines; but 'to grapple with complexly realized persons and to dare to face them in the tragic or sordid crisis of real life is to rise to a higher plane of art'. *Jude* exposed 'the reality of marriage... for the first time in our literature', demonstrating that human sexual relations were not 'as simple as those of the farmyard' (Cox 1970: 300–15).

Hardy told Florence Henniker in June 1896 that he had 'imagined before publishing' *Jude* that it would 'considerably lower my commercial value' but in fact he was 'overwhelmed with requests for stories' (*Letters* II 122). He did not, however, change his mind about abandoning fiction. After revising 'The Pursuit of the Well-Beloved' for volume publication in 1897, he wrote to William Archer to explain that he should not expect another 'novel from me':

zest is quenched by the knowledge that by printing a novel which attempts to deal honestly & artistically with the facts of life one stands up to be abused by any scamp who thinks he can advance the sale of his paper by lying about one. (II 206)

The rumour persisted, as Max Beerbohm recalled in 1904, that Hardy had abandoned fiction 'disheartened by the many hostile criticisms of *Jude the Obscure*', a rumour he resolutely resisted (Cox 1970: 336). Critics continued to recognise *Jude* as a protest novel. For Phelps in 1910 it was 'shriek of rage', 'revolting' in every sense, 'hysterical and wholly unconvincing' (399) while for Manning in 1912 it was only in his latest work that Hardy's nature found 'its most complete expression'. Abercrombie's monograph of 1912 called it 'a fierce, burning revolt against the evil it conceives', a savage protest against 'the measureless injustice of man's state in the world'. He noted the paradox that

Even while existence is being arraigned as an unjust evil, the sense of justice is thereby impassioned to a flame of activity, profoundly *enjoying* itself and its own warmth, and sending a glow of its indignation through the whole consciousness that contains it.

(Abercrombie 1912: 143)

Jude, in other words, was written not only, as Hardy told Gosse, for those 'into whose souls the iron has entered' (*Life* 513) but for those who enjoyed shaking their fists at God, the universe, society and everything else wrong with the world.

Jude retained the power to shock its readers, bringing down the wrath of G. K. Chesterton, who famously labelled Hardy the 'village atheist brooding and blaspheming over the village idiot' (Chesterton 1925: 143), and T. S. Eliot, who presented him as the 'Arch-blasphemer' (Marsh 1998: 325), responsible for 'the intrusion of the *diabolic* into modern literature' (Eliot 1934: 54). Subsequent critics such as Guerard have noted the novel's continuing ability to cause outrage among 'the moralistic and optimistic middle classes' (Guerard 1949: 37). Not only was it 'untimely' in the Nietzschean sense of 'acting counter to [its] time' but it continues 'to confound readers with undiminished intensity across a hundred years' (Neill 1999: 89). Joss Marsh presents it as the climax of her account of blasphemy in nineteenth-century England, noting the similarity of the games Hardy played with the Bible with the games played by rationalist journals such as the *Freethinker* (Marsh 1998).

Jude is indeed a blasphemous book. It is possible to read *Tess* (or at least to make a film about it) and fail to notice its strong anti-theological elements. But this is hardly possible in a book whose hero is named after an obscure first-century Christian apostle and martyr, who travels from *Mary*green to *Christ*minster, the city he calls the 'heavenly Jerusalem', symbolising the union of piety and knowledge, and who models himself on his mentor Christ, whose vicar he wants to become. David Lodge has noticed the extent to which Jude's life follows that of Jesus, from the parody of his baptism in the opening phase to his coming to 'Jerusalem' for his final passion (Lodge 1981: 112–13), an analogy well captured in Michael Winterbottom's attaching the music of Bach's St Matthew's Passion to this scene in his film *Jude*.

The parody of Christ's baptism is particularly shocking because it is not a dove that descends upon the head of Hardy's protagonist as he mimics his Saviour's words, 'Christminster shall be my Alma Mater; and I'll be her beloved son, in whom she shall be well pleased' (*JO* 38; cf. Matt. 3:17) but a pig's pizzle, by the side of which, dangling from the bridge, he begins the courtship of Arabella. Jude's religious ambitions continue to be undermined by his sexual desires; he ogles Sue as she goes about her 'sweet, saintly, Christian business' surrounded by ebony crosses and prayer-books' (88) and again in the cathedral as the choir intone the question from Psalm 119, 'Wherewithal shall a young man cleanse his way?' (93). He recites the words of St Paul to the Corinthians (worried at their promiscuity) almost as if they might have a magic charm to cure him of his infatuation, as a form of 'mumbo-jumbo' (97; cf. Marsh 1998: 275). Sue meanwhile is conducting her own pagan rites before the naked statues of Venus and Apollo, passed off as St Peter and Mary Magdalen, reading Gibbon and reciting Swinburne's lament that the 'pale Galilean' has conquered (94–5). She also attacks the historical claims of the ancient Jerusalem, finding 'nothing first-rate about the place, or people . . . as there was about Athens, Rome, Alexandria, and other old cities' (106). As in *Two on a Tower*, Hardy places his explicit attacks on Christianity in the mouths of a character, thereby escaping personal responsibility for them.

Jude's attempts to follow Christ continue to founder. After he recites the creed drunkenly in Latin for a bet, telling his audience that it 'might have been the Ratcatcher's Daughter in Double Dutch' for all they could tell (122), he returns home, pausing by the well, 'thinking as he did so what a poor Christ he made' (124). He proceeds to theological training in Melchester, however, planning to 'begin his ministry at the age of thirty – an age which much attracted him as being that of his exemplar when he first began to teach in Galilee' (130). When this ambition also fails as a result of his continuing attraction to Sue, the narrator once again takes the opportunity to undermine orthodox teaching on the incarnation: He might fast and pray... but the human was more powerful in him than the Divine' (207). The biblical citations become more and more shocking as the novel, like the gospels, reaches its narrative climax in the passion. Sue underlines the similarities, on seeing Phillotson in the crowd, 'He is evidently come up to Jerusalem to see the festival like the rest of us' (329), and on recognising their mistake: 'Leaving Kennetbridge for this place is like coming from Caiaphas to Pilate'(330). The three bodies of the children hanging from their hooks behind the door can be seen as a grotesque pastiche of the crucifixion although it is on ceasing to sleep with Sue that Jude echoes the evangelists: 'let the veil of our temple be rent in two' (354; cf. Mark 15:37–8, Matt 27:51, Luke 23:45). Father Time, as we have seen, is clearly identified as the Suffering Servant of Isaiah 53, groaning for the rashness of his parents, and dying for their misfortunes (337) while the couple are left to cope with their loss to the ironic tones of Psalm 73, 'Truly God is loving unto Israel' and to the uncomfortable words of St Paul, 'We are made a spectacle unto the world' (337; cf. I Cor. 4:9).

Hardy refuses to relent, presenting Sue's guilty self-laceration before the cross, her belief that the innocent children suffered 'to bring home to me the error of my views' (361), as an indictment of the doctrine of atonement. 'They were sacrificed,' she tells the incredulous Jude, 'to teach me how to live' (363). Such primitive belief in a vengeful, bloodthirsty God can have no place in Jude's heart, although he tells her that the verses on charity from Corinthians 13 'will stand fast when all the rest that you call religion has passed away' (362). The epigraph to the whole novel cites another Pauline verse, 'The letter killeth', characteristically omitting the words that follow, 'but the spirit giveth life' (2 Cor. 3:6).

Hardy's attack on Christianity in this novel is clearly partial and one-sided. His point, however, is that the Christianity of his day is itself a partial and one-sided interpretation of the documents (Sue herself edits the New Testament chronologically to give a better understanding of the growth of early Christianity). Like many of Hardy's novels, *Jude* dramatises a number of acts of reading and interpretation. Ramon Saldivar calculates 'at least thirty-two letters indicated or implied in the novel, ranging from one-line suicide notes... to full-sized' epistles, not to mention all the inscriptions and carvings which 'reinforce the importance of the letter in the text' (Saldivar 2000: 38). Jude himself has been likened to Thomas Pooley, sentenced to imprisonment for

chalking blasphemous words on a gate and 'holding blasphemous conversations with a labourer and a policeman' (Marsh 1998: 297). He too
succeeds in citing Scripture against its intentions, as in the words from
Job he chalks on the gates of Biblioll College, 'I have understanding as
well as you' (*JO* 118; cf. Job 12:3).

The phenomenological point, as Saldivar explains, is that 'the written
word does not allow access to the thing in itself, but always creates a
copy, a simulacrum' (Saldivar 2000: 39). The theological point, for
Hardy at least, is that contemporary Christianity, built upon a partial
and untenable interpretation of its original documents, is itself a false
copy of the original. In Jude Hardy creates a Jesus-figure who strives to
emulate his mentor, struggling like him against the conventional beliefs
and prejudices of his time, only to be 'crucified' by his society. Not
surprisingly, as we have seen, it was not just Jude but his creator who
would suffer at the hands of his outraged readers and critics.

The Well-Beloved: the end of realist fiction

The two versions of *The Well-Beloved*, the serial version published from
October to December 1892 in the *Illustrated London News* as 'The Pursuit
of the Well-Beloved' and the novel published five years later as a supplement to the Osgood, McIlvaine Wessex Novels, are so different as to be
regarded as 'alternative texts' (Ingham 1989: 97). Hardy, who had originally written 'The Pursuit' for Tillotson's Fiction Bureau, told Clement
Shorter, editor of the *Illustrated London News*, who presumably bought
the magazine rights from Tillotson's, 'The tale is of a light discursive
nature. Whether my single eye to the Bolton Journal has influenced the
writing I cannot tell, but I naturally contemplated a provincial audience'. No cutting would be required, he had blandly assured Tillotson's:
it could be 'circulated freely in schools and families – nay in nurseries'
(Johanningsmeier 1997: 130–1). The prospectus he produced for them,
as well as promising a fair sprinkling of 'peers, peeresses, and other
persons of rank and culture' and a variety of scenes, from 'drawing
rooms of fashion to the cottages and cliffs of a remote isle', contained
the usual assurance that it could not 'offend the most fastidious taste',
being 'equally suited for the reading of young people, and for that of
persons of mature years' (Purdy 1954: 95). This may not seem an entirely
accurate description of a tale involving uncontrollable lechery, bigamy
and fetishism but it does describe the kind of story Tillotson's expected.

The *Illustrated London News*, an 'up-market picture magazine' which
specialised in current events rather than fiction (*W-B* 366–7), was clearly

proud to be publishing Hardy, prefacing the first issue of the serial with a whole-page portrait of the newly famous author (CI 431) followed by an article by Frederick Greenwood on 'The Genius of Thomas Hardy' (435). The illustrations by Walter Paget drew attention to the autobiographical nature of the story, the older Pearston of parts 2 and 3 bearing a marked resemblance to Hardy himself, most notably in the moustache and thinning hair. Most of the autobiographical elements in the text, however, would only be observable by later readers of the *Life*. When Pearston lists some of the 'earlier incarnations' of his well-beloved in chapter seven of the serial, including a girl on horseback who 'turned her head, and . . . smiled' (*PW-B* 32), the link to a similar moment in Hardy's youth is clear (*Life* 29). Similarly, when the narrator recounts the way Pearston would pursue a pretty face glimpsed 'in omnibus, in cab, in steam-boat, through crowds, into shops, churches, theatres, public-houses, and slums' (*PW-B* 42–3), later readers can compare similar passages in the biographies of Hardy recording his fascination with girls 'in fluffy blouses' on the tops of buses (Gittings 1978: 454) or 'women glimpsed in the street, in railway carriages, on the tops of omnibuses, or indeed in any public place' (Millgate 1982: 112–13).

The similarity of other characters in the serial to well-known figures on the London social scene encouraged a reading of 'The Pursuit' as a *roman à clef*: Lady Channelcliffe is recognisable as the real Lady Portsmouth while the dinner at Lady Speedwell's resembles a similar occasion at Lady Jeune's. Alfred Somers, the painter in the novel, shares a number of character traits with Hardy's painter friend Alfred Parsons, while Nichola Pine-Avon, whom Somers eventually marries, appears to have been based on Rosamund Tomson (Millgate 1982: 329). The serial seems designed to gratify Hardy's aristocratic female admirers and to titillate the curiosity of readers of the *Illustrated London News*.

'The Pursuit' is altogether more titillating than *The Well-Beloved* itself. It begins with its philandering hero destroying the evidence of his misspent past, burning 'several packets of love-letters, in sundry hands' while musing cynically on their authors (*W-B* 9) and continues with him abandoning the 'nice' Avice for the more glamorous Marcia, over whose drying underwear he indulges in fetishistic reverie, tracing the delicate patterns and fabrics which 'seemed almost part and parcel of her queenly person' before kissing 'each of the articles of apparel' (28). This scene, toned down in the volume, is matched by later scenes which remain in both versions, such as his excitement at the 'pit-pat of naked feet, accompanied by the brushing of drapery' when he keeps the second Avice captive in his London flat (101). He also returns suspiciously to pocket the 'little boot' of the third Avice after rescuing her from the rocks (124, 361). Only in a very special sense could these scenes be said to appeal to the 'most fastidious taste'.

The serial is also far more outspoken in its denunciation of marriage than the final version of the novel. In the serial, Pearston makes the mistake of marrying the glamorous Marcia whereas in the novel they separate soon after practising the coyly-labelled 'island custom'. The serial depicts a fierce row between 'these hastily wedded ones' in which 'they talked in complete accord of the curse of matrimony'. Marcia, like Sue Bridehead, objects to being 'her husband's property', like 'one of his statues that he could not sell' (39). Their 'common residence', however, lasts for four years, during which she continues to argue and to fling statues at him, before they finally agree to separate, leaving each other free to follow their 'own matrimonial laws' (42), which appear to allow for bigamy. Both versions of *The Well-Beloved* portray Pearston continuing to be plagued by sexual desire and pursuing a variety of young women around London. As in all Hardy's novels, it is the distance, the inaccessibility of the object, which increases his desire (Miller 1970). He manages, like his creator, to sublimate some of his sexual drive into artistic creativity, discovering in doing so that 'he was hitting a public taste he had never deliberately aimed at, and mostly despised' (*W-B* 44). It is as if Hardy is consciously satirising the popularity of his early fiction and its 'tasteful' eroticism.

The attack upon marriage is renewed in the serial as Pearston falls in love with two more generations of the Caro family, finally marrying the third Avice, who is young enough to be his grand-daughter. Ashamed at the disparity in their age, however, and discovering that she too has a prior attachment, 'the conviction grew that, whatever the rights with which the civil law had empowered him, by no law of nature, of reason, had he any right to partnership with Avice against her evident will' (144). Like Phillotson in *Jude the Obscure*, he challenges conventional wisdom by refusing to exert his legal rights as a husband and allowing the third Avice to return to her former lover. He attempts suicide, only to be rescued and nursed back to health by a mysterious figure who turns out to be the aged Marcia. The serial ends with the hysterical laughter of its protagonist, laughing uncontrollably at this absurd 'ending to my would-be romantic history' (168). 'The Pursuit of the Well-Beloved', it could be argued, in the interest of the candour for which Hardy had been calling throughout the 1890s, subjects its readers to some of the more grotesque elements in the relations between the sexes.

In the novel, as Patricia Ingham has observed, the women are much more independent:

> the first Avice makes clear that she will not conform to the Island custom of a trial marriage ... Likewise it is Marcia who ... decrees the end of their affair ... The third Avice takes her life into her own hands and elopes before he can complete their marriage.
>
> (W-B xxviii)

The focus is less on the appalling institution of marriage and more on the artistic temperament of its sculptor-protagonist, now spelt Pierston. Its subtitle, *A Sketch of a Temperament*, underlines this, as does the Preface, which calls him 'a fantast', subject to the same 'delicate dream which in a vaguer form is more or less common to all men' (171). He comforts himself during his infatuation with the second Avice with the thought that his peculiar temperament is responsible for his artistic creativity:

> he would not have stood where he did stand in the ranks of an imaginative profession if he had not been at the mercy of every succubus of the fancy that can beset man. It was in his weakness as a citizen and a national unit that his strength lay as an artist ... (251).

When he realises at the end of the novel, after being nursed back to health from an illness rather than attempted suicide, that his capacity both to create and to respond to art has disappeared along with all susceptibility to female beauty, his primary emotion is relief. 'Thank Heaven I am old at last,' he announces. 'The curse is removed' (333). He and Marcia settle happily on the island, surprised only by the interest their neighbours take in their marriage, which is the only marriage in this version of the story.

Hardy's account of the novel's reception dwells on the moral critique: 'certain papers affected to find unmentionable moral atrocities in its pages – quite bewildering to the author' (*Life* 303). The only contemporary review strongly to attack the novel, however, was the *World*. Most of the others, as Millgate remarks, were 'extremely favourable, if occasionally a little puzzled' (Millgate 1982: 382–3). The first batch of reviews, in fact, were unanimously positive. The *Daily Chronicle* (18.3.97) celebrated Hardy's 'richest stroke of humour', 'a fantastic tale ... told with diverting freshness'. Edmund Gosse, who had described himself in a private letter to Hardy four days earlier 'all glowing from "The Well-Beloved" ... a little the worse for your aphrodisiac nectar' (DCM 2721), wrote more circumspectly in the *Saturday Review* (20.3.97), welcoming a return to beauty after the 'squalid' and 'ugly' elements of *Tess* and *Jude*. The *Graphic* (20.3.97) felt confident that 'Mrs. Grundy may for once be happy, or at least reasonably so, over a book by Mr. Thomas Hardy' while the *Daily Mail* (23.3.97) also found 'no faintest trace of disfiguring indecency' in it. The *Westminster Gazette* (24.3.97) had nothing but praise for a 'most accomplished and cutting piece of satire', which was 'somewhat sardonic' but not 'disagreeable', containing 'nothing squalid or violent'. Even the *Christian World* (25.3.97) reported it 'free from disgusting realism' if inclined to suggest 'dubious situations'. The omission of all references to the 'island custom', it thought, would have made the book 'entirely fitted for family reading'. The *Literary World* (26.3.97) also welcomed the fact that it had 'few features in common with its two most recent predecessors', being 'free from the grosser traits that sent staid matrons into hysterics of wrath'. The *Speaker* (27.3.97) argued that the novel escaped being 'ridiculous by the real genius', 'the charm' and 'glamour' shown in its execution, while the *Academy* (27.3.97) also felt that Hardy alone could have succeeded with this 'extreme case'. It complained about some 'gratuitously unpleasant' phrases and pronounced this 'a wrong road' for Hardy to have taken, one unworthy of his genius, only for Hardy to reply, in a letter to the *Athenaeum* (3.4.97), explaining that the 'ultra-romantic' nature of the tale was in part a result of Tillotson's request for 'something light'. The protagonist, he insisted was 'an innocent and moral man throughout'. In its defence, the *Academy* of the same date quoted a number of other complaints about the 'ridiculous' nature and 'inadequacy' of the protagonist.

Hardy claimed by now to have become 'review-proof' (*Life* 303). What he seems to have found offensive about the review in the *World* (24.3.97) was its sneering and sarcastic tone. It cannot have helped that this was applied especially to his attempts to discuss high society, 'for the sympathetic and refined delineation of which Mr. Hardy has always displayed such a notorious aptitude'. The review proceeded to complain of his 'Wessex-mania'. It gave an absurd account of the plot of the novel, characterised as 'cabbage thrice', before comparing it with Richard Le Gallienne's prurient *Quest of the Golden Girl*, in which the protagonist, like Pierston a lingerie fetishist, embarks on a walking tour in search of wife, a quest finally satisfied by a Piccadilly prostitute (Pilgrim 1991: 130).

Hardy's letters to friends about this review suggest that he was seriously concerned about the possible damage to his reputation (and presumably his earnings). 'That a fanciful, tragi-comic half allegorical tale of a poor Visionary pursuing a Vision should be stigmatized as sexual and disgusting,' he told George Douglas, was 'a piece of mendacity hard to beat' (*Letters* II 154). Douglas reassured Hardy that at a dinner party that weekend all had agreed on 'the feebleness of the article' in the *World* in contrast to the 'enjoyment' provided by the novel, which he was happily reading to his mother, who dared to criticise it but 'wanted him to read on' (DCM 2131). Hardy continued to complain about 'that extraordinary stab in the back of my poor innocent little tale' (*Letters* II 156–7). Gosse attempted to comfort him in the face of 'unjust detraction', which he characteristically attributed to 'some smart feather-headed woman, grinding some axe of her own' (DCM 2722), but Pearl Craigie was able to identify the reviewer as a (male) pupil of W. P. Ker, Professor of English at University College London, himself 'one of your faithful' (DCM 1192). But Gosse was not to be deflected from leading a counter-attack, a carefully orchestrated chorus of reviews designed to reassure the reading public about the moral rectitude of their leading novelist.

Gosse's second review of this novel, in the *St James Gazette* (31.3.97), began by deploring the way in which Hardy had been subject to 'an extraordinary amount of adverse criticism'. Now he welcomed the way in which he came 'forward, smiling, with a capricious idyll, very whimsical and pleasant, in which no fists are shaken at the vault of heaven'. Similar support was forthcoming from Richard Le Gallienne, writing in the *Star* (29.3.97) to defend Hardy's portrait of a temperament 'not so abnormal or exceptional ... that there need be such an outcry as already mounts to heaven from Philistia'. An 'element of the ludicrous' necessarily attached to 'middle-aged men in love with washer-maidens' but Hardy's treatment of the subject was elevated by the 'poetry and pathos of the book'. Similar defences appeared in the *Globe* (5.4.97), which argued that the novel had 'been taken too seriously in many quarters' as if it were a 'transcript from life' rather than a 'fantasy'. It might not be 'one of Mr. Hardy's masterpieces' but it was 'a very enjoyable performance'. The *New Age* (8.4.97) too found in this novel 'none of the grim realism and sordid description' of *Jude*, 'nothing to offend even the most squeamish reader'. Britten in the *Athenaeum* (10.4.97) thought it evinced on Hardy's part a 'desire to renew ... pleasant relations with his readers' (Cox 1970: 318). George Douglas in the *Bookman* (May 1897) also found in the novel a return to the pleasant qualities that marked Hardy's earlier work. American reviews expressed similar relief that Hardy had turned away from the squalor of *Jude*: William Lyon

Phelps in the *Book Buyer* (May 1897) found *The Well-Beloved* more 'palatable' than that earlier novel while William Morton Payne in the Chicago *Dial* (16.5.97) thought 'all lovers of good literature would rejoice to learn that the "blue devils" had been exorcised'. The New York *Critic* of May 1897 found the novel 'thin, meagre and bony' while the Boston *Literary World* (15.5.97) thought only its 'charming style' rescued it from 'complete dullness'.

Hardy clearly put much time and effort into canvassing editorial support, attempting to repair the damage to his reputation inflicted by the *World*. A letter from G. E. Buckle, editor of *The Times*, assured him that 'what the World has said will not have the slightest effect with our reviewer, who will judge entirely for himself' (DCM 1532). *The Times'* review, however, when it finally appeared (8.6.97), after (ironically?) flattering Hardy on being 'sturdily independent...and sublimely contemptuous of censure', proceeded to criticise his final novel as a not altogether 'persuasive...poem in prose' whose later scenes were 'unpleasing' and whose denouement was 'sad and cynical almost to tragedy'. After this initial spate of reviews, the world appears largely to have forgotten about *The Well-Beloved*. Critical references to it were slight and mostly dismissive. Edward Wright in 1904 found 'no probability in characterisation or plot' (Cox 1970: 362), a judgement echoed by W. L. Phelps in 1910 complaining of its 'absurd' and 'whimsical plot...a plot that would wreck any other novelist' (399). Abercrombie dismissed it as 'frankly fantastic', unlike all Hardy's other novels in requiring to be 'read just for the sake of its idea, not for the verisimilitude of its substance' (Abercrombie 1912: 71–4). Writing in the *Edinburgh Review* in 1918, Gosse noted its similarity to some of Hardy's poetry, which was also often concerned by the superiority of the dream to the fact (460).

Other novelists were distinctly unenthusiastic. Katherine Mansfield dared to criticise the novel in a letter of 1918 to Middleton Murry (himself an ardent admirer of all Hardy's work) calling it '*appalingly [sic] bad, simply rotten* – withered, bony and pretentious'. Having 'hugged it home from the library as though I were a girl of fifteen', she found herself reacting violently to its 'pretentious, snobbish, schoolmasterly vein'. 'If a man is wonderful,' she continued, 'you want to fling up your arms and cry 'oh do *go on* being wonderful' (O'Sullivan 1989: 100–1). Lawrence called it 'sheer rubbish, fatuity' (Lawrence 1978: 480). Almost the only novelist to have liked it seems to have been Proust, who read it in French translation in 1910 and found it 'a fertile companion in my life of physical and moral suffering' (Healey 1994: 56). His notebooks admire the novel's architectural symmetry while *A la recherche du temps perdu* reworks its central themes: the treachery of love and time as a process of decay redeemed only by art (Casagrande 1987: 112–19).

Hardly any critic for three-quarters of a century had a good word to say about *The Well-Beloved*. J. W. Beach was forced to fit the novel anachronistically into the period of 'Relapse' since the plot so clearly taxed 'the credulity of the most confirmed readers of Hardy' (Beach 1922: 128). A. J. Guerard observed that it was 'not the worst book ever published by a major writer' but 'certainly one of the most trivial' (Guerard 1949: 67). As late as 1971 Millgate noted that Hardy's final novel had been 'largely ignored by recent critics' (Millgate 1971: 190). In his introduction to the New Wessex Edition of 1975, however, Hillis Miller announced that it was 'one of the most important nineteenth-century novels about art', not only closing 'the great sequence of Hardy's own novels' but 'bringing to an end the form of prose fiction characteristic of the Victorian novel'. Its self-conscious awareness of 'the fictionality of fiction', according to Miller, marked it as more Modernist than Victorian:

> most Victorian novels at least superficially maintain the illusion that they are imitated or copied from some extralinguistic reality. They present themselves as a species of history. They are, moreover, committed to the notion that the stories they tell have definite contours, a beginning, a middle and an end. The end is especially important. It is the *telos* of the whole, the goal towards which the protagonist has been tending. The end of a Victorian novel retrospectively sums it up. The ending gives the story a definitive meaning in the death of the protagonist or in a marriage justifying the traditional conclusion: 'They lived happily ever after.' Twentieth-century fiction seems likely to be more ostentatious in putting these mimetic and teleological assumptions in question.
>
> (Miller 1975: 12–16)

No reader of Hardy, of course, would expect a happy ending, but even his other novels of the nineties, *Tess* and *Jude*, ended definitively, with the tragic death of their protagonists. *The Well-Beloved*, however, anticipates postmodern writers such as Fowles (himself, of course, a self-conscious follower of Hardy) by supplying alternative endings, neither of which is definitive. The serial version, as we have seen, leaves readers with the hysterical laughter of its demented protagonist while the novel allows him all-too-sensibly to settle into his marriage of prosaic friendship with the aged Marcia.

Part of Pierston's problem, as Miller argues, is that he is doomed not to a linear progress, the development characteristic of the *Bildungsroman* in general and the *Kunstlerroman* in particular, but to cyclical repetition both in his life and in his art. The linearity and teleology of classic realist fiction gives way to a tantalising and frustrating circularity. The opening chapter of the revised novel introduces the cyclical theme, presenting the return of the native to his island, at whose 'infinitely stratified walls of oolite' (or limestone, the sedimentary rock comprised of the bones of dead fish), he gazes while meditating on Shelley's lament for 'The melancholy ruins/Of cancelled cycles' (*W-B* 179). This stone, of course, provides the material for his sculptures, as he sublimates his desire into 'One shape of many names', that other quotation from Shelley which Hardy added as an epigraph to the title page of the novel. Hardy added epigraphs not only to the title page but to each of the three parts of the novel to increase the cyclical quality of this novel, its clear enactment of literary art's recycling of language (Pilgrim 1991: 130; Miller 1982: 161). Pierston is fascinated by the recycling of life into art, the natural into the cultural, languishing on the London wharves to 'contemplate the white cubes and oblongs' of his native island as they are unloaded for recycling in metropolitan art and architecture (*W-B* 239).

Pierston's courtship of the three Avices illustrates the cyclical processes of nature, of desire and of genetics. Miller draws attention to Hardy's reading in 1890 of August Weismann's *Essays on Heredity*, which propounded 'a theory of the immortality of the germ plasm' (Miller 1982: 169), that genetic inheritance which produces the visible repetition of similar features in the faces of each generation of the Caro family. Hardy's poem, 'Heredity', the 'germ' of which appears in Hardy's diary under the date of 19 February 1889 (Purdy 1954: 194) displays a similar fascination with this recycling of family features, which alone can be seen as

> The eternal thing in man,
> That heeds no call to die.

> (*CP* 407–8)

The 'ultimate grimness of the human condition', however, becomes not so much 'the universality of death but the fact that it may be impossible to die', to come to a definitive end. Not only Pierston's lovemaking and art, in other words, but his life, is doomed to a repetition which, like the lovers on the vase in Keats's 'Ode on a Grecian Urn' can never achieve its goal (Miller 1982: 169, 173).

Genealogical continuity and variation, Tess O'Toole has claimed, is at the heart of all narrative, which requires the linking of units that may be similar but which cannot be identical. Realistic family sagas such as *The Forsyte Saga* 'flesh out the genealogical pattern with a richness of quotidian detail' and 'place the family history within the context of an account of contemporary society' (O'Toole 1993: 207). Hardy's three generations of heroines, however, cut off as they are upon their lonely 'island', lack the accoutrements of realism. They also lack the variety of 'normal' families, appealing to Pierston precisely because they appear the same: 'Anne or otherwise,' he tells the second generation of this family gene-pool, 'you are Avice to me' (*W-B* 237).

Pierston's fixation upon the 'One shape' of the same name also underlines his emotional incapacity for development. He at times laments his 'inability to ossify' (287), to grow old gracefully and to mature. 'In his heart,' he muses on falling for the second Avice, 'he was not a day older than when he had wooed the mother at the daughter's present age. His record moved on with the years, his sentiments stood still.' He even envies 'those of his fellows who were defined as buffers and fogies – imperturbable, matter-of-fact, slightly ridiculous beings' who were responsible for 'populating homes, schools, and colleges ... and giving away brides'. They at least 'had got past the distracting currents of passionateness' (245). As in the poem, 'I Look into My Glass', in which the persona longs for his heart to grow old along with his body, instead of shaking 'this fragile frame at eve/ With throbbings of nonontide' (*CP* 72), Pierston, catching sight of his reflection in the cold light of day, laments that he should 'have been encumbered with that withering carcase, without the ability to shift it off for another' (*W-B* 305). To Avice the Third, learning for the first time of his wooing of the two earlier generations, he appears 'a strange fossilized relic' (306).

At the end of the novel, Pierston reports the local gossip to Marcia:

They say, 'those old folk ought to marry; better late than never.' That's how people are – wanting to round off other people's histories in the best machine-made conventional manner. (334)

Hardy, however, at this stage of his career, was damned if he was going any longer to pander to what 'people' wanted, to provide them with the conventional endings they expected. He was damned too if he would publish any more novels. A diary entry of October 1896 records his belief that he could 'express more fully in verse ideas and emotions which run counter to the innert crystallized opinion – hard as rock – which the vast body of men have vested interests in supporting' (Millgate 1982: 382). *The Well-Beloved* at many points strains after the qualities of verse, echoing poems on similar themes. Hardy also wrote a poem entitled 'The Well-Beloved' dramatising a similar distance between the ideal object of men's dreams and the real women on whom they project their desire. Other poems echoed in the novel, as Patricia Ingham has shown, are 'The New-comer's Wife', describing crabs clinging to the face of a drowned man, and 'The Souls of the Slain', describing the ghosts of those slain in battle off Portland (*W-B* 342, 355). The 'poetic' qualities of the novel as a whole are part of Hardy's abandonment of fiction for verse.

The Well-Beloved, Hardy's final farewell to fiction, deliberately flouts the conventions which characterise the Victorian novel. It cannot be read as a *Bildungsroman* since its central character displays no *Bildung*. It fails to qualify as a family saga since the three generations of the Caro family betray so little variation. For a time, it operates as a society novel, but Pierston finally rejects London society for the isolation of the island. More positively, as Patricia Ingham has demonstrated, *The Well-Beloved* is highly metafictional, offering a critique, almost an abjuration, of Hardy's whole career as an artist, which, like Pierston's, is founded upon the attempt to mould women into a preconceived artistic ideal (Ingham 1989: 98–102). In the words of John Fowles, it reveals 'fiction at the end of its tether', 'a nausea at the fictionality of fiction . . . a dread of once more entering an always ultimately self-defeating labyrinth' (Butler 1997: 30). Hardy, like his protagonist, was sick of his art. Since he no longer relied upon his readers for a living, he could settle, again like his protagonist, into a prolonged and peaceful retirement. In 1897 finally, the words applied to 'the late Mr. Pierston' by 'gourd-like young art-critics' in the last lines of the novel must have seemed appropriate to Hardy too: 'his productions are alluded to as those of a man not without genius, whose powers were insufficiently recognized in his lifetime' (336). But longevity would alter that.

Bibliography

For abbreviations and details of works by Hardy, see pages ix–x.

Manuscripts

The Dorset County Museum (abbreviated DCM) holds the correspondence to Hardy cited in the text, plus three scrapbooks of his reviews marked 'Personal', 'Prose' and 'Poetry' respectively. Copies of these scrapbooks, not always complete or fully legible, were issued on microfilm by EP Microfilm Ltd of Wakefield in 1976 (reel 6) and can be found in some university libraries and, of course, the British Library.

The British Library holds the massive Macmillan Archives in 564 volumes at Add. MSS. 55281–55845.

The National Library of Scotland holds the Correspondence and Records of Smith, Elder and Company. The correspondence relating to Hardy is in MS. 23171, reproduced on microfilm by Adam Matthew Publications of Marlborough, Wiltshire, in Part 2 of their series of Nineteenth Century Literary Manuscripts (reel 1).

Reviews

I have not had space to include a complete list of contemporary reviews of Hardy's novels (cited in brackets in the text by journal and date). Where the review has been reprinted I have cited the relevant volume (for example Lerner 1968, Cox 1970, Clarke 1993). The most complete published list of all reviews of Hardy can be found in Gerber (1973).

Books and Articles

Abbott, Claude Colleer, ed. (1935) *The Correspondence of G. M. Hopkins to Robert Bridges*, London: Oxford University Press.

Abercrombie, Lascelles (1912) *Thomas Hardy: A Critical Study*, London: Martin Secker.

Aldington, Richard (1924) *Literary Studies and Reviews*, London: Allen & Unwin.

Allingham, Philip V. (1994) 'Six Original Illustrations for Hardy's *T* Drawn by Sir Hubert Herkomer, R. A., for *The Graphic* (1891)', *THJ* 10 no.1: 52–70.

——(1995) 'Robert Barnes' Illustrations for Thomas Hardy's *MC* as Serialised in *The Graphic*', *Victorian Periodicals Review* 28: 27–39.

——(1998) 'The Original Illustrations for Hardy's *T* Drawn by Daniel A. Wehrschmidt, Ernest Borough-Johnson and Joseph Syddall for *The Graphic*', *THA* 24: 3–50.

Allingham, Philip V. (2001) 'Sensation Novel Elements in *The London Graphic*'s Twenty-Part Serialisation of Hardy's *MC*', *THY* 31: 34–64.

Altick, Richard D. (1957) *The English Common Reader: A Social History of the Mass Reading Public, 1800–1900*, Chicago: University of Chicago Press.

—— (1989) *Writers, Readers and Occasions: Selected Essays on Victorian Literature and Life*, Columbus: Ohio State University Press.

Archer, William (1904) *Real Conversations*, London: Heinemann.

Asquith, H. H (1928) *Memories and Reflections, 1852–1927*, 2 vols, London: Cassell.

Austin, Linda M. (1989) 'Hardy's Laodicean Narrative', *Modern Fiction Studies* 35: 211–22.

Baker, Ernest A. (1907) 'The Standard of Fiction in Public Libraries', *Library Association Record*, vol. 9.

Baldick, Chris (1983) *The Social Mission of English Criticism, 1848–1932*, Oxford: Clarendon Press.

Ball, David (1987) 'Tragic Contradiction in Hardy's *W*', *Ariel* 18: 17–25.

Bayley, John (1987) 'A Social Comedy? On Re-reading *W*', *THA* 5: 3–21.

Beach, Joseph Warren (1922), *The Technique of Thomas Hardy*, Chicago: University of Chicago Press.

Beatty, C. J. P. (1975) 'Introduction' to *DR*, London: Macmillan, pp.11–33.

Beauman, Nicola (1987) *Cynthia Asquith*, London: Hamish Hamilton.

Beegel, Susan (1984) 'Bathsheba's Lovers: Male Sexuality in *FMC*', *Tennessee Studies in Literature* 27: 108–27.

Bell, Anne Olivier, ed. (1977–84) *The Diary of Virginia Woolf*, 5 vols, London: Hogarth Press.

Bennett, Andrew, ed. (1995) *Readers and Reading*, Harlow: Longman.

Bicknell, J. W., ed. (1996) *Selected Letters of Leslie Stephen*, 2 vols, Basingstoke: Macmillan – now Palgrave Macmillan.

Blain, Virginia (1986) 'Introduction', in Collins 1986: vii–xxi.

Blatchford, Robert (1894) *Merrie England*, London: Clarion Press.

—— (n.d.) *My Favourite Books*, London: Clarion Press.

Bliss, Arthur (1970) *As I Remember*, London: Faber & Faber.

Bloom, Harold, ed. (1988) *Thomas Hardy's MC*, New York: Chelsea House.

Blunt, Wilfrid (1964) *Cockerell*, London: Hamish Hamilton.

Booth, Bradford A. and Mehew, Ernest, eds (1994–5) *The Letters of Robert Louis Stevenson*, 8 vols, New Haven: Yale University Press.

Boulton, James, ed. (1979–93) *The Letters of D. H. Lawrence*, 7 vols, Cambridge: Cambridge University Press.

Boumelha, Penny (1982) *Thomas Hardy and Women: Sexual Ideology and Narrative Form*, Brighton: Harvester Press.

—— (1993) '"A Complicated Position for a Woman": *HE*', in Higonnet 1993: 242–60.

—— (1999) 'The Patriarchy of Class: *UGT, FMC, W*', in Kramer 1999: 130–44.

—— (2000) ed., *JO: Contemporary Critical Essays*, Basingstoke: Macmillan – now Palgrave Macmillan.

Boyle, Thomas (1989) *Black Swine in the Sewers of Hampstead*, New York: Viking.

Brady, Kirstin (1999) 'Thomas Hardy and Matters of Gender', in Kramer 1999: 93–111.

Brake, Laurel (1993) '"The Trepidation of the Spheres": The Serial and the Book in the Nineteenth Century', in Myers 1993: 83–101.

——(1994) *Subjugated Knowledges: Journalism, Gender and Literature in the Nine-teenth Century*, Basingstoke: Macmillan – now Palgrave Macmillan.

Brantlinger, Patrick (1998) *The Reading Lesson: The Threat of Mass Literacy in Nineteenth-Century British Fiction*, Bloomington: Indiana University Press.

Brennecke, Ernest (1921) *Thomas Hardy: Poet and Novelist*, London: Longmans, Green and Co.

——(1925) *The Life of Thomas Hardy*, New York: Greenberg.

Brown, Douglas (1954) *Thomas Hardy*, London: Longman.

Brugmans, Linette F., ed. (1960) *The Correspondence of Andre Gide and Edmund Gosse*, London: Peter Owen.

Buchan, John (1923) *A History of English Literature*, London: Thomas Nelson.

Bullen, J. B. (1986) *The Expressive Eye: Fiction and Perception in the Work of Thomas Hardy*, Oxford: Clarendon Press.

Burnett, John (1977) *Useful Toil: Autobiographies of Working People from the 1820s to the 1920s*, Harmondsworth: Penguin [1974].

Burnett, John, Vincent, John, and Mayall, David, ed. (1984–9) *The Autobiography of the Working Class: An Annotated Critical Bibliography*, 3 vols, Brighton: Harvester.

Butler, Lance St. John, ed. (1989) *Alternative Hardy*, London: Macmillan – now Palgrave Macmillan.

——(1997) *Thomas Hardy after Fifty years*, London, Macmillan – now Palgrave Macmillan.

Calder, Robert (1989) *Willie: The Life of W. Somerset Maugham*, London: Heine-mann.

Calinescu, Matei (1993) *Rereading*, New Haven: Yale University Press.

Carpenter, Richard C. (1964) *Thomas Hardy*, New York: Twayne.

Casagrande, Peter (1971) 'The Shifted "Centre of Altruism" in *W*: Thomas Hardy's Third "Return of a Native"', *ELH* 38: 104–25.

——(1987) *Hardy's Influence on the Modern Novel*, Basingstoke: Macmillan – now Palgrave Macmillan.

Cecil, Lord David (1943) *Hardy the Novelist: An Essay in Criticism*, London: Constable.

——(1976) 'Hardy the Historian', in Drabble 1976: 154–61.

Chapman, Frank (1934) 'Revaluations (IV): Hardy the Novelist', *Scrutiny* 3: 22–37.

Chapman, Raymond (1990) 'The Reader as Listener: Dialect and Relation-ship in *MC*', in Leo Hickey, ed., *The Pragmatics of Style*, London: Routledge, pp. 159–78.

Charteris, Evan (1931) *The Life and Letters of Sir Edmund Gosse*, London: Heine-mann.

Chase, Mary Ellen (1927) *Thomas Hardy from Serial to Novel*, New York: Russell & Russell.

Chesterton, G. K. (1925) *The Victorian Age in Literature*, London: Williams & Norgate.

Chew, Samuel C. (1921) *Thomas Hardy; Poet and Novelist*, New York: Longmans, Green & Co.

Child, Harold (1916) *Thomas Hardy*, London: Nisbet.

Clarke, Graham, ed. (1993) *Thomas Hardy: Critical Assessments*, Mountfield: Helm Information, 4 vols.

Clayton, Jay (1997) 'The Voice in the Machine: Hazlitt, Hardy, James', in Jeffrey Masters, Peter Stallybrass and Nancy J. Vickers, eds, *Language Machines: Tech-nologies of Literary and Cultural Production*, London: Routledge, pp. 209–32.

Cline, C. L., ed. (1970) *The Letters of George Meredith*, 3 vols, Oxford: Clarendon Press.

Clodd, Edward (1916) *Memories*, London: Chapman & Hall.

Collins, Vere H. (1928) *Talks with Thomas Hardy*, London: Duckworth.

Collins, Wilkie (1986) *No Name*, ed. Virginia Blain, Oxford: Oxford University Press [1862].

——(1989) *Armadale*, ed. Catherine Peters, Oxford: Oxford University Press [1866].

——(1992) *The Law and the Lady*, ed. Jenny Bourne Taylor, Oxford: Oxford University Press [1875].

Compton-Rickett, Arthur (1933) *I Look Back: Memories of Fifty Years*, London: Herbert Jenkins.

Connell, John (1949) *W. E. Henley*, London: Constable.

Coustillas, Pierre, ed. (1970) *George Gissing: Essays and Fiction*, Baltimore: Johns Hopkins University Press.

——ed. (1978) *London and the Life of Literature in Late Victorian England: The Diary of George Gissing, Novelist*, Brighton: Harvester.

Cox, R. G., ed. (1970) *Thomas Hardy: The Critical Heritage*, New York: Barnes & Noble.

Cross, Nigel (1985) *The Common Writer: Life in Nineteenth-Century Grub Street*, Cambridge: Cambridge University Press.

Cross, Wilbur L. (1969) *The Development of the English Novel*, New York: Greenwood Press [1927].

Cruse, Amy (1935) *The Victorians and Their Books*, London: George Allen & Unwin.

Cunningham, Valentine (1975) *Everywhere Spoken Against: Dissent in the Victorian Novel*, Oxford: Clarendon Press.

——(1994) *In the Reading Gaol: Postmodernity, Texts, and History*, Oxford: Blackwell.

D'Agnillo, Renzo (1993) 'Music and Metaphor in *UGT*', *THJ* 9: 39–50.

Dalziel, Pamela (1995) 'Exploiting the *Poor Man*: The Genesis of Hardy's *DR*', *Journal of English and Germanic Philology* 94: 220–32.

——(1996) 'Anxieties of Representation: The Serial Illustrations to Hardy's *RN*', *Nineteenth Century Literature* 5: 84–110.

——(1998) '"She matched his violence with her own wild passion": Illustrating *FMC*', in Pettit 1998b: 1–32.

Darlow, T. H. (1925) *William Robertson Nicoll: Life and Letters*, London: Hodder & Stoughton.

Davidson, Donald (1940) 'The Traditional Basis of Thomas Hardy's Fiction', *Southern Review* 6: 162–78.

Davies, Margaret Llewelyn, ed. (1977) *Life as We Have Known It*, London: Virago [1930].

Davies, Sarah (1993) '*HE*: De-mythologising "Woman"', *Critical Survey* 5: 123–9.

Dawson, W. J. (1905) *The Makers of English Fiction*, London: Hodder & Stoughton.

De la Mare, Walter, ed. (1930) *The 1880s: Essays by Fellows of the Royal Society of Literature*, Cambridge: Cambridge University Press.

Dessner, Lawrence J. (1992) 'Space, Time and Coincidence in Hardy', *Studies in the Novel* 24: 154–72.

Devereux, Jo (1992) 'Thomas Hardy's *PBE*: The Heroine as Text', *Victorian Newsletter* 81: 20–3.

Douglas, George (1900) 'The Wessex Novels', *Bookman* 17: 110–12.

——(1928) 'Thomas Hardy: Some Recollections and Reflections', *Hibbert Journal* 26: 385–98.

Downey, Edmund (1905) *Twenty Years Ago*, London: Hurst & Blackett.

Drabble, Margaret, ed. (1976) *The Genius of Thomas Hardy*, London: Weidenfeld & Nicolson.

Draper, R. P., ed. (1975) *Hardy: The Tragic Novels*, London: Macmillan.

——(1987) *Thomas Hardy: Three Pastoral Novels: A Casebook*, Basingstoke: Macmillan – now Palgrave Macmillan.

Duffin, Henry Charles (1937) *Thomas Hardy*, Manchester: Manchester University Press [1916].

Dutta, Shanta (2000) *Ambivalence in Hardy: A Study of his Attitude to Women*, Basingstoke: Palgrave – now Palgrave Macmillan.

Eagleton, Terry (1971) 'Thomas Hardy: Nature as Language', *Critical Quarterly* 13: 153–62.

——(1976) *Criticism and Ideology*, London: Verso.

Easingwood, Peter (1993) '*MC* and the Irony of Literary Production', *THJ* 9, no.3: 64–75.

Ebbatson, Roger (1977) 'Thomas Hardy and Lady Chatterley', *Ariel* 8 (1977) 85–95.

——(1986) 'Introduction' to *PBE*, Harmondsworth: Penguin.

——(1993) *Hardy: The Margin of the Unexpressed*, Sheffield: Sheffield Academic Press.

——(1997) 'Hardy and Zola Revisited', *THJ* 13, no.1: 83.

Eddy, Spencer L. (1970) *The Founding of the 'Cornhill Magazine'*, Muncie, Indiana: Ball State University.

Edel, Leon, ed. (1974–84) *Henry James Letters*, 4 vols, Cambridge, Mass., Harvard University Press.

Eliot, Simon (1994) *Some Patterns and Trends in British Publishing 1800–1919*, London: Bibliographical Society.

Eliot, T. S. (1934) *After Strange Gods: A Primer of Modern Heresy*, London: Faber & Faber.

Ellis, Havelock (1940) *My Life*, London: Heinemann.

Ellis, S. M. (1919) *George Meredith: His Life and Friends in Relation to His Work*, London: Grant Richards.

Ellmann, Richard, ed. (1966) *Letters of James Joyce*, 3 vols, London: Faber & Faber.

Enstice, Andrew (1979) *Thomas Hardy: Landscapes of the Mind*, London: Macmillan.

Exman, Eugene (1967) *The House of Harper: One Hundred and Fifty Years of Publishing*, New York: Harper & Row.

Feltes, N. N. (1986) *Modes of Production of Victorian Novels*, Chicago: University of Chicago Press.

——(1993) *Literary Capital and the Late Victorian Novel*, Madison: University of Wisconsin Press.

Fisher, Joe (1992) *The Hidden Hardy*, Basingstoke: Macmillan – now Palgrave Macmillan.

Fleishman, Avrom (1971) *The English Historical Novel*, Baltimore: Johns Hopkins Press.

Flint, Kate (1993) *The Woman Reader, 1837–1914*, Oxford: Clarendon Press.

Flower, Desmond, and Maas, Henry, eds (1967) *The Letters of Ernest Dowson*, London: Cassell.

Flower, Newman, ed. (1932) *The Journals of Arnold Bennett*, 3 vols, London: Cassell.

—— (1950) *Just As It Happened*, London: Cassell.

Flynn, Elizabeth A. and Schweickart, eds (1986) *Gender and Reading: Essays on Readers, Texts, and Contexts*, Baltimore: Johns Hopkins University Press.

Ford, Ford Madox (1938) *Mightier than the Sword*, London, George Allen & Unwin.

—— (1971) *Memories and Impressions*, London: Bodley Head.

Forster, E. M. (1990) *Aspects of the Novel*, Harmondsworth: Penguin [1927].

Freund, Elizabeth (1987) *The Return of the Reader: Reader-Response Criticism*, London: Methuen.

Frith, W. P. (1888) *My Autobiography and Reminiscences*, London: Richard Bentley.

Fuss, Diana (1989) *Essentially Speaking: Feminism, Nature and Difference*, London: Routledge.

Garland, Hamlin (1934) *Afternoon Neighbours: Further Excerpts from a Literary Log*, New York: Macmillan.

Garnett, David, ed. (1938) *The Letters of T. E. Lawrence*, London: Jonathan Cape.

Garson, Marjorie (1991) *Hardy's Fables of Integrity: Woman, Body, Text*, Oxford: Clarendon Press.

Gatrell, Simon (1980) 'Hardy and the Critics', *Cahiers Victoriens et Edouardiens*, 12: 19–43.

—— and Juliet Grindle, eds (1983) *T*, Oxford: Clarendon Press.

—— (1985) 'Introduction', *UGT*, Oxford: Oxford University Press, xi–xxiii.

—— (1986a) 'Middling Hardy' *THA* 4: 70–90.

—— ed. (1986b) *'The Return of the Native': A Facsimile of the Manuscript with Related Materials*, New York: Garland Publishing.

—— (1988) *Hardy the Creator: A Textual Biography*, Oxford: Clarendon Press.

—— (1993) *Thomas Hardy and the Proper Study of Mankind*, Basingstoke: Macmillan – now Palgrave Macmillan.

Gerber, Helmut. E. and Davis, W. Eugene, eds (1973) *Thomas Hardy: An Annotated Bibliography of Writings about Him*, De Kalb, Illinois: Northern Illinois University Press.

Gerin, Winifred (1981) *Anne Thackeray Ritchie: A Biography*, Oxford: Oxford University Press.

Gibson, James (1980) 'Hardy and His Readers' in Page 1980b: 192–218.

—— (1996) *Thomas Hardy: A Literary Life*, Basingstoke: Macmillan – now Palgrave Macmillan.

—— ed. (1999) *Thomas Hardy: Interviews and Recollections*, Basingstoke: Macmillan – now Palgrave Macmillan.

Gittings, Robert (1975) 'Introduction' to *HE*, London: Macmillan.

—— (1978) *Young Thomas Hardy*, Harmondsworth: Penguin [1975].

—— (1980) *The Older Hardy*, Harmondsworth: Penguin [1978].

—— and Manton, Jo (1979) *The Second Mrs Hardy*, London: Heinemann.

Gladstone, William Ewart (1994) *The Gladstone Diaries*, ed. H. C. G. Matthew, 14 vols, Oxford: Clarendon Press.

Glynn, Jennifer (1986) *Prince of Publishers: A Biography of George Smith*, London: Allison & Busby.

Godwin, Geraint (1929) *Conversations with George Moore*, London: Ernest Benn.

Goldring, Douglas (1943) *South Lodge: Reminiscences of Violet Hunt, Ford Madox Ford and the English Review Circle*, London: Constable.

Goode, John (1980) 'Hardy and Marxism' in Kramer 1980: 21–7.

—— (1988) *Thomas Hardy: The Offensive Truth*, Oxford: Blackwell, 1988.

Gosse, Edmund (1893) *Questions at Issue*, London: Heinemann.

—— (1925) *Silhouettes*, London: Heinemann.

Gould, F. J. (1923) *The Life-Story of a Humanist*, London, Watts & Co.

Graham, Kenneth (1965) *English Criticism of the Novel*, London: Clarendon Press.

Granville-Barker, Harley, ed. (1929) *The 1870s: Essays by Fellows of the Royal Academy of Literature*, Cambridge: Cambridge University Press.

Graves, Robert (1957) *Goodbye to All That*, London: Cassell [1929].

Green, Laura (1995) ' "Strange [in]difference of sex": Thomas Hardy, the Victorian Man of Letters and the Temptations of Androgyny', *Victorian Studies* 38: 523–47.

Greenslade, William (1987) 'Edward Carpenter on *JO*: An Unpublished Letter', *English Language Notes* 24: 37–8.

Gregor, Ian (1974) *The Great Web: The Form of Hardy's Major Fiction*, London: Faber & Faber.

Gribble, Jennifer (1996) 'The Quiet Women of Egdon Heath', *Essays in Criticism* 46: 234–57.

Griest, Guinevere L. (1970) *Mudie's Circulating Library and the Victorian Novel*, Newton Abbot: David & Charles.

Grigson, Geoffrey (1974) 'Introduction', *UGT*, London: Macmillan, 11–23.

Grimsditch, Herbert B. (1925) *Character and Environment in the Novels of Thomas Hardy*, London: H. F. & G. Witherby.

Grindle, Juliet M. (1979) 'Compulsion and Choice in *MC*' in Smith 1979: 91–106.

Grogan, Lady (1909) *Reginald Bosworth Smith: A Memoir*, London: James Nisbet.

Gross, John (1969), *The Rise and Fall of the Man of Letters*, London: Weidenfeld & Nicolson.

Grosskurth, Phyllis (1980) *Havelock Ellis: A Biography*, London: Allen Lane.

Guerard, Albert J. (1949) *Thomas Hardy: The Novels and Stories*, London, Oxford University Press.

Hall, Anne (2001) *'Peter Ibbetson* (1891): Literary References in the Wheelbarrow Scene', paper at the conference on the 1890s at Newcastle, July 2001.

Hall, Edith (1977) *Canary Girls and Stockpots*, Luton: W. E. A.

Hall, N. John, ed. (1983) *The Letters of Anthony Trollope*, 2 vols, Stanford, Cal.: Stanford University Press.

Hankin, C. A., ed. (1983) *The Letters of J. Middleton Murry*, London: Constable.

Hardy, Barbara (1974) 'Introduction', *T-M*, London: Macmillan, pp. 11–33.

—— (1975) 'Introduction', *AL*, London: Macmillan, pp. 13–30.

—— (1985) *Forms of Feeling in Victorian Fiction*, London: Peter Owen.

Harper, J. H. (1912) *The House of Harper*, New York: Harper.

—— (1934) *I Remember*, New York: Harper.

Hart-Davis, Rupert, ed. (1979) *Selected Letters of Oscar Wilde*, Oxford: Oxford University Press.

—— ed. (1981) *Siegfried Sassoon Diaries, 1920–1922*, London: Faber & Faber.

—— ed. (1983) *Siegfried Sassoon Diaries, 1915–1918*, London: Faber & Faber.

—— ed. (1985) *Siegfried Sassoon Diaries, 1923–1925*, London: Faber & Faber.

Harvey, Geoffrey, ed. (2000) *Thomas Hardy, Tess of the d'Urbervilles: A Reader's Guide to Essential Criticism*, Cambridge: Icon Books.

Hattersley, Roy (1983) *A Yorkshire Boyhood*, London: Chatto & Windus.

Healey, Frank. G. (1994) 'Proust and Hardy – An Update', *THJ* 10: 51–7.

Hedgcock, F. A. (1911) *Thomas Hardy: Penseur et Artiste*, Paris: Librairie Hachette.

——(1951) 'Reminiscences of Thomas Hardy', *National and English Review* 137: 220–8 and 289–94.

Heilman, Robert B. (1979) '*The Return:* Centennial Observations', in Smith 1979: 58–90.

Hennelly, Mark M. 'The Unknown "Character" of *MC*' (1995), *Journal of Evolutionary Psychology* 16 (1995) 92–101 and 272–84.

Hepburn, James, ed. (1966) *Letters of Arnold Bennett*, 4 vols, London: Oxford University Press.

Higonnet, Margaret R., ed. (1993) *The Sense of Sex: Feminist Perspectives on Hardy*, Urbana: University of Illinois Press.

Hilson, Oliver, ed. (1938) *Gleanings in Prose and Verse from the Literary Life-Work of Sir George B. Douglas, Bt.*, Jedburgh: privately printed.

Hind, C. Lewis (1921) *Authors and I*, London: John Lane.

——(1926) *Naphtali: Being Influences and Adventures While Earning a Living by Writing*, London: John Lane.

Hobson, Harold (1978) *Indirect Journey: An Autobiography*, London: Weidenfeld & Nicolson.

Hochstadt, Pearl R. (1983) 'Hardy's Romantic Diptych: A Reading of *AL* and *TT*', *English Literature in Transition* 26: 23–34.

Hodgkins, James Raymond (1960) 'A Study of the Periodical Reception of the Novels of Thomas Hardy, George Gissing, and George Moore', University of Michigan, PhD.

Hoggart, Richard (1957) *The Uses of Literacy*, London: Chatto & Windus.

Holub, Robert C. (1984) *Reception Theory: A Critical Introduction*, London: Methuen.

——(1992) *Crossing Borders: Reception Theory, Poststructuralism, Deconstruction*, Madison: University of Wisconsin Press.

Horne, Alastair (1990) *Macmillan: 1894–1956*, Basingstoke: Macmillan – now Palgrave Macmillan [1988].

Horne, Lewis (1982) 'Passion and Flood in *FMC*', *Ariel* 13: 39–49.

Horne, Philip, ed. (1999) *Henry James: A Life in Letters*, London: Allen Lane.

Houghton, Walter E., ed. (1966–89), *The Wellesley Index to Victorian Periodicals*, 5 vols, Toronto: University of Toronto Press.

How, M. A. De Wolfe (1919) *The Atlantic Monthly and Its Makers*, Boston: Atlantic Monthly Press.

Howard, David, Lucas, John and Goode, John, eds (1966) *Tradition and Tolerance in Nineteenth-Century Fiction*, London: Routledge & Kegan Paul.

Howard, Jeanne (1977) 'Thomas Hardy's "Mellstock" and the Registrar General's Stinsford', *Literature and History* 6: 179–201.

Howarth, Patrick (1963) *Squire: 'Most Generous of Men'*, London: Hutchinson.

Howe, Irving (1968) *Thomas Hardy*, London: Weidenfeld & Nicolson.

Howells, W. D. (1901) *Heroines of Fiction*, 2 vols, New York: Harper.

——(1959) *Criticism and Fiction and Other Essays*, ed. Clara Marburg Kirk and Rudolf Kirk, New York: New York University Press.

—— (1969) *My Literary Passions*, New York: Greenwood Press [1895].

—— (1993) *Selected Literary Criticism*, ed. Ulrich Halfmann and others, 2 vols, Bloomington: Indiana University Press.

Hughes, Linda K., and Lund, Michael (1991) *The Victorian Serial*, Charlottesville: University Press of Virginia.

Hughes, Winifred (1980) *The Maniac in the Cellar: Sensation Novels of the 1860s*, Princeton: Princeton University Press.

Hunt, R. W., Philip, I. G and Roberts, R. J., eds (1975) *Studies in the Book Trade*, Oxford: Oxford Bibliographical Society.

Hunter, Shelagh (1984) *Victorian Idyllic Fiction: Pastoral Strategies*, London: Macmillan – now Palgrave Macmillan.

Huxley, Leonard (1923) *The House of Smith Elder*, London: Smith Elder.

Hyatt, Alfred H., ed. (1906) *The Pocket Thomas Hardy*, London: Chatto & Windus.

Ingarden, Roman (1973) *The Cognition of the Literary Work of Art*, trans. Ruth Ann Crowley and Kenneth Olson, Evanston, Illinois: Northwestern University Press.

Ingersoll, Earl (1990) 'Writing and Memory in *MC*', *English Literature in Transition* 33: 299–309.

Ingham, Patricia (1976) 'The Evolution of *JO*', *Review of English Studies* 27: 27–37, 159–69.

—— (1989) *Thomas Hardy*, Hemel Hempstead: Harvester Wheatsheaf.

Irvin, Glenn (1988) 'Hardy's Comic Archetype: *UGT*', *THJ* 4: 54–59.

Iser, Wolfgang (1974) *The Implied Reader: Patterns of Communication in Prose Fiction from Bunyan to Beckett*, Baltimore: Johns Hopkins University Press.

—— (1978) *The Act of Reading: A Theory of Aesthetic Response*, Baltimore: Johns Hopkins University Press.

—— (1993) *The Fictive and the Imaginary: Charting Literary Anthropology*, Baltimore: Johns Hopkins University Press.

Jackson, Arlene M. (1981) *Illustration and the Novels of Thomas Hardy*, London: Macmillan – now Palgrave Macmillan.

Jacobus, Mary (1975) 'Tess's Purity', *Essays in Criticism* 26: 318–38.

—— (1979) 'Tree and Machine in *W*' in Kramer 1979: 116–34.

—— (1986) *Reading Woman: Essays in Feminist Criticism*, London: Methuen.

—— (1999) *Psychoanalysis and the Scene of Reading*, Oxford: Oxford University Press.

Jameson, Fredric (1981) *The Political Unconscious: Narrative as a Socially Symbolic Act*, London: Methuen.

Jauss, Hans Robert (1982) *Toward an Aesthetic of Reception*, trans. Timothy Bahti, Brighton: Harvester.

Johanningsmeier, Charles (1997) *Fiction and the American Literary Marketplace: The Role of Newspaper Syndicates, 1860–1900*, Cambridge: Cambridge University Press.

Johnson, H. A. T. (1976) 'In Defence of *T-M*', in Pinion 1976: 39–59.

Johnson, Lionel (1911) *Post Liminium: Essays and Critical Papers*, ed. Thomas Whittemore, London: Elkin Matthews.

—— (1923) *The Art of Thomas Hardy*, London: Bodley Head [1894].

Jones, Doris Arthur, (1930) *The Life and Letters of Henry Arthur Jones*, London: Victor Gollancz.

Jones, Lawrence (1965) '*DR* and the Victorian Sensation Novel', *Nineteenth-Century Fiction* 20: 35–50.

——(1978) ' "A Good Hand at a Serial": Thomas Hardy and the Serialization of *FMC*', *Studies in the Novel* 10: 320–34.

——(1980) 'George Eliot and Pastoral Tragicomedy in *FMC*' *Studies in Philology* 77: 402–25.

——(1989) '*UGT* and the Victorian Pastoral', in Colin Gibson, ed., *Art and Society in the Victorian Novel*, Basingstoke: Macmillan – now Palgrave Macmillan.

Jones, Mervyn (1999) *The Amazing Victorian: A Life of George Meredith*, London: Constable.

Jordan, John O. and Patten, Robert L., eds (1995) *Literature in the Marketplace: Nineteenth-Century British Publishing and Reading Practices*, Cambridge: Cambridge University Press.

Joshi, Priya (1998) 'Culture and Consumption: Fiction, the Reading Public, and the British Novel in Colonial India', *Book History* I: 196–220.

Kearney, Anthony (1986) *John Churton Collins: The Louse on the Locks of Literature*, Edinburgh: Scottish Academic Press.

——(1987) 'John Morley's "On the Study of Literature" and Hardy's *JO*', *Notes and Queries* 232: 499–500.

Keating, Peter (1991) *The Haunted Study: A Social History of the English Novel, 1875–1914*, London: Fontana [1989].

Keith, W. J. (1965) *Richard Jefferies: A Critical Study*, London: Oxford University Press.

Kelly, John, ed. (1986, 1994, 1997) *The Collected Letters of W. B. Yeats*, 3 vols, Oxford: Clarendon Press.

Kettle, Arnold, ed. (1972) *The Nineteenth-Century Novel: Critical Essays and Documents*, London: Heinemann.

Kincaid, James (1979) 'Hardy's Absences' in Kramer 1979: 202–14.

King, Jeanette (1978) *Tragedy in the Victorian Novel*, Cambridge: Cambridge University Press.

——(1992) '*MC*: Talking about Character', *THJ* 8, no.3: 42–6.

Kramer, Dale, ed. (1979) *Critical Approaches to the Fiction of Thomas Hardy*, London: Macmillan.

——ed. (1980) *Critical Essays on Thomas Hardy: The Novels*, Boston: G. K. Hall.

——ed. (1981) *The Woodlanders*, Oxford: Clarendon.

——ed. (1999) *The Cambridge Companion to Thomas Hardy*, Cambridge: Cambridge University Press.

Krissdottir, Morine, ed. (1995) *Petrushka and the Dancer: The Diaries of John Cowper Powys 1929–1939*, Manchester: Carcanet Press.

Lago, Mary and Furbank, P. N. (1985) *Selected Letters of E. M. Forster*, 2 vols, London: Arena; Cambridge, Mass.: Belknap Press.

Laird, J. T. (1975) *The Shaping of* T, Oxford: Clarendon Press.

——(1980) 'New Light on the Evolution of *T*', *Review of English Studies* 31: 414–35.

Lamont, Corliss, and Lamont, Lansing, eds (1979) *Letters of John Masefield to Florence Lamont*, London: Macmillan.

Lang, Cecil Y., ed., *The Swinburne Letters*, 6 vols, New Haven: Yale University Press.

Langdon, Richard G., ed. (1978) *Book Selling and Book Buying: Aspects of the Nineteenth-Century British and American Book Trade*, Chicago: American Library Association.

Law, Graham (2000) *Serializing Fiction in the Victorian Press*, Basingstoke: Palgrave – now Palgrave Macmillan.

Lawrence, D. H. (1978) 'Study of Thomas Hardy', in *Phoenix: The Posthumous Papers of D. H. Lawrence, ed. Edward D. McDonald*, Harmondsworth: Penguin [1936].

Layard, George Somes (1901) *Mrs Lynn Linton: Her Life, Letters and Opinions*, London: Methuen.

Lea, F. A. (1959) *The Life of Middleton Murry*, London: Methuen.

Leavis, F. R. (1948) *The Great Tradition*, London: Chatto & Windus.

Leavis, Q. D. (1932) *Fiction and the Reading Public*, London: Chatto & Windus.

Lecercle, Jean Jacques (1993) 'The Violence of Style in *T*', in Widdowson 1993: 147–56.

Lee, Vernon (1923) *The Handling of Words*, London: John Lane.

Lerner, Laurence and Holmstrom, John, eds (1968) *Thomas Hardy and His Readers*, London: Bodley Head.

Liebman-Kleine, JoAnne (1987), 'Reading Thomas Hardy's *MC*', *Reader* 17: 13–28.

Lock, Charles (1992) *Thomas Hardy: Criticism in Focus*, Bristol: Bristol Classical Press.

Lodge, David (1981) *Working with Structuralism*, London: Routledge & Kegan Paul.

Lonoff, Sue (1982) *Wilkie Collins and His Victorian Readers: A Study in the Rhetoric of Authorship*, New York: A. M. S. Press.

Lothe, Jakob (1999) 'Variants on Genre: *RN, MC, HE*', in Kramer 1999: 112–29.

Lovell, Terry (1987) *Consuming Fiction*, London: Verso.

Lubbock, Percy, ed. (1926) *The Diary of Arthur Christopher Benson*, London: Hutchinson.

Ludwig, Richard, ed. (1965) *Letters of Ford Madox Ford*, Princeton: Princeton University Press.

Lund, Michael (1994) *America's Continuing Story: An Introduction to Serial Fiction, 1850–1900*, Detroit: Wayne State University Press.

Lynd, Robert (1919) *Old and New Masters*, London: T. Fisher Unwin.

Maas, Henry, ed. (1971) *The Letters of A. E. Housman*, London: Rupert Hart-Davis.

MacCarthy, Desmond (1931) *Portraits*, London: Putnam.

—— (1932) *Criticism*, London: Putnam.

—— (1935) *Experience*, London: Putnam.

McCarthy, Lillah, *Myself and My Friends*, London: Thornton Butterworth.

Macdonell, Annie (1894) *Thomas Hardy*, London: Hodder & Stoughton.

Machor, James L., ed. (1993) *Readers in History: Nineteenth-Century Literature and the Contexts of Response*, Baltimore: Johns Hopkins University Press.

McDonald, Peter D. (1997) *British Literary Culture and Publishing Practice, 1880–1914*, Cambridge: Cambridge University Press.

McNeillie, Andrew, ed. (1986–1994) *The Essays of Virginia Woolf*, 4 vols, London: Hogarth Press.

Mair, G. H. (1914) *Modern English Literature: From Chaucer to the Present Day*, London: Williams & Norgate.

Mairet, Philip (1936) *A. R. Orage: A Memoir*, London: J. M. Dent.

Maitland, F. W., (1906) *The Life and Letters of Leslie Stephen*, 2 vols, London: Duckworth.

Mallett, Phillip, ed. (2000) *The Achievement of Thomas Hardy*, Basingstoke: Macmillan – now Palgrave Macmillan.

Marcus, Stephen (1969) *The Other Victorians: A Study of Sexuality and Pornography in Mid-Nineteenth-Century England*, London: Corgi [1966].

Marrot, H. V. (1935) *The Life and Letters of John Galsworthy*, London: Heinemann.

Marsh, Joss (1998) *Word Crimes: Blasphemy, Culture, and Literature in Nineteenth-Century England*, Chicago: University of Chicago Press.

Martin, Robert Bernard (1985) *With Friends Possessed: A Life of Edward Fitzgerald*, New York: Athenaeum.

Marx, Karl (1977) *Karl Marx: Selected Writings*, ed. David McLellan, Oxford: Oxford University Press.

Mason, D. G. (1991) 'Hardy and Zola: A Comparative Study of *T* and *Abbé Mouret*', *THJ* 7, no.3: 89–102.

Mason, Michael (1988) 'The Burning of *JO*', *Notes and Queries* 233: 332–4.

Matthew, H. C. G., ed. (1994) *The Gladstone Diaries*, 14 vols, Oxford: Clarendon Press.

Mattheissen, Paul F., and Millgate, Michael, eds (1965) *Transatlantic Dialogues: Selected American Correspondence of Edmund Gosse*, Austin: University of Texas Press.

Mattheissen, Paul F., Young, Arthur C., and Coustillas, Pierre, eds (1990–97) *The Collected Letters of George Gissing*, 9 vols, Athens, Ohio: Ohio University Press.

Maugham, W. Somerset (1948) *Cakes and Ale*, Harmondsworth: Penguin [1930].

May, Charles E. (1974) '*FMC* and *W*: Hardy's Grotesque Pastorals', *English Literature in Transition* 17: 147–58.

Mays, Kelly J. (1995) 'The Disease of Reading and Victorian Periodicals', in Jordan 1995: 165–194.

Meredith, George (1978) *An Essay on Comedy and the Uses of the Comic Spirit*, New York: Scribner [1877].

Meynell, Viola, ed., (1940) *Friends of a Lifetime: Letters to Sydney Carlyle Cockerell*, London: Jonathan Cape.

——(1942) *Letters of J. M. Barrie*, London: Peter Davies.

——(1956) *The Best of Friends: Further Letters to Sydney Carlyle Cockerell*, London: Rupert Hart-Davis.

Miller, J.Hillis (1966) 'The Geneva School', *Critical Quarterly* 8: 305–21.

——(1970) *Thomas Hardy: Distance and Desire*, Cambridge, Mass.: Harvard University Press.

——(1975) 'Introduction', *W-B*, London: Macmillan, pp. 11–21.

——(1981) 'Topography in *RN*', *Essays in Literature* 8: 119–34.

——(1982) *Fiction and Repetition: Seven English Novels*, Oxford: Blackwell.

Millgate, Michael (1971) *Thomas Hardy: His Career as a Novelist*, London: Bodley Head.

——(1982) *Thomas Hardy: A Biography*, Oxford: Clarendon Press.

Mills, Sara, ed. (1994) *Gendering the Reader*, Hemel Hempstead: Harvester Wheatsheaf.

Mitchell, Judith (1993) 'Hardy's Female Reader', in Higonnet 1993: 172–87.

——(1994) *The Stone and the Scorpion: The Female Subject of Desire in the Novels of Charlotte Brontë, George Eliot and Thomas Hardy*, Westport, Conn.: Greenwood Press.

Moore, George (1936) *Conversations in Ebury Street*, London: Heinemann [1924].

——(1972) *Confessions of a Young Man*, ed. Susan Dick, Montreal: McGill-Queens University Press [1888].

Moore, Jerrold Northrop (1984) *Edward Elgar: A Creative Life*, Oxford: Oxford University Press.

Moore, Kevin Z. (1982) 'The Poet within the Architect's Ring: *DR*, Hardy's Hybrid Detective-Gothic Narrative', *Studies in the Novel* 14: 31–42.

Morgan, Charles (1943) *The House of Macmillan*, London: Macmillan.

Morgan, Rosemarie (1988) *Women and Sexuality in the Novels of Thomas Hardy*, London: Routledge.

—— (1992) *Cancelled Words: Rediscovering Thomas Hardy*, London: Routledge.

Morrell, Roy (1965) *Thomas Hardy: The Will and the Way*, Kuala Lumpur: University of Malaya Press.

—— (1976) 'Some Aspects of Hardy's Minor Novels', in Pinion 1976: 60–73.

Morrison, Elizabeth (1995) 'Serial Fiction in Australian Colonial Newspapers', in Jordan 1995: 306–24.

Morrison, Ronald D. (1992) 'Reading and Restoration in *T*', *Victorian Newsletter* 82: 27–35.

Moses, Michael Valdez (2000) 'Agon in the Marketplace: *MC* as Bourgeois Tragedy', in Wolfreys 2000: 170–201.

Mossman, Mark (1998) 'Unique Individualities, United Communities: *UGT* as Hardy's Workable World', *THJ* 25: 20–5.

Moulton, Richard G. (1895) *Four Years of Novel Reading: An Account of an Experiment in Popularizing the Study of Fiction*, London: Isbister and Co.

Moulton, W. Fiddian (1926) *Richard Green Moulton*, London: Epworth Press.

Murry, J. Middleton (1920) *Aspects of Literature*, London: Collins.

Myers, Robin and Harris, Michael, eds (1993) *Serials and Their Readers, 1620–1914*, Winchester: St. Paul's Bibliographies.

Mylett, Andrew, ed. (1974) *Arnold Bennett: The Evening Standard Years*, London: Chatto & Windus.

Nash, Andrew (2001) 'The Serialization and Publication of *RN*: A New Thomas Hardy Letter', *The Library* 2: 53–9.

Neale, Catherine (1993) 'DR: The Merits and Demerits of Popular Fiction', *Critical Survey* 5: 115–22.

Neill, Edward (1999) *Trial by Ordeal: Thomas Hardy and the Critics*, Columbia, SC: Camden House.

Nemesvari, Richard (1990) 'The Anti-Comedy of *T-M*', *Victorian Newsletter* 77: 8–13.

Nevinson, Henry W. (1905) *Books and Personalities*, London: John Lane.

Newbolt, Henry (1942) *The Later life and Letters of Sir Henry Newbolt*, London: Faber & Faber.

Newsome, David (1980) *On the Edge of Paradise: A. C. Benson, The Diarist*, London: John Murray.

—— ed. (1981) *Edwardian Excursions: From the Diaries of A. C. Benson, 1898–1904*, London: John Murray.

Nicholson, Nigel and Trautmann, Joanne, eds (1975–1981) *The Letters of Virginia Woolf*, 6 vols, London: Hogarth Press.

Nicoll, W. Robertson (1913) *A Bookman's Letters*, London: Hodder & Stoughton.

Nietzsche, Friedrich (1996) *On the Genealogy of Morals*, trans. Douglas Smith, Oxford: Oxford University Press [1887].

Norris, Christopher (1987) *Derrida*, London: Fontana.

Nowell-Smith, Simon (1964) *Edwardian England, 1901–1914*, London: Oxford University Press.

—— ed. (1967) *Letters to Macmillan*, London: Macmillan.

Nunokawa, Jeff (1992) 'T, Tourism, and the Spectacle of the Woman' in Linda M.Shires, ed., *Rewriting the Victorians*, London: Routledge.

Ogden, Daryl (1993) 'Bathsheba's Visual Estate: Female Spectatorship in *FMC*', *Journal of Narrative Technique* 23: 1–15.

O'Hara, Patricia (1997) 'Narrating the Native: Victorian Anthropology and Hardy's *RN*', *Nineteenth-Century Contexts* 20: 147–63.

Ohmann, Richard (1996) *Selling Culture: Magazines, Markets, and Class at the Turn of the Century*, London: Verso.

Olmsted, John Charles (1979) *A Victorian Art of Fiction: Essays on the Novel in British Periodicals, 1870–1900*, New York: Garland.

Orel, Harold (1984) *Victorian Literary Critics*, Basingstoke: Macmillan – now Palgrave Macmillan.

Orwell, George (2000) *Coming Up for Air*, Harmondsworth: Penguin [1939].

Orwell, Sonia and Angus, Ian, eds (1968) *The Collected Essays, Journalism and Letters of George Orwell*, 4 vols, London: Secker & Warburg.

O'Sullivan, Vincent, ed. (1989) *Katherine Mansfield: Selected Letters*, Oxford: Clarendon Press.

O'Toole, Tess (1993) 'Genealogy and Narrative Jamming in Hardy's *W-B*', *Narrative* I: 207–21.

Ousby, Ian (1984) 'Class in *DR*' *Durham University Journal* 45: 217–22.

Owen, Harold and Bell, John, eds (1967) *Wilfred Owen: Collected Letters*, London: Oxford University Press.

Page, Norman (1977) *Thomas Hardy*, London: Routledge & Kegan Paul.

——ed. (1980a) *Thomas Hardy: The Writer and His Work*, New York: St. Martins Press – now Palgrave Macmillan.

——ed. (1980b) *Thomas Hardy: The Writer and His Background*, London: Bell & Hyman.

——ed. (2000) *Oxford Reader's Companion to Hardy*, Oxford: Oxford University Press.

Palmer, D. J. (1965) *The Rise of English Studies*, London: Oxford University Press.

Panton, J. (1908) *Leaves from a Life*, London: Eveleigh Nash.

Paterson, John (1959) '*RN* as Antichristian Document', *Nineteenth Century Fiction*, 14: 111–27.

——(1960a) *The Making of 'The Return of the Native'*, Berkeley: University of California Press.

——(1960b) 'The Genesis of *JO*', *Studies in Philology* 57: 87–98.

Paul, Charles Kegan (1899) *Memories*, London: Kegan Paul, Trench, Trubner & Co.

Peck, John (1981) 'Hardy's *W*: The Too Transparent Web', *English Literature in Transition* 24: 147–53.

Peterson, Carla L. (1985) *The Determined Reader: Gender and Culture in the Novel from Napoleon to Victoria*, New Brunswick: Rutgers University Press.

Pettit, Charles P. C. ed. (1994) *New Perspectives on Thomas Hardy*, Basingstoke: Macmillan – now Palgrave Macmillan.

——ed. (1998a) *Celebrating Thomas Hardy: Insights and Appreciations*, Basingstoke: Macmillan – now Palgrave Macmillan.

——ed. (1998b) *Reading Thomas Hardy*, Basingstoke: Macmillan – now Palgrave Macmillan.

——(2000) 'Merely a Good Hand at a Serial? From *PBE* to *FMC*' in Mallett 2000: 1–21.

Phelps, William Lyon (1910) *Essays on Modern Novelists*, New York: Macmillan.
—— (1939) *Autobiography with Letters*, New York: Oxford University Press.
Pilgrim, Anne C. (1991) 'Hardy's Retroactive Self-Censorship: The Case of *W-B*' in *Victorian Authors and Their Works: Revision Motivations and Modes*, ed. Judith Kennedy, Athens: Ohio University Press.
Pinck, Joan B. (1969) 'The Reception of Thomas Hardy's *RN*', *Harvard Library Bulletin* 17: 291–308.
Pinion, F. B., ed. (1974) *Thomas Hardy and the Modern World*, Dorchester: Thomas Hardy Society.
—— ed. (1976) *Budmouth Essays on Thomas Hardy*, Dorchester: Thomas Hardy Society.
Poovey, Mary (1984) *The Proper Lady and the Woman Writer: Ideology as Style in the Works of Mary Wollstonecraft, Mary Shelley, and Jane Austen*, Chicago: Chicago University Press.
Potter, Stephen (1937) *The Muse in Chains*, London: Jonathan Cape.
Poulet, Georges (1980) 'Criticism and the Experience of Interiority', in Tompkins 1980: 41–9.
Pound, Reginald and Harmsworth, Geoffrey (1959) *Northcliffe*, London: Cassell.
Powys, John Cowper (1934) *Autobiography*, London: John Lane.
—— (1938) *The Pleasures of Literature*, London: Cassell.
Pritchett, V. S. (1969) *A Cab at the Door, An Autobiography: Early Years*, London: Chatto & Windus.
Purdy, Richard Little (1954) *Thomas Hardy: A Bibliographical Study*, London: Oxford University Press.
Rabiger, Michael (1989) 'Hardy's Fictional Process and His Emotional Life', in Butler 1989: 88–109.
Radford, Andrew (2001) 'The Unmanned Fertility Figure in Hardy's *W* (1887)', *Victorian Newsletter* 99 (Spring): 24–31.
Radway, Janice (1991) *Reading the Romance: Women, Patriarchy and Popular Literature*, Chapel Hill: University of North Carolina Press [1984].
Raleigh, Lady (1926) *The Letters of Sir Walter Raleigh*, 2 vols, London: Methuen.
Reid, Forrest (1928) *Illustrators of the Sixties*, London: Faber & Faber.
Rideing, William (1912) *Many Celebrities and a Few Others: A Bundle of Reminiscences*, London: Eveleigh Nash.
Riesen, Beat (1990) *Thomas Hardy's Minor Novels*, Berne: Peter Lang.
Rimmer, Mary (1993) 'Club Laws: Chess and the Construction of Gender in *PBE*' in Higonnet 1993: 203–20.
Riquelme, John Paul, ed. (1998) *Thomas Hardy: T*, Boston: Bedford Books.
Robertson, P. J. M (1981) *The Leavises on Fiction*, London: Macmillan – now Palgrave Macmillan.
Rose, Jonathan (1992) 'Re-Reading the English Common Reader: A Preface to a History of Audiences', *Journal of the History of Ideas* 53: 47–70.
—— (1993) 'What Did Miners Read?: Miners' Libraries in South Wales, 1920–50', *Publishing History* 34: 75–6.
—— (2001) *The Intellectual Life of the British Working Classes*, New Haven, Conn.: Yale University Press.
Rothenstein, William (1932) *Men and Memories: Recollections of William Rothenstein 1900–1922*, London: Faber & Faber.
Rowse, A. L. (1942) *A Cornish Childhood*, London: Jonathan Cape.

——(1988) *Quiller-Couch: A Portrait of 'Q'*, London: Methuen.

Rutland, William R. (1938) *Thomas Hardy*, London and Glasgow: Blackie.

Saintsbury, George, *The English Novel*, London: J. M. Dent.

Saldívar, Ramon (2000) '*JO*: Reading and the Spirit of the Law', in Boumelha 2000: 32–52.

Sampson, George (1941) *The Concise Cambridge History of English Literature*, Cambridge: Cambridge University Press.

Sanders, Andrew (1978) *The Victorian Historical Novel 1840–1880*, London: Macmillan.

Saunders, Max (1996) *Ford Madox Ford: A Dual Life*, 2 vols, Oxford: Oxford University Press.

Schmidt, Barbara Quinn (1984) 'Novelists, Publishers and Fiction in Middle-Class Magazines, 1860–1880', *Victorian Periodicals Review* 17: 142–53.

——(1985) 'In the Shadow of Thackeray: Leslie Stephen as Editor of the *Cornhill Magazine*', in Joel H.Wiener, ed., *Innovators and Preachers: The Role of the Editor in Victorian England*, Westport, Conn.: Greenwood Press.

Schweik, Robert C. (1975) 'Character and Fate in *MC*' in Draper 1975: 133–47.

Seymour-Smith, Martin (1994) *Hardy*, London: Bloomsbury.

Sharp, Evelyn (1933) *Unfinished Adventure: Selected Reminiscences from an English-woman's Life*, London: John Lane.

Sherren, Wilkinson (1902) *The Wessex of Romance*, London: Francis Griffiths.

Shires, Linda M. (1993) 'Narrative, Gender, and Power in *FMC*', in Higonnet 1993: 49–65.

Short, Clarice (1958) 'In Defense of *Ethelberta*', *Nineteenth-Century Fiction* 13: 48–57.

Short, Michael (1990) *Gustav Holst: The Man and His Music*, Oxford: Oxford University Press.

Shorter, Clement (1897) *Victorian Literature: Sixty Years of Books and Bookmen*, London: James Bowden.

Showalter, Elaine (1979) 'The Unmanning of the Mayor of Casterbridge' in Kramer 1979: 99–115.

Shumaker, Jeanette (1994) 'Breaking with the Conventions: Victorian Confession Novels and *T*', *English Literature in Transition* 37: 445–62.

Siemens, Lloyd (1984) 'Hardy among the Critics: The Annotated Scrapbooks', *THA* 2: 187–90.

Silverman, Kaja (1993) 'History, Figuration and Female Subjectivity in *T*', in Widdowson 1993: 129–46.

Singleton, Frank (1950) *Tillotsons, 1850–1950*, Bolton: Tillotson.

Slack, Robert C. (1957) 'The Text of *JO*', *Nineteenth-Century Fiction* 2: 261–75.

Small, Ian (1996) 'The Economics of Taste: Literary Markets and Literary Value in the Late Nineteenth Century', *English Literature in Transition* 39: 7–18.

Smith, Anne, ed. (1979) *The Novels of Thomas Hardy*, London: Vision Press.

Smith, Sydney (1926) *Donald Macleod of Glasgow*, London: James Clarke.

Snell, K. D. M. (1985) *Annals of the Labouring Poor: Social Change and Agrarian England, 1660–1900*, Cambridge: Cambridge University Press.

Spector, Stephen J. (1988) 'Flights of Fancy: Characterisation in Hardy's *UGT*', *English Literary History* 55: 469–85.

Spivak, Gayatri Chakravorty (2000) 'Feminism and Critical Theory' in David Lodge and Nigel Wood, eds, *Modern Criticism and Theory: A Reader*, London: Longman, pp.476–93.

Spring, Howard (1942) *In the Meantime*, London: Constable.

Springer, Marlene (1983) *Hardy's Use of Allusion*, London: Macmillan – now Palgrave Macmillan.

Squire, J. C. (1930) *Sunday Mornings*, London: Heinemann.

Squires, Michael (1974) *The Pastoral Novel: Studies in George Eliot, Thomas Hardy, and D. H. Lawrence*, Charlottesville: University Press of Virginia.

Stannard, Martin (1986) *Evelyn Waugh: The Early Years*, London: Dent.

Stave, Shirley (1995) *The Decline of the Goddess: Nature, Culture, and Woman in Thomas Hardy's Fiction*, Westport, Conn.: Greenwood Press.

Steig, Michael (1970) 'The Problem of Literary Value in Two Early Hardy Novels', *Texas Studies in Literature and Language* 12: 55–62.

Stephen, Leslie (1875) 'Art and Morality', *Cornhill* 32: 91–101.

Stewart, Garrett (1996) *Dear Reader: The Conscripted Audience in Nineteenth-Century British Fiction*, Baltimore: Johns Hopkins University Press.

—— (1998) ' "Driven Well Home to the Reader's Heart": *T*'s Implicated Audience', in Riquelme 1998: 537–51.

Stewart, J. I. M. (1963) *Eight Modern Writers*, Oxford: Oxford University Press.

Stimpson, Felicity (2000) 'Reading in Circles: An Examination of the Work of the National Home Reading Union from 1889 to 1900', MA thesis, University of London.

Straus, Ralph (1942) *Sala: The Portrait of an Eminent Victorian*, London: Constable.

Sullivan, Alvin, ed. (1984) *British Literary Magazines: The Victorian and Edwardian Age, 1837–1913*, Westport, Conn.: Greenwood Press.

Sumner, Rosemary (1981) *Thomas Hardy: Psychological Novelist*, New York: St. Martin's Press – now Palgrave Macmillan.

Sutherland, J. A. (1976) *Victorian Novelists and Publishers*, London: Athlone Press.

—— (1989) *The Stanford Companion to Victorian Fiction*, Stanford, Cal.: Stanford University Press.

—— (1991) 'Tinsley Brothers' in Patricia Anderson and Jonathan Rose, eds, *British Literary Publishing Houses, 1820–1880*, Detroit: Gale Research, 299–303.

—— (1997) *Can Jane Eyre Be Happy?*, Oxford: Oxford University Press.

Swinnerton, Frank (1950) *The Georgian Literary Scene, 1910–1935*, London: Hutchinson.

Symons, Arthur (1927) *A Study of Thomas Hardy*, London: Chas Sawyer.

Taylor, Richard H. (1982) *The Neglected Hardy: Thomas Hardy's Lesser Novels*, Basingstoke: Macmillan – now Palgrave Macmillan.

Thackeray, William (1853) *The English Humourists of the Eighteenth Century*, London: Smith, Elder.

Thomas, Jane (1999) *Thomas Hardy, Femininity and Dissent: Reassessing the 'Minor' Novels*, Basingstoke: Macmillan – now Palgrave Macmillan.

Thompson, Bonar (1934) *Hyde Park Orator*, London: Jarrolds.

Thwaite, Ann (1984) *Edmund Gosse: A Literary Landscape, 1849–1928*, London: Secker & Warburg.

Tillyard, E. M. W. (1958) *The Muse Unchained*, London: Bowes & Bowes.

Tinsley, William (1900) *Random Recollections of an Old Publisher*, London: Simpkin, Marshall, Hamilton, Kent & Co.

Todorov, Tzvetan (1988) 'The Typology of Detective Fiction', in *Modern Criticism and Theory*, ed. David Lodge, London: Longman, pp.157–65 [1966].

Toliver, Harold E. (1962) 'The Dance Under the Greenwood Tree', *Nineteenth-Century Fiction* 17: 57–68.

Tompkins, Jane, ed. (1980) *Reader-Response Criticism*, Baltimore: Johns Hopkins University Press.

Trible, Phyllis (1984) *Texts of Terror: Literary-Feminist Readings of Biblical Narratives*, Philadelphia: Fortress Press.

Trollope, Anthony (1938) *Four Lectures*, ed. M. L. Parrish, London: Constable.

—— (1950) *An Autobiography*, London: Oxford University Press [1883].

Tuchman, Gaye (1989) *Edging Women Out: Victorian Novelists, Publishers, and Social Change*, London: Routledge.

Turner, Michael L (1968) 'The Syndication of Fiction In Periodical Newspapers, 1870–1939: The Example of the Tillotson "Fiction Bureau"', Oxford B.Litt.

—— (1975) 'Tillotson's Fiction Bureau' in Hunt 1975: 351–78.

—— (1978) 'Reading for the Masses: Aspects of the Syndication of Fiction in Great Britain', in Langdon 1978: 52–72.

Turner, Paul (1998) *The Life of Thomas Hardy: A Critical Biography*, Oxford: Blackwell.

Vann, J.Don (1985) *Victorian Novels in Serial*, New York: Modern Language Association.

Vincent, David (1982) *Bread, Knowledge and Freedom: A Study of Nineteenth-Century Working Class Autobiography*, London: Methuen.

—— (1989) *Literacy and Popular Culture, 1750–1914*, Cambridge: Cambridge University Press.

Ward, Mrs. Humphry (1918) *A Writer's Recollections*, London: Collins.

Watts, Cedric, ed. (1999) *JO*, Peterborough, Ontario: Broadview Press.

Webb, R. K. (1955) *The British Working Class Reader, 1790–1848*, London: Allen & Unwin.

Weber, Carl J. (1946) *Hardy in America: A Study of Thomas Hardy and His American Readers*, Waterville, Maine: Colby College Press.

—— (1965) *Hardy of Wessex*, London: Routledge & Kegan Paul [1940].

Weiner, Seth (1978) 'Thomas Hardy and His First American Publisher: A Chapter from the Henry Holt Archives', *Princeton University Library Chronicle* (1978) 134–57.

White, R. J. (1974) *Thomas Hardy and History*, London: Macmillan.

Widdowson, Peter (1989) *Hardy in History: A Study in Literary Sociology*, Routledge: London.

—— ed. (1993) *T: Contemporary Critical Essays*, Basingstoke: Macmillan – now Palgrave Macmillan.

—— (1994) '"Moments of Vision": Postmodernising *T*', in Pettit 1994: 80–100.

—— ed. (1997) *Thomas Hardy: Selected Poetry and Non-Fictional Prose*, Basingstoke: Macmillan – now Palgrave Macmillan.

Wilkinson, Louis, ed., (1943) *The Letters of Llewelyn Powys*, London: John Lane.

Willey, Basil (1970) *Cambridge and Other Memories, 1920–1953*, London: Chatto & Windus.

Williams, Harold (1911) *Two Centuries of the English Novel*, London: Smith, Elder.

Williams, Merryn (1972) *Thomas Hardy and Rural England*, London: Macmillan.

Williams, Merryn and Williams, Raymond (1980) 'Hardy and Social Class', in Page 1980b: 29–40.

Williams, Raymond (1970) *The English Novel: From Dickens to Lawrence*, London: Chatto & Windus.

—— (1975) *The Country and the City*, St Albans: Paladin [1973].

Wilson, Charles (1985) *First with the News: The History of W. H. Smith, 1792–1972*, London: Jonathan Cape.

Wilson, Jean Moorcroft (1998) *Siegfried Sassoon: The Making of a War Poet*, London: Duckworth.

Wing, George (1976) 'Middle-Class Outcasts in Hardy's *AL*', *Humanities Association Review* 27: 229–38.

Wittenberg, Judith Bryant (1983) 'Early Hardy Novels and the Fictional Eye', *Novel* 16: 151–64.

—— (1986) 'Angles of Vision and Questions of Gender in *FMC*', *Centennial Review* 30: 25–40.

Wolfreys, Julian ed. (2000), *MC: Contemporary Critical Essays*, Basingstoke: Macmillan – now Palgrave Macmillan.

Woodward, E. L. (1942) *Short Journey*, London: Faber & Faber.

Woof, Emily (2002) Conversation, 10.1.02, about her role as Grace Melbury in Phil Agland's film of *W*.

Woolf, Virginia, (1990) *A Passionate Apprentice: The Early Journals, 1897–1909*, ed. Mitchell A. Leaska, London: Hogarth Press.

Wotton, George (1985) *Thomas Hardy: Towards a Materialist Criticism*, London: Gill and Macmillan.

Wright, David (1978) 'Introduction', *UGT*, Harmondsworth: Penguin, 11–22.

Wright, T. R. (1986) *The Religion of Humanity: The Impact of Positivism on Victorian Britain*, Cambridge: Cambridge University Press.

—— (1989) *Hardy and the Erotic*, Basingstoke: Macmillan – now Palgrave Macmillan.

Ziff, Larzer (1966) *The American 1890s: The Life and Times of a Lost Generation*, Lincoln: University of Nebraska.

Index

9 780333 962602